PRAISE FOR

All We Ever Wanted Was Everything

by Janelle Brown

"**A withering Silicon Valley satire** . . . From the ashes of their California dreams, the three [women] must learn to talk to each other instead of past each other, and build a new, slightly more realistic existence—but not without doses of revenge and hilarity. [Janelle] Brown's hip narrative reads like **a sharp, contemporary twist on *The Corrections*.**"   —*Publishers Weekly*

"Through humor, some deft plot twists, her eye for absurd detail and her ability to reveal the inner lives of her characters [Brown] manages to . . . temper sharp irony with a dose of mercy."

—*Newsday*

"**Vibrant.**"   —*Elle*

"Janelle Brown expertly takes the social temperature of those gated communities exclusive to new money and finds a chill that inhabits the growth of family life."   —New York *Daily News*

"A soapier, more summery version of Franzen's biting social commentary . . . Her tale of one family's implosion is **a deliciously fun satire that manages to raise interesting questions about the American Dream.**"   —*Boston* magazine

all

we ever wanted

was

everything

a novel

JANELLE BROWN

SPIEGEL & GRAU
NEW YORK
2009

2009 Spiegel & Grau Trade Paperback Edition

Published in the United States by Spiegel & Grau, an imprint of The Random House Publishing Group, a division of Random House, Inc., New York.

The SPIEGEL & GRAU Design is a trademark of Random House, Inc.

RANDOM HOUSE READER'S CIRCLE and colophon is a trademark of Random House, Inc.

Originally published in hardcover in the United States by Spiegel & Grau, an imprint of The Random House Publishing Group, a division of Random House, Inc., in 2008.

Library of Congress Cataloging-in-Publication Data
Brown, Janelle.
All we ever wanted was everything : a novel / Janelle Brown.
p. cm.
ISBN 978-0-385-52402-5
1. Rich people—California—Santa Clara Valley (Santa Clara County)—Fiction.
2. Divorce—Fiction. 3. Mothers and daughters—Fiction. 4. Santa Clara Valley
(Santa Clara County, Calif.)—Fiction. 5. Domestic fiction. I. Title.
PS3602.R698A79 2008
813'.6—dc22
2008009237

Printed in the United States of America

www.randomhousereaderscircle.com

8 9 7

BOOK DESIGN BY JENNIFER ANN DADDIO

We are all failures; at least, the best of us are.

—J. M. BARRIE

all we ever wanted was everything

one

june in santa rita is perfect, just perfect. the sun sits high in the sky—which is itself just the right shade of unpolluted powder blue—and the temperature averages a mild eighty-three. It isn't too hot to play tennis. Silk doesn't stick. The pool at the club is cool enough so that swimming is refreshing, and the summer fog that usually creeps in off the ocean is held at bay, its gray tentacles undulating right off the shore.

Janice Miller wakes up on the last Monday of the month to the sound of a song from her youth playing softly on the radio alarm clock. In the vast king bed, where the impression from her husband's body has already grown cold, the lyrics wash over her as she drifts up toward consciousness: "Imagine me and you, I do/I think about you day and night/It's only right/To think about the girl you love/And hold her tight/So happy *together*!" A frivolous little tune, one she hasn't heard in decades, and yet she can suddenly recall every word, even the cover of the album. The record had been a bribe from one of her mother's transient postdivorce boyfriends, and ten-year-old Janice had played the song over and over ad nauseam until the record finally disappeared during one of their moves. Thirty-nine years later, and Janice is once again hooked in by that uplifting refrain, the curious minor key: "So happy *together!*"

She yawns widely; she did not sleep well the night before. Paul crept out of bed at four in the morning in order to make it to the stock exchange before the starting bell, and although he tiptoed around silently in the dark—trying not to wake her, though she really wouldn't have minded if he had kissed her good-bye, not today—she had tossed and turned for the next few hours. Really, though, she was too giddy with anticipation to sleep well anyway. This song, dredged up from the dusty archives of her consciousness, feels like an appropriate soundtrack for the day. "I can see me lovin' nobody but you/For all my life!" The refrain matches her upbeat mood.

Glancing at the clock, Janice is jolted out of her reverie—it's seven forty-five, almost two hours since the stock market opened. She turns the radio to a news station, cutting off the last refrain of the song ("So happy tog—"), and climbs out of bed. She takes a shower, listening with one ear as she lingers under the two-way adjustable head, but hears nothing about Applied Pharmaceuticals. The morning news—a heat wave in the South, fifty-four dead in a suicide bombing in Israel, a congressman caught taking handouts from lobbyists—plays as she makes the bed, folding in hospital corners and placing the dozen or so pillows, shams, bolsters, and decorative blankets in their designated positions. There's still nothing by the time she's dressed in her tennis whites, and, itching with impatience, she finally goes downstairs to turn on the coffeepot. En route, she snaps on the television in the family room so she can watch CNBC through the kitchen door as she prepares an egg-white frittata with feta and roasted zucchini for her daughter Lizzie.

The frittata sizzles on the stove, the nutty aroma of browning butter warming the kitchen while Janice watches the set with one eye and waits (nearly jumping out of her skin, she can hardly stand it anymore) for the commentator to drop the name Applied Pharmaceuticals. Finally, at eight-thirty, the chesty redhead perched behind the anchor desk clears her throat and turns to the camera. ". . . And now, the stock market story of the morning, the meteoric ascent of Applied Pharmaceuticals, whose IPO shares are currently sitting at a hundred thirteen dollars and a quarter only two hours after opening bell."

Janice gasps in surprise. Below the commentator, the stock ticker crawls across the bottom of the screen and—*there it is,* APPI, and her heart palpitates again—she sees that yes, it's true: $113! And if Paul—if *they*—possess 2.8 million stock options that means. . . . The rush of blood in her ears makes it hard to hear the rest of the report: "Experts cite the strategic timing by CEO Paul Miller, riding the wave of the booming biopharm industry, for this impressive Nasdaq debut, despite the fact that the company's much-anticipated new drug, Coifex, has yet to arrive in pharmacies . . ."

Janice has the urge to scream or jump up and down or run around the house or *something,* but that would wake Lizzie up and alarm the neighbors. Instead, she just smiles and automatically moves back to the stove to put the frittata in the oven. Inside, though, she feels like she's exploding and wishes she had someone to share the news with, just to make it more *real.* She can't call her friends—it would come off as bragging. There's her elder daughter, Margaret, in Los Angeles, but Margaret always seems to be so busy with that magazine, and, considering the precariousness of their relationship these days, it's probably not a good idea to pester her at work. Besides, Margaret would probably balk at the sums of money at stake and make some kind of comment about ethnic cleansing in Darfur that would make Janice feel materialistic and selfish. And Lizzie isn't really an option either. They haven't explained to Lizzie exactly what this IPO will mean to the Miller family's bottom line, because at fourteen Lizzie is far too young to need to worry about these kinds of financial matters. Besides, they don't want it to go to Lizzie's head.

Instead, she goes to the phone and dials Paul's cell. The call goes straight to voice mail, which is not a surprise—he had warned her that his day would be madness—but she leaves a message anyway. "Paul, I saw it on television," she says, trying to keep her voice calm and collected but squeaking a bit nonetheless. "And it's *thrilling*. We did it! Don't eat before you come home—we're going to celebrate tonight, okay? Would eight o'clock give you enough time to get back down here from San Francisco? I am just so *proud . . .*" She stays on the phone for a minute, feeling the impulse to babble on, but curbs it and hangs up.

And although Janice is just a bit frustrated that, once again, Paul is impossible to get ahold of, she cheers herself with the knowledge that this is finally the end of all that. This day has loomed in her calendar for almost a year now, a period during which she has become intimately familiar with the machinations of the stock market and the vagaries of the pharmaceutical industry and the interior workings of the FDA, while, simultaneously, becoming less and less familiar with her own husband. Every few days, he has had to jet off to Reykjavik or Brunei or Kobe on the Applied Pharmaceuticals IPO road show, in order to convince investors to part with ridiculous sums of money. The rest of the time, he's been in his office in a sprawling industrial park in Millbrae, with a view of the sludgy gray San Francisco Bay, working until he collapsed on his leather couch.

During the long weeks that Paul's been absent, Janice has sometimes stood before his medicine cabinet in their bathroom, gazing at the little plastic bottles of green Coifex pills lined up in a row and thinking about him. She'd taken a Coifex once, just to see what it felt like when Paul took it, curious about what it would do—not that she was going bald herself, but maybe it would bring back some of the natural blond or make her hair somehow softer—but the pill had mostly made her feel bloated. It was as big as a kalamata olive, almost too big to swallow: another innovation of Paul's, who had argued that larger pills appealed to men's need for masculine potency. Janice thought that was a bit ridiculous; but then again, no one ever said that product marketing made sense.

She kept one pill in her pocket, though, and would turn it round in her hand sometimes, fondling the pebbled surface of the pill as if it were a rabbit's foot or a good-luck charm. And that wasn't so silly after all, was it? Because the charm worked, and today the IPO is over, and it looks like those unwieldy green pills will be paying her family's bills for a long, long time to come. Which means that Paul will finally have time at home again, giving them a chance to return things to the way they were before all this Applied Pharmaceuticals insanity began. She imagines their marriage as a pendulum: They have grazed the bottom and are poised at the beginning of an upswing.

The old grandfather clock in the living room chimes out the half hour, which means that it's time to get down to the country club for her tennis date with Beverly. She finishes her coffee, puts the mug in the dishwasher, and gathers her car keys, errand lists, and tennis racket. There is much to be done today; she has been planning a grand fête for tonight, something as memorable as the day promises to be. The evening lies before her, as vivid as a magazine spread: Janice, crisply attired in a flattering new dress, her family assembled around a table heaped high with a home-cooked feast, everyone tipsy on champagne, everyone so filled up with love and abundance that they could almost burst. The only disappointment is that Margaret won't be there to celebrate with them, having dispensed with Janice's request that she use her father's IPO as an impetus for a long-overdue visit home with a mumbled excuse about publishing schedules.

Lizzie has still not gotten up yet by the time Janice leaves for town, so she just sets the frittata on the counter under a towel with a note (*At tennis. Eat me. Have a good day. Love, Mom*). Then she slips out the door, starts up the Porsche Cayenne, and drives down the oak-lined streets toward town.

The low morning sun blinks at Janice through the canopy of leaves as she navigates through the residential streets. The neighborhood is still quiet—a new local ordinance, voted into law by citizens grown weary of predawn bulldozers, has forbidden any construction before nine o'clock—and the enormous half-built villas that Janice passes on nearly every block loom blankly with their windows gaping, their gray facades still raw concrete. Sometimes it is difficult to remember how Santa Rita looked just two decades ago, when she and Paul and Margaret first moved into a modest, ranch-style home; before the technology industry explosion turned the sleepy bedroom communities of Silicon Valley into boomtowns; before the bulldozers began scraping up those postwar ranch homes and replacing them with multimillion-dollar Tuscan villas and Craftsman mansions and goliath Spanish missions complete with screening rooms and temperature-controlled wine cellars and five-car garages; before Janice and Paul and their friends realized how much money was within their grasp if only they bullied their way into it.

Over the years, Santa Rita has become an enclave for Silicon Valley's super-rich; Janice has watched her friends and neighbors march into ludicrous wealth, buoyed by the information age and stock options and seven-figure salaries. It's a community made affluent by acronyms—CEOs and VCs and IPOs and MBAs—a community where the lowest common denominator is actually astronomically high. And now, Janice realizes, after years of swimming along in the wake of these wild successes—doing quite well for themselves but certainly not doing *spectacularly*—she and Paul have finally joined their ranks. As she drives by, Janice eyes a particularly sizable villa with a separate guesthouse and at least a two-acre lot—not that there's anything wrong with the 5,200-square-foot Colonial they moved to seven years back. Still, she can't help luxuriating in the knowledge that they could afford even better now, if they so chose.

As she pulls into town, Santa Rita's main street is coming to life. The Italian café expels a steady stream of husbands on their way to work with their steaming commuter mugs; in the plate-glass window of the gym, young women half-dressed in jog bras (so blithe about their public display of bare flesh, and still firm enough to get away with it) churn away on treadmills. The specialty shops and designer boutiques and gourmet restaurants remain shuttered, and in front of them, the ornamental magnolia trees that line the sidewalks are weeping soft pale petals, each the size of a child's hand, down onto the parking spots below.

As she drives, she composes a master plan for the day. After tennis with Beverly, she'll get her hair done for tonight. Then, the grocery store. For dinner, she's preparing Cornish game hens with peppercorn-honey glaze, butternut-squash gnocchi with duck confit, and chocolate-lavender pots de crème, and, for appetizers, her melon puffs and maybe those lemon-ahi crostini that she was saving for next month's cocktail party. She'll need to pick up flowers, some candles, a bottle of champagne. Then her new dress, waiting at the tailor's.

Janice regards her schedule with satisfaction, each errand a stepping stone on a path that will logically deposit her, by day's end, back at home.

As she's driving, that song pops back into her head again. "If I should call you up/Invest a dime/And you say you belong to me/And ease my mind/Imagine how the world could be/So very fine/So happy *together!*" In the privacy of the car, Janice tries singing the tune out loud, thinking that maybe this will release her from its grip, but instead she just sounds ridiculous (she never could carry a tune).

Randy—that was the name of her mother's boyfriend, the one who gave her the album; she remembers it now. They must have been living, where, Indiana? Michigan? Sometimes her childhood feels so out of focus. After her parents divorced when she was seven and her father moved off to Ohio (where he promptly died in a car accident), Janice's school years were spent drifting around the Midwest, as her mother found and lost work, and moved them from decrepit apartment to the spare bedroom of a relative's house to motel and back again. Mostly, her mother worked as a cleaning lady for the enormous homes on the shores of the Great Lakes, dusting porcelain knickknacks and polishing mahogany. After school, Janice would often sit at the kitchen tables of these grand houses, watching her mother mop floors, and feel a sense of protectiveness (*Her* mother! Cleaning *their* toilets!) but also shame (Her *mother*! Cleaning their *toilets*!).

From those years, Janice acquired a taste for gourmet food— tinned sardines and salty caviar, boxes of water crackers and hand-cut Italian pastas and briny cornichons, which her mother fed her as an after-school snack from the pantries of her employers. Sometimes, when no one was home, she would wander through the palatial bedrooms upstairs and linger in the girls' rooms. These were studies in pink, always, and she would examine their contents like a visitor to a museum: postcards from summer vacations in the south of France, stiff sateen-upholstered daybeds heaped carelessly with porcelain dolls, snapshots of boyfriends strategically stuffed into the carved mirror of a vanity. Mementos of lives lived without fear or pain or *worry.* Before she left, she would occasionally take a souvenir—a mohair sweater, a silk blouse with a loose button, a scarf of snagged cashmere extracted from the bottom of a forgotten pile. She could never wear these things outside, of course. She kept her purloined wardrobe in a cardboard box at the back of a closet, behind the secondhand corduroy skirts her mother bought for her at Henny Penny's Shop-n-Save, and played dress-up as a treat for benchmarks achieved: an A on her French exam, a date at the drive-in, a scholarship offer to a good college out West. With the expensive fabrics against her skin, she would imagine herself propelled toward some shiny future that winked at her from a distance, like a mirror catching the sun and reflecting back the promise of a more perfect life.

Her senior year, she reluctantly sold her collection at a consignment shop in order to help cover the car payments for their sputtering Buick, just a few months before her mother's latest useless boyfriend vanished with the keys. One kleptomaniac done in by another. In retrospect, she can almost laugh at the irony, although it certainly didn't seem funny at the time.

the monumental iron gates of the country club loom on her left as she leaves town and enters the foothills, with their pine forests and wildflower-filled meadows. The Forest Heights Country Club, once an estate owned by a tycoon who made his fortune selling shovels during the California Gold Rush, is situated on two hundred acres just north of town. Its meandering gardens have been replaced by a golf course; the stable has room for twenty-eight mounts and an equestrian ring out back; and a phalanx of tennis courts flank the two Olympic-sized swimming pools. The estate's sprawling stone mansion is now the club's main building, and from its grand ballroom—kept in its original, parquet-floored grandeur, and normally used as the club restaurant—you can look over the grounds, an expanse of manicured green that rises up to meet the sky.

Janice parks her SUV in the side lot, already filled with the cars of the morning golfers, and walks out toward the tennis courts. The *pock-pock-pock* of tennis balls bouncing off clay echoes across the grounds, but when Janice arrives down at the courts Beverly is nowhere to be seen. Janice waits for her at the edge of the courts and watches Linda Franks rally with Martha Grouper. Back and forth the ball sails, and Janice averts her eyes from the women's frantic lunges, wondering if she looks as stiff as they do when she plunges after a ball. Ever since she pulled a ligament in her elbow in the spring tournament, she's grown more aware of her age, of the vague creaking in her joints and the slowness of her muscles to fire.

Martha finally sends Linda flying backward in pursuit of a perfectly sliced backhand, then walks over to the low fence and leans toward Janice, gesturing her in close. Horizontal sweat lines dampen the yellow knit of Martha's tank top, marking the exact location of the folds of her stomach. Janice unconsciously touches her own belly, which is definitely pushing against her waistband but has not yet succumbed to gravity in the way that her rear end and hips have. Fifty is looming, just a year off now, and she sometimes thinks she can see her looks falling away by the day. Men don't stare at her on the street anymore, the way they used to. Worse, she and Paul haven't had sex in six months, and although he's been overwhelmed by the IPO and she hasn't felt much of a sex drive herself, she can't help but worry that he has stopped desiring her altogether. Tonight, she thinks. Tonight she will initiate it.

"I bet *you're* in a good mood today," Martha says, pushing

up her visor and dropping her sunglasses down so ᵗ
peer directly into Janice's eyes. "It's all over the n
saying you've gone Forbes 400—what, trillionaires?"

The number, Janice has already calculated in her head, is
actually around $300 million—it is surreal to even summon
up the figure—but she wouldn't dare tell Martha that. Still, she
can't quite prevent the grin of embarrassed pleasure that
pinches her face. "Oh, please. We both know it's just numbers
on paper. Stock options are just accounting figures, not actual
money." *Yet,* she thinks.

"What on earth does a person do with so much money?"
Martha marvels, as though it's an utter mystery to her, despite
the fact that Janice knows that Martha's husband, Steven, a
venture capitalist specializing in wireless technology, has already made his own fortune. (Their vacation home in Aspen
has eight—*eight!*—bedrooms.) Nonetheless, Martha's question
has crossed Janice's mind many times lately. Not that the
Millers *need* much, but suddenly they have been catapulted into
that upper strata of Santa Rita society that can have *anything it
wants.* What Janice has told no one—not Paul, not even Margaret, the one person who she thinks might appreciate this—is
that when she imagines what she might afford now, the only
thing she truly covets is art. A painting. Specifically (and yes,
it's ludicrous, but . . .) she covets a van Gogh, one like those
she saw a few years back when they last visited France. Janice
had spent a rainy day at the Louvre by herself—Paul was back at
the hotel taking business calls—and had felt a curious sense of
liberation as she walked the great halls alone, addressing the
stoic museum guards in her somewhat rusty French. Egyptian
antiquities, Greek sculpture, Italian Renaissance, Impression-
ism: She took in each one in order, spending no more than
ten minutes in each room, making sure not to skip the smaller
galleries, carefully noting every important piece. She wanted
to absorb it *all,* methodically, sequentially. But when she got to

the van Gogh exhibition she came to a dead stop. She had seen photos of his work before and found them interesting, but this—the paintings themselves—was something else entirely. The violence of the paint applied in furious layers so thick that she could see the impressions of the artist's fingers, clawing at the canvas—she felt like she'd been slapped. The color! As vivid as a hallucination. There was something wild and abandoned in that gallery, and she stood there, trembling, unable to leave the room for well over an hour. She never made it to see the Dutch Masters.

She imagines one of those paintings hanging over the mantel in her living room and shivers at the thought of what it might let into her home. Not that they could (or should) buy an $80 million painting. Still, they could start with a minor drawing—like the landscape study she earmarked in the Sotheby's catalog last month—and work their way toward a collection. They could become patrons of the arts, even start a foundation, and she could take guided tours across Europe to really cultivate a discerning eye. She envisions paintings in the de Young Museum limned by placards boasting *From the Collection of Paul and Janice Miller.* A suitable title for a generous life, well-lived.

Regardless, the truth is that what she might *buy* with all that money sometimes feels besides the point; mostly she just likes to think of this money as a safety net, vast and tightly woven, a guarantee that from this point on everything will be okay. Her children will never have to worry about money, ever; they will never suffer the gnawing panic of wondering where the rent will come from, the way she once did.

Everyone always says that the early years of struggle are the happiest, but Janice knows better than that. A photograph in an old album of hers shows Paul in the tiny peeling bathroom of their very first apartment, the one above the dry cleaners in San Francisco that smelled like mold, extending his fingertips so that he is touching both walls; the grin on his face says, "Look at me, slumming it!" But Janice remembers taking that photograph and thinking, *He has no idea,* even as she laughed along with him. Because in the morning, he would leave for his job and she would be alone in that depressingly familiar apartment with Margaret, a fussy and demanding baby even if she was the first of their friends' children to toddle and talk, and that sense of shared adventure would dissipate. She battled an oblique discontent, a sense that she had run up against a wall without any doors, and even though she had every reason in the world to love where she was—beautiful baby! charming husband! a whole apartment of her own to work on!—somehow she didn't feel satisfied. Perhaps it was just the couch? If they could just get rid of that avocado plaid Sears couch and get a nice leather one? The miscarriages came, then, one after another, like a punishment; and Paul began to work longer and longer hours, pulling himself rung by rung up the corporate ladder, a snappish companion even when he was home to admire the secondhand side table she'd spent all day decoupaging. It wasn't until later—when they'd bought their first house, had some money to spend and room to breathe, gave up on a second child—that she discovered a sense of peace. Janice can remember a morning, their ninth anniversary, when they went up in a hot air balloon over the Napa Valley, on an obscenely expensive whim, and she looked over at her husband and realized that his eyes were bright with excitement and free of worry, and he looked back at her and laughed and she felt like they'd seen each other for the first time in years. Napa Valley unfolded below them, a blanket of green vines planted in reassuring geometric rows, and farther out was the ocean, where they could see the clouds rolling in, but where they floated the sun was hot and the sky clear. Janice remembers thinking then that they'd made it through the worst years and now they were being lifted up, lifted like the balloon, and feeling pure joy. When had that feeling waned? Sometime after Lizzie was born, she thinks, once Paul was swept up in the technology boom, once Margaret had abandoned them for another life. Maybe it's time to plan another trip to Napa, another balloon ride.

Janice checks her watch as Martha and Linda finish their game. It's nine-thirty, and Beverly is a half hour late, which is so unlike her—Beverly, like Janice, is of the school that believes that promptness is a sign of respect—and when Janice finally calls her at home to see whether she forgot, no one answers. Perhaps there's been an emergency with her son, Mark? Janice feels a vague sense of anxiety, a slight pull in the fabric of her morning. She waits fifteen more minutes, trying Beverly's cell phone, too, and then gives up altogether. As she walks back up to the car she struggles to remember another time when Beverly failed to appear for a date and can't recall a single incident.

The loss of her morning game throws Janice's plans off and she arrives back in downtown Santa Rita half an hour before her hair appointment, annoyed at the upheaval of her meticulous schedule. To kill time, she picks up a box of truffles at the patisserie—cardamom and black pepper chocolates for him, violet and rose petal creams for her, and walnut-cinnamon for Lizzie—and a $150 bottle of Dom Pérignon that the gentleman at the wine cellar describes as "transcendent" (blatant hyperbole on his part, perhaps, but she is compelled nonetheless). She leaves both in the car, worried that they'll melt and spoil, while she goes to have Peggy doctor her graying roots back to their original blond.

Janice reclines in the salon chair, finding it difficult to lose a tension that's settled in between her shoulder blades (excitement? anxiety? she can't tell), while Peggy—who seems out of sorts this morning, her eyes puffy and her responses terse—slaps the stinging peroxide on Janice's scalp. By the time her hair is blown out and coaxed into submission around her shoulders, Janice can tell that the color is a little too brassy this time, a shade too yellow—the color, she thinks, of a woman trying to cling to youth, rather than of one aging with grace. Peggy watches her staring at herself in the mirror, and Janice forces a smile. "Thank you," she says. "It's lovely." She will *not* let this ruin her day, she decides, and when it comes time to pay the bill, she impulsively adds a $100 tip—a little something to improve Peggy's spirits. Besides, if today isn't the day for frivolous generosity, when is?

As she leaves the salon, she checks her cell phone and is frustrated that there is still no message from Paul. The stock market won't close for another hour, though, and it's probably too much to expect him to call before then. Janice tucks the phone in her bag and shoulders on to the grocery store, where they have no Cornish game hens at all, the ahi looks mangy, and the cantaloupe that she needs for her melon puffs is completely unripe. As she stands in the produce aisle, morosely contemplating the rock-hard melons, Cecile Bellstrom clips by in her jogging suit, a quart of orange juice in her hands. "Janice!" Cecile exclaims. She pauses, and then bursts out: "Okay, I just can't stand here and pretend that I don't know, but of course I do, I saw the news just like everyone else, so I just wanted to say congratulations! Couldn't happen to a nicer family!"

This lifts Janice back up, out of her strange slump, and she bounds off toward the florist, where she picks up an armful of stargazer lilies for the dinner table. On the way back to her car she spies Noreen Gossett, who just last weekend had been in a golf foursome with her and Beverly—their daughters are in the same class, although Noreen's rather self-entitled daughter, Susan, has never shown the slightest bit of interest in Lizzie— and she perks up in anticipation of yet another flattering conversation. But instead of coming over to say hello, Noreen twitches and then jerks sideways as if someone had seized her shoulders, veering off without even a wave.

Janice comes to a halt, seized by confusion. She can feel the heat radiating off the parked cars around her as they bake in the midday sun. What could she have done to offend Noreen? Is something wrong? She has a sudden flash of understanding that the news of the Miller family's new fortune will not be taken well by everyone and that she is not the only person in town who's ever suffered a twist of jealousy at her neighbor's successes. But maybe it's just that Noreen didn't see her after all, Janice tries to reassure herself. She restlessly pulls out her cell phone and checks it again—ten to one, the stock market closing any minute—before continuing on toward the tailor.

The tailor is two blocks up Centerview Avenue, and Janice glimpses herself in every window she walks past: the organic Italian deli (yes, the hair is definitely too yellow), a real estate agency whose plate glass is hidden underneath photographs of Beaux Arts estates (her tennis skirt is exposing far too much cellulite), and the shop that sells four hundred kinds of artisanal soap (has her chin always had that wobble in it?). A throng of teenagers slump over the wrought-iron sidewalk tables outside the Fountain, eating French fries; the expressions of ennui on their faces suggest that summer, only a week in, has already become a chore. Janice smiles at them as she passes, trying to recall if she knows any of their parents, but they gaze at her without interest. The traffic on the street has picked up—it's the lunchtime rush—and someone is honking persistently, slamming down on their horn over and over.

At the tailor shop, the owner, an efficient elderly Chinese lady named Mrs. Chen—her fingers, Janice often tells her friends, move as quickly as hummingbirds—sits hunched over a suit, framed by plastic garment bags hanging on the rack behind her. Janice's own dress, a dark blue Calvin Klein sheath that she had to purchase slightly too large in the chest in order to fit over her hips, is already waiting for her by the cash register, and she tries it on behind the faded curtain that serves as a dressing room. The minute Janice pulls the dress over her head, she knows something is wrong: It wedges at her armpits, with her arms trapped helplessly in the fabric, and refuses to go farther.

"I think you took it in too much," she calls.

Mrs. Chen peeks around the curtain, seemingly unperturbed by the sight of Janice in tennis panties and a jog bra. She tugs firmly down on the dress, and there's a sound of popping thread. "You too big," Mrs. Chen observes mildly, yanking the garment back over Janice's head.

Janice picks up her tennis shirt to shield her nakedness. "You measured me," she complains. "I certainly haven't changed sizes in the last week."

Mrs. Chen examines the seams of the dress and picks at the zipper. "No worry, I can fix," she says. "You come back next week." Janice looks down at the dress—feels the image of herself as the stylish and still-attractive wife effortlessly serving her family a gourmet meal fading away—and is taken aback when tears well up in her eyes. She blinks them back before Mrs. Chen can see them. It's just a dress, she reminds herself; just a bad haircut, a missed game, an unripe melon.

"Fine," she says. "It's not a problem."

As she returns through the sheltering oaks toward her house—the car radio, tuned to the news, announces that the Nasdaq has closed up thirteen points but mentions nothing about Paul's company—Janice goes back over her day. She senses that things have shifted out of alignment, like a house that's slipped off its foundation; trying to identify the origin of this feeling, she fixes on Beverly once more. Something was definitely wrong this morning—it's not like Beverly not to call—and she is suddenly overwhelmed with a rush of concern for her friend. *Maybe,* she thinks, *if I just sort that out, everything else will fall back into line.* When she reaches the edge of town, instead of turning toward her house, she impulsively turns right, toward Beverly's.

The Weatherloves live in a two-story Tudor with a shake roof and green shutters. The Fourth of July is still a week away, but Beverly has already hung up bunting and a flag and planted red and white impatiens in the flower beds by the front door. Beverly's BMW is not in the driveway. Janice rings the doorbell, peering through the front window into the dim living room, but sees no sign of life. She can hear footsteps echoing through the hallway, though, bare feet thudding along the wood floors toward the door.

When the door swings open, Beverly's teenage son, Mark, stands there, sullen and silent, his hooded sweatshirt yanked over his head despite the heat, his eyes bloodshot, his mottled skin angrily mapping every red pimple.

"Hello, Mark. Is your mother here?" Janice asks.

"No," he says. His voice is nasal and stuffy—has he been crying?

"Where is she?"

"She's gone," he says, which elucidates nothing at all. Janice stands looking at him dumbly, pondering that word: *Gone? Gone where? Gone to the grocery store? Gone away?* She looks at the boy—he's definitely been crying, and despite her general alarm she feels a stab of tenderness for the dour child.

"Mark, is everything okay?" She steps toward him, her hand half-lifted, tugged by a desire to pull him into her bosom. But Mark shrugs and punches the door slightly toward her, as if to block her way.

"I'm fine," he says. "Thanks. I'll let her know you were here." And then he closes the door, leaving Janice baffled on his front steps. There is nothing for her to do but go back home and hope that she's making something out of nothing. A forgotten date, a crying kid—it could be anything and nothing at all. But she remembers a confession Beverly made a few months back, after a couple of Bloody Marys in the club lounge, about how her relationship with Louis had been strained for some time, and she can't help but wonder now if Louis has left her. If she doesn't hear back from Beverly by the morning, Janice decides, she'll come marching back and sit on her friend's doorstep until Beverly tells her what's wrong.

She pulls into her own driveway just after two and sits in her car for a moment, gazing up at her house. They painted it a pale yellow several years back, the color of a cashmere sweater, and the house seems to glow in the afternoon sun. It's a graceful, regal building, in a classic Georgian Colonial architectural style, with manicured hedges and pilasters framing the front entrance and ivy creeping up the siding, a house that makes her feel like she's a part of some great American tradition. Looking at it, she experiences relief, as if she's ridden out a small squall and has arrived back in a safe port.

But inside, the house is too quiet. The answering machine is silent: no messages. Janice's breath is loud in the empty kitchen as she puts away the groceries and the champagne, echoing off the stainless steel appliances, the Calphalon pans hanging above the kitchen island on their custom-designed iron rack, the yellow-veined granite counters. In the back garden, James, her new pool boy, has arrived for his biweekly visit. He pushes his net slowly against the current of the water, lifts a single leaf, swings the pole to the side of the pool, and taps the net to deposit the leaf on an accumulating pile of soggy greenery. Janice watches him from the kitchen window. When he looks up, she waves at him, and he lifts a hand and smiles. A worm of sweat rolls down his brow as he upends a jug of chlorine into the deep end.

Janice sets the oven to preheat and quickly begins arranging the stargazer lilies into a centerpiece, with one eye on the clock: She is already behind on her cooking, and she needs to clean, too (her housekeeper, fired earlier in the month when Janice discovered that the liquor cabinet was suspiciously empty, has yet to be replaced). As she sets the table with the good silver, she snaps the television back on and, standing in the middle of the living room with her arms crossed against the chill of the air-conditioning, learns that the Applied Pharmaceuticals stock has closed out the day at 141¼. She absorbs this news neutrally, unable to conjure the breathless excitement she had only six hours earlier. Instead, she just feels weary: weary of taking all of this in on her own, weary of waiting for her husband to call her. Despite his schedule, he should have *wanted* to share the excitement, the second it happened. In this moment of weakness, what creeps in is the sneaking suspicion that her enthusiasm for reviving their marriage is not matched by her husband, that she is going to have to do all the work.

But she perseveres with her table settings, folding three napkins into swan shapes, the way she always has for special occasions, just like Paul's mother showed her so many years ago. The first time Paul took her back to his parents' house in Connecticut for Christmas, her senior year of college, it felt like she had stepped into one of those homes her mother had once cleaned. There was the tree, decorated with matching gilt ornaments made of real glass; the homemade stuffing, not from a box; the napkins folded like origami; the sharp-scented pine boughs over the front portico. A portico! Cunning crystal salt and pepper shakers shaped like Christmas trees! The scene winked at her with such familiarity that she almost wept. When Paul's mother asked her whether her own mother would miss her at the holiday, Janice thought of her, working an extra shift for the overtime pay and then eating a microwaved turkey dinner alone, and lied. "No," she said. "She's eating with friends. She's baking a ham."

Despite the cordial napkin-folding lessons, Paul's mother

had been less than thrilled to hear, months later, about their shotgun wedding. Janice always suspected that Elaine had more ambitious aspirations for her only son's wife, a suspicion that was finally confirmed a few years back, during their last visit to Connecticut, where an Alzheimer's-addled Elaine was decaying in a senior citizens' home. Elaine had grabbed Janice's arm with her ropy hands. "I know you," she had croaked, her breath sour in Janice's face. "You're the tramp that trapped my son."

It wasn't quite that simple. If fifteen-year-old Janice had imagined college as a place where one went to meet a rich husband, twenty-year-old Janice had grown beyond that. This Janice—Jan to her friends—was a French major known, within her sorority, for her bohemian streak. During her first year at the university, an art history professor had written on one of her essays that she had a "sharp mind and an artistic spirit," and she had taken him at his word. She read Balzac in the original French, took classes in ceramics (producing a series of very respectable teapots), sewed her own skirts, learned to cook pot-au-feu. She even took up smoking Gauloises at parties and liked the way they conferred upon her an appearance of continental nonchalance. By her junior year she was planning a postgraduation year in Paris, where her thesis adviser said he might be able to arrange a job at a student travel agency. Sometimes, when she looked in the mirror, she was thrilled by herself.

Paul came as a surprise, a quiet and intense MBA student who materialized by her elbow at a sorority mixer at the beginning of her senior year and doggedly pursued her throughout the fall. When he looked at her, sometimes, she felt like a valedictory prize he had claimed as his own, and she would blush at how much this pleased her. By his side, she experienced a new stillness: He could calmly command a room like that, tilt it toward him until he seemed to be at its vortex. And yet he was vulnerable to her too. One night, they drank too much Chianti, and he told her about his banker father's expectations for him and his mother's patrician coldness and cried real tears, and she knew she was in love.

Of course, she hadn't *intentionally* forgotten to take the pill; not at all. The pill just passed through her mind, like water through a sieve. Graduation was looming, just a few months away, and the question of her future was growing less clear by the day. She had the job lined up in Paris and a room in the home of a young couple who were friends of friends of friends, but Paul no longer smiled benignly when she talked about leaving, as if her year abroad were some charming quirk; instead he glowered like she was betraying him. But if he was so angry with her, why didn't he ask her to stay? Even though she wasn't quite sure what her answer should be if he did beg her not to go, she grew increasingly concerned when he didn't. Would he just *allow* this casual amputation? The thought made her ill. She spent most nights motionless and frozen under the old cotton sheets, unable to sleep. Lying there, in a black fugue, she would remember the smooth pink oval, wrapped in tinfoil and buried in her makeup bag in the bathroom, and think: *I should get up and take the pill. I can't forget the pill.* And then the next thing she knew it would be morning and she'd be on her way to class and she would have forgotten entirely that she'd never taken it. And she wouldn't remember again until three days later, when she guiltily gulped down four pills in a row with a glass of milk. She should have said no when Paul crawled in her bed, the way she usually would when this happened, should have told him of her mistake and insisted on a condom, but she didn't have the willpower to turn him down, not now when he was so distant anyway. And so she lay in bed afterward as he slept beside her in a warm placid sleep and tried to forget that she had forgotten.

She could have gotten an abortion—there were girls who

did, even some who treated it like a badge of honor—but the truth was that she never even considered it as an option. When she got the test results back, she was surprised by the pang of pleasure she experienced: Here it was, her future as a wife and mother, the mistress of a beautiful home overlooking a lake somewhere, decided for her just like that; and it was strangely, comfortingly, familiar, like slipping on an old favorite dress she had forgotten she owned.

She knew Paul wouldn't flee when she told him she was pregnant, just as she knew that she was relinquishing herself into good hands. And maybe she would be giving something up, but wasn't this comfortable life of the potential Mrs. Miller far more promising, long-term, than any impulses she might have followed on her own?

The day after she told Paul she was pregnant, he took her out to the park overlooking the bay, where children were flying kites in what felt like hurricane-force gales. The setting sun caught in the fog over the city and rimmed the gray clouds with nuclear hues. Spring was late, and the temperature was just slightly above freezing. They walked to the retaining wall to look out at the water, and he dropped to one knee.

The grass was muddy but he gamely let his khakis sink into the dirt. He pulled out a black velvet box and held it in his hands. She broke out in goose bumps at the sight.

"I know it's been hard lately," he said, each hoarse word rising stiff and slow. "And I'm really sorry about that. But Janice, you have to know that from the very first moment I saw you, I knew you were a very unique woman, someone who is just so full of life. I can't think of anyone I would rather have as the mother of my children. So maybe this is all very sudden—sooner than we'd wanted—and we have a lot to figure out, but I'm really optimistic. Optimistic about us. We'll make a great team." He paused. The wind lashed hair across Janice's cheeks. "I love you."

Janice had started crying when his knee hit the grass, from relief and joy, and in part because of the sea salt that was being whipped into her eyes by the wind. He opened the box, revealing a simple gold band with a tiny chip of a diamond. Modest but tasteful. By the time he said the words "Will you marry me?" she was sobbing so hard she could barely hear him.

"Yes, yes, yes," she said. "Of course I will. I'm so glad you want me."

She let him slide the ring onto her finger and smiled, feeling strangely split, as if she'd triumphed and failed at the same time. Was this supposed to be the happiest moment of her life? She mostly felt dizzy, as if she'd just been sucked into a cyclone and was floating there in circles above the ground. Paul must have noticed the strange expression on her face as she looked at the ring on her finger, because he stood up and took her hand, covering it with his.

"Don't worry, I'm going to get you a bigger one soon," he said. "If we're going to do this, we'll do it right."

Twenty-nine years later, she can track the progress of their marriage—and Paul's rise through the corporate ranks—by the stack of velvet boxes in her armoire. He did get her a bigger ring, four years later, after her first miscarriage (the second and third miscarriages merited a peridot necklace and a pair of garnet earrings, respectively). And a 3-carat princess-cut diamond arrived nine years after that—long after she had taken her doctor's advice and given up trying to have another child—when they were surprised by her pregnancy with Lizzie. And lastly, for their twenty-second anniversary, seven years ago, a 5.1-carat Asscher-cut diamond, with 1.5-carat baguettes, set in a platinum band—a stone that matched Paul's latest position as CEO of an Internet start-up, their new four-bedroom house, and the Porsche SUV in the driveway. This was a diamond so big, in fact, that at first she found herself embarrassed by its ostentatiousness and nostalgic for the modest diamond she had once worn—until she saw Beverly's fortieth-birthday present from Louis, a 7.8-carat Harry Winston shocker that drooped off her finger, and realized that size was always relative.

Janice wonders, abstractly, what this new success will merit. *Maybe,* she thinks, *he'll arrive home tonight with another velvet box to install in the armoire,* and she tries to muster the excitement for this, but mostly she just wants him to come home.

The doorbell rings before the phone does. From the kitchen, where she is disassembling the duck for the confit, she runs to the door, wiping her hands on a dish towel. She finds a young man about Margaret's age standing on her doorstep, with a faded rainbow fringe of hair that's been smashed down by his motorcycle helmet. His motorcycle boots are covered in mud, and she wishes that he hadn't stepped on her handwoven "Welcome to Our Happy Home" doormat, which she made out of dried lavender from the garden earlier in the spring. In his black leather jacket and jeans he reminds her vaguely of Bart, Margaret's boyfriend, who also rides a motorcycle; at least Bart doesn't dye his hair pink, though that's about all she can say on his behalf.

In one hand, the man holds a manila envelope; in the other, a clipboard. "Messenger delivery," he says, and shoves the clipboard at her. "Sign here."

Janice wipes her hands dry in order to sign on the dotted line and tries to remember anything she might have ordered. Tearing the manila envelope open, she finds a white envelope inside with a familiar return address: Applied Pharmaceuticals, 220 Analgesic Loop, Millbrae, California. She stands there, just looking at it, and is suddenly terrified to open it. She resists this feeling as she breaks the seal of the envelope, but when she extracts a note written on Applied Pharmaceuticals letterhead (she immediately recognizes, without even looking at it, Paul's signature on the bottom) she registers no surprise at all. *Of course,* she thinks, as a cloud of doomed in-evitability descends over her.

The letter, typed on cream-colored paper, reads:

Janice,
As you know, today is a day of big changes for me. And so it seems as
good a day as any to start fresh. There's no easy way to tell you this, so
I'm just going to be blunt: I think we both know that our marriage has
become a sham. I haven't been happy for years and, though I'm sure
you would never admit it, I don't think you've been happy either. We
need to escape this claustrophobia, have the chance to find real passion
before it gets too late. That's why I've decided to file for divorce. My
lawyer will be in touch. I'm confident that you'll come to agree with
me that it's for the best.

Paul.

He has signed it in bright green ink, a green that she rec-ognizes as coming from the fountain pen she bought him to match the green of the Coifex logo, the same green as those pills.

Janice clutches her dish towel in one white-knuckled hand. She looks down at the word "Happy," woven in lavender buds on the doormat. ("So happy *together!*") She looks up again at the messenger, still loitering on the doorstep, and realizes that he is hoping for a tip.

"One minute," she says. She turns blindly back into the house, bumping into a chair en route to the kitchen, grabs her purse from the counter, and returns to the front door. As the messenger watches her, she pulls out a Prada wallet and finds only twenties.

"Here," she says, and shoves one at him.

"Hey, thanks!" he says, palming the bill into the pocket of his motorcycle jacket. He smiles. "Thanks a lot."

As the messenger's engine coughs to life, Janice scans the

letter again, her hands vibrating so that the words smear before her. Janice is not sure where Paul has learned these turns
of phrase, which sound like they were cribbed from a romance
novel: How did Paul, who composes only business plans, who
reads nothing but biographies of billionaire corporate executives, come up with florid ideas like "find real passion" and
"escape this claustrophobia"? What on earth does that mean?

For a few crucial seconds, her mind seizes up around these
anomalies, refusing to consider the bigger matter: that her
husband has just left her. She is dizzy, and black spots spin in
the sun before her eyes. She looks down at the ground again,
trying to focus herself, and can't help noticing through her
blurring vision that the messenger has left a shiny smear of
mud across her mat.

her hands are shaking so hard that she can
barely dial. And even then, she has to call his cell phone five
times before he picks up. Surely, she tries to convince herself,
she is misinterpreting his note; it's some kind of mistake. But
when he eventually answers his phone, he does so with two
simple words: "Hello, Janice." A statement of fact, a tribute to
the magic of caller ID, and with the blank utterance of those
four syllables she knows that it is, in fact, true. Her husband is
leaving her, because only that would explain the total lack of
affection in his voice. "I assume you got the letter," he says.
"I'm sorry, but I thought that would be the easiest way . . ."

"I don't understand," she says, reeling from the finality in
his words. Her own voice cracks unattractively. "Where did this
come from?"

"It had to be this way," Paul says. Janice is bewildered by
how mild and rational he sounds, as if he were a dentist in-
forming her that he is about to extract her molars. "But this
isn't the time to talk about it. I'm still at work."

"Find a private place to talk then," says Janice. "This is important, Paul. This is our *life.* What do you *mean,* a sham?"

"I think you know what I mean," he says.

Janice walks to the doorway of her dining room and stares at the table, at the centerpiece of stargazer lilies erupting like fireworks, at the crystal stemware ascending across each setting. Somewhere behind Paul, she can hear the pop of a champagne cork. She thinks of the champagne chilling in their own refrigerator and swallows. "No. I don't know what you mean," she says, and although this isn't quite true, she also isn't ready to admit this to him, especially now. "I mean . . . I *need* you."

"You don't need me," Paul says. "You've never needed anyone in your life. That's half the problem. The only thing you seem to *need* from me is to pay the bills."

"That's ridiculous. You're not making any sense."

"Look," says Paul. "Tell me the last time we had an actual conversation about anything of significance. We've been on autopilot for years, and, frankly, I don't see why either of us should have to settle for that."

"I'm perfectly capable of an actual conversation, Paul," says Janice, horrified by the pleading in her own voice. "Just because we haven't had one lately doesn't mean we can't. Let's talk now. Or later. We can get a counselor to help us talk."

"It's beyond that," says Paul. "We moved beyond that years ago."

Janice tries to say something, but all she can do is breathe shallowly into the phone. Her own damp inhalations echo in her ears. "Who are you?" she says, furious. "I don't know this Paul."

"That's exactly my point," Paul says, and his logic silences her. Behind him, she hears a woman's voice, muttering something. In this context she can't quite place the voice, but the tone is familiar. *Someone from Paul's office,* she thinks. *How horrible, that a coworker might be overhearing this.* Paul covers the mouthpiece with his hand, so that all she can hear is the muffled vacuum of a receiver pressed against flesh.

Paul comes back on the line. "Janice," he begins, but then from the background the woman's voice cuts through his words, louder now, almost shrill. "You have to tell her," the woman says. "She needs to know."

Recognition hits her abruptly, and when it does, it's as if a bucket of ice water has been thrown in her face. All the premonitions of the day total together, finally, and she is stunned by what they add up to, by her inability to have seen it sooner. "Is that Beverly with you?" She can barely get the words out.

There is a telling void on the other end. Paul clears his throat and says nothing.

Janice drops the phone like a hot dish and stares at it, lying there on the floor, her heart pounding frantically. After a minute, the line disconnects itself and starts to beep insistently, in time with the throbbing vein at her temple.

a few minutes later, when she is sitting stiffly on the couch, frozen in shock, she finds herself staring fixedly at their wedding photo framed in crystal on the side table. It was taken after the brief ceremony they had in South Lake Tahoe two weeks after Paul proposed: a snapshot of herself, in gloves and a borrowed white sheath dress just a little too tight around the stomach, looking up at Paul with her arms flung around his neck, and Paul in his suit, looking into the camera with a startled expression, as if someone behind the camera had just said, "Boo!" She thinks of the words of their vows: "In sickness and in health. For richer and for poorer."

That is what marriage is, she thinks; it's not about some sort of childish notion like "passion," because the grown-up truth is that life, partnership, love, is *hard*. It takes work, in good times and bad. It takes *sacrifice*. She had thought Paul felt that, too: a respect for the institution of marriage, the center and stability it provides. And yet he's throwing all that away because, why? For *Beverly*?! Divorce: just the thought of it makes her ill. *It's the lazy way out,* she thinks. It's not like she's been blissfully happy all the time, either, but you are *supposed* to keep trying, even when your husband looks like a chilly balding stranger on the other side of the dinner table, even when you hear him talk impatiently on the phone to his ailing mother and realize that he is capable of cruelty, even when he leaves you alone night after night and doesn't even try to make it up to you. You stick with it, because marriage and family are sacrosanct. A fortress against a difficult world. Maybe things haven't been perfect lately—she'll grant Paul this—but why is he so quick to give up? She thinks of Beverly, her *best friend,* coaxing her husband away with open arms and open thighs, and feels ill—ill that Beverly could do this, and ill that Paul would succumb so easily.

Janice tries to imagine her life without Paul and is overtaken by a surge of feeling, as if she's falling off a tightrope and realizing as she plummets downward that there is no net below her. She grabs the photograph and hurls it across the room as hard as she can, so that the glass shatters into a hundred pieces against the mantel. And then she stands in the living room, motionless, as the silence restores itself, the crash vanishing in the vacuum of wall-to-wall carpeting and brocade drapes. And then she bends to pick up the shards—she doesn't want Lizzie stepping on them barefoot—before going to the kitchen to swipe the bottle of champagne from the refrigerator.

two

four hundred miles south, in los angeles,
Margaret Miller's phone is ringing again. It shivers to life in
the passenger seat of her car, belting out a shrill electronic
arpeggio, its screen illuminating in phosphorescent blue as
the red "Call" light flashes. The phone teeters on the far edge
of the passenger seat. Margaret has to stretch for it, one hand
on the steering wheel, one eye on the traffic on Beverly Boulevard, her dress pulling tight under her thighs. It's just beyond
her reach.

The phone rings again, the same three bars of a mangled
Chopin étude ringtone that she once found acceptably benign
but that, these days, makes her want to scream. The ringing
phone starts her pulse racing; she feels as jumpy as a gazelle.
She reaches a little farther, the thin vintage cotton of her dress
complaining again at the strain—she can feel a seam pop under her arm—and her Honda swerving slightly, until her fingertips scrabble ineffectually against the phone's metallic case.

She should just turn the damn thing off, but she's afraid she'll miss an important call, *the* important call, the one that will turn everything around. The provenance of this call is not clear to her—perhaps it will come from her so-called investor, Stuart, a call in which he tells her that he's changed his mind entirely and wants to do the financing after all. Or—less likely—from Bart, her ex, telling her not to worry about his e-mail. From her father, perhaps, with an offer Margaret can't (even if she should) refuse. But something—right? Margaret has never considered herself an optimist—optimism being for hopeless idealists like Anne Frank (who, let's face it, in the end perished in a death camp) and mung-bean-chewing Age of Aquarius types—but for the last few years she has been living on the fumes of hope, and she's not quite ready to give up.

And yet. In the back of her mind, a red light flashes in time with the cell phone's call light: Danger. Danger. Danger. Margaret blinks and realizes that the brake lights of the car in front of her have lit up. She jerks upright just in time to jam her own brakes on. Her tires belch burnt rubber, while behind her a chorus of horns condemn her driving skills. Stopped at the intersection, her heart pounding, Margaret lurches all the way across the seat and grabs the phone.

The caller ID reads "RESTRICTED NO." She knows better than to answer that. She drops the phone into her purse instead. The ringing stops, abruptly, mid-trill.

The light turns green, the traffic around her accelerating heavy-footed into the gap. The evening sun setting directly ahead burns blinding circles into Margaret's retinas as she steers her whining Honda down Beverly Boulevard toward Acqua Trattoria, noting the time on the car's clock display and berating herself for being so late. She'd walked out of her apartment in Echo Park three times, hesitating twice just outside the door and then turning to go back inside, thinking, *I can still skip it, I'll just call Josephine and tell her I'm sick.* But she finally left anyway, lured by the promise of a night out with her girl-friends—always so *intelligent,* always doing such *interesting* things—in which she won't be sitting at home mulling over her various intractable problems.

Still, it was stupid to come, considering. A salad. She'll just order a salad. That can't possibly cost more than, what, fifteen dollars? With a glass of wine, maybe twenty-five, thirty. That's not *exactly* in her budget—*nothing* is in her budget anymore—but it's not wildly extravagant either.

The phone jolts to life again, this time emitting one long beep. A text message. Margaret flips the phone open and reads: "VZW MSSG: Your VZ Wireless bill 60 days past due. CC declined. Bal due $126.30. Service terminated tmrw unless immediate pmt."

Not *now.* "Shit," she says out loud. On her right looms a Bank of America, and, spying an empty meter, she swerves between a BMW and a Hummer and parks the car amid another cacophony of honks. She sits behind the wheel for a moment, sweat beading at her hairline. *It's no big deal,* she thinks. *I can fix this.* So her credit card was declined again, and her checking account has been frozen—she still can use cash, right? She'll just drop by the cell phone store tomorrow morning and pay it off in person. What other bills require her urgent attention? The rent, yes, but the landlord, a nice old gentleman named Al, loves her—she fed his portly Persian cat when he went to visit his grandchildren last month—so surely he'll be lenient for just one more month. FedEx? Not a priority. Cable? Already turned off, along with her home phone. The gas and electric bill? Yes, that one is frighteningly overdue. On-the-verge-of-being-cut-off overdue. Will-have-to-cook-with-candles overdue if she doesn't come up with $142 quickly.

Bart? The words of the e-mail she received this morning from her ex-boyfriend drift back. "Margaret—I know it's been a while and I haven't wanted to bug you about this until we both had some space to cool down, but it's time we talked about the $12,000+ you owe me. I saw your dad on the news the other day, by the way. Lucky him. I'd rather you paid me back in full, of course, but if nothing else let's establish a payment plan. Bart." Sneaky Bart with his oh-so-coy mention of her father's IPO. He *knows* she'd never ask her family for money. He *knows* that she has always prided herself on her utter independence from her family, and that even the suggestion would upset her beyond all belief. And God knows he doesn't really need that money, anyway—not when, according to last week's *Variety*, which featured the headline "CAA Nabs Boffo Payday for Up-and-Comer Johnson," Bart's going to be paid $1.2 million for his next film role. (The *Variety* story ran with a photo, the old head shot she knew well—she had been there when he'd had it taken, making ridiculous faces at him so that he'd relax for the photographer—and she hadn't been able to force herself to throw the magazine away but had tucked it, instead, deep in a file box.)

No, Bart isn't on the top of her priority list anymore.

She'll just take out enough cash to cover the cell phone and electricity bills, plus some money for dinner. As she runs to the ATM, tripping on the sidewalk in her thrice-resoled heels, dizzy from the rush-hour exhaust fumes and the glare of sun on parched concrete, she flips through the cards in her wallet and selects one—surely she still has a little cash left in her savings account? But the ATM machine ruminates on the card, tasting it, and spits it right back out. Growing anxious, Margaret rifles through her wallet. The MasterCard is maxed out, and so are her Visa and Discover cards . . . but what about the Bank of America business account? Maybe she could get an advance on that. The machine considers the plastic rectangle and then blinks the phrase INSUF⁵CIENT FUNDS at her, in all caps. INSUF⁵CIENT FUNDS, INSUF⁵CIENT FUNDS.

The cell phone in her purse—an aged brown leather satchel

that has seen better days—chooses that moment to start ringing again. RESTRICTED NO. All caps, again. INSUF⁵CIENT FUNDS. The machines are *yelling* at her! The machines are just like her mother, who, in her e-mails, always nags her in capital letters: "DON'T FORGET YOUR GREAT-AUNT EDNA'S BIRTH-DAY AGAIN PLEASE." "WE'D VERY MUCH LIKE YOU TO COME HOME FOR THANKSGIVING THIS YEAR SINCE YOU DIDN'T LAST." "Don't forget your TEN-YEAR REUNION, honey—Kelly Maxfield told me that it's LABOR DAY WEEKEND and it would be a SHAME to miss." The missives make Margaret grit her teeth: Why does Janice bother crafting these artfully passive-aggressive guilt trips if she's just going to SCREAM THEM IN ALL CAPS? Anyway, Margaret didn't *mean* to forget Aunt Edna's ninety-second birthday last year (she hasn't seen her in a decade anyway). And if she skipped Thanksgiving it was only because, as usual, she had to work straight through the holiday to finish editing the cover story for the January issue of *Snatch,* her magazine— though, of course, that's the kind of focus and dedication her mother would never really understand, having never held a real job in her entire life.

The ATM spits out her card. The only card left in her wallet is the new American Express she received last month, the card that has a cash-advance option with a usurious 29 percent interest rate—the card she swore she'd use only for emergencies, but if this isn't an emergency (no phone! no electricity!), what is? The machine—thank God—offers her the option of a cash advance. She hits SELECT and punches in $300.

RESTRICTED NO., whoever it is, gives up as Margaret retrieves three crisp hundred-dollar bills from the machine and tucks them in her wallet. As she walks back to her car, she gulps down a not-at-all refreshing lungful of humid air, blots her damp hairline with a tissue, and tries to calm down. She'll find a way to pay the advance back next week, before the interest accumulates; but at the back of her mind that red alert is going off again: Danger. Danger. Danger.

She's twenty minutes late by the time she arrives at Acqua and grows even later as she drives around looking for a parking space. She is unwilling to relinquish $4.50 to the line of exhausted-looking Armenian valets lining the sidewalk and, honestly, embarrassed to pull her rusting Japanese import up amid all the shiny sports coupes and German sedans. Instead, she finds parking seven blocks away and half-jogs back along the empty sidewalks toward the restaurant, the straps on her heels cutting blisters into her feet. She arrives at the restaurant feeling limp and sticky and examines her reflection in the window before entering. Too many hours in front of a computer have left her with a permanent hunch, her head leading her body by a good three inches, her sharp chin pointing the way. Dye jobs and haircuts have long gone the way of dentist visits and new underwear and other unnecessary luxuries, so that her hair has reverted to its natural, prematurely gray-flecked muddy brown and hangs limply to the center of her back. At least her eyes are an arresting cornflower blue tonight, but that's just because the whites are so bloodshot. She looks like hell.

Inside the door, Margaret maneuvers around a two-story wall built entirely of glass blocks filled with water, inside which brilliantly-colored betta fish petulantly float. The foyer is blocked by a clot of immaculately attired Hollywood aspirants, living the Los Angeles cliché: the fashionable emaciation, the glowing tans, the second-skin designer jeans and pillowy cleavages hoisted toward the ceiling by complicated undergarments. The hostess, who looks like a Slavic supermodel, with her sunken cheeks and jutting clavicles, assiduously ignores everyone, including Margaret.

Who chose this place? Josephine? Alexis? Margaret avoids coming to the West Side of Los Angeles; it's like there's a beauty tax charged for the privilege of being in proximity to such dewy, manicured—no, *manufactured*—youth. At twenty-eight, Margaret feels *old* when she comes to Hollywood. She considers her hair, pulled back into a limp ponytail, and her vintage 1950s polka-dotted housedress, slightly discolored under the armpits, and feels frumpy. But at least she's being an individual, she tries to cheer herself. Unique. Quirky. No fashion victim, not Margaret. Even if she *had* that much money, she wouldn't succumb to $300 jeans.

Once she would have seen this restaurant as a sort of petri dish, a culture to be studied under a microscope. Los Angeles might not have seemed the most logical place in the world to start a pop-feminist magazine for young women—New York, yes, San Francisco or Seattle, sure, but not the city dismissively referred to as "La-La Land"—but when Margaret had moved here with Bart four years earlier and started *Snatch* she'd thought of Los Angeles as a source of material. This was the lair of the entertainment-industrial complex that shaped the world's perceptions, and living in the belly of the beast endowed her, as a media critic, with authority.

Running a magazine had been her secret fantasy since high school, when she served as the film critic for the *Fillmore High Bugle* (trying, futilely, to convince her classmates that they should eschew Jim Carrey for Federico Fellini). As long as she could remember, she'd felt like she had something she needed to tell the world, and after she'd finished her double major in media studies and women's studies at Cornell, then completed her master's at U.C. Berkeley—and, critically, met Bart—she'd identified exactly what that something was: America's young women were adrift in a culture of consumerism, celebrity worship, and vapid pop entertainment; with *Snatch,* she would cut through the crap. *Snatch: Because Girls Can.* It would be a new voice for young women, one that looked at pop culture with a critical eye, identifying unrealistic body images and sexist clichés; a voice that embraced real female sexuality and encouraged strong role models. *Snatch* would be the antidote to *Us Weekly*. She would help change the face of contemporary entertainment and make feminism relevant to young women again—women like her sister, Lizzie, who already suffered from a troubling addiction to tabloid magazines.

Except that four years on, and especially after the events of the last week, she's starting to wonder whether anyone has actually been listening to her. Certainly here, at tony Acqua, where the spray tans abound, it appears that she's made no difference at all. Margaret discovers that her eyes are filling with tears and blinks rapidly so that her mascara doesn't end up on her chin.

But then she sees Josephine, Claire, and Alexis seated at a table near the back, waving frantically to catch her attention, and locates the necessary stamina required to pin a grin on her face and shove her way through the crowd. Josephine—the queen of the evening, the beloved birthday girl, the celebrated screenwriter—sits at the head of the table, slurping at a crab leg with eyes closed in pleasure. There is a pile of presents by her feet—oh God, Margaret forgot a present! A bottle of expensive-looking champagne is cooling in an ice bucket, and a heaping platter of raw seafood dominates the center of the table. It looks like the entire Pacific Ocean has been emptied onto the plate.

"Happy thirtieth," Margaret says, reaching down to bestow a parched air kiss on Josephine's moisturized cheek. "Sorry I'm late, but, you know. Traffic." From across the table Claire kisses her fingers and waves them through the air, magic fairy pixie dust of love sprinkled from her tiny hands, the pale fingers still carelessly crested with blue specks of paint from her art studio. Alexis merely grunts, too busy dismantling a lobster claw with a pair of stainless steel pliers and scattering bits of its flesh across her lap.

"This really is so barbaric," Alexis complains, throwing down the shell. "Why did we order this, again? I'm not sure I like to be so hands-on with my dinner's demise."

"Oh, don't be such a grump," says Josephine, who—God bless her—is blithely wearing an African-print headwrap with her black cocktail dress and doesn't look the least bit ridiculous. Margaret's old grad school friend radiates Pan-Ethnic Urban Goddess: Her toffee skin shiny and plump, she oozes comfort and well-being and for a half second Margaret hates her for that. Josephine pushes a dish of green liquid toward Alexis as she scoots over to make room for Margaret. "Try the wasabi dipping sauce."

"I'm allowed to be a grump," says Alexis. Her thick black bangs fall over her eyes, which are makeup-free and puffy from lack of sleep: Alexis thrives on a state of near exhaustion and grows jumpy and even more irritable when not under extreme stress. "I had a dismal day on set. My DP got sent to rehab and the record label slashed the budget in half and now the singer refuses to wear the pink Victorian wig she said she wanted to wear just last week. Remind me why I haven't quit directing music videos yet?"

Margaret struggles to sympathize but can only muster a small shake of her head. "Because you get paid ten thousand dollars a day to do it," she says, hoping that this doesn't come across quite as bitter as it feels rolling off her tongue. When she met Alexis, three years ago, after Alexis directed the no-budget independent film Josephine had written (the film that had, in fact, ended up going to Sundance and jump-starting both their careers), Alexis and her then roommate Claire were so broke they'd been sharing a *studio* apartment. How had things changed so quickly?

"Ouch," says Alexis. "And yet. So true."

Josephine pushes the tray of seafood toward Margaret. "Oyster?" she asks. "Japanese."

"Oh, no," Margaret says, sizing up the seafood pile and doing some mental addition about its cost. "I'm not that hungry. I'm just going to have a salad." She eyeballs the bottle of champagne as Claire pours her a glass; a bottle of Dom Pérignon's got to be, what, eighty dollars? A hundred? Surely they won't expect her to share the bill for that since, after all, she didn't order it. But just one teensy glass would really hit the spot.

A waiter materializes behind her and silently hands her a menu. It lists only three salads; the cheapest, microgreens with anchovy foam, is $18. Dismayed, Margaret scans the menu, but the only item any cheaper is a side dish of mashed potatoes for $13, which, regardless of its ludicrous price ($13 for potatoes?), she would simply look silly ordering as her main course.

"The microgreens, please," she tells the waiter. "And that's it." Margaret sees him glance at her, size her up, and write her off as just another anorexic actress picking at lettuce. Margaret wants to explain to him, *I don't have an eating disorder, really; I'm just on a budget!* but he's already turned on his heel and vanished. The smell of roasting salmon from the kitchen makes Margaret's stomach gurgle loudly—the only thing she's eaten today is mac-n-cheese from a box—and she resists the urge to gobble down the forbidden lobster tails. Instead, she takes a dinner roll and slathers it thickly with butter.

Claire, who needs a booster seat to see over the pile of discarded oyster shells, says something no one can hear over the blaring electronica sound track. She has cropped her blond hair into a Mia Farrow pixie, exposing tiny shell-like ears hung with oversized gold chandelier earrings, which Margaret knows were purchased from the proceeds of Claire's last solo art show; she'd sold one of her photographs—a full-sized self-portrait of herself naked except for leather chaps, titled *Hairless Claire*—to the pop star Bobby Masterston. Margaret tries not to stare at the earrings, or at Josephine's Balenciaga purse or Alexis's cashmere hoodie. She tries not to care—she knows perfectly well that she shouldn't care, that doing so is just succumbing to an advertising-driven culture of consumption, and why should it really matter whether the dress she's wearing has a designer label or whether the car she's driving has leather seats, as long as she's attired and gets where she needs to be? Isn't that the whole *point* of everything she's been writing? But the bitter realization is that Margaret *does* care. She cares when she's invited over to Alexis's new house, a gorgeous midcentury oasis with an ovoid swimming pool and views all the way to Santa Monica, whereas her own home is a sweltering studio apartment in a concrete-block building that smells of mold and cat urine. She cares when her friends go on two-week vacations at four-star yoga retreats in Bali, while she can't even scrape up enough cash to make it across the border to Rosarito Beach. She cares about her friends' increasingly expensive wardrobes, their automobiles, their furniture, their stereo systems, and, most of all, their enviable professional successes.

It was easy, initially, to pretend that all the people in their social group were equals. Struggling artists, writers, filmmakers, actors, everyone in their mid-twenties: creative talents with big goals and small budgets. Margaret, as the impoverished editor of her own magazine, had felt that she was among peers. But at some point their paths diverged, and as they came up against their thirties her friends had started to make real money—selling screenplays, directing films and music videos, holding art openings—whereas she was still on a yard-sale budget. It was easier, when she was with Bart, to ignore the financial gap between them: Bart was also starting to make money, lots of money, and he insisted on paying for Margaret on those occasions when she balked at $15 martinis, and on anteing up more than his half (specifically, his 85 percent) for the charming little Spanish bungalow they were renting in Los

Feliz. But now he's gone, and so is the bungalow and so are the martinis, and what has replaced them in the last four months is the credit card debt that compounds daily. And though Margaret had thought she was just paces behind her friends, about to catch up any day, now she knows that she is miles behind. Maybe not even in the race.

Claire is still speaking in her soft little feather voice, but Margaret can't understand a word she's saying. Josephine cups her hand to her own plump lobe. "We can't hear you, honey," she shouts. "Speak up."

Claire cranes her neck and speaks louder. A few of her words drift over the music ". . . Margaret know . . . celebrating . . . news about Josephine's mppffh . . . ?"

Margaret turns to Josephine for translation, but Josephine is looking down at her plate, waving her hand vaguely. "It's nothing," Josephine says. "Nothing's signed yet. It's all hot air." Her elusiveness is alarming; Margaret does not like to be the only person at the table who doesn't know what everyone is talking about.

Across the table, Alexis leans over and shouts, "Josephine's new screenplay was bought by Disney. They see it as a vehicle for Ysabelle van Lumis. Impressive, right?"

Claire, gingerly pinching a limp pink shrimp by its tail as it drips cocktail sauce, looks up with a horrified expression on her face and stares bullets at Alexis. Josephine coughs, and under the table Margaret feels a shoe graze her shin en route to Alexis's. "Ouch," Alexis says. "That hurt."

"What?" says Margaret, growing increasingly concerned.

"Nothing," says Josephine.

"Oh, come on," says Margaret, looking around the table and trying to interpret the stricken looks on her friends' faces. "You know that I already know Ysabelle van Lumis is going to be in *Thruster* with Bart. You don't have to avoid mentioning his name with me. I'm not *that* fragile."

There is an awkward silence, and no one looks directly at Margaret. She peers at Alexis, the most likely person to give it to her straight. "Is he dating her? Ysabelle van fucking Lumis?"

Alexis leans in, her brows crumpled, and sighs. "Well, they were seen holding hands during dinner at the Ivy last week. 'Canoodling,' according to, well, a certain celebrity magazine whose name we shall not speak for your sake. So read into that what you will."

Margaret feels a peculiar twisting somewhere around her esophagus. She's not sure which is worse—the knowledge that her friends (and anyone else reading *Us Weekly*) now know more about Bart, the man she lived with for well over three years, than she does herself or the intimation that her ex-boyfriend appears to have bounced back from their breakup so quickly (and with a bona fide movie star, no less!), whereas she has yet to delete his picture from her computer's screen saver.

"It's just a rumor," Josephine says soothingly. "I mean, come on. You know how full of shit those tabloids are. Hand-holding means nothing these days, anyway."

Margaret knows that hand-holding is not, in fact, nothing, but right this moment she knows that she can decide between feeling even worse than she already does by imagining her ex-boyfriend mid-coitus with a cream-faced underaged starlet, or having another glass of champagne. She decides she would rather have the champagne. She swallows her doubts, tilts the glass back, and lets the last of the bubbles tickle their way along her throat. Josephine quickly refills her flute.

"Tell me what your screenplay is about," Margaret says, changing the subject.

Josephine cocks her head, puts a finger to her chin, and strikes a pose. "Log line: High-concept teen romance. A modern adaptation of *Wuthering Heights* in the milieu of a Laguna Beach teen beauty pageant." She looks at Margaret and wrinkles her nose. "Really, it's the kind of trash you're going to eviscerate in *Snatch.*"

The entrées arrive at this opportune moment, giving Margaret a chance to gather herself. She looks down at her plate, where a mountain of shrubbery floats on a fishy-smelling pool of foam. The aroma of her friend's entrées—mounds of sea bass smothered in potato-olive puree, Madeira-soaked steaks still bleeding on the plate—makes her feel anemic.

"Oh, I wouldn't do that to you," she mutters, feeling vaguely ashamed. This isn't exactly true—she would do that. She's done it before, much to the detriment of her relationship with Bart. Perhaps now she'll be wise enough to think twice before she does a critical review of one of her friend's projects. But, of course, she won't have the opportunity anymore, will she?

Damn Stuart Gelkind. For more than a year he strung her along, promising her that *Snatch* was going to be the linchpin in the new alternative-publishing empire he was starting, the edgy female title that would sit on the magazine stands along with *Mother* (his planned eco-activism magazine) and *AMP* (his magazine devoted to unsigned indie bands) and *New Sprout* (the raw-foods title). He was going to purchase *Snatch* for a sum that seemed, to Margaret, breathtakingly large—$425,000, plus options! Together, they were going to turn *Snatch* into an even bigger, better magazine. Glossy covers. Full-color photos. Celebrity interviews (inspiring ones, of course, like indie-movie actresses and hip female politicians). *Paid contributors.* With Gelkind's backing *Snatch* would be more than a struggling feminist zine run out of Margaret's apartment; it would be a new kind of young women's magazine, a twenty-first-century anti-consumerist *Sassy,* a real mainstream publication that inspired girls to think for themselves.

All Margaret had to do was keep *Snatch* afloat for a few more months (and then a few more, and just a few more, until more than a year had passed), build up circulation to make the publication more appealing to the investors Gelkind was lining up, and when the financing finally came through they would be ready to go. It was a sure thing, Stuart vowed, and she believed him. He was, after all, the son of conservative publishing magnate Maxwell Gelkind, and even if Stuart's interest in this project sometimes seemed more about spiting his father than about his real commitment to independent publishing, certainly the kid had access to people with very deep pockets. The future looked very promising, and if Margaret found herself paying what otherwise would have seemed an extravagant sum for the lawyers to negotiate the acquisition agreement, and the FedEx bills for all those documents, and the direct-mail solicitations that Stuart had suggested would build up circulation, and the new copier and the glossy paper, it had seemed an unimpugnable investment.

And although Margaret had a momentary twinge about selling out, she told herself that this was a different form of capitalism than, say, her father's predatory variety of business. She would take ads only from enlightened companies—organic food chains, indie-rock labels, cosmetics not tested on animals—and only ads that were empowering to women. She even splurged by hiring two freelance ad salespeople to focus on just that. And if, after six months, they hadn't actually sold many ads, she consoled herself with the fact that setting a new paradigm always took time.

And then, last Friday, just a week ago, with the investors finally confirmed and the acquisition papers ready to sign, Stuart had asked to meet her at the Coffee Explosion on Sunset. She knew something was wrong when he didn't pay for her soy latte; he had *always* paid for her latte, a gesture one part noblesse oblige and one part future employer.

Stuart, sweating in his Brooks Brothers shirt, stared into the crème of his macchiato and refused to meet her eyes.

"Look," he said. "There's no easy way to say this so I'm just going to be frank. We're not going to be able to buy your magazine."

Margaret could feel the blood draining from her face. She had a mental flash of the pile of bills on her desk, a stack of unopened envelopes two inches thick, waiting for Stuart's long-promised check to finally arrive. There was a moment of silence before she was able to stammer, "Who is 'we'? I thought 'we' was you?"

"The investors I brought in," Stuart said, now gazing resolutely out the window as if fascinated by the parking lot. "They decided that *Snatch* didn't really have a viable business model after all. You have to admit, the circulation hasn't exactly skyrocketed this year, despite the direct-mail solicitations—"

"We have fifteen thousand subscribers," Margaret protested, her voice strangled by the tennis ball that had seemingly lodged in her throat. "That's still pretty good."

"I know, I know," said Stuart. "But the investors I brought in . . . well, they had a different vision. Bigger, you know? It's a pretty limited audience you're reaching. I mean, you know how hard it's been to sell ads. The investors still think that I should do a women's magazine, but just something a little more *fun*. Honestly, Margaret, you know how much I love *Snatch*, but it's just too . . . fringe to be mainstream. I mean, the last issue had a ten-page spread of vibrator reviews? With how-to diagrams!"

"Forty-six percent of all women own vibrators—what's fringe about that?" She did cringe, though, just a little, remembering the editorial she had written for the issue—an essay she'd composed in a drunken stupor one evening two weeks after Bart left—in which she'd declared vibrators the "great liberating tool of the female masses, making men totally irrelevant and putting women in charge of their own sexual destinies."

Stuart shrugged. "Well, it's not going to sell in Peoria."

Margaret seethed. She took an angry swallow of her latte and looked around the café, at the screenwriters busily tapping away at their laptops, at the retirees meticulously consuming every word of their daily *Los Angeles Times,* at the bored barista jittery from stolen espressos. She felt, suddenly, more angry than upset at Stuart's self-entitled carelessness. "You promised me," she hissed. "Do you know how much I spent—of my own money!—to make this happen? And now you're just walking away and leaving me holding the bill?"

"Well, if it makes you feel any better, I'm probably going to ditch *New Sprout,* too," he said, shrugging. "Raw food is too last year."

She grabbed for the most hurtful thing she could say to him. "God, you're just like your father."

Stuart looked at the bottom of his coffee cup, as if waiting for it to refill magically. "Well, it turns out he has kind of a point. I don't want to, like, lose money. This was supposed to be an investment. I mean, I know you hate greedy capitalists and all that, but this is a business, you know?"

And that was that. *Snatch*—her baby—was dead, murdered by Stuart Gelkind; though if Margaret was going to be honest with herself, the magazine had been on life support before Gelkind ever came around. The day of its death, *Snatch* was $92,000 in the hole. To be more specific, Margaret was $92,000 in the hole, since she had been paying all the bills out of her own pocket (or, more specifically, off her numerous credit cards) for the last year anyway. To be *really* specific, Margaret was exactly $92,548 in the hole, according to the math that she had done on Monday, a few days after Stuart dropped the bomb, as she fiddled with her pocket calculator and watched her father's company go public on CNBC. (That was three days ago, though, so the figure is probably higher now. Which means Margaret owes $92,548 plus three days of criminal interest to MasterCard, American Express, Visa, and one or two other credit card companies, all of whom want it back. Now.)

All that Monday, the first weekday she hadn't worked in months, maybe years, she'd sprawled on her couch in an uncharacteristic stupor, chain-smoking cigarettes and watching CNBC—the cable hijacked from an upstairs neighbor—while fanning herself with a six-month-old copy of *Granta.* She was hypnotized by the endless loop of inscrutable symbols scrolling by on the bottom of the screen; every twenty minutes her father's symbol—APPI—would swim by, and her pulse would quicken, and the bills would go ignored for a few minutes. The numbers crept upward, always. She wondered what each fraction represented to her father: A hundred thousand dollars? Five? A million? What had he done to *deserve* that kind of money—prey on male vanity with overpriced placebos? And then she thought of her own numbers creeping ever higher, each minute adding more interest to the bottom line of her credit card debt. Not to mention the money she owed Bart. It was incredible that her father's portion of just one of those Nasdaq fractions—one-quarter! one-half!—was probably more than her entire debt.

The thought had flickered across her mind then—just as it did this morning when Bart e-mailed, and just as it does even now, as she gazes down at her $18 microgreens—that one call to her parents would, in all likelihood, make her financial problems go away. But she refuses to do it; she has too much pride to go groveling back to Mommy and Daddy. She just *knows* that they have been waiting for her to fail for four years now—she can just imagine the "I told you so"s she'd hear when they found out about the magazine's demise. She can already hear the lectures about fiscal responsibility, see the disappointed faces reflecting on her "lost potential." So why give them an excuse to judge her? (This may be, she suspects, the reason she still hasn't summoned the strength to tell them that she and Bart broke up, either.)

And besides . . . just maybe . . . maybe there's still a chance she could resuscitate *Snatch.* Right? Stuart could change his mind and call. Better yet, she could do it by herself: She could find funding elsewhere. Or the ad salespeople could suddenly materialize with an enormous buy (never mind the fact that on Monday she'd told them, along with her other two part-time staffers, that *Snatch* was on a publishing hiatus). Or . . . something. She's just not ready to succumb to the fact that it's over, and until it's *really, truly* over there's no reason to tell her parents. She can fix this.

Anyway, she hasn't even had the opportunity to tell her parents about *Snatch*'s demise; her parents still haven't bothered to return the message she left on Monday, congratulating her father on his IPO, and she certainly isn't going to call them twice.

Then again, if they called her and just offered up some money of their own volition, maybe she wouldn't say no. Like a grant. Or an investment. But no: That would be a cop-out, too. If she'd absorbed one lesson from her father it was that self-reliance was paramount to self-worth, and it was already bad enough that she'd let Bart lubricate her lifestyle for so long. It would be even worse to skim money off her father; doubly bad that she would be profiting off the morally bankrupt pharmaceutical industry. This was her responsibility. Shaking off these thoughts, she forks up a pile of microgreens and leverages it toward her mouth. Everyone is staring at her. "Hmmm?" she asks.

"I just asked how *Snatch* was doing," says Alexis. "When's that acquisition going to happen?"

The microgreens are quite heavenly, actually, salty and redolent of the sea. Margaret pauses, considers the pillaged mountain of oyster shells, the sweating bottle of chilled champagne, the sparkly gold chandelier earrings ($3,400 at Fred Segal—Margaret was there when Claire bought them), and makes herself smile. She doesn't have the energy for anything else.

"Oh, very soon," she says vaguely.

Josephine smiles widely and grips Margaret's forearm with a broad hand. "That's *so great,*" she says. "We are *so* proud of you, you know? You did it! With your little magazine!"

And although Margaret winces at the word "little," she can't help but grin back, too caught up in Josephine's enthusiasm to feel guilty about lying to her friend yet again. For just a moment, her successes—imagined or not—are equivalent to those of her glamorous peers. She is in the race again. *Yes,* she thinks, *I will revive* Snatch. *I will make it work.* She looks around at her smiling, encouraging friends and thinks, *This is going to be okay.*

"A toast!" squeaks Claire, lifting her champagne glass. "To Margaret, the magazine mogul!"

"Yay, Margaret!" echoes Alexis.

Margaret smiles shyly, letting the alcohol flush her cheeks. She is lifted too high by all the champagne bubbles and the warm and fuzzy cheer to worry about the phone calls or about Stuart or about her debt to her ex-boyfriend or even about *Snatch* anymore; and she is also too high to panic when the bill finally arrives and is an astonishing $912.

Alexis yanks the bill away from Josephine's groping hand. "Our treat," she says. She points a finger at Josephine and orders: "Plug your ears." Josephine sighs, compliantly cupping her hands over her ears, and hums to herself to block out their conversation.

"Okay, so that's $304 each, not including tip, which makes it more like $350 each," says Alexis, digging into her purse. "Not as bad as I thought, actually." For just a moment, Margaret feels as if an elevator inside her has lost control and plummeted into her intestines. *They're splitting?* But she didn't even taste the lobster! She sacrificed her entrée! She quickly steadies herself and puts her game face back on. No, it's fine, she thinks, letting the bubbles lift her up again. It's just *money.* She reaches for her wallet, wondering if somehow an extra $50 will have materialized in its folds during the course of her meal.

Claire leans in toward Alexis and whispers, "But Margaret only had a salad . . ."

"Right," says Alexis. "Okay, then, you and I will cover, let's say, $375 each, and Margaret can chip in $275." She looks at Margaret and raises an eyebrow. "Fair?"

"Absolutely," Margaret replies, hanging tenuously on to her equanimity. "It's Josephine's birthday." She pulls out the wallet and extracts the three hundred-dollar bills, fanning them out. She lays them down on the table with a slap and discovers that this actually feels rather good. There is power that comes with just flinging away $300 like that, she thinks—a comfort in the bravado of a splurge. Now she can see why her friends like coming to places like this, and she feels herself an equal to them. This feels so great that when Claire reaches into her purse to get Margaret $25 in change, Margaret even waves her off.

But deep in her purse, the cell phone has started ringing again. For a brief second, Margaret is able to hang on to her high spirits and believe, optimistically, that this call might finally be a good one, the one she's been superstitiously waiting for, the mystery phone call that will somehow turn everything around. She sits there, frozen with indecision, torn between hoping and knowing better, between answering it and pretending that the cell phone so rudely ringing at dinner isn't hers all.

Josephine has taken her hand away from her ears and is pointing at Margaret's purse. "Whose phone keeps ringing?" she says. "Margaret—I think that's yours."

Alexis and Claire turn to stare at her, too. Margaret looks down at her purse as if she has never seen it before—but now, even without reaching in, she can see the cell phone's illuminated display, blinking, RESTRICTED NO.—and freezes. The champagne bubbles rapidly pop, one by one, bringing her suddenly back down to terra firma. And with six eyes fixed on her, with the burden of her friends' faith in her riding heavily down, she feels like she has no choice but to answer it. Even though she knows better, her hand plunges down into the satchel's leather depths, almost as if it has a will of its own, and comes back out with the cell phone, vibrating in her palm like a fish. She flips it open—the table silent, her friends watching her expectantly—and lifts it, excruciatingly slowly, to her ear.

"Hello, is this Margaret Miller?" asks the metallic woman's voice on the other end.

Margaret gazes at the tabletop for a long minute, trying to think of the correct answer to this question. She touches a finger to a particularly large bread crumb on the table and, when it sticks to her finger, brings it up to her mouth. She crunches the morsel between her teeth, chewing it twenty times, as if it were the last bite of food she will ever eat.

"Yes," she finally says in a flat voice, knowing exactly who the person on the other end is—it doesn't matter which one of them it is, there are a half dozen of them, maybe a dozen, but they are all the same. They have been torturing her for weeks now, months, disembodied robotic voices calling to collect her soul. RESTRICTED NO.

"I'm calling from the collection agency on behalf of MasterCard," the woman barks. "We've left eighteen messages for you already and sent you four notices in the mail. We would like to discuss the $22,353 debt on your credit card. Are you aware that if this is not paid expeditiously MasterCard has the right to take you to court and put . . ."

Margaret pulls the phone away from her ear, slowly, methodically, and shuts it so gently that it doesn't even make a click. She puts it back in her purse and looks back up at her friends. They are studying her very strangely. Claire appears vaguely panicked, Alexis's brow is wrinkled, and even Josephine is frowning with concern. This time, Margaret can't muster a smile.

"Is everything okay, Margaret?" asks Claire, her voice a nervous squeak. "You look pale."

"Wrong number," Margaret says, and stands up so suddenly that the room begins to spin. She stabilizes herself with a hand on the table, her other sweaty palm clutching the handle of her purse. *Oh my God,* she thinks. *I just threw away my last $300—on microgreens. Three hundred dollars. At 29 percent interest! I owe a hundred thousand dollars and I spent my last buck on a salad?* "I'm not feeling so well, actually," she stammers.

"You're leaving? You can't leave!" Josephine moans. "We have a table reserved at that new Russian vodka lounge!"

"No," Margaret says, "I think I need to go home." Without waiting for the usual formalities, she begins the long, agonizing walk toward Acqua's front entry, back past the almost-famous starlets and the Slavic hostess and the men in their Prada suits, and feels for all the world like a convicted prisoner shuffling out of the courtroom.

by the time she reaches her apartment, in the back of a moldering eighties-era apartment complex marred by graffiti tags from the nearby gangs, Margaret is descending so rapidly into despair that she is not in the least surprised to see a note taped to her front door. She opens it carefully and reads it in the dim light of the hallway. Written on blue notepaper in spidery old-fashioned script, it reads, "Margaret— Your rent is two months late. I regret it's come to this, but if I don't receive the past rent by the end of next week, I'm going to have to ask you to move out. Thanks, Al."

She crumples the note in her fist, stuffs it in her purse, and unlocks the door. All she can think of is her bed: If she can just go to sleep now, maybe in the morning everything will be better. In the dark, she gropes for the light switch and flips it on. Nothing happens. She stands in the main room—the only room—of her apartment, in the dark, listening to the traffic below. She can hear the Hernandez family in the studio apartment next door, their three children bickering, their Spanish soap opera so loud that she can make out the individual words: *¡Soy así que perdido—el amor de mi vida ha funcionado lejos con mi hermana gemela!* The night air in her apartment is hot and stale and smells like decaying cheese. The louvered blinds leak thin bars of sulfurous yellow light from the streetlamps outside.

She tries the light switch in the kitchen. Nothing. Margaret can't even muster the energy to cry. She sits down abruptly on the kitchen linoleum, which is sticky and worn, and then crumples back and stares at her ceiling from a prone position on the floor. In the dark, the cottage-cheese ceiling of her apartment looks oppressively close, an optical illusion as if the apartment above her is coming down to smother her.

It's all over, she thinks. *The magazine, Bart—everything.* She is about to be homeless, in debt, and jobless, and the thought of starting over—of sleeping in Josephine's spare bedroom, starting at zero in a new career, trying to date again—is too awful to bear. Maybe she can just run away, she thinks. Hide somewhere, far from the credit card companies, far from Bart, far from her friends and family and anyone else who might see how lost she's become. She wants to be anywhere but here.

The cell phone in the purse, still hooked over her shoulder, begins to ring, and the first three bars of that goddamn

Chopin étude are the final straw that turn Margaret's stupor
into fury. She sits up with a jerk, grabs the phone out of her
purse, and is about to hurl it across the room and against the
wall so that it never rings again—they're going to turn the
damn thing off tomorrow anyway—when she notices the caller
ID. LIZZIE, it says. LIZZIE. LIZZIE.

She stares at it for a minute, wondering if this is some
kind of cosmic message. But of course it's just her sister. Still,
Margaret is so relieved by the sight of her sister's name—so
grateful that, for once, it's not someone demanding her
money—that despite her dismal mood, she flips the phone
open.

"Lizzie?" she says.

"Margaret!" Her sister's voice on the end of the line is
high-pitched and childish. "It's Lizzie."

"I know," says Margaret, smiling despite herself. "I just
said your name, remember?"

"Oh," says Lizzie. "Hey. Have you talked to Mom?"

"No . . ." says Margaret, confused by the intensity of
Lizzie's question.

Lizzie sighs, a heavy whoosh of breath, as if the weight of
the world perched on her shoulders is crushing her flat. It is
the kind of dramatic sound that fourteen-year-old girls often
make when they consider the tragedy of their small lives, but
for some reason it gives Margaret pause. The sigh sounds real.
"Yeah, well. Mom needs you to come home," Lizzie continues. "Actually she didn't say that, but I think it's probably a
good idea because Dad's gone and she's, like, freaking out?
Did you know Dad left? I guess you don't if you haven't talked
to her. She's, like, freaking out. Anyway, do you think you
could come home?"

In the sweltering dark, on the filthy kitchen floor, Margaret smiles.

three

by the time margaret's car turns up the
driveway, at dusk on Monday, Lizzie has been sitting in the
living room window, waiting, for nearly three hours. During
that time, she has worked her way through eleven rice cakes
smeared with peanut butter, two trashy magazines, a liter of
lemonade, and one forbidden Snickers bar stealthily purchased that afternoon from the local 7-Eleven, which she
wolfed down only when she was 100 percent sure that her
mother, upstairs cleaning Margaret's room for the second
time today, wouldn't catch her eating it. When Margaret's
Honda finally crunches through the gravel and ticks to a stop,
Lizzie is so giddy with sugar and anticipation that she wrenches
open the front door before her sister has even unbuckled her
seat belt. She flings herself at the car, tripping on her cork
platform sandals, so that Margaret, extricating herself from
the front seat, is nearly knocked backward by Lizzie's embrace.

"Hey," Margaret says, her voice muffled and small from inside Lizzie's curtain of hair. "Hey there, Lizzie. Hey."

Lizzie rests for a moment there, catching her breath, her head buried in Margaret's shoulder. Her sister smells like French fries. Then Lizzie straightens herself and tugs on the bottom of her cutoff shorts. "God, I'm so glad you're home," she says, her words tumbling out uncontrolled. "Things are really weird here. Mom is kind of freaking me out. I thought I was going to have to give her a Valtrex or something . . ."

"Valtrex?" Margaret looks confused. "The herpes medication?"

"No, the stuff that makes you all chilled out," says Lizzie.

"Oh, you mean *Valium*," Margaret laughs.

"Whatever," Lizzie says, and sighs. Margaret always has this effect on her—unintentionally reminding Lizzie how stupid and naïve she really is, as if she'd only yesterday shoved her Barbies into the shoe box in the back of her closet. As Margaret extricates a duffel bag from the passenger seat, Lizzie cups her hands on the dusty glass of the windshield so that she can peer into the back of the car. It's full of cardboard boxes. "What are those?" she asks.

"Oh, just . . . nothing," Margaret says. "A few things I thought I'd store here. Where is she, anyway? Mom?"

"She's upstairs," says Lizzie. "Cleaning. Again. It's been weird. First she was in, like, denial about Dad, kept setting the table for him and everything, and then she suddenly got depressed, and then two days ago she went all psycho and started cleaning. All night long, even. Like I said, it's kind of like she needs a *Valium*."

They pause in the driveway, the unspoken subject hanging heavy between them. Lizzie glances up at the window and, deciding that Janice isn't watching, leans in close. "So, have you talked to Dad at all?"

Margaret looks at Lizzie, measuring her up. "No, but I got an e-mail from him. Saying it was all going to be okay. A total cop-out, if you ask me. He really should have called."

"I got one, too!" The e-mail had arrived in her in-box two days after her father had left: "I'm sure that by now your mother has told you that we're going to be divorcing. I know this may be hard, but we're going to be fine. I'm going to be giving your mom some space while we get used to these changes and I'm going to be traveling a lot in the next month or two for work, but you and I will spend some time together later this summer. Maybe miniature golf?" This had given Lizzie pause, especially since her father had never taken her minia-ture golfing in his life. She suddenly had a vision of a future filled with custody visitations, and was boggled by the implau-sibility of going to the movies with him alone, or visiting the zoo together, or doing whatever kids do with their divorced dads. "Regardless, there's no need for you to worry," the e-mail went on. "I'm sure you won't need to testify. And no matter what your mother may say, this isn't all my fault. Be good. Love, Dad."

Lizzie had read the e-mail a dozen times, trying to figure out what, exactly, it meant. Don't worry about *what*, specifi-cally? *What* was whose fault? And what did he mean by "good"? But mostly she had wondered to herself why he hadn't just called her instead of writing an e-mail. What, he didn't even want to *talk* to her anymore? Somehow this small detail was far more painful than the fact that her father had left them at all.

Her father's departure hadn't really come as a surprise to her. At breakfast the day after he left, when Mom had fed her that line about Dad "taking some time," she'd known imme-diately that he was gone. His leave-taking, in a way, had been pretty gradual: he'd been around less, and less, and less, until it seemed normal to not have him around at all. He spent most of the spring on the road for the business thing he was doing.

On the weekends, if he wasn't attending a conference some-place, he was at the golf course or off at "business dinners." But mostly it seemed like he was avoiding them.

The only reliable time to glimpse him had been at break-fast, and even then she was afraid to speak to him: The un-spoken rule for years had been that no one should speak to Dad until he'd finished his coffee. While Lizzie and her mother chatted, he would retreat behind his *Wall Street Journal*, randomly interjecting terse commands—rarely more than five words at a time, never lowering the paper. "Fire her," he'd say, registering Mom's complaints about the cleaning lady who was supposedly drinking their booze. "Just *sell* it," about the unreliable Porsche. "Not while I'm still breathing," regarding Lizzie's desire to go to Mexico on spring break. His patience, Lizzie sensed, was finite and had probably been entirely used up years ago.

She isn't happy that he's gone—after all, he's her *father*—but it is, in a weird way, a kind of relief. She hadn't realized how much she'd been holding her breath in anticipation of the moment when Dad just never came back from a business trip at all. And now that he hasn't, she can stop wondering whether he never will. Maybe life without him won't be so bad. It could just be her and her mom. And Margaret, now that she's back.

Except that, the truth is, it feels pretty horrible to be dumped like an old pair of tennis shoes, left by the curb. And then there's the Beverly issue, which makes everything even weirder and more complicated and upsetting. Lizzie tugs on a chunk of streaked hair and tries to read the expression on Margaret's face. "So . . . did Dad mention anything about Beverly in his e-mail?"

"Beverly?" Margaret looks confused.

"Mom's friend. Beverly Weatherlove. Her tennis partner. Remember?"

"What about her?"

"I guess . . ." Lizzie pauses, looking for the right words. "I guess he left us to be with her."

Margaret stands there blankly, her mouth hanging slightly open, as if she can't quite understand what Lizzie has said. "You mean, ran off with her? As in, an affair?"

Lizzie nods. "I think so."

"Holy shit," says Margaret. "Mom told you this?"

Her mother had not, in fact, told Lizzie this. The person who had decided it was her sacred duty to fill Lizzie in on the lurid details of her father's sex life was Susan Gossett. Susan— the swim team record holder in the 200-meter backstroke, the first girl in class to get her hair professionally highlighted, in possession of a perfect pair of 32C breasts that every guy in class lusted after but only a rare few were allowed to touch—had filled Lizzie in after summer swim camp at the rec center last Thursday, just three days after her father had left. She had timed her locker-room assault perfectly, waiting until the exact moment when Lizzie was prying the damp swimsuit from her goose-pimpled behind and feeling particularly vulnerable.

"Hey, Lizzie, I heard that your dad is, like, totally doing it with Beverly Weatherlove," Susan had told her in a voice coated with sugar, twirling the gold locket around her neck. "They're staying in a hotel together in San Francisco. A *suite.* My mom heard it from Leslie Beck's mom, who heard it from Mrs. Baron. It's *such* a scandal. Are you, like, totally upset?!"

Lizzie's brain had frozen solid at Susan's words, incapable of absorbing this nugget of information. Her father? Beverly Weatherlove? Beverly with her Clairol-blond bob and puckering brown cleavage? Her mother's tennis partner and clone? It was unfathomable. As Lizzie stood there, wordlessly churning, dripping chlorinated water on the locker-room floor, Susan took one step back and said loud enough for the whole locker room to hear, "Didn't you do it with Mark Weatherlove? So wouldn't that be, what, incest or something? That's so disgusting." All pretense of sweetness gone, Susan gazed at her with the beady focus of a hawk about to claw a field mouse to pieces.

Lizzie's fingernails cut sharply into her own palms, leaving small raw crescents. *Don't cry,* she thought, *that's the kiss of death.* She followed the thin wire of pain back to the center of her chest, coiled it into a deep wobbly breath. Mark's face swam into view: the sprinkle of acne across his forehead, the strange juggy ears that made his hair stick out on the side. Mark, her classmate, the son of her mother's best friend, the dork with whom she had been saddled for years at family barbecues and pool parties and group campouts.

"Mark? Nasty," she said, trying to capture just the right note of bored nonchalance as she grabbed a T-shirt to pull over her head. She thrust her head through and met Susan's blue eyes again. "You must really have a sick mind if you think *that.*" Inside, though, her mind raced: Had Mark told Susan that they'd slept together? Why had he lied? What else had Susan heard, anyway? Were people talking? What did they *know*?

Her cheeks were so hot she could practically hear the water sizzling as it trickled down the edges of her face. Lizzie had given up trying to figure out the logic of Fillmore High's social atmosphere: Why some people got to eat lunch on the grass on the main quad and others were banished to the patch of dirt behind the science room, why only certain music (Bobby Masterston: yes; the Hurly Burly Boyz: no) was acceptable to blast from your car stereo in the parking lot, why girls who wore Abercrombie & Fitch were so resolutely opposed to those who dared show up in Tommy Hilfiger. There were rules, and Lizzie had furiously studied them, even if she'd never been given the guidebook that explained why they existed in the first place. For years, of course, she hadn't been in play at all—she wasn't exactly *losing* the game, but she was irrelevant to female classmates like Susan, which was almost as bad. Only lately had she entered the field, to discover that she had become a focus of their hostility, and she was still unsure what that meant in terms of score.

That Thursday, though, it seemed clear that she had lost a round. Susan stepped away, edging back toward the door. "I only report what I hear," she said, then vanished before Lizzie could formulate another response. A low din returned to the locker room as the rest of the girls returned to their swimsuits and hair dryers and mascara. This felt like that recurring dream, Lizzie thought miserably, the one where she showed up at a party and realized, when everyone began to lob water balloons at her, that she was wearing a cowgirl costume and it wasn't a costume party. She wanted to run to the bathroom to release the tears of humiliation that had welled up under her lashes, but that seemed like a bad idea. Instead, she glanced around; almost everyone averted their eyes, except Becky Jackson. Becky screwed up her nose, crossed her eyes, and mouthed the word "bitch," thumbing her finger toward the door. Lizzie felt a quick stab of gratitude: Becky was a friend who could always be relied upon. Her only friend, actually. Kind, solid, earthy Becky, always good for an extra Snickers bar or a ride to the mall, even if she sometimes seemed kind of, well, *young*.

Lizzie went straight home after swim camp, her heart still thudding uncomfortably in her chest, her skin itching from the chlorine. She ached indefinably, not quite upset enough to cry, but hollow like a Russian nesting doll. Her father? An affair? How come she hadn't known? She felt she'd been given a glimpse into a secret world of adults that she'd never known existed, one that was perilously close to her own world, and couldn't quite put a handle on what it all *meant*. She had a flash of her father doing it with Beverly (where? in a cheap hotel? in the back of Beverly's BMW station wagon?), and it made her queasy.

The house was hot and stuffy and silent, with the doors closed to the afternoon breeze. "Mom?" she called out, but there was no response: Janice was out. She slid across the parquet of the entry hall, her flip-flops squeaking on the wax, and thunked up the stairs. The house was designed in L-shaped wings that met in the center at a sweeping mahogany staircase that unrolled like the tongue of a panting dog. Downstairs, the musty living room and terrifying dining room—done all in white, an invitation for Lizzie's inevitable cranberry spills and scuff marks—dominated the east wing. She usually gravitated instead toward the west, where the vast kitchen stretched across the length of the house (offering views in both directions as well as access to the Sub-Zero), next to the family room, with its 422 channels of nonstop entertainment. Upstairs, the girls' bedrooms were to the left, from the top of the staircase; master and guest bedrooms to the right. It was entirely possible to stand at the end of the girls' wing and shout as loud as you could and never be heard at the other end—mostly because the upholstery was so lush that it seemed to suck all the sound from the rooms. The drapes were thick brocade; the cream carpet piled an inch thick; the furniture heaped with down-filled cushions in velvets and tweeds. Sometimes, as Lizzie walked down the hall, she would whack the walls with the side of her hand until it throbbed, just to remind the house that she was, in fact, alive.

Shaken by Susan's news, that day, she found herself inexplicably drawn toward the master bedroom, the main locus of mystery in the house. What did she expect to find there—answers? hidden love letters? her father, doing it with Beverly Weatherlove? Certainly, she didn't expect to find her mother, lying down in the middle of the day.

When she pushed open the door, she saw that the blinds were drawn, with only a little daylight leaking from behind the swagged curtains to illuminate the silhouette of an unmade bed. Lizzie hit the light switch with the edge of her palm and then froze in alarm: Her mother was lying on the bed, fully dressed in a cerulean velour tracksuit with a gel mask over her eyes. A bottle of Côtes du Rhône sat on the nightstand, leaving a cherry ring on the wood. A half-empty tumbler held loosely in her right hand listed dangerously. One of Lizzie's father's suits, covered with dust, lay on the bed beside her.

At the sound of the door, her mother twitched, letting a little wine splash onto the linen. "Paul?" she called out, struggling to heave herself to her elbows. She pushed the gel pack to the top of her head—it caught back her fine blond hair like a headband—and blinked twice at Lizzie with enlarged pupils. "Oh. Sorry, honey. How was swim camp?" Janice put the glass back down on the side table and dabbed at the spilled wine with the edge of her palm.

Lizzie took a step forward. "Are you okay?" she asked.

Janice sat up against the pillows, fanning her flaming cheeks with her left hand. The gel mask had left deep creases in the thin skin surrounding her eyes, giving her the appearance of a stunned owl. "Just a little under the weather," Janice said, but her voice was as parched and thin as dust. "I think it might be allergies. All the pollen in the air this time of year."

"Oh," Lizzie said, not quite sure how to address this obvious untruth. Her mother smelled faintly tangy, like stale alcohol. Was she *drunk*? Lizzie stared at her mother with alarm: Her mother *never* got drunk. "Um, are you sure?"

Janice nodded, her head wobbling and bumping the headboard with each jerk.

Lizzie swallowed hard. She'd spent the last few days waiting for her mother's collapse—waiting for some clue that might reveal exactly how Lizzie was supposed to react to her father's departure—but her mother hadn't shed a single tear that Lizzie had witnessed. Instead, she had behaved as if nothing had changed. She sat at dinner—ignoring the empty place setting, where her father had not come to the table—and quizzed Lizzie about her day at swim camp. She put together shopping lists and continued to thumb through *Gourmet,* compiling the menu for an upcoming cocktail party. She drove to her Wednesday morning Pilates class and got her nails wrapped by Ellie. But the pitch of her chatter had ascended several octaves, until it had taken on a shrill quality. Lizzie felt as if she were watching a delicate crystal vase teeter on the edge of a tall shelf, aware that it could come crashing to the ground at any minute but too far away to stop it.

That Thursday, Lizzie was relieved that something had finally changed, although this particular collapse wasn't exactly what she'd had in mind. She'd expected something a bit more basic: tears, for example. This felt more like a black hole that had sucked all the emotion from the room. The emptiness was frightening. She took a tentative step forward. "Mom? Are you sad about Dad?"

Janice stiffened. "We're not going to talk about your father right now, okay?"

Lizzie tried to hold her tongue, pressing it to the roof of her mouth as hard as she could, but the question slipped out anyway. She couldn't help it. "Mom, I heard something today about Beverly Weatherlove?" she asked, then instinctively winced in anticipation of her mother's response.

But nothing happened at all. Janice just pressed her fingers to her temple. "Could you bring me a few aspirin? I have a headache."

Lizzie sighed and sidled into the bathroom to paw through the cabinets, sending a pair of tweezers and an empty bottle of Vicodin onto the tile in the process. Returning to the bedroom, Lizzie plopped two Tylenol into her mother's outstretched hand. Janice clenched her fingers around them. "Do you want water?" Lizzie asked, but Janice was already washing the pills down with the wine.

"You're my angel," Janice said, and reached out to pat Lizzie on the wrist. "I just need to sleep this off. But I'll make you dinner later."

"Mom . . ." Lizzie began.

Her mother closed her eyes. "Don't," she said, strangling the end of the word. The room fell silent again. Lizzie could hear the faint whine of the neighbors' dog, barking in the distance. The air tasted hot. She waited by the bed for a minute, but Janice didn't open her eyes. Instead, she pulled the gel mask down again and slid down the pillows until she was lying flat, her hair fanning out behind her on the sheets.

Lizzie slipped out the door. Downstairs, she picked up the phone and dialed her sister in Los Angeles. This was too much to deal with alone, she decided. Margaret would know what to do. She always knew everything. She would come home and make everything okay again.

Except that Margaret is here now, and her presence isn't nearly as reassuring as Lizzie had thought it would be. Something about her sister's appearance makes her nervous, although she can't quite pin down why. She has always been jealous of her sister's skinny-girl metabolism: Margaret has a take-it-or-leave-it attitude toward food, whereas Lizzie is an unfortunate lifelong member of the clean-plate club. (If Lizzie forces herself to eat a salad for dinner, she'll dream that night of Twinkies and fried chicken, tuna sandwiches dripping with mayonnaise, and chocolate chip cookies fresh from the oven.) But now Margaret is a total *twig*: When she went in for a hug on the driveway, Lizzie could feel the angles of Margaret's collarbones, the gaping of the terry-cloth sundress around her chest. Maybe it's just because Lizzie, in her four-inch platform sandals, is taller than her, but the weird truth is that Margaret seems *diminished*.

They walk up the driveway and toward the house, Lizzie

carrying Margaret's laptop case, Margaret heaving the duffel over a fragile-looking shoulder. "So," Lizzie says, eager to get started with the fun gossip. "How's Bart?"

"He's fine," says Margaret, quickly. Lizzie waits for her to elaborate, but she doesn't. Lizzie bites her tongue. Maybe in Los Angeles it's not considered cool to talk about your famous boyfriend. Maybe it's about acting like that kind of thing is just totally normal. Still, she is dying to know everything about the Hollywood life she reads about in the tabloids, and Margaret is always so *stingy* with those kinds of details.

She changes tactics. "Have you been to any Hollywood parties lately?" she asks. "What celebrities have you seen?"

"Lizzie, celebrities aren't really as interesting as you think they are," says Margaret, giving her a sidelong look. "You really should stop buying those trashy magazines. They're just going to make you feel insecure. Don't you read the magazines I send you? I had a big editorial in the February issue about that."

"Of course," says Lizzie, although the truth is that she finds *Snatch* boring and difficult to read. Too many ten-dollar vocabulary words, not enough celebrity gossip: It makes Lizzie's brain hurt to try to follow along, although she found the vibrator pictures in the last issue very educational. Still, she smiles gamely at her sister. "Did you bring the new issue for me?"

But Margaret doesn't answer. Instead, she stops at the door to the house, with its formidable brass knocker, and looks Lizzie up and down. "You've lost more weight, haven't you?" she says, changing the subject.

Lizzie feels herself beaming. She had wondered when Margaret would notice. "Thirty-seven pounds now. You can tell?"

"Of course. You look terrific. Not, of course, that you looked bad before, mind you. Marilyn Monroe was a size fourteen, did you know that? The cult of thin is just a recent development in human evolution. But, anyway, you look great. Really great. You should be proud of yourself."

Lizzie smiles and shrugs, hoping to look casually indifferent. "It's the swimming."

"I figured it wasn't the elocution lessons," Margaret says and smiles as they walk into the house and head up the stairs in search of their mother.

in the beginning of eighth grade, a year and a half earlier, Lizzie's mother signed her up for classes in etiquette, ballet, and elocution. "For grace, poise, and eloquence," Janice explained to Lizzie. Lizzie hated them all. She was terrible at ballet. Her pliés were mushy, her pirouettes wobbly, and the way the elastic on the leotard squished the fat on her thighs depressed her. Etiquette was the most useless thing she'd ever learned: Snails were disgusting, she'd never in a million years eat one, so why did she need to learn the proper fork for escargot? And elocution was even worse. Mrs. Grimley would make her trill her *r*'s over and over and over again until she thought she would hyperventilate.

The classes were filled with gawky, awkward girls, girls with surgical-looking headgear, or with erupting acne, or crippling shyness, or who were overweight and lumpen like herself. The lot of them spent their weekly internment miserably chewing on their hair and trying to shrink as far into the corners as possible, lest the teacher call on them. Lizzie felt like she'd been banished to the island of misfit toys.

"Light and feminine! Like a robin on a branch! Rrrrrobin!" Grimley would command, as she cruised up and down the line of cowering teenagers. She would, without fail, pick out poor Rebekah Steinberg—six feet tall, with a deadly lisp and so self-conscious she would blush if you even looked at her—and force her to repeat phrases like "Why yes, sir, I'd be delighted for this dance," except that in Rebekah's mouth it came out like a bowl of oatmeal mush and you knew that no boy was ever going to give her the opportunity to botch that sentence. And Lizzie, while pitying Rebekah, would inch that much farther away, aware that befriending other social pariahs might diminish her status even more. She was cooler than this class, she knew; sure, she was a little chunky, but her personality wasn't crippled, like many of these other girls'. Maybe she wasn't at the top of the social spectrum, but she hadn't yet hit the bottom either.

"It's not going to kill you to learn a little poise," Janice said when Lizzie complained. "You're going to be a young lady soon. I wish someone had taught *me* these kinds of things when I was your age—I remember how petrified I was the first time I ate dinner at your father's parents' house. . . . Don't laugh, Lizzie, these things are important. Think about it: What will happen when some boy you like takes you out to dinner and he sees you talk with your mouth full?"

"But, Mom," Lizzie protested, "most boys in my class think table manners means shoving French fries up your nose."

"Well, that doesn't make them right," said her mother. "Really, honey, good manners will take you far in life. Trust me."

And so, for a while, Lizzie tried. Maybe her mother was right—what was keeping boys from asking her out was that she didn't properly turn out her toes and didn't enunciate her *t*'s. Maybe the reason her father was so rarely home for dinner was not that he was really busy at work but because he couldn't stomach watching Lizzie shovel spaghetti Bolognese down with the salad fork.

Though she diligently attended classes and practiced her posture in front of the mirror at home, it didn't make a difference. After over a year of lessons in ladydom, Lizzie could properly ask for the salt to be passed but she had gained another eleven pounds and still tripped over her feet and had failed to fill her Saturday nights with dates, or anything, for that matter, besides the occasional MTV marathon with Becky. Instead, she climbed in the SUV with her mother every week and wanted to cry, seeing the grim, determined look on her mother's face. It was a kind of punishment, she decided. It was obvious to Lizzie that her mother secretly wished she could take her back and replace her with a perfect daughter, some skinny, poised, anemic ballerina.

Janice, after all, had perfect table manners and perfect diction and didn't really walk—she levitated through rooms with satisfyingly dainty clicks of her heels. And apparently all this came naturally to her, since she had never taken etiquette classes herself. Unlike Lizzie, she had the tiny bones of a sparrow. It was totally unfair. And everyone loved her. She always had a party to go to, and the phone rang constantly, and even though she was nearing fifty Lizzie sometimes saw men turning to watch her mom on the street. Lizzie only attracted attention from the weirdos.

"Don't let Mom force you to take those classes," Margaret said when Lizzie called to complain. "She made me do it, too. It's some bizarre thing from growing up poor; she believes these are advantages she's conferring on you, but what she's really doing is shoehorning you into some stereotyped fantasy of womanhood. Right? So just stand up to her—tell her to stop reinventing her own childhood through you. Or just sign up for extracurricular activities at school instead. That's what I did."

But Lizzie secretly thought her mother was right. She *was* ungainly. Her only real friend was Becky, who didn't have any dates either and sometimes picked her nose when she didn't think anyone was looking. Instead of hanging out in the parking lot of the Pizza Stone after school, where the cool kids liked to go, Lizzie mostly sat in her bedroom and plucked the hair out of her legs with tweezers. She'd only kissed two boys: one was a captive victim during a spin-the-bottle game at summer camp in seventh grade and the other was Mikey Bronstein, the alto saxophonist from band class, who was sweet but wore thick Coke-bottle glasses and still let his mother pack him crustless bologna sandwiches in brown paper bags for lunch. He'd taken her to a freshman football game, held her hand, and called her his girlfriend. Mortified by his enthusiasm, she'd dumped him within a week.

Not long after Lizzie tipped the scales at 168 pounds, she arrived downstairs one morning to find an egg-white omelet on the table rather than her usual bowl of Frosted Flakes. "Honey," Janice said, as Lizzie balked, "don't you think you would feel better if you lost a little bit of weight?"

"No," Lizzie said. "I'll be miserable no matter what I weigh." But she knew this wasn't true; didn't skinny girls have more fun, get more boyfriends, attract more attention?

"Don't be so pessimistic," Janice said. "It'll be fun. We'll do it together." She patted her own thighs, underneath the pleats of her tweed slacks. "I've got to do something about my cellulite, too." And Lizzie imagined living like her mother, who had been on a diet as long as she could remember, who nibbled on green vegetables and cottage cheese rather than French fries and chocolate popcorn in order to maintain her figure, and she wanted to cry. Her future spread out before her, a barren wasteland with all the joy and grease stripped out.

But maybe if she was skinny, Lizzie thought, she would get attention from boys. Dates. Love. And that would be even better than chocolate popcorn. So she did it. She stopped her lunchtime raids of the vending machines in the cafeteria, cut out the secret trips to McDonald's that she usually made on the way home from school, and stopped hoarding candy bars under her bed. She ate the tofu salad and skinless chicken and mounds of steamed spinach that her mother prepared without once making a face or holding her nose.

It was about this time, the fall quarter of her freshman year, that she joined the swim team—initially because it provided an easy way for her to bail on the etiquette and elocution lessons, per Margaret's advice, and then because she found she actually enjoyed it. And, amazingly, between the exercise and the self-restraint, she found the scale registering lower and lower: 162 pounds, 157, 149. Clothes began to hang off her, and she thought she could actually see cheekbones. Her mother, she could tell, was pleased. Lizzie began to look forward to her mother's little exhalation of pleasure when the scale registered a drop, pushed harder just to impress her. Even her father noticed the change, dipping his *Wall Street Journal* one morning to examine her over the top of the business section. "Lookin' good, pumpkin," he said before turning the page. It made her week.

When she hit the twenty-pound mark, Janice lent Lizzie her platinum card and sent her on a shopping spree. Lizzie filled her closet with trendy new things, dumping the baggy cargo pants and oversized T-shirts, the dresses she'd stealthily purchased in the Generous Juniors department, and replacing them with neon-pink halter tops and denim miniskirts. She couldn't wait for the moment when she could put on something sexy—a fancy cocktail dress, maybe even heels?—and walk out the front door on a date with a cute boy while her parents watched from the kitchen window.

And it worked: Losing all that weight got her the attention she wanted. That, and much, much more.

by the spring of her freshman year, it seemed like Lizzie had been dying to lose her virginity forever. She felt it hanging like a yoke around her neck. Girls in her class had been bragging about their sexual conquests for years: starting with Frenching and feel-ups in sixth grade, moving on to blow jobs and fingering (a phrase she found both obscene and banal—some cross between an alien probe and playing the piano) by eighth, and then, once they reached high school, going "all the way." It happened like clockwork: There would be a party at somebody's house over the weekend—the parents having disappeared for a vacation in Hawaii, graciously enabling their children to roll a keg into the chaperone-free living room—and on Monday, girls would show up at school with squared shoulders and a fresh familiarity with the male anatomy. ("Oh my God, his penis, like, curved!" "He—so gross—had hair on his *back*!") They dropped like flies all freshman year, judging by the conversation in the girls' locker room. Virginity flew out the window, blossoms of used condoms bloomed in wastepaper baskets all across town, sheets were furtively dumped in spin cycles with extra bleach before Mom and Dad's town car picked them up at the airport.

Lizzie wanted it so badly she was almost embarrassed. It wasn't like she believed that losing her virginity was somehow going to be a ticket to womanhood—just like getting her period for the first time had been more of a messy pain in the ass than the entrée to some feminine sisterhood that Margaret had promised. It was more that she wanted to be in the inner circle, to have those terms—clitoris? smegma? pearl necklace?— mean something to her, too. You either knew or you faked it, and she was tired of faking it, tired of nodding sagely while she listened in, uninvited, to yet another whispered tale of deflowering or requited lust, as if she could totally relate, when in fact she couldn't. Losing your virginity was the ultimate sign of social success, she decided: It meant that you were the object of desire, that a boy wanted you so badly that he couldn't control himself. She wondered when her mom had lost her virginity. Surely *she* hadn't been a virgin on her wedding day.

And neither would Lizzie, thanks to Justin Bellstrom, the indisputable star of Millard Fillmore High's swimming team.

Her first spring regional swim meet had happened in Sacramento the last week of March. Her mother was playing in the spring tennis tournament at the club, and her father was off on the IPO road show, so Lizzie had gone in the team bus without them, not sure whether she was relieved that they wouldn't be there embarrassing her or disappointed that they wouldn't see her swim competitively. And although she didn't win a blue ribbon at the meet, she did place third in the 100-meter breaststroke time trial. She tried calling her mom on her cell phone to give her this piece of news, but her mother didn't answer—she was probably on the court. Lizzie didn't bother leaving a message.

That was the weekend Justin cruised to first-place in the men's freestyle. As he stood on the pedestal at the end of the race to receive his award, leering at the cheering crowd, Lizzie thought he looked like one of those Greek gods they were studying in her Ancient History class. Adonis. Maybe Hermes. (Or was that the one with the weird clubfoot?) Anyway: Justin's sun-bleached waves shone, faintly green from chlorine damage (Justin, famously, refused to wear a swim cap), and she could see the downy hair on his legs, growing thicker toward his crotch. He was wearing a fake gold tooth someone had given him as a joke, and when he smiled his trademark dimpled smile, you could see it glint. When they announced his name, he pumped his fist in the air in victory, then quickly turned, yanked down the top of his Speedo, and mooned the crowd with a pale, bumpy behind. Anyone else, the coach would have benched for that stunt, but not Justin. He could get away with anything.

As he was climbing off the pedestal, his gaze snagged on Lizzie's. Shockingly, he winked at her with one big, pink-rimmed eye—wickedly, as if they'd just shared some secret. She could feel her face burning with pleasure. Was it a message? Had his mooning been some kind of display just for her? Had he secretly had a crush on her all this time and she'd just not known it? It seemed so unlikely—Lizzie and Justin Bellstrom? It would never happen. It was as unlikely as a peacock dating an orangutan. But—and here she caught herself—why not? She'd just hit the thirty-one-pound mark on her diet, and maybe he'd noticed the cute new halter top she was wearing. Maybe he'd even noted her performance in the time trials that morning. Stranger things had happened.

Lizzie decided right then and there that he was the one. She didn't want to lose her virginity to a nice boy like Mikey Bronstein; she wanted a heartthrob, the kind of boy everyone would look at and admire. Justin was in an entirely different league than she was, which was why, of course, he was perfect. She had visions of herself trading up, leaping a few rungs up the social ladder of Fillmore High. God, wouldn't Susan Gossett and her friends just *die* if they saw Lizzie walking down the halls of Fill High arm in arm with Justin!

Later that night, after several hours of watching pay-per-view movies with Becky in their hotel room, she announced that she was going to the vending machine and left to search the shabby hallways of the Sacramento Wander Inn (doubles only $39 a night), trying to find Justin. The entire hotel had been booked with swimmers from around the state. The coaches either didn't care about the debauchery or had fallen asleep and weren't aware of it or had given up and retired to the hotel bar. When she pressed her ear to the doors of various hotel rooms, she thought she could hear faint echoes of orgies taking place inside. In one room, the sounds of shrieking laughter and breaking glass; in another, gunfire from a television; in another, the rhythmic thump of a headboard drilling the wall. The industrial carpet of the hallways was littered with abandoned beer bottles, empty pizza boxes, and the occasional puddle of vomit. She picked her way through gingerly, from the fifth floor through the first, stepping over a passed-out teenage boy in the stairwell, tiptoeing around the groups of whispering girls clustered outside hotel room doors who glanced blankly past her as she squeezed by.

After half an hour of wandering, she was ready to give up and go back to her own quiet hotel room, where she'd left Becky watching *Blind Date* on cable. She stood waiting by the elevator, trying not to inhale lest she accidentally get a whiff of the potted fern next to her, into which someone had recently urinated. When the elevator door slid open, there was Justin, prone on the floor with his arm wrapped lasciviously around a pillow. He opened one bloodshot eye and stared at her.

"Party central, going up," he said. "Have any beer?"

The stench of booze wafted through the air and hit her in the face. She inched into the elevator and let the door slide closed, but didn't press any buttons. Instead, she drummed up the conversational opener she'd been practicing in her head all night. "Congratulations on winning the freestyle," she began. But standing over him like that made her feel awkwardly large, so she crouched down on her haunches and started again. "I thought that was really funny what you did today. You know, when you won."

Justin squinted at her. "What about vodka? Have any of that? Pot? I'll take anything."

"Um, no," she said, taken aback. She tried to return to the script. "I really like your technique. The way you, um, breathe every fourth stroke?"

Justin rolled over onto his back and hugged the pillow to his chest. "Who are you?" he asked.

Lizzie's stomach sank. "Lizzie," she said. She stood up and hit the button for her floor. The elevator lurched and began to rise. "Lizzie Miller. I'm on the swim team with you. I do the breaststroke."

"Oh, right," he said. "Lizzie. Lizzie of the breaststroke. Lizzie of the breasts. Lizzie, know where we can get some beer?"

"No," she said.

"I think I might have some alcohol in my room," he said. "I just can't remember where my room is. Do you know where my room is?"

The elevator slid to a stop, and the doors opened to reveal two kids slurping at each other's faces. Justin and Lizzie watched for an endless few seconds, the air filled with suggestion and the liquid sound of spit being exchanged, before Lizzie hit the "Door Close" button with her fist. The doors slid shut again, and the elevator rose. She considered her options: he was clearly a mess, but when else would she be alone with Justin Bellstrom?

"What does your room key say?" she asked.

Justin propped himself up against the mirrored wall of the elevator. His curls were flattened on one side, with cigarette ash caught in the front. He dug in the pocket of his jeans and pulled out a room key with the number 302 on it. He looked up at Lizzie with frank admiration. "Wow, you're really smart."

Lizzie shrugged. "Logic," she said.

"Wanna come have a drink?"

The hair on her forearms prickled up, as if she'd just put her finger in a light socket. Her heart began to race. "Sure," she said, more nonchalantly than she felt.

Room 302 was at the end of the corridor. She followed Justin as he reeled down the hallway, bouncing from wall to wall like a pinball and stopping at each door to squint at the number and compare it to his key. He dropped the pillow and left it behind. She picked it up and took a quick whiff. It smelled like scalp. At the door, he fumbled with the key, attempting to insert it upside down. She grabbed it from him and let them in.

The hotel room was hazy from cigarette smoke, and all the sheets had been ripped from the bed and piled in a heap by the television. His roommate, whoever he was, was gone. Justin crawled over, flung himself facedown on the pile of sheets, and rummaged under the bed. He emerged with a plastic jug of blue liquid and held it up over his head.

"Victory is mine," he said.

"What is that?" Lizzie asked.

"Everclear. With blueberry Kool-Aid."

"Everclear?"

"Grain alcohol. Hundred and fifty-one proof. This stuff will get you fucked up." He lifted the bottle and took a swig before handing it to Lizzie. She paused and smelled it—it made the hair in her nose stand on end—before taking a gulp. The alcohol felt like it was peeling a layer off the inside of her throat, and the Kool-Aid left a gummy sugar coating on the inside of her mouth. She choked and dribbled blue juice down the front of her T-shirt.

"Um," she said. "That's awful."

"Yeah, isn't it? It's the bomb."

With Justin watching, she gamely took another swig. Already she could feel the heat radiating from her belly up to her chest and out through her fingertips. She had tasted alcohol before—the occasional swig from her parents' abandoned glasses after dinner, a whole glass of champagne snuck at a bar mitzvah last year—but she had never experienced anything like this. It was, she decided, a pleasant sensation. It made her feel weightless, almost like she was swimming. She took the bottle out of Justin's hands and swallowed again. She lay back on the pile of sheets next to Justin, and stared up at the pebbled ceiling; someone had managed to stick a wad of gum on it.

Justin lit a cigarette and took a puff. "Isn't this lame? I hate this shit."

"Cigarettes? Yeah, they're kinda gross."

"Nah. Swim team. I only do it because my mom makes me. She thinks it will get me into a good college. But I hate all this gwoooo . . ." He burped. "I mean, giving up my weekends. Sacramento sucks, you know? I wanna stay home and party with my friends. Fucking six-in-the-morning wake-up. It's too much work."

"I don't know," said Lizzie. The cigarette was making her nauseous and light-headed and she could feel sweat beading up at her temples. "I think it's fun to be good at something."

"Are you good at swimming?"

"I'm getting better. I guess I'm pretty decent." She blushed. When she looked up, Justin had rolled onto his side and was examining her intently. He reached out and pulled a strand of her hair over her eyes, so that she was peeking out from behind it.

"Hey," he said. "Didn't you lose a bunch of weight or something?"

She nodded, finding her tongue incapable of motion. Instead, she took another gulp of the booze, which rendered her limbs immobile, too. The gum on the ceiling was beginning to undulate in a peculiar way.

Justin crawled closer. She could feel the warmth of his skin through the cotton of her shirt, so near that all she need do was shift her hand an inch and she would make contact. She was petrified. *This is the moment of my reinvention,* she thought. *I can be anyone.*

"Do you have a crush on me?" Justin asked. He paused. "It's okay if you do."

She closed her eyes so she wouldn't have to see his response and nodded. With her eyes closed, she felt like she was on a merry-go-round spinning at top speed. *Please,* she thought to herself, *please when I open my eyes let him be madly in love with me.* She counted to three and opened them. Justin was leaning in, looking straight down at her from five inches away. His eyes, she noticed, were pale blue, almost the color of the water in the school swimming pool. She thought she could feel the blood pulsing through her veins, in time to the whacking of her heart.

Before she could second-guess herself, she lurched upward, closing the space between them, and kissed him. He didn't seem the slightest bit surprised.

His tongue was sloppy and tasted like a raw steak tenderized with ash and lemons, and their noses bumped in the dark. *Thank God,* she thought, and closed her eyes again. She had to concentrate very hard on breathing through her nose and she could feel saliva dripping down her chin. The alcohol washed over her in waves, carrying her gently along the tides, tugging away her T-shirt, her jeans, her bra and panties, until she found herself, six minutes later, naked and exposed on the opposite shore.

Later, she would try to dredge up the details of losing her virginity and come up with very few. It hadn't really hurt—maybe she was anesthetized by the Everclear?—but it hadn't exactly felt fantastic either. It was, she decided, much like when she'd had a root canal and the dentist gave her nitrous before he fired up his drill: kind of unpleasant and violent and lovely and blurry all at the same time.

What *was* nice was afterward, when they lay there naked, and she could hear his slowing breath by her ear. His sweat dripped onto her stomach, and she didn't wipe it away. She'd never been so close to a boy in her life, flesh pressing against flesh, hair in each other's faces. Her father wasn't really the hugging type, and her mom didn't count. So this is what intimacy is, she thought. This is what it means to be close to someone. This is what it feels like to be beautiful. It's this simple.

"Thanks," he said. "That was fun."

They lay there in silence for a few minutes, as the air-conditioning kicked on and goose bumps rose on their naked skin. A knock sounded at the door. Lizzie froze, afraid to breathe, as the voice of Coach Jones drifted through the plywood. "Lights out, kids. Set your alarms for six A.M." She could hear him walk away and knock on the door of the next room over.

"I should go," Lizzie whispered, hoping that Justin would ask her to stay. Justin didn't reply. She craned her neck and looked down at where he lay on her chest. He'd passed out. His mouth hung open, and she could see that his tongue had turned blue from the Kool-Aid. She had to use both hands to push him off her. He flopped to the floor and began to snore. Lizzie scrubbed herself clean with a wad of toilet paper in the bathroom and reluctantly got dressed, feeling like every article of smelly clothing she put back over her naked skin further erased the momentous thing that had just occurred. Then she let herself out. She stumbled back to her room, where she found Becky asleep in the middle of the bed, hugging a teddy bear to her chest.

Justin didn't call her. Not that she'd given him her number, but secretly she hoped he'd look it up anyway. When she saw him in the hallway at school the next week, he smiled and waggled his fingers and even mouthed a "hello" as he walked by with his friends. She thought she saw—*wait, did he?* Yes. He winked. And this time it was for real, it was meant for her.

Becky watched this interaction with bewilderment. "Since when are you and Justin Bellstrom friendly?" Becky asked.

And Lizzie just smiled, a mysterious smile that she thought looked maybe a little like the Mona Lisa, and let the warmth of her secret intimacy suffuse her. She saw the puzzled look on Becky's face and thought she might pop right out of her own skin, she was so happy.

.   .   .

maybe it was true that losing her virginity was kind of a disappointment. Justin wasn't madly in love with her after all, and he didn't want to be her boyfriend. But it cracked open a sealed door in the social strata of Millard Fillmore High. Justin would, on occasion, come talk to her after swim team—just to say hello—and some of Justin's guy friends began nodding to her in the hallways too. She began to find notes shoved in her locker, inviting her to the parties she'd always felt excluded from before; notes asking if she wanted to hang out after school to do homework together; notes wondering if she wanted to come by when parents were out of town.

Her mother had been right: Lose the weight, learn to hold your fork correctly, and you'd have all the dates you could dream of. Boys liked her after all. Besotted with her new popularity, she ended up having sex with Justin's friends, too. More than one of them. Actually, six.

She marveled at the attention; it was unreal. Never before had she shown up at a party and found herself surrounded by boys from her class, who seemed to hang on her every word, who made sure her hands were never empty. They thoughtfully retrieved her pint glasses of rum and Coke purloined from liquor cabinets; cans of Pabst Blue Ribbon purchased by a gracious older brother; bongs generously filled with foulsmelling skunkweed that someone had purchased at the grammar school playground. She drifted through the end of her freshman year on a cloud of booze and pot, intoxicated as much by the sudden male attention as by the alcohol. And if the boys didn't necessarily hang out with her at school, exactly, it was okay, too; the social hours after school and on the weekends were when the alternate Lizzie came into existence. She felt just a little like Cinderella: the coal-covered drudge that—after the school bell rang—turned into a prom queen with endless boyfriends.

She seemed to walk an inch taller. She begged more money

from her mother to buy high heels, visited the hairdresser at the mall and got her brown hair streaked with blond for the first time, even went on a shopping spree at Walgreens and bought a whole drawer full of makeup. So what if the girls at school still didn't really talk to her; if, in fact, they seemed to be snubbing her more than usual. And maybe she didn't spend as much time with Becky anymore, but Becky was a pill these days. Her idea of a wild and crazy Saturday night was watching a corny old Meg Ryan movie and plying a Ouija board with questions about their future husbands. Lizzie had no time for fuzzy romantic visions anymore; she had the real deal. She had boys paying attention to her *now*. Even if Justin, who she still had a hopeless crush on, was dating a cheerleader and limited his interactions with her to a "Yo, Lizzie!" and a slap on the back.

Her mother, in turn, was thrilled that her daughter had so many social engagements—and with the children of her friends, too! "I'm glad you're having fun," she told Lizzie, as Lizzie headed out to yet another party. "Ten o'clock curfew, keep your cell phone on, and don't forget to thank your hosts, remember?"

Being with a boy was amazing. She was in love with it all: The significant looks in the kitchen, so dense with meaning and portent. The lingering touch on the thigh, the waist, the hand, followed by the invitation to go upstairs and "check out the house." Then, the closed door and the beating heart. Naked skin exposed to the air. For those minutes, when she was being grabbed, touched, kissed, desired, she felt like she was floating, suspended in gossamer threads high above the earth. They really liked her, they found her totally irresistible. She bounced from one boy to the next and back, hooking up with each guy for a week or two, maybe a weekend, maybe just a night, before the next would swoop in. If she closed her eyes, sometimes she could even pretend it was Justin who was kissing her.

"Brian told me you were really hot," said Tom Liverbach, right after they had sex in the walk-in closet at a party one weekend in May. "He was totally right." The fact that they were talking about her made her bloat with pride—she was being *discussed,* as an object of group desire!—though she felt a vague twinge of concern that perhaps they weren't talking about her in precisely the way a girl would want to be talked about. Each time she launched into a whirlwind courtship with a new guy, eventually leading to a sweaty bout in a sticky twin bed or a lunchtime make-out session at the back of the football field, she secretly wondered whether this guy would be the one. Whether this time he would stick around for a month, or two, or even longer. And they never did. Which made Lizzie just a little bit worried. They weren't, like, using her for sex, were they? *Everyone* was having sex, weren't they? Plus, it felt so good that it seemed stupid to worry about it. What was the phrase Margaret had used to describe herself? "Pro-sex feminist." She wasn't quite sure what that meant, but it sounded good. Maybe that's what she was.

And as she slept with her fifth and, finally, sixth suitor, she did feel a growing modicum of pride. When she listened to other girls talk about their hookups in the bathrooms now, she realized that some of them didn't actually know what they were talking about after all. (She knew from experience, for example, that the male anatomy did not taste like chicken, despite Jennifer Hillbrand's announcement in the girls' locker room.) She saw her female classmates staring at her in the hallways of school with darkly curious eyes, bending in toward each other like willow trees in anticipation of the moment when she would be out of earshot, and she *knew* that they were talking about her. They would, wouldn't they? Girls in her class had always gossiped about other girls who had sex, but now she understood that they did this just because they were jealous, because she had all the power. She had proven herself desirable despite it all, had even bested them in the sexual competitions. (She had, after all, slept with more than a few of their crushes and ex-boyfriends, including the ex of her avowed enemy Susan Gossett, Max Grouper, just a week after they had broken up.) She squared her shoulders, reminded herself that she was *winning* for once.

But then school came abruptly to an end in June, and most of the guys in her class headed out to Munich, where they were currently chugging beer as part of the freshman class annual "European Educational Adventure." Now, once again, Lizzie's Saturday nights are devolving into *Pretty Woman* reruns with a bowl of buttered popcorn at Becky's house. Lizzie wonders if anyone misses her. So far, she hasn't gotten any postcards. Not even from Justin.

today, lizzie lets margaret lead the way up the stairs. They pass the family portraits that line the upstairs hallway—one taken every Christmas, framed in carved gilt. Paul is always in a white button-down and a Christmas-tree tie, Janice in a red or green silk blouse and a collection of discreet holiday-themed earrings (sterling silver reindeer, porcelain bugle boys, miniature ceramic wreaths). As children, the girls are gussied up in frilly holiday dresses; later, they wear the annual Christmas sweaters their grandmother Ruth sent from Indiana (hand-knitted in an astonishing array of mutated Rudolphs and demonic elves) with sullen expressions. In the final one, taken last Christmas, Margaret is mid-blink and Lizzie looks like she is about to vomit, probably because of all the eggnog she drank that afternoon.

At the landing, Lizzie pauses. The breakdown four days earlier had been an anomaly; that evening, Janice had returned to the kitchen at dinnertime as usual, pretending that nothing had happened. The news that Margaret was coming home for a visit had, in fact, sent Janice into a new flurry of activity—Margaret's room had to be aired out, special shopping lists made up, flowers picked from the garden and arranged in the entry. If anything, Janice is more herself today than ever, almost vibrating with activity. Already, Lizzie thinks, Margaret's return is making everything better. Lizzie still can't erase the image from her head, though: her mother on the bed, lying as still as a corpse, with a glass of wine in her hand.

"Mom?" Margaret calls.

Janice materializes in the doorway of the bedroom that is designated as Margaret's, despite the fact that Margaret has slept there less than ten nights in the last four years. She is dressed in a fresh shirtdress, with an apron over it, and she has rubber gloves pulled up to her elbows, a sponge in her hand. Her blond hair has been scraped back into a low chignon, and her blue eyes are pale and luminous. She doesn't look depressed at all, Lizzie thinks; in fact, she looks like she might have just applied the same cleaning and polishing to herself that she just gave to the windows.

"Margaret!" Her mother turns toward the bedroom, then back to the foyer, trying to decide whether to drop the gloves and sponge before she approaches for a hug. "I didn't hear your car in the driveway or I would have come down. What time is it? I wasn't expecting you yet. . . . Did you leave early? Because otherwise you must have driven much too fast if you're already here. How fast were you driving?"

"Hi, Mom," says Margaret. And in the weariness of Margaret's reply to their mother's barrage, Lizzie remembers that her sister and her mother fight, have fought for years, and worries that perhaps Margaret's presence is not going to make everything better after all.

"Just a minute," Janice says, racing into the bedroom to drop the sponge in a bucket by the window and shoving the rubber gloves into her apron pocket. Lizzie and Margaret follow her inside. That accomplished, Janice swoops in and squeezes her elder daughter so hard that Margaret visibly winces—Lizzie, remembering the feel of Margaret's ribs jutting from under the dress, winces along with her—and then stands back to look Margaret up and down. "Well, don't you look pale! I'd think you were living in Alaska, not Los Angeles, if I didn't know better." She gives Margaret another hug, closing her eyes as she does it.

Margaret looks very tired suddenly, almost on the verge of tears, as if her mother is squeezing her like a sponge. "How are you doing, Mom?" she replies, ignoring her mother's questions. "I've been worried about you."

"Oh, please." Janice shakes her head. "I'm fine, just fine. Well, obviously I've had better weeks, but I'm feeling fine now." She pauses. "Really fine," she says again. Her eyes dart to the window and back several times, as if she's looking for any last errant smudges to scrub.

"Mom—" begins Margaret.

Janice cuts her off. "When you drove in did you see the new house they're building at the end of the street? They're putting an entire bowling alley in the basement. Who needs a bowling alley? Home theater, yes, I understand, but bowling? They're from India . . ." She pauses, as if finishing the sentence in her head, and then leans forward and sniffs the air around Margaret's face, wrinkling her nose. Lizzie just knows this is going to piss Margaret off, and she braces herself for Margaret's reaction. "Do you smell like smoke? Have you been smoking? Please tell me you aren't smoking again."

"I won't, then," Margaret says, her voice growing more terse by the second.

"Did you stop for lunch? I have a mushroom quiche in the fridge. I could fix you up that, and a salad—"

"I had a burger," Margaret replies. The entire room is

crackling with tension. Margaret and Janice always seem to fight about stupid, insignificant things like how much coffee Margaret drinks and why the country club has a men's-only grill and how Congress is full of reactionary fascists, and it makes Lizzie want to cover her ears and climb underneath the covers and sing a Hilary Duff song as loud as she can until they stop. Still, she realizes, there is a comfort to their vocal sparring. It's better, at least, than the silent way her mother and father seemed to fight. That kind of fighting felt like spreading poison, whereas this is just an explosion, like fireworks, hot and violent but over quickly.

"Well, I guess that means you aren't a vegetarian anymore?"

"Not really," says Margaret.

"Well, *that's* good," Janice says, reaching out to touch Margaret's bare upper arm. "You've gotten so *skinny* down there. Please don't tell me you're doing another one of those weird L.A. diets, with the raw food or the macrobiotic whatever or the one where you don't eat anything but lemon juice—it's all so cultish. Whatever happened to good old-fashioned meat? For God's sake, we're at the top of the food chain for a reason."

"Have you ever seen the inside of a slaughterhouse?" Margaret asks, frowning. "Do you *know* how they treat those cows before they become your sirlion burger?"

"Margaret, please. Can we not?"

Margaret sighs and walks over to the bed. She picks up one of the plaid pillows and hugs it in front of her like a shield. Lizzie lets her breath out slowly, relieved that Margaret has decided not to take the bait. Janice follows her to the bed and starts fluffing the pillows beside her, swapping a plaid pillow for a polka-dotted pillow, then shifting them back again.

Lizzie pipes up. "I'm thinking of being a vegetarian." She isn't, really, but suddenly it seems like a good idea, if only to insert herself into the conversation. "Does it count if you eat shrimp?" Neither Margaret nor Janice respond. Lizzie looks down at the floor and scuffs her shoe in the carpet, making the pile stand up in the shape of a heart, feeling useless.

"How long were you planning to stay?" Janice asks.

"As long as you need me," says Margaret, gesturing vaguely.

Janice shakes her head. "Well, of course I'd love for you to stay as long as you can manage, but I don't *need* anything." Something about her last words makes Janice blink and pause, and then she continues on: "Your mother is capable of holding it together, hard as that may be for you to believe." Lizzie, sensing her mother's lie, hopes that Margaret doesn't take this as carte blanche permission to leave again. Not yet.

But Margaret examines their mother closely, as if gauging every line in her crow's-feet, every tender spot underneath her eyes. She glances at Lizzie, then back at Janice. "Mother, are we going to talk about what's going on?"

Janice just sighs, puts her fingers to her temple, and looks at the floor. She seems to be speaking to the nap of the carpet. Her voice drops three octaves. "Margaret. Please. Right now, I just want to be happy that you're home."

Margaret shakes her head, and Lizzie, watching her, has a comforting realization: Margaret, indomitable Margaret, has just been equally shut out by their mother. They are *both* not in the know, which means that Lizzie finally has someone on her side. She smiles to herself and pushes her toe out to smooth the nap of the rug, erasing the heart.

The two women stand there, stuck in a kind of standoff but not quite sure where to aim next. Janice buckles first. She jerks toward Margaret, opens her arms wide, and sweeps in for yet another hug, crushing Margaret into her shoulder. "I really wish you would visit more often," Janice sighs. Lizzie watches them press together, feeling once again like the third wheel, and wonders whether she should just leave. Perhaps the only reason Janice and Margaret fight so much is because Janice loves Margaret more, anyway. But then Janice looks up and beckons Lizzie over with a quick wave of the hand. "Come here, Lizzie," she says. Lizzie shuffles over and lets her mother pull her into a group hug. The two sisters hang helplessly in their mother's grip like rag dolls.

"Just us girls—that's nice, right?" Janice says. She has tears in her eyes, and one translucent drop worms its way through her foundation, exposing a trail of raw pink flesh underneath. Up close, Lizzie can see that the reason Janice's eyes look so blue today is that her pupils are tiny and the rims of her eyes are red, as if she hasn't slept in days. "Let's try to have some fun, okay?"

Lizzie feels a tiny crumb of dread. She can't imagine having much fun with her mother in this state. Her shoulder aches from where Janice's knuckles are pressing in.

Her mother releases them. "Well," she says, and gives them the satisfied look that a shopkeeper might give to a floral arrangement that's just been placed in a window for display. "Why don't we go have some tea? I made lemon cookies." She sweeps them toward the door and follows them down the hall toward the stairs.

Margaret steps aside to let their mother go down the stairs first and grabs Lizzie's arm as she starts to follow, pinching it hard. She raises one eyebrow until her face freezes into a semispastic contortion and then flares her nostrils at Lizzie. After a moment Lizzie nods, sagely, as if she knows exactly what Margaret intends to say with this curious expression, but she hasn't got a clue.

four

there is nothing so comforting as the pro-
duce aisle of a gourmet supermarket. Janice pushes her cart
briskly past the bins and marvels at the feats of engineering
around her. Towers of oranges, each one a perfect miniature
sun. The summer peaches, gently fluffed by a loving grocer
until their fuzz stands on end. The eggplants, tumescent and
purple, jury-rigged into stacks that defy gravity. Janice can't
help but admire the symmetry, the smartly contrasting colors,
the little chalk signs that denote the contents of each bin:
"Organic frisée, imported from Peru, $6.99 a pound. Woody
and delicious."

When she was in college, organic produce looked nothing
like this. It was sold out of dark little stores that smelled pow-
dery and rancid, like wheat germ, and the produce was mealy
and spotted and full of bugs. When she'd first arrived on the
West Coast in the 1970s, she had shopped at a co-op near the
campus, both because it was cheap and in the spirit of adven-

ture. She remembers cooking Paul an apple pie a few months into their courtship and the horror she felt when he paused and stared down at a tiny, ossified worm on his fork. "Death by sugar," he said before folding the worm into his napkin. "Not a bad way for a worm to go." He kept eating anyway, but Janice couldn't force down another bite.

She stops in front of a display of fresh McIntosh apples, polished until Janice can see a thousand tiny reflections of herself in their ruddy cheeks. That's an idea: She will bake an apple pie, a dessert so banal and rudimentary that she hasn't made one in years, maybe even decades (she usually gravitates more toward the culinary fireworks of a coffee-walnut mousse torte or a cherry Armagnac Pavlova); right now the idea of a good old-fashioned American dessert sounds almost therapeutic. Janice deftly picks out ten of the largest, roundest, most brilliantly streaked fruit—careful not to upset the precarious tower—and sets them down on the bottom of the cart, on top of the frisée, so that they won't bruise. She notices that her hands are trembling and she shakes them to make it stop.

She trots the cart down past the fresh herbs in the refrigerated bins, just as the sprinklers hiss on. She pauses for a brief second and—she can't help it, it looks so cool and enticing, and she feels just a tiny bit wobbly—tips her head in, just over the dill, tilts it up, and lets the mist come down over her face and neck. It feels marvelous, as soft and delicate as a feather, dampening the top of her blouse, catching in her hair. She is reminded of a trip she once took to Hawaii with Paul—a walk in a tropical rain forest, a waterfall that she longed to step under but didn't dare, lest she ruin her sundress and sandals. Only now can she sense the bliss that comes with that kind of abandon.

"Janice?"

The voice seems to come from a thousand miles away. Janice steps back with a jolt, realizing with alarm what she has done, and opens her eyes. Water is in her lashes, she can't really see, but she recognizes Barbara Bint by the throatish rasp of her voice.

"Barbara," she says, as she frantically mops the water from her face with the sleeve of her blouse, patting her cheeks dry in a vain attempt to cover the damage. "How are you?"

Barbara Bint stands in front of her, blocking the path to the leeks with a cartful of Slim-Fast and Diet Coke. Janice can't think of a person she'd less like to see. There is nothing really *wrong* with Barbara, it's just that she is a bit too enthusiastic. Like a puppy that won't stop licking your foot, no matter how much you discourage it. If there is a charity planning committee Barbara will undoubtedly volunteer for the most demeaning tasks no one else will touch; if there is a Thanksgiving church feed for the poor, Barbara will be stuffing the donated turkeys at four A.M.; if there's a death in the neighborhood, Barbara's the first person to arrive with a casserole and a tear-stained face. And then there's Barbara's overt religiosity, an acquisition after the death of her husband (a fall from a ski lift, right before Barbara's eyes, horrible) five years ago and a slightly gauche novelty in a neighborhood of understated religion. Barbara now talks about God in the same familiar way poor people in the Midwest did: as if he lived in the double-wide next door and was coming over that night for a Hamburger Helper dinner. Janice doesn't much go for religion, but if she did, she would do it in a discreet, pious sort of way. She wouldn't, for example, pray under her breath for God's hand to guide her club before she tried to sink a putt on the fourteenth hole.

Today, Barbara wears white pedal pushers, through which Janice can see the ridged line of her underwear. Barbara always looks half put together—the gray roots visible under her brown rinse, the chipped pedicure visible through her sandals, the collar of her polo shirt splattered with spots of grease—as if after all the energy she expends on the rest of the world she has none left to attend to herself. Something about this makes Janice want to slap her.

Barbara reaches out to touch Janice's forearm. It feels like Barbara is grasping her from behind a plastic curtain; her face seems watery and opaque. Janice closes her eyes for just a second, hoping that when she opens them Barbara will have disappeared, just an apparition. No such luck—she still stands there, her mouth pursed.

"How am I?" says Barbara. "Oh, nothing new to report. But Janice"—and Janice cringes at the sight of Barbara's eyes welling up with sympathetic tears—"how are *you*? Not to sound nosy but . . . I've heard."

Janice feels a stab of irritation—why couldn't Barbara Bint just *pretend* she hadn't heard?—but her mind is moving too quickly to really focus on Barbara for long. As she stands there, her thoughts race forward: If she's serving apple pie she should switch the entrée from wasabi-baked grouper with edamame salad to perhaps a fennel-orange roasted chicken, side dishes of potato gratin and broccoli rabe with garlic. She must pick up some baking soda. Does she have baking soda? She can't remember.

She shifts her legs, which telegraph their desire to keep marching forward.

"I'm doing well," says Janice, realizing that Barbara is waiting for an answer. "I'm just fine."

Barbara lowers her voice. "Just fine? I mean, Janice, I'm glad to hear it. Really. But—you know if things are hard you can always talk to me—"

"Really, Barbara, I'm *fine*. Margaret's home, and we have a lot on our agenda for her visit," she lies. "Plus, I'm catching up on a bunch of projects that I've been putting off for *years*. My attic—God, you wouldn't believe the state of my attic. Why do we even bother saving all these *things* if all they do is grow dusty and forgotten up under the rafters? And attract vermin, too. Seems pointless, doesn't it. What was my point? Anyway, yes, I've been too busy to . . ." Realizing that she's lost her train of thought, Janice attempts to rectify the situation by clearing her throat. "Right. All is well, Barbara. Please don't worry. I'm fine." She notices she's grinding her teeth, and forces her jaw to relax.

"Well, you don't *look* fine," says Barbara, and points over Janice's shoulder. Janice turns, catching sight of herself in the mirror above the herbs. Her hair is matted from the water, and mascara is smeared under her eyes, and her white blouse, translucent from its soaking, reveals the shape of her beige underwire bra and the pooch of her stomach underneath. She is a drooping mess, and this strikes her as being very, very funny, so she starts to laugh, a curious sort of hiccuping laugh that just makes Barbara step in closer and grip Janice's arm even harder.

"Ow," says Janice. She tries to control the hysteria, wills her teeth to stop jittering. "Careful of my tennis elbow, Barbara."

Barbara drops her hand quickly but doesn't move back. "You know Luella Anderton?" Janice nods, unsure why Barbara is bringing up the treasurer of the local PTA. "Well, she's dating a lawyer these days. Her divorce lawyer. Just a year after Bill left her. Remember? I'm just saying . . . there is life after. Stay positive."

"Thank you, Barbara," says Janice, whose legs threaten to move of their own accord. She can't seem to focus on Barbara's face. She desperately wants this conversation to come to an end. Already she can feel the bubble of her goodwill beginning to wane, the enthusiasm for her pie vanishing before a descending darkness. Barbara has never seemed to understand the Santa Rita code of silence in the face of ugliness. Doesn't she understand that offers of help only succeed in making all the pain real? *Go away, Barbara,* she thinks. *You're ruining everything.* She breathes in to calm herself and smells sage, thick and druggy. "I'll keep that in mind."

"I've said this before, but it bears repeating: You really should come to our Monday night Bible-reading group. Just for the company, if nothing else," Barbara presses on.

Janice puts a hand on her cart and pushes it a foot in the opposite direction. The apples wobble at the bottom. "I really have to go, Barbara. The girls are waiting for me at home and we're going to do some baking."

Barbara steps forward, forcing Janice to take another step away, and whispers conspiratorially. "I mean it, Janice. My door is always, always open for you."

"Knock, knock," Janice says faintly. She escapes to the frozen foods aisle and tries to restore herself to her previous brisk efficiency. But even as she weaves her way up and down the aisles, grabbing fresh vanilla bean and fennel seed and shallots—baking soda, don't forget the baking soda—she feels the melancholy beginning to creep over her again. The store is all out of crème fraiche, which means she'll have to make another stop or else make do with whipping cream. Someone has broken a bottle of orange pop in aisle 2, and the filthy fizzing puddle slops up into her sandal; her toes grow sticky with orange sugar water. And then, when she gets to the checkout, there are only two lines open and ten people in each of them, while a cashier sits at an unopened register and slowly counts out stacks of nickels. *Don't they have machines that do that?* Janice thinks. As she inches forward, she glances at her watch: It's one forty-five, which means that James, the pool boy, will be arriving any minute. And he usually stays less than half an hour, which gives her barely enough time to make it home. She thinks of what's waiting for her at the house and feels the back of her throat tickle in anticipation.

Janice is prepared with her credit card, swiping it through the machine before the clerk has even finished checking her groceries. She races through the parking lot, the cart shuddering over the bumpy asphalt, and uses the alarm remote to preopen the back of the SUV so that by the time she arrives at the car all she has to do is thrust the bags in the trunk and jet off. She is in a race against the pain she can feel coming on, an oily pool that will start at the back of her head and work its way through her entire body until she feels like one enormous, rawly exposed nerve.

Now that she's out of the grocery store she realizes, with mortification, that she just stuck her head in the produce-section sprinklers in front of Barbara Bint, the busybody, who will probably go ahead and tell the whole damn neighborhood. Which means that Beverly and Paul will surely hear about it— and as these names pop into her head, Janice is again assaulted by the nauseating image that has been lurking on the periphery of her consciousness, waiting for her guard to fall: Beverly and Paul naked in a hotel room, a writhing mass of sweat and flesh like something from a cheap pornographic movie. Her husband! Her best friend! How could he? How could *she*? The horror bubbles up, uncontrollable, and she presses her foot heavily on the accelerator until she is going eighteen miles over the speed limit. All she wants to do is get home in time to catch James before he leaves. And so she rolls through a couple of stop signs on the way home, watching in her rearview mirror for traffic cops while she reapplies mascara with one hand, and pulls into the driveway behind Margaret's hideously rusted Honda, just in time to see James heaving his bottles of chemicals into the back of the pickup truck. He pushes a mass of black curls out of his eyes with the back of his hand, smiles at her, and waves.

"James!" cries Janice, leaping from her car. "I'm glad I caught you."

by the time janice makes it through the door

with the groceries, the ice cream is beginning to get soft. Still, she pauses by the phone in the hallway and checks whether the light on the answering machine is blinking. It isn't. She presses "Play" anyway, just to make sure, but the machine only beeps angrily at her. Paul still has not called, and it's been well over a week.

There is also a growing pile of mail, including the latest copy of *Paris Match.* She glances at the cover—some European pop star she doesn't recognize. She has been meaning to cancel her subscription for years. She never reads it anymore except to peruse the photos of the royals, and the truth is that three decades in Santa Rita have nearly obliterated whatever fluency in French she might once have had. And yet, year after year the magazine keeps arriving in her mailbox, a tether to something half-forgotten.

Below the *Paris Match* she finds a FedEx packet that was delivered in her absence. Janice stands at the table, the grocery bags slipping in her arms, and considers this. A FedEx would seem to require immediate attention, but she finds she doesn't have the heart to open it. She's not in the mood for bad news, and God knows good news rarely comes by express mail.

Her impulse is to go straight to the bathroom and address the darkness that has been descending since she saw Barbara at the supermarket, but she has to put down the groceries first. In the kitchen, though, she finds Margaret at the table, studying the movie section of the paper, and revises her plan.

It is two-thirty in the afternoon, but Margaret is still in her pajamas. Or, rather, Lizzie's pajamas, since it appears that Margaret neglected to bring any of her own. They are pink, with flowers embroidered on the front of the shirt, matching the pattern on the drawstring pants. The pajamas hang on Margaret, making her look small and girlish, and for a minute Janice feels a pang for the child Margaret once was, the little girl who wouldn't go to bed if Janice didn't read her *Where the Wild Things Are,* the little girl who played Wendy in her second-grade class's rendition of *Peter Pan,* long before she eliminated pink from her wardrobe in favor of an all-black costume and began meeting Janice's every utterance with undisguised impatience.

"Where's the coffee?" asks Margaret, by way of a greeting. "I can't find it."

"Did you just get up?" Janice glances at the clock as she fits the ice cream into the freezer. Margaret notices her glance.

"I didn't set an alarm clock. I'm on vacation, Mom. I never get to sleep in L.A."

Janice thinks of saying something—well, lazybones, *I* was up almost all night and managed to reorganize the photo albums *and* scrub out the refrigerator while you were sleeping—but bites her tongue, because she'd rather get through at least a few days of Margaret being at home before they start to fight. Their conversations always seem to devolve into combat so quickly, and she's never precisely sure how it starts. She looks at Margaret and longs to grab her, squeeze her until the stressed expression lifts from her face and Margaret can't help but hug her back.

"Did you know your car is leaking coolant in the driveway? Isn't it time you bought yourself a new one? That thing doesn't look *safe*." Janice eyes her daughter, optimistic that, for once, she'll accept some maternal wisdom.

But Margaret just frowns. "It gets thirty miles to the gallon and it gets me where I need to go. When are you going to swap your gas-guzzling, oversized, and totally unnecessary SUV for something more ecologically responsible? Like, say, a hybrid?"

Janice shakes her head. "I might have a glass of white wine," she says, changing the subject. "Do you want some wine? A spritzer, maybe."

"Wine?" asks Margaret, a confused look on her face. "You're offering me wine for breakfast? Has hell frozen over?"

"Well, I'll have a glass of wine then, and I'll make you some coffee."

"Thanks," Margaret says, and for a moment it seems like peace will reign. Janice puts on a pot of coffee and, for good measure, slips two slices of French bread into the toaster. She finds a half bottle of chardonnay in the fridge and pours herself a generous glass, sipping at it as she unpacks the groceries. The wine helps take the edge off, but she wonders, too, how long she has to wait. The kitchen is warm and sunny, and Janice pauses by the sink to let the light fall on her face. She can smell the jasmine in the garden, light and sweet and summery.

"Do you have any plans while you're here?" asks Janice.

"Oh, you know," Margaret says vaguely. "Just figured I'd help around the house. Sit by the pool. Catch up on my reading. Why, you ready to get rid of me already?"

"Don't be ridiculous," says Janice. But truth is that Margaret's unexpected arrival on the front doorstep *has* made Janice nervous. She feels a rebuke in Margaret's presence, as if Margaret is judging her, blaming her for Paul's departure. It has always been this way: Janice has *always* felt like a black hole of blame, a repository for her daughter's judgment. She's sure that, if ever forced to take sides, Margaret would side with Paul.

Perhaps Margaret's visit home *is* an olive branch, a gesture that she wants to erase all the awkwardness between them. She wants to believe that Margaret really arrived here because she felt compelled by daughterly empathy. But she suspects, somewhere deep in her heart, that Margaret's motives aren't that pure; there is something gray and dark hanging around her daughter that Janice fears is the aura of disappointment. She is afraid to ask; she would rather not know, not right now, not when things are how they are.

"How are things with your magazine?" she asks, hoping that this vague question will suffice. She can't make herself say the magazine's name. When Margaret, as she was moving to Los Angeles, had announced that she was starting a new publication for women, Janice had initially been excited—her daughter hadn't thrown away all that talent and education and promise to chase after a boy after all. A magazine! She imagined, in her mind, something like *Vogue* or even *Glamour* and, for a moment, envied her daughter's ambition. Excited, that is, until she heard what Margaret had named her project and began to realize what kind of magazine it was.

"Snatch what?" Janice had asked, confused.

"It's a double entendre," said Margaret. "I'm reclaiming the word 'snatch.' Snatching it back, as it were." And still Janice didn't understand; she felt stupid, like her daughter was laughing at her, until suddenly the meaning of the word sank in, and what replaced the humiliation was a feeling of horror.

"Oh, Margaret," she said, while her daughter listened, bemused (as if she thought Janice's morals were funny!). "That's not really funny, at all. I can't imagine who would buy a magazine named that. Will bookstores even stock it with that kind of title?"

Margaret went silent and refused to talk about it any further. And although ever since an issue has arrived in the mail in a manila envelope for Lizzie every month, Margaret has never sent one to Janice. But Janice takes the old issues, when Lizzie is done with them, and saves them in a cupboard in the family room. And every once in a while, she opens the cupboard and flips through an issue, regarding her daughter's strident writings with a mix of pride and shame. Her daughter is so smart—Janice is struck, sometimes, by the fluency of her prose and the vigor of her arguments—and yet there is so much anger in her magazine. Janice can't help wondering, too, if the pointedness of her daughter's feminism is aimed at her, a rebuke, as it were, of Janice's choice of home and family over ambition. "Anachronistic" was the word Margaret used when she wrote about stay-at-home mothers. Janice often consoles herself with the idea that Margaret will understand, someday when she has a family of her own, how priorities change; how fantasies about career and adventure grow irrelevant the minute you have a baby in your arms who adores you, relies on you, greedily consumes your very essence. How life isn't always what you anticipate it will be like when you're young and idealistic, and the grace comes in learning to love what you have chosen instead. Sometimes, Janice also wonders whether the person she is trying to convince of this is not her daughter but herself.

"Oh, *Snatch* is fine, the usual," Margaret says in answer to Janice's question, a response (what is "the usual"?) that somehow doesn't relieve Janice's concern but that will do for the moment. Margaret flips through the paper, then looks up at Janice. "I saw you talking to that guy. Is he the pool boy?"

Janice's heart races for just a minute, but Margaret doesn't know—how could she? "Yes. James. He comes twice a week. He's new—came recommended by the neighbors."

"He's cute," says Margaret. "In a slacker kind of way." Janice pictures James, his tanned thin body and curly nest of black hair, the lazy brown eyes and damp reek of physical labor, and thinks that he is not the type of boy she would have liked at Margaret's age; he is more fey and sensitive than masculine. Nor would she have had a crush on the pool boy. Her aspirations, she thinks, were always loftier than that.

"Is he? Well, he certainly could stand to take a shower more often," Janice says. She polishes off the glass of wine and pours herself another. Margaret watches her with a puzzled expression and seems about to say something. She is stopped by the ringing of the telephone.

Margaret and Janice both freeze. Janice doesn't move to answer it. If it's Paul, she doesn't have the energy to talk to him in front of Margaret.

"Are you going to answer that?" Margaret asks as something odd flickers across her face, a mix of alarm and fear. (*Is she afraid of confronting Paul, too?* Janice wonders.) But she grabs at the phone before Janice can answer. She presses the receiver to her ear, glancing sideways at Janice, and then after a moment she sighs—was that relief? or dismay? Janice can't quite tell—says, "No thanks," and drops it back down into its cradle.

"It was a telemarketer," she says.

"Were you expecting a call from Bart?" Janice knows she shouldn't ask, but she can't resist.

Margaret walks to the sink, so that her back is to Janice, and washes her hands. "Not really."

Janice flails blindly, wishing for the best. "How is Bart, anyway? Is he still acting?" She hopes this last question doesn't sound too passive-aggressive; of course, she knows perfectly well that Bart is still acting, but she can't help but let a slight bit of her distaste creep into her voice.

She met Bart only once, over a dismal meal at L'Étouffée, and instinctively disliked him. He was utterly indifferent to her and Paul, showed nothing but contempt for their sur- roundings, and responded coldly to their futile attempts to connect with him. He practically laughed in her face when she mentioned how much she had loved a recent production of *Les Misérables*. He'd shown up at L'Étouffée—of all places—in mo- torcycle boots and with grease under his nails, and he ate off the back of his fork; he pawed at her daughter; and what was even more killing was that when he walked out halfway through the meal, Margaret—the astonishing grad student who had every opportunity in the world lined up before her—followed him like a devoted puppy. Then followed him off to a precar- ious life in a faraway city where she had no job prospects. It just made no sense that after a lifetime of overachieving, Mar- garet could suddenly *settle* like that. What was she chasing? Or running from? Janice still doesn't understand: Was it her? Was it Paul? She had found herself inexplicably angry at her daughter, as if Margaret was betraying Janice with her flighty whims. Still, perhaps she shouldn't have *told* Margaret that her boyfriend was an "arrogant good-for-nothing." Or that she was wasting her life by dumping a good job at Stanford University—*right here! at home!*—in order to move to L.A. with an unemployed actor. It certainly hadn't opened Margaret's eyes or prevented her departure, and apparently it *had* discouraged her from visiting home. Four visits in four years, not including this one. So little.

"Yes, of course he's still acting." Margaret speaks with infinite patience, as if dealing with a very slow child.

"His character was killed off that show he was on, right?"

"They capsized his boat in a freak tropical storm. Tragic accident. Broke thousands of teenage girls' hearts." Janice had tuned in a few times out of dismal curiosity and hadn't been surprised when it wasn't her taste. Some twenty-something soap opera that took place in Malibu, with a lot of promiscuous sex and purposeless characters and gratuitous swearing. It was the kind of sensationalist pablum intended to corrupt kids' minds, and she'd forbidden Lizzie to watch it. But she'd noted, too, the vaguely impressed looks on her friends' faces when she mentioned the name of the show, as if all Bart's obvious character flaws were made irrelevant by the validation of prime-time television, and so, now and again, she'd mention his name with an eye roll of exasperation—"that *boy* Margaret lives with"—just to watch their eyes bulge with suppressed interest.

"So what's he doing now?"

"He's the lead in a new movie."

"Really. What's it about?" Janice registers the unsurprising sensation of disappointment: She is not unaware that she has been waiting for Bart to fail, proving to Margaret that she was right about him all along.

"I'm not sure. Something about cars."

"Well! Maybe we could all go see it, together."

Margaret smiles unconvincingly, a smile that can't disguise the fact that she would rather die than sit in a movie theater watching Janice watch Bart. "Oh, definitely."

The mystery of her daughter's life sometimes makes Janice want to weep. Trying to pry information out of her is like trying to yank the tenacious thistles from the vegetable garden. The harder she pulls, the more likely it is that the thistle will break off at the base and she'll never get the critical roots up at all. She finds herself wishing that Margaret would be just a little bit more like the Maxfields' daughter, Margaret's old classmate Kelly. Helen Maxfield is always bragging about how her daughter is her best friend, how Kelly married a nice banker and started a successful public relations firm, how she comes for dinner every Friday. Helen's maternal display often gets on Janice's nerves (surely no child is *that* saintly), but still, sometimes she finds herself watching with pure naked envy when Helen brings her daughter and son-in-law and new grandchild to the club for Sunday brunch—the way they lean their heads together to laugh at shared jokes, Kelly sometimes clutching her mother's hand in a moment of shared humor. She can't remember the last time Margaret touched her impulsively.

"You know, the Moores' son, Nelson, just finished the California bar exam. He's living in the neighborhood, rented a house just a few blocks away from his parents. Remember him, he was a year ahead of you?"

"The kid with the harelip?"

"He's had plastic surgery. You should give him a call while you're in town. I remember he had the biggest crush on you back in grade school."

"Mother. Please."

"I just thought you'd like to socialize." Janice busies herself washing the apples for the pie, polishing each with a dishrag before placing it on the counter for slicing. She notices that her hands are jittering again, almost as if they were detached from the rest of her body. She watches as they dance across the counter, grappling with an apple, fidgeting with a knife, tapping against the ceramic tiles, before she wills the hands together and clenches them in front of her. She senses Margaret's inexplicable annoyance falling between them like a dark curtain and knows that no matter what she says she is doomed. It exhausts her. The kitchen falls silent, except for the ticking of the Viking range as it heats up.

"So, how long do you think you'll keep doing that magazine?" Janice asks, still striving toward some conversational end goal she's not sure she wants to reach but unable to stop herself nonetheless.

Margaret grabs an apple and takes a bite of it. "Mom," she says as she munches away, "I'd really rather not talk about the magazine. I get it: You hate the magazine. You think I'm wasting my time."

Janice jabs at an apple with her paring knife and watches the naked halves rock back and forth on the counter, their exposed white flesh now vulnerable to the brown creep of oxidization. "I don't hate it, honey," she says, knowing that she's pushed it too far. "I'm happy you've got something you're excited about." She peeks at Margaret, who looks decidedly unexcited. Janice just can't resist—the words spill out of their own volition, despite the warning message that her brain sends to her mouth. "Though I still don't understand how you can make a living doing it."

Margaret looks at Janice queerly. "I'm doing just fine, Mom," she mumbles, then bites into the apple again, sending juice splattering to the floor and bringing a decisive end to that subject. "Anyway, can we please stop talking about me? Aren't there more important things to talk about right now? I mean, it's time we talked about the obvious question. What's going on with Dad?"

Janice freezes. She should have expected this, but still, she has managed thus far to avoid answering anyone's questions. She is silent for a minute. "I don't know," she says finally. This is true: She has looked at the situation from every angle, trying to find a way to stitch everything back together seamlessly. Instinctively, she wants Paul back from Beverly. She tells herself that she must somehow convince him that he has made a grievous mistake, that he needs to come back to her and repair the rift he has torn in their world. But this response doesn't take into consideration the raging fury she feels at the betrayal, the *humiliation* Paul has forced upon her. Part of her wants him and Beverly to rot in hell forever. And yet these are the same feelings that Janice does not want to think about in the first place. So the question of what to do about this disaster just circles around and around in her head, like one of those snakes eating their tails, making her feel worse and worse. It's easier to ignore it, and what's sitting in her purse right now, just waiting for her—*It*—makes ignoring it that much easier. "Do you really want to talk about this?" Janice asks hopefully. "I'd really rather hear what's going on in your life."

"You won't talk about the divorce?" Margaret shakes her head in disbelief. "This affects all of us. You and Lizzie *and* me."

Janice holds up one palm, as if to halt the word in its path through the air before it can make its way to her eardrums. "Margaret, *stop*. Your father and I need to talk before . . ." She hesitates. ". . . before anything else is decided. We're a long ways off from . . . what you're talking about; we are simply . . . *separated*. Taking time off, which isn't so unusual in a long-term marriage. And who are you to say otherwise, missy? Your father's clothes are still all hanging in the closet and everything he owns is here, here in *our house*, so calling this the end of our marriage seems rather premature, don't you think?"

She listens to herself blather on, wincing reflexively at her obvious defensiveness but incapable of just shutting up. The back of her head begins to throb, and she looks up at the clock and thinks, *Surely I've waited long enough.*

"Premature? Mom, he's *gone*. He's off with *someone else*. And *you're* drinking wine in the middle of the afternoon. Have you considered what's going to happen to . . ." Margaret pauses. ". . . all that IPO *money*? And what about custody of Lizzie? Who's going to get the house? What are you going to *do*? You could end up *on the street*!"

Margaret's voice has gotten screechy and hysterical, as if the end of the world is coming, and Janice suddenly can't bear to hear another word from her mouth. She drops the halved apple in her hand, letting it bounce and bruise on the kitchen floor, and turns to Margaret in a fury, the paring knife still gripped in her palm. "Who are *you* to tell me how things are in *my* marriage? I've been married for twenty-nine years. You, you run off with some . . . actor . . . and live with him for a few years and suddenly you know everything about relationships? Don't you *dare* tell me what commitment is all about."

Margaret looks at the knife with bulging eyes and steps back a foot. She lifts her hands, palms toward Janice and fingers spread, muttering just below her breath, "Okay, okay. Fine." Janice thinks she sees genuine fear in her daughter's face, and the momentary flicker of victory vanishes as she realizes that she is waving a knife at Margaret. Though it's hardly a real knife, just a stubby little thing that needs sharpening; so Margaret's dramatic display is really quite unnecessary. Janice drops the knife to the cutting board but is still unable to meet Margaret's eyes. She bends over, picks the halved apple off the floor, and plucks a stray hair from its white flesh. She feels herself sinking, rapidly, into the quicksand. Where is her purse?

"I'm going to the ladies' room," she says, standing up.

"The ladies' room? Why don't you just call it a bathroom?" says Margaret.

"I call it a ladies' room because I am a lady, unlike some of the other residents of this house, who would prefer to be slobs or pigs," snaps Janice, and tries to walk, not run to the downstairs bathroom, snatching her purse from the counter en route. With the door closed, she sits on the toilet and rifles through the handbag, hands shaking. She finds the Ziploc bag, fumbles with the seal, and fishes out the little packet of It.

She taps the white crystalline powder onto the marble counter and carves out a thin line with the edge of her Neiman Marcus credit card. Eyeing this, she tips just a bit more out, and then, with a rolled-up twenty-dollar bill, snorts It up her nose.

It makes her eyes water, and she sits on the toilet, dabbing at the corner of her eyes with a square of quilted bath tissue, so that her mascara won't melt. She can taste something bitter and viscous dripping down the back of her throat, but she doesn't mind it anymore, because she knows that what follows it is relief.

She is getting better at this, she thinks. The first time she did It, she was riveted by this gritty rail of fire in her nose and throat. She thought she must have broken something or done something wrong. She'd followed James's instructions to the letter—the credit card, the dollar bill, the pinned nostril—but she hadn't expected the raw power of It. The only drugs she'd ever taken were marijuana—once or twice in college—and painkillers, but this felt so much *dirtier*. She had stared at herself in the mirror, thinking that her face surely must look different after this violation. A flicker of a memory—a scene from some movie about gangsters, a pile of cocaine and a man with his nose dipped in it like a contestant in a pie-eating competition—had flashed through her brain and she'd panicked: Had she made a terrible mistake? He had called this crystal meth, not cocaine; he had *said* it was medicinal, but what if he had lied?

And then her anxiety winked away as the drug did its work. She closed her eyes and felt a brightening wash through her. It was that same feeling that she feels today, right *now:* a spreading warmth that immediately erases the tension in her head and then melts slowly over her body, like ice cream softening in its tub. In a minute, she feels totally remade. She can face anything now.

She is careful to flush the toilet before she leaves the bathroom, just in case Margaret is listening.

there is a legitimate reason for It, of course.

She strained her elbow in the April tournament at the club, chasing after a sliced volley that Beverly could have easily returned but didn't (Beverly always was a little lazy on the upper court), leaving it up to Janice to save the match. They had lost anyway—the first time in three years—and the pain in Janice's elbow sent her to Dr. Brunschild, who prescribed her two weeks of total arm rest and a week's worth of Vicodin.

She was amazed by how pleasant the Vicodin was—delightful, even, not only eliminating the pain in her elbow but also bequeathing her a quiet sort of elation. When she walked, it was as if she were sliding slowly through silk. Still, she felt guilty about the pills; the pain in her arm wasn't terrible, and taking medication she didn't *really* need seemed dangerous. She stopped, but tucked the rest of the bottle away in her medicine cabinet, just in case the pain came back.

That particular pain hadn't come back, though another one had descended in its place. Janice discovered the bottle in her bathroom cabinet the Monday Paul left her for Beverly. She stood there, the half-empty bottle of champagne in one hand, slowly rolling the Vicodin bottle in the palm of the other. The pills rattled provocatively: eight left. And she thought, *Why not?* After all, this was a pain far worse than a strained muscle or broken wrist. This was a pain worse than childbirth, even, because with childbirth you are being given a gift; worse, too, than the death of her mother from cancer last year, because that slow demise at least had a sense of eventuality to it, of an ending due to come. No, this kind of loss was a living loss, one packed with anger and remorse and self-doubt.

As she stood there in front of the medicine cabinet, she

thought of what Paul had said. "Claustrophobia"? *He* felt claustrophobic? She was the one who should feel claustropho-bic—her life was the one that took place within the confines of this house, the yard, the local supermarket and the shopping center and the country club. She was the one who had to be present and available whenever her children and husband needed her. Meanwhile, Paul was off on a business trip every week; he visited a half dozen countries a month. He apparently even had the leisure time to go off and screw her best friend. Who was he to complain? She thought about picking up the phone again and screaming until her lungs gave out, but she couldn't muster the will to do it.

She took a pill instead. And then, twenty-two minutes later, mercy. The combination of Vicodin and champagne erased everything, leaving only the most ghostly pencil shav-ings of fury and shame. She spent the rest of that afternoon wandering around the house in a euphoric calm. She stood in the garden for a long, long time, overwhelmed by the sugared scent of the summer roses. She spent hours enthralled by cooking shows on TV. Just as *soon* as she felt better, she was go-ing to run out and buy an immersion circulator so that she too could make lamb *sous vide* with balsamic sorbet! Paul and Bev-erly barely crossed her mind; when they drifted in, like feather down, she found it amazingly easy to blow them away.

"He'll come home," she reassured herself. "He will come to his senses. Everything will be fine." She set the table for supper—and, despite everything, set a place for him anyway, wondering whether positive thinking might somehow lure Paul home. In this mild stupor, she told Lizzie only that her father was taking some time off and would be gone for a little while, and when she saw that Lizzie thought Janice was refer-ring to a business trip, she didn't bother to explain.

Janice told herself that it was an extraordinary situation and she wouldn't take the Vicodin again. But when she woke up the next day in the empty bed and thought she would tear her hair out and break the china into a million pieces or burn the house down, it was obvious what she needed to do. She didn't have room for anger in her life, and if people with, say, insomnia occasionally took Ambien to help them sleep, why couldn't she prescribe herself some Vicodin temporarily to relieve this rage?

She floated through the next two days on a cloud, unperturbed and full of energy, popping a Vicodin every time she felt the fuzzy edges beginning to sharpen again. It *was* as if Paul was on just another of his business trips—hadn't he spent the better part of the year gone, anyway?—and she thought: *Yes, I can live like this, in this limbo state.* Thoughts of divorce and infidelity barely crossed her mind.

And then she ran out of pills.

She called Dr. Brunschild for a refill on Thursday morning. "My elbow hurts," she said.

"Again?" he said. "Or still?"

"Still," she said, unsure if this was a plausible answer and hoping he hadn't already seen her playing out on the club courts.

"Have you been playing on it?"

"Not really," she lied. "It's too painful. Maybe I need more Vicodin?"

"No, if it's still hurting you, you may have torn something. You could need surgery. I think you should come in and see me."

She couldn't lie to him in person, of course. So she demurred, then stood there, in her empty bedroom, as hopelessness fell over her. Looking forward, she could see only pain, like a monster waiting to devour her. And suddenly she understood the impulse to murder—this was *Paul's* fault, all of this, and he should suffer as she was suffering.

She flung open the doors to the closet and considered the

line of Paul's suits. They marched along the back of the closet, in a palette that ranged from gray to black, summer weight to heavy woolens, the coordinating shirts hanging just below. Ties hung crisply from a rotating rack. Shoes were in position below, again matched by color, each shoe polished to a shine and stuffed with a cedar shoe tree to keep its shape. Janice thought of the endless hours she had spent at Thomas Pink and Neiman Marcus, selecting those 44R suits, those matching ties and dress shoes and shirts with meticulous care. The hours she spent designing an organizational system for the closet that would guarantee that Paul would never leave for a predawn meeting accidentally wearing a black suit with a brown shoe. The shirts she had taken to be dry-cleaned and pressed until they snapped on their hangers. She could have been a translator at the U.N., or a fashion designer in Paris, or gone to culinary school, and instead, she'd spent the last thirty years doing *this,* for a man who seemed to believe that it had turned her into some kind of ogre.

With one arm, Janice swept the shirts off the rack and into a pile on the floor. They lay in a satisfying heap, wrinkling, wasting hours of her exertions. Then she attacked the suits, which, being heavier, required more effort. The pile grew. Woolens and gabardines and worsteds lay in heaps. She began to perspire. The contents of the bureau came next: socks, underwear, handkerchiefs, T-shirts, pajamas, golf clothes, each drawer turned upside down and emptied onto the floor. The personal effects: They would go too. She dumped the contents of his jewelry box into the pile.

The mountain of Paul's possessions on the floor of the closet looked disappointingly small. She wanted it to be enormous, a massive purge. She stepped into the bedroom and looked around: pictures. Paul was all around her, smiling out from a dozen photographs, from the bedside table, the top of the bureau. Janice swept these away. Yes, she was throwing away images of Margaret and Lizzie and herself in the process, but they would take more photos, this time *without* Paul.

She continued her rampage down the stairs, removing, as she went, the annual Christmas family portraits. Paul's stiff, false smile—no, she never wanted to see it again. At the bottom of the stairs, she stacked all twenty-eight of the photographs in a precarious tower; then she made her way to the kitchen, where, after tucking back a glass of wine, she unearthed a box of super-strength Hefty bags from under the sink.

All told, Paul's presence in the house filled up seven Hefty bags. This was a good start, Janice thought as she stuffed the stiff fabrics into the black plastic, hangers and all. The sharp edges of the photographs poked holes through the bags. The shoes left polish marks on the pristine white golf shorts. But Janice didn't care, not at all. Soon, her velour tracksuit was soaked through with sweat and streaked black from the dust at the back of Paul's closet.

Janice dragged the first Hefty bag down the staircase, letting it land with a thunk against each step, and then on out the front door toward the curb, where the garbage and recycling bins were already awaiting their weekly pickup. From inside the bag came the crunch of broken glass. She tried to lift it over her shoulder, but the bag, loaded with suits, was too heavy. She dropped it to the driveway and tried to drag it behind her with both hands, but the plastic didn't glide along in gravel the way it had on the hardwood floors. The bag resisted her and snagged in the sharp stones. She gave it one more heave and heard the sound of ripping plastic as the bottom of the bag split open and Paul's clothes spilled out onto the gravel.

"Piece-of-crap bag," Janice exploded. "Super-strength, my ass." She kicked at a camel-colored overcoat with her foot and watched it tumble through the chalky white dust, and then she broke into hysterical, furious sobs. Sat right down in the gravel and screamed.

When she came back to herself, after what must have been five minutes, it felt like she was emerging from a red haze. Her jagged breaths came slower and more smoothly, and she gazed out onto the street, at the Ferns' new house on the other side of the road, at the drapes pulled shut in the Upadhyays' living room. She realized that the neighbors, if they were looking out the window, had just been graced with quite a spectacle. *Thank God,* she thought, *there's no sign of life across the street.* Madness; this was madness. She was completely out of control. What was she going to do, tear the whole house down in order to destroy everything Paul had ever touched? Make a fool of herself in front of the entire neighborhood? And what would Lizzie think when she arrived home from camp to see her mother behaving like an escapee from a lunatic asylum? This was not rational, not at all. She was *better* than this. She thought again of the gentle embrace of the Vicodin: If drugs were what was required to regain control of the situation, then she would simply have to find more, despite Dr. Brunschild. For normalcy's sake. For Lizzie's sake.

She gathered Paul's possessions into her arms and, cradling them, carried everything back upstairs. It took three trips, as she darted from driveway to doorway to avoid being seen by any passersby. The suits were marred with dust and grit, which Janice scrubbed away with a damp cloth and a lint brush before hanging them back on the rack. She emptied the six other sacks, returning each item to its place. She rehung the photographs in the stairwell. The two broken photographs she put in the back seat of her SUV, to be taken to the frame shop for repair. When she was done, she drank an entire bottle of wine and crawled into bed. When Lizzie found her there, later that afternoon, Janice couldn't even sit upright, and the alarmed expression on Lizzie's face only firmed up Janice's resolve. That, and the news that Margaret was going to be coming home. There was no way Margaret was going to see her like this. She needed to get more Vicodin, in order to pull herself together. But how?

the day after her breakdown, janice woke up hungover and irritated. It was hot in the house, despite the air-conditioning, and Janice found herself gravitating toward the cool, clean water of the pool.

She stood at the far end of the pool, took a deep breath to prepare for her dive, and stopped—something smelled odd. A skunk, she thought at first—the neighborhood had suffered a plague of skunks the previous summer—but the scent triggered something in her memory (the dark couch of a party in college, a joint dripping hot ash) and she realized: Someone was smoking pot.

The smell was coming from the dark recesses of the garden behind the pool shed. Lizzie was her first thought. *Lizzie's in back smoking pot.* Janice tore back around the poolhouse, even as in her mind she registered the fact that not only was Lizzie far too young to be tempted by drugs yet (wasn't she? God, she hoped so), but she was off at swim camp anyway.

She almost tripped over the pool boy, who was crouching by a pansy bed with a joint the size of his thumb stuck firmly in his mouth. James's eyes were closed, and he sucked on the dark brown butt with the intensity of a newborn child at its mother's nipple. After inhaling for a long, deep minute, he opened one eye, then both, and blinked twice, as if Janice might just be a hallucination.

When she cleared her throat, he jumped to his feet, tripping over his sneakers. "I'm sorry, Mrs. Miller," he said and bent over, frantically stubbing out the joint in the dirt. And then, as if reading her mind—as she thought to herself, *Ash in my pansies!*—patted some dirt over the dirt that he had just soiled with his joint. And then, as she still watched in astonishment, dug that dirt up with his fingers and shoved it in his pocket, along with the crumpled joint stub.

Janice was stupefied into silence. "Are you going to fire me?" asked James, looking up at her.

She *should* fire him. That was the right thing to do. What kind of kid smokes pot on the job? How could she trust him with dangerous chemicals in her pool when his brain was addled with intoxicants? What if he tried to give some to Lizzie?

"I think that's only appropriate, don't you?"

"Look, I'm sorry, but it's just pot," he said. "It's as benign as having a . . . glass of wine."

"I've smoked pot," she snapped at him. "I know what it is."

And then James, oddly, winked at her. "Well, in that case . . . do you want some?" he asked. "It's not a problem. I have plenty. What would you like? Thai stick? Humboldt green?"

Janice stared at him, stunned by his audacity. Her pool boy was offering her *drugs*? How bizarre, and how totally inappropriate. Should she call the police? She looked around, as if there might be an audience with whom she could share her bafflement at this scenario. James watched her struggle with the situation, a placid smile on his face. And then, as she considered and reconsidered his flabbergasting offer, the dots connected, from the dirt in his pocket straight up to her medicine cabinet on the second floor. Here it was, exactly what she needed. But—she couldn't. The pool boy? No. How mortifying. She shouldn't. Before she had time to think about it any more, she did.

"No. I don't care for marijuana," she said, her heart racing. "But maybe you could . . . help me with something else."

"Help you?"

"Yes," she said, not quite sure how to go about this. It had been hard to avoid pot altogether in the seventies, but even during her most suggestible moments at college she certainly had never bought it—or any illegal drug—herself. Not that Vicodin was a drug, though. It was a prescription medicine.

"Well," she began. "What I'm trying to say is, maybe you know something about where to get . . . things."

He looked at her, his face toasted brown from long days outdoors. And then he smiled, a delighted grin that revealed a wide winsome gap between his nicotine-stained teeth. "Things? Can you be more specific?"

"I need some Vicodin." She paused, feeling James's inscrutable smile in her gut. What must he think of her? "I hurt my elbow playing tennis, and my prescription ran out but my doctor is out of town. Do you know where to get that kind of thing?"

James squinted. "Not really. I don't do prescription medicine. You could get that in Mexico, though, if you wanted."

"Oh," she said, and felt humiliated, half naked and lumpy in her bathing suit before this slight young man. "It's the pain," she said, by way of explanation. "It's really unbearable. I can't even put a foot on the court unless I have painkillers. But I really shouldn't have asked. I'm sorry." She took a step away, hoping to escape.

But James didn't appear alarmed. "Don't worry. I get it, Mrs. Miller," he said, nodding seriously. "I think I can help you."

"Any kind of painkiller would do, actually."

"I've got something better than Vicodin—stronger, and it won't make you drowsy." He had a curious expression on his face, but he smiled at her beatifically.

"Not a prescription drug, though?"

"Sort of—it's in a lot of other drugs," he said. "Crystal. Heard of it?"

Janice racked her brain—hadn't she seen a special on TV about this recently? Something about that conservative talk-show host who had been sent off to jail? "It's not OxyContin, is it?"

"Nah," said James. "Look, it's not totally harmless, but it will definitely help you feel no pain, if that's your problem. And it gives you lots of energy."

Janice hesitated.

"And it helps you lose weight, too. If you're interested in that kind of thing. I know personally that a bunch of other women in Santa Rita take it. It's kind of like a diet pill, in a way. But better."

This tipped the scales for Janice. "How much would it be?" she asked.

"You'd want . . . what, half a gram?" Janice nodded, having no idea what exactly a gram represented. "That'd be fifty bucks."

"Fifty dollars? Vicodin costs a fraction of that at the pharmacy."

James laughed. "Yeah, well, I don't accept any insurance. Sorry."

She paused. She knew better than this, and yet something in her felt reckless. She closed her eyes and had a sudden vision of herself at twenty in a patterned shift dress and long flaxen hair, gesturing widely with a Gauloise. When she opened her eyes, James was still there. "How soon could you get it?"

"Later today?" James said. "I'll need to talk to—"

"Please," she said quickly, sensing how fragile her grasp on this moment really was. "I don't need the details."

"Not a problem." He hiked the pool net over his shoulder, as if he were a javelin thrower about to send the pole flying over the pool into the bougainvillea. "I assume this means I'm not fired after all?"

"No. I guess not."

"Well, anything you need. I'm your man."

"Thank you," said Janice, who thought she felt better already. "Oh, and James?"

"Yeah?"

"Don't smoke pot in my garden. The neighbors might smell it. And it's really not good for you, you know."

"Sure," he said. "I won't do it again. Thanks again, Mrs. Miller."

"Please," she said. "Call me Janice."

by the time janice reemerges from the bathroom, Margaret has vanished from the kitchen. Janice goes to work on the pie with renewed energy, quickly and efficiently sifting flour, squeezing lemons, measuring out sugar by the tablespoon (her hand still shakes slightly, she notices). The butter is too cold; she takes it out of the fridge and sets it on the counter to warm. She'll have to wait to finish the pie. She glances at the clock: It is now three in the afternoon. Her fingernails rap agitatedly on the granite countertop. Her mind races from one thought to another, settling on each for precisely two seconds before it forgets and moves on to the next. She feels marvelously alive, marvelously *in the moment*, implacable and unperturbed.

She picks up the morning paper Margaret left on the table and turns to the business section to study the Nasdaq listings. APPI has gone up another one and a quarter points, making the shares worth $148.75, which, by Janice's mental calculations, means that the 2.8 million shares they own are worth roughly $3.5 million more than yesterday. Funny money. She thinks of the FedEx in the hallway whose contents she suspects she knows already and reminds herself, *Half of that money is yours.* Over $200 million dollars—my God, she can do whatever she wants with it now, without even asking Paul. This thought thrills her for a minute and then nauseates her, as if she'd just eaten an entire bag of marshmallows in one sitting.

Janice folds the newspaper neatly closed, walks it over to the trash compactor (acutely aware of the racing pulse at the back of her neck), and throws it on top of a pile of eggshells and onion skins. She hits the "On" button and listens to the whole mess grind down into a muffin-sized cube. Then she goes to work chopping the butter into the flour, kneading it into dough, and noticing how sticky and wonderful it feels between her fingers. She should do this every day.

Margaret materializes through the kitchen door again, wearing the same shapeless sundress with the dangling hem she had on yesterday. Did she not bring any other clothes home with her? "I'm going out," she announces.

"Oh, don't do that," Janice says. "I'm just about to make a pie. Lizzie will be home any second and I thought maybe we could play a game together. We have Pictionary? Or Monopoly. Hearts—do you remember how much you loved to play hearts when you were little? Lizzie should be here any second."

And yes, just then Lizzie walks in the door from swim camp, carrying her wet swimsuit in a string bag over her shoulder and looking somewhat boiled from a day spent immersed in chlorine. "See!" crows Janice.

"What's going on?" asks Lizzie. Lizzie is all round and soft and sun-kissed, tottering in her unwieldy shoes. Her baby girl, her miracle child. After all those years of miscarriages, after sex had come to feel like a game of roulette, after they'd taken her doctor's advice and given up trying (so much so that they'd rarely had intercourse at all), she'd been so surprised by her pregnancy that she hadn't actually believed it until she'd held the purple squalling infant in her arms. At the time, Janice had felt blessed—Lizzie had saved her marriage, she'd thought then, though now she wonders whether her second child was just a distraction from her crumbling relationship. It doesn't matter: Lizzie will always be her baby.

"I'm baking a pie," says Janice. "Apple. You like apple pie, right?"

Lizzie ogles the dough. "I thought I was supposed to be on a diet."

"Well, I'm cheating on my diet, too," says Janice. "Want to roll out the dough?"

Lizzie drops her swim bag on the floor, and chlorinated water begins to make a puddle by the back door. She happily grabs a rolling pin and thwacks it into the pile of dough on the counter. Flour goes flying in all directions, and Janice thinks of the mess this will make of the floor, but discovers that it doesn't bother her a bit. The idea of mopping actually fills her with pleasure. She rapidly slices the apples into perfect, even wedges and squeezes lemon over them, to save their color, before starting on the lattice for the top of the crust. If she's going for traditional American kitsch, she might as well go all the way. Serve it up on a checked tablecloth, wearing a frilly apron. The thought makes her hiccup a giggle.

Lizzie breaks a piece off the dough and eats it, watching Janice out of the corner of her eye. Janice says nothing.

"So, Lizzie, how was your day? How was camp? Getting faster?"

"Good," says Lizzie. She breaks off another piece of dough and crams it into her mouth. "I shaved a half second off my time in the five-hundred meter."

Margaret is still standing by the back door, waiting for Janice. "Mom, we need to finish our discussion about . . . you know," she starts. "Maybe not now, but let's pick a time. I might be able to help."

"Discussion about what?" asks Lizzie.

"I don't need help, Margaret," Janice says, and turns to Lizzie to change the subject. "Do you have any social plans this week, Lizzie? Any parties you're going to?" Lately, Janice has noticed, Lizzie has been staying at home on Saturday nights again, and this concerns her. For a while, during the spring, it seemed like Lizzie had started making some friends, and while perhaps it's just that the summer is quiet because everyone is off on vacation, she worries that Lizzie is reverting to her old, antisocial ways. Lizzie spends far too much time by herself, her social life starting and ending with Becky. Friends are so important at that age. It pains Janice to think that her daughter might be lonely. Hasn't she done everything she can to make sure that her daughters were shown the easy path through life, easier than her own? And yet no matter what she does, she can't quite protect them from cruel schoolmates and shiftless boyfriends and the vicissitudes of youth.

"Maybe you want to join some kind of activity group, with all your spare time this summer," she continues, feeling chatty. "I think there's a tennis tournament for teens at the country club."

Lizzie sighs. "I don't like tennis. You know I don't like tennis."

"Well, maybe you could start a knitting club," she says. "I hear knitting is very trendy these days. I could teach you how— I used to knit when I was in college. I made a sweater for your father once. They have kits, now, I think, for beginners. It's actually a very social activity. You'd be surprised." Lizzie doesn't respond, having apparently given up on rolling out the crust in order to stuff her face with dough.

"Want to leave some for the pie, Lizzie?" says Janice, and Lizzie abruptly stops chewing, her mouth bulging with pie dough, her eyes frozen in fear. Janice gives up and takes the dough, pressing it quickly into the pan, arranging the apples in symmetrical circles, and sprinkling the top with cinnamon and sugar. She places the lattice over the top and has the pie in the oven within minutes. She looks around the room, jittery with energy. Now she can clean. Where is the mop? She turns to see Margaret still standing behind her, watching, and quickly averts her gaze, worried that, if given a direct glimpse into Janice's eyes, Margaret might somehow see straight into her mind and know exactly what she has just done in the bathroom.

"Mom? Are you okay?" Margaret says, staring at Janice.

Before Janice has to answer, the doorbell rings. "That's the door!" she chirps. "Is anyone expecting someone?"

Lizzie shakes her head no. "Well, maybe it's a package delivery," says Janice, although she recalls that FedEx has already come and gone today. For a second she wonders, *Could it be Paul?* But why would he ring the bell? Then she decides it is more likely a neighbor or a friend coming by to see how Janice is holding up. She is thankful that, if that's the case, they will be walking into an idyllic domestic tableau. No train wreck here. No. Train. Wreck. Heeeeere! But at the door, instead, is Paul's personal assistant, Evan. Evan is in his early thirties—awfully old to be an assistant, Janice has always thought—and prematurely balding. Unlike older men who use the comb-over or the close crop to disguise their hair loss, youthful Evan has chosen to disguise his receding hairline by wearing a baseball cap with the Coifex logo on it. Janice is annoyed that he doesn't take the hat off when she opens the door.

"Hi, Janice," says Evan. "How are you?"

Taken aback, Janice nods, choosing not to be overly friendly with Evan until she knows what, exactly, he is here for. "I'm fine. How may I help you?"

"I've come to pick up Mr. Miller's things," Evan says, and shoves his hand deep in the pockets of his khakis. He pulls out a folded piece of paper. "He gave me a list."

Janice is aware of Margaret's presence behind her, so close that she can feel her hot breath against her neck. She doesn't turn around. "His work papers, I assume? They're in his office in the back."

Evan won't look at her but instead unfolds the paper and stares at it as if he is reading it for the first time, though he clearly isn't. "No, Mrs. Miller. Mostly his personal belongings. His clothes."

"Oh," says Janice, suddenly dizzy. "Well, come in." She watches him walk through the door and lets him start up the stairs before she calls up after him.

"Wait," she says. He pauses mid-step and turns around slowly. "Take off your hat. We don't allow hats in the house." Evan nods and removes his hat, folds it in half, and shoves it into his pocket. Janice notices that underneath the hat, Evan's remaining hair is greasy and creased.

She follows Evan up the stairs and is followed, in turn, by Margaret and Lizzie, trailing a cautious ten feet behind. Evan seems to know his way to the bedroom already—it appears that Paul has drawn him a map on a piece of paper—and immediately walks into Paul's closet and begins pulling down wool suits, shoes, rugby shirts, chinos, and polo sweaters. He takes the suitcases off the top shelf—he seems to already know that the gray suitcases are Paul's, whereas the burgundy ones are Janice's—and begins to throw the clothes into them, willynilly.

"Oh, don't do it like that," she says, unable to prevent herself from moving forward to help. "Fold them, at least."

But Evan shakes his head and blocks her way to the suitcases. "Really, this is fine. We'll just have them pressed."

She steps back and lets her hands flutter aimlessly by her sides. They itch to do something—to fold a shirt, to tuck a pair of shoes into a shoe bag, to smack Evan over his smug head with a sweater. She senses It throbbing through her veins, keeping her from doing anything stupid or rash, but senses, too, that its copacetic thrall isn't as strong as it was just a few minutes ago.

Evan picks up a beige summer suit that is lying on the

chaise, a casualty of her Hefty-bag incident, covered with scuff marks and smudges. Can Evan tell that she has mistreated Paul's suit? Is he judging her for that? "That needs to be cleaned," Janice informs him, trying to snatch the suit from his grasp. "You shouldn't take it."

"We'll take care of it," Evan answers. He points to the top of the dresser. "That's his jewelry case, right? He wants his cuff links."

Margaret and Lizzie are standing in the doorway of the closet. Lizzie's mouth hangs open, and Margaret's hands are clenched in front of her, radiating fury. It is their presence more than Evan's curt efficiency that makes Janice feel like she is about to fall apart, despite It. She moves to the door and waves her daughters out. "Leave," she says. "Just leave."

Evan looks up. "If this is awkward, I don't really need you to be here, either, Janice," he says. "I'll be quick. I know where everything is. He told me."

Janice nods, feeling more helpless, she thinks, than she has ever felt in her life. "I'll leave you alone," she says, desperate to get down to her purse. It's only been an hour since her last dose and James said she should wait at least four, but maybe just a little tiny bit more would help. "Let me know if you need anything."

"Actually, if you don't mind, he wants his golf clubs? I think he said they're in the garage?"

But Janice stands there, unable to tear herself away from the spectacle, until a high-pitched shriek splits the air. Janice jumps, her hands flying up in an involuntary spasm of panic, and she realizes that it's the smoke alarm going off downstairs. She can hear the neighbor's Labrador retriever barking wildly through the ringing in her eardrums and the bleating of the alarm. Evan freezes, his hands buried in Paul's sock drawer, and stares at Janice until she turns and bolts from the room.

She races down the stairs, smelling burning sugar. In the

kitchen, tendrils of black smoke drift, snakelike, from the oven up to the ceiling. She grabs the nearest dish towel—the oven mitts are not in their usual spot by the stove—yanks open the oven door, and grabs the scorching pie plate. It burns right through the rag, searing the flesh on her hands. She flings the pie dish away instinctively and watches it skitter across the kitchen floor as charred bits of apple splatter across the tile. The glass plate cracks right through the center. She thrusts her hands in the sink and runs cold water over her palms as the smoke alarm continues to go off. Smoke billows from the superheated pie plate, which, Janice realizes, is now burning a mark into her cherry wood floor.

Lizzie and Margaret materialize in the kitchen behind her.

"I can't believe he sent his *envoy* to do his dirty work," says Margaret. "How cowardly. You can't possibly still think he's coming back, Mom."

"Are you okay?" asks Lizzie. "Did you burn yourself?"

Janice shakes with fury. "Make the goddamn alarm stop right now!"

Lizzie and Margaret look at each other, waiting for the other person to take action.

"Um, how do you turn it off?" asks Lizzie.

"Oh, *I'll* do it, I'll do it, I'm the only person in this entire house who knows how to do anything!" Janice shouts, and she lifts her hands from the running water—contact with the air makes them throb—and grabs a broom from the broom closet and stomps over to the smoke alarm, which hangs over the kitchen door. She takes the broom and tries to push the alarm off its screw, and when that doesn't work after two tries she gives up and thwacks the alarm, and then thwacks it again and again until the white plastic breaks open and the battery comes spilling out and little bits of plastic get in her hair. The alarm whines to a stop.

"Mother," begins Margaret, but Janice cuts her off.

"Oh, shut up! Just shut up, Margaret!"

Margaret shuts up. Lizzie stares at them with bulging eyes, looking from Janice to Margaret to Janice again.

Janice takes a deep breath. "I'm going to go upstairs and take a nap," she says in an even voice. She turns, grabbing the bottle of chardonnay off the counter, and leaves.

She encounters Evan on the stairway, lugging suitcases bulging with Paul's possessions. "Fuck you," she says as she passes. He stops in surprise and stands there speechless as she continues past.

She marches up, up the stairs, down the hall and into the bedroom, where the closet door has been neatly shut, leaving no sign of the devastation that has just taken place inside it. She finishes the bottle of wine and climbs beneath the sheets.

but she cannot come even close to sleep, and she curses the chemicals that keep her eyes dry and open. She tosses and turns. Twilight creeps in, what's left of the day staggers off into the sunset, and she can hear clanking dishes in the kitchen downstairs, the rattle of Margaret's car in the driveway leaving and then returning. The television comes on in the downstairs den, and canned laughter drifts up the stairs. As the sun eventually sets, a silence slips down over the house like a tea cozy. Janice can hear nothing but her own breath. She lies there in profound discomfort, hating Paul, hating her life, hating every decision she has ever made that has brought her here to this bed at this moment. She thinks of her purse downstairs, the little packet hidden inside, but can't muster the will to go downstairs and face her daughters again, so she just lets her high fade away with the day. In its place comes a throbbing headache.

At nine, there's a soft knock on the door. Janice doesn't lift her head.

"I don't want dinner," she says to the closed door. "I'm not hungry." But Lizzie opens it anyway, peeking cautiously around the jamb. She has a plate in her hand; and on that, a piece of apple pie.

"I thought you'd want some," says Lizzie.

Janice stares at the pie, not understanding. "That's not the pie that burnt, is it?"

"No," says Lizzie, looking down at the plate. "It's a new one. We made it."

"You baked a pie?"

"It's pretty good. Not as good as yours, though." Lizzie proffers the plate in clenched hands. "Margaret had to get more apples from the store, and I don't think they were the right kind because they were kind of mushy."

Janice stares at the pie, which is oozing sugar goo, and feels a deep pure sadness for the first time since Paul has left. She tries to open her mouth to tell Lizzie how thoughtful and sweet she is, to let her know that having Lizzie and Margaret as daughters is the only thing she could get up out of bed for right now, but nothing comes out except a strange hiccup. She can feel her jaw working, like a fish gasping for water. When Janice doesn't reach forward to take the pie, Lizzie sets it down gently on the nightstand and tiptoes out, closing the door quietly behind her. It isn't until Lizzie leaves the room that Janice lets the tears come. She takes a bite of the pie as she cries. Too sweet and a bit dry. Fork to mouth, fork to mouth, she eats two bites, and then three, but her stomach protests. She has no appetite. She puts the plate on her nightstand and lets the pie grow cold and congealed at her side.

margaret bolts upright in bed and, for a
moment, has no idea where she is. The room isn't familiar.
Nothing about it reminds Margaret of the room she grew up
in. Although her childhood belongings were transferred when
her parents moved to this house, and carefully rearranged by
her mother, somehow Janice managed to get it all wrong. A
row of Margaret's least-tattered and, therefore, least-loved
dolls rescued from the depths of her old closet have been
arranged on the top of the bureau. A few photographs of long-
lost high school friends—last seen during Thanksgiving break
of her sophomore year of college—are framed on a shelf. An
assembly of gold-plated debate team and academic triathlon
and chess club trophies have been polished and prominently
displayed. It takes a few minutes to quell the disturbing feeling
that she has been transported through time back into a
scrubbed-clean version of her childhood, sanitized, all angst
removed. The dog-eared *Last Tango in Paris* poster and Clin-

ton/Gore '96 campaign bumper stickers weren't saved from her former bedroom walls. Apparently, they didn't go with the new sage color scheme.

Judging by the light coming through the windows, it's already midday. Margaret rolls out of bed, stumbles over to the armchair, and pulls on her favorite orange terry dress, a dress she has been wearing almost nonstop since her arrival home; the idea of putting together another outfit, of even thinking about making herself presentable for the outside world, is somehow too much to bear. Besides, she sold most of her other clothes back in Los Angeles. After a week of wear, the dress smells pleasantly gamy. Squinting in the bright afternoon sun, Margaret heads downstairs to the kitchen, toward the scent of brewing coffee.

As she reaches the bottom of the stairs, her mother materializes in the front hall with a rag and furniture polish in her hand.

"Good morning!" In her postsleep bloat, Margaret is stunned by how striking her mother is, even when her husband has just left her, even when she is *cleaning.* She is cleaning in a dress, for God's sake. She is coiffed and polished and well preserved, like those actresses you see extolling the virtues of Ziploc freezer bags and lemon-scented Pledge in television ads, women who may be pushing fifty but who are constantly asked if their daughters are their sisters. Margaret looks down at her own threadbare dress, reflects on her toenails, marred with scarlet flecks from a three-month-old home pedicure, thinks of the kinky gray strands that have begun sprouting along her hairline, and mulls over the utter unfairness of it all.

Margaret has always understood that no matter what she might achieve she still isn't what Janice wants her to be: a *good* girl, polite and charming and feminine, a respectful daughter and pillar of Santa Rita society. She never has been, and though she wishes this didn't bother her and she knows that it shouldn't, she's infuriated to discover, time and time again, that it *does.* Being near her mother drains her, saps her of any strength, and makes her feel like half a person. It's as if she has never shaken free of, say, the day of her graduation from grade school when she spilled punch down the front of her white lace dress right before walking down the aisle to collect her "diploma" and saw the look of anguish on her mother's face. Her mother never said anything, but Margaret could feel the frustration in her mother's hands as she used scratchy brown paper towels to scrub the red Kool-Aid off the front of Margaret's dress in the auditorium bathroom. Janice herself would never have tripped, Margaret knew. Margaret may have attended an Ivy League college, received two degrees, and started her own magazine, yet proximity to her mother, even now, makes her feel like she is nine and deserves a spanking.

Her mother is still talking, seemingly unaware that Margaret hasn't responded. "It's really such a beautiful day out. I brewed you some coffee. Really, you should quit drinking so much coffee. It will give you an ulcer, you know. There's cream in the fridge. Are you really wearing that dress again? Didn't you bring anything else to wear? Maybe you should go down to the shopping center and buy yourself some new clothes. I think they have outdoor concerts at lunchtime during the summer. At the mall, I mean. Why don't you call Kelly Maxfield? Remember her? I saw her mother at the club last week, she says Kelly always asks about you. You've lucked out with the weather—all this sun, yes yes, global warming, I know, but I was just out in the tomato garden, and with this sunshine my heirlooms are growing like mad. So, an upside, right? Oh! Look! I just moved the couch from the wall and there's your grandmother's favorite old brooch underneath . . . I've been looking for it since . . ."

Margaret nods vaguely and wanders away before her mother's effluent soliloquy ends. From the kitchen, as she's pouring the coffee, she hears her mother start up the vacuum cleaner. She can't help herself: *No wonder Dad left,* she thinks. Her mother is exhausting.

As she drinks her first cup of coffee, she remembers that spring morning in first grade when her father issued her an invitation to accompany him on his Sunday golf game. She sat in the passenger seat of the golf cart, wearing blinding new sneakers and white shorts, gripping a bottle of warm Gatorade. The thrill of being in her father's company—alone, without her mother!—was almost too much to bear. She felt she'd been granted entry to a secret society; even their conversation (Margaret offered her insights into Velcro shoelaces, her new *Lady and the Tramp* record, friendship bracelets, and other timely subjects, as her father occasionally nodded to acknowledge her presence) came sprinkled with glitter. The sun, perched high above them, freckled her bare shoulders.

Somewhere around the fifth tee, her father pulled a tissue-thin piece of blue paper from his breast pocket, a paper that Margaret immediately identified as her report card. With alarm, she watched him unfold it, concerned less about the grades—which were, as usual, all "above satisfactory"—than the teacher's note penned in red ink at the bottom: "Margaret continues to excel at her scholastics, but I am concerned that she is a bit bossy. She needs to work on her people skills and learn to become more of a team player."

Her father gazed at the report card for a minute, then tucked it back into his breast pocket and peered down the manicured fairway to the red flag a half mile away. He winked at Margaret. "Get me my five-iron?"

Margaret clambered down from the seat and selected the golf club numbered 5 from the collection bristling from the leather bag strapped to the back of the cart. The club was taller than her by at least an inch.

She handed it to her father and watched him tee up his shot, arcing the club through his practice shots just beside the ball. *Swish* went the club. *Whoosh. Whish.* The gleaming metal bit through the air. Finally, she could take the suspense no longer.

"Are you mad?" she asked.

"Mad?" Paul tore his gaze from the flag and stared down as if he'd just noticed her. He arched one hairy eyebrow at her. "Now, what do you think I would be mad about?"

"About what Mrs. Winston wrote on my report card."

Paul leaned the club against his thigh and wiped his hands. "Not at all. 'Team player' is just another way of saying pushover," he said. He reached out and tweaked her chin. "I'm proud of you. My teachers used to say the same thing about me. It's just a way of maintaining the lowest common denominator as the status quo. Do you know what that means?"

Margaret was not quite sure what this meant—something to do with math, she thought—but she liked the idea that her father might also have had a teacher like Mrs. Winston, who was old and smelled like mothballs and never called on Margaret in class even though Margaret stuck her hand in the air for almost every question.

"So," her father said. "Do you know what you want to do when you grow up?" He lined up the shot once more and, with a quick roll, sliced the ball through the air. It lolled to the right, arced back left, and landed with a soft bounce just a few feet from the little red flag. Margaret watched it fly, her breath caught in her throat. She could smell the sharp sour grass clippings collected on the edge of the green, and it reminded her comfortingly of the lawn at home.

"Yes?" she said, sensing that this was what he wanted to hear, although the subject was not, in fact, one she had spent much time considering yet.

"And?"

Margaret cast her eyes around the golf course, wondering

if the answer was hidden somewhere. She considered the impression from her rear end on the leather seat of the golf cart, and the eucalyptus trees dripping ghostly arms of foliage down across the edge of the golf course. She stared at the label of the Gatorade bottle and then, looking far ahead at the next tee, the backs of a middle-aged couple teeing up. The man had his arms around the woman, his hands covering hers as he helped her with her swing. "Um. Get married?"

A dark look flickered across Paul's face and Margaret knew that this was not the correct response. "Margaret, really? Get married? That's all you can think of? You can't imagine something bigger than that?"

"You don't think I should get married?" This shattered her. Wasn't that what everyone did? You fell in love and then you got married and had babies. She tried to think of an adult who wasn't married. Even Mrs. Winston was married.

Paul leaned in. "Well. It's complicated, kiddo. You know what it's like when your mother makes you go sit in your room by yourself as punishment, to think about the mistakes you've made, right?" Margaret, who had indeed suffered this indignity more than once, nodded. "Well, marriage is kind of like that, sometimes." He gazed down the fairway, then turned back and smiled at Margaret. "Do you get what I'm saying? About not hurrying into marriage and commitment?"

Margaret nodded again, although she did not in fact quite get it. There was a mosquito bite on her behind that itched, but Margaret was afraid to scratch it.

Paul seemed satisfied with this response. "Good. So don't rush. You can do anything you want, Margaret. You could become a lawyer or go into business or become a scientist. You're good at math, right?"

"I'm best at spelling," she said, relieved to have something to offer to the conversation. "Do you want me to spell 'Mississippi' for you? M–I–double S–I–double S–I–double P–I. I can spell 'onomatopoeia' too."

Her father laughed. "What languages are they teaching you?"

"English?"

Paul considered this. "Okay. Well, when they get around to language courses, don't waste your time on French, no matter what your mother says. It's useless. Better to take German or Japanese."

Margaret wished she'd brought her notebook and pencil. "Okay," she said. "I'll remember."

"So tell me again. What do you want to do when you grow up?"

Margaret considered the question only briefly. "Be a businessman?" she said.

He knocked his fist gently under her chin. "That's my girl." And Margaret knew this was the right answer. She had been escorted into the inner circle of her father's love. He pulled another golf ball from his pocket, fingered the dimpled surface, and leaned over to balance it on the tee. He stood up and handed Margaret the five-iron. "Go ahead, give it a go."

Margaret grasped the enormous club with both hands and spread her feet wide for leverage. The club, sticking almost straight out from her belly, made a tripod that she struggled to keep upright. She fixed her eyes on the ball and took a wide flailing whack. A rooster tail of grass and dirt rose up in the wake of her swing. She had missed by six inches.

It wasn't until the day of Margaret's fifteenth birthday that she did the math and realized that she had been born only six months after her parents got married. And it took her until college before it dawned on her that this was what her father had been hinting at, that day on the green: Her mother had trapped him into marrying her by getting pregnant. Could it be? She'd seen photographs of her mother from her university days—she wore bell-bottoms and smoked cigarettes and looked like someone Margaret might have been friends with. She spoke French, a language of incomparable sex appeal, studied by people with an expansive view of the world. It was shocking to imagine that this woman could so completely betray her education and the ideologies of her age (she was living in San Francisco during the heyday of second-wave feminism, for God's sake) and resort to the oldest trick in the book.

In a way, the surprise now is not that her father left her mother but that it took him two decades to do it. Margaret wouldn't have pegged him for cheating on Janice, although, when she considers the ruthlessness with which he has always conducted his business transactions, it's perhaps not surprising that some of that would leak into his personal life, too. Despite it all, she can't help feeling pity for the woman in the other room, so obviously overcompensating for what just happened with a vacuum and a feather duster.

Margaret takes the newspaper off the kitchen table, pours herself a second cup of coffee, and ambles out the door, down the driveway to the street. She climbs up on a low brick wall on the edge of the property, out of sight of the house, and pulls a pack of cigarettes from her pocket. Lungs pumped full of revivifying tar, Margaret surveys the two-story villas that line the lane, looming threateningly over the edge of their property lines.

Though the technology gold rush didn't really hit Santa Rita until after Margaret left for college, she felt its tremors long before that. By the time she started high school, Silicon Valley's growing prosperity had begun leaching into the neighboring suburbs. Each day she drove to Fillmore High in the old Suburu station wagon she'd inherited when Janice traded up for a new Audi and parked beside the brand-new Cabriolet convertibles and BMWs her classmates had received for their sixteenth birthdays. She remembers, vividly, a day in

sophomore tennis class when she watched a classmate systematically destroy the graphite tennis racket her tech-CEO father
had given her for her birthday. "It wasn't the one I asked for,"
the girl explained, smashing the racket against the concrete
until it snapped. "But he'll buy me another if I tell him this
one broke." Margaret looked down at her old racket, a beat-
up one she'd owned since she was eleven, and felt not shame
but fury at the waste of it all.

Things have only gotten worse since she left. The town's
moneyed modesty is vanishing under a veneer of generic
opulence, the homes just this side of tacky. Every year, when
Margaret comes to visit, there is a new behemoth villa replacing some simple midcentury one-story ranch home. This
trip, it's a ten-thousand-square-foot pinky-beige Spanish-
Mediterranean just across the road, its front yard still raw, the
landscaping too young to cover the fresh dirt despite the gar-
deners Margaret can see fussing over the budding foliage. At
the head of the driveway stands a mailbox, a replica in miniature of the house behind it, emblazoned on one side with
"The Ferns" in gold script.

Margaret's father had always pointed to the accumulating
wealth around them and said it was proof positive that anyone
could make it in life. "These people weren't born rich," he
would say. "They have just gotten a good education, worked
hard, and stayed disciplined."

But as Margaret sees it, the wealth around them—both here
and in Los Angeles—seems to have far more to do with luck
than with some sort of meritocracy: It's all about being in the
right industry, at the right company, at the right time. Certainly, she can no longer see a clear path toward this kind of
success herself.

The week she has been home at her parents' house has been
oddly blissful, despite her father's continuing absence, despite
her mother's infuriating cheerfulness, despite the fact that the

nuclear family she grew up in has clearly disintegrated since she's been gone. It's been, for Margaret, a week of blessed incommunicado: a week without ringing phones or bills arriving in the mail or collection agencies knocking at her door. For the first time in years, she has no deadlines for *Snatch,* no stories that have to be written, no writers who have to be paid, no advertisers that need to be placated. She feels cocooned here, invisible. No one, not her friends, not her creditors, knows where she is.

It took hardly any time at all to pack up her entire life: She was on the road by Monday, a week after her father's company went public, just a few days after her sister's call. She sold everything she owned—her futon, her desk, that ludicrously expensive copy machine, the contents of her wardrobe, her collected works of Simone de Beauvoir—in an impromptu sidewalk sale that netted a depressing $732, not even enough to make the minimum payment on one card. What didn't sell fit easily into the back of the Honda: a few boxes of second-hand books and magazines and yellowing papers, a random clutch of clothing in black plastic garbage bags, a few knick-knacks of sentimental value. Some people are expansive, as big as houses; the sum of her life, on the other hand, is smaller than a standard Japanese hatchback.

How long will it take before her friends notice that she's gone? More to the point, how long will it take for the bill collectors to find her? She considers the BMW parked in the neighbors' driveway, acutely aware that she is in need of a game plan for paying the cards off, a strategy for setting everything right as quickly and unobtrusively as possible so that she can return to Los Angeles and reassemble her life. With all the money in the air in Santa Rita it would seem as if she could just stick out her tongue and catch it, like a snowflake, in her mouth. She flips the newspaper over to the back page to peruse the want ads. There are depressingly few options. "GET PAID

TO TEST CONDOMS" (she has no one to have sex with, let alone safe sex), "EGG DONORS NEEDED: Ages 21–25" (at twenty-eight, she isn't even qualified for this, she notes). There are help-wanted ads for paralegals and bike messengers and exotic dancers in San Francisco (she considers this last one for just a minute and then dismisses it), but none for literary types with graduate degrees and a photographic memory of *The Society of the Spectacle.* Unless you count the ad looking for a typist.

Anyway, she doesn't want her family to know the truth, and if she suddenly took a full-time job it would undoubtedly raise questions that she doesn't want to answer yet. As it is, she's already been studiously avoiding any meaningful conversation with her mother, in fear that everything might come flooding out of her—the debt, the crushing failure of her magazine, the demise of her relationship, the collection agencies hounding her day and night.

Jumping off the brick pedestal, she stubs her cigarette out underfoot and pitches the newspaper into the recycling bins lined up by the front curb. Reluctant to go back into the house just yet, she instead paces down the block, thinking through her options. Her flip-flops send rocks flying. She stops, abruptly, at a telephone pole halfway down the road.

A xeroxed flyer in neon pink is affixed to the pole with pushpins. "WANTED: Upbeat part-time workers for local summer temp job. Must be responsible, educated, and a good multitasker. Quick cash! Lots of fun. Call Carly: (650) 555–9221." A fringe of phone numbers has been cut into the bottom of the flyer. *Quick cash!* Her heart thumps arrhythmically at the sight of these words. She tears off a number and slips it into her pocket, then looks over at the Ferns' villa, where a Mexican gardener is administering fertilizer with an eyedropper to some freshly planted rosebushes. He eyes Margaret suspiciously and she quickly turns and heads home.

As she walks up the driveway, a red Chevy truck—rusting

hood, dented fender—rattles to a stop beside her. Hand-painted letters on the side read, "Cool Pools," and early REM blasts over the radio, rattling the windows. A jumble of nets and buckets and jugs of chemicals ricochet around the back. As she approaches, the pool boy climbs out of the front seat and, his back to her, scratches a scrawny rear end through the seat of tattered jeans. James. She's only seen him through the windows before; up close, she can tell that he is a little younger than her, with dark unruly curls that hang down to his shoulders, and even cuter than she'd thought. He pulls a net from the back of the truck, turns, and sees Margaret. He plants the pole on the ground and smiles, revealing a two-millimeter gap between his teeth. The effect is sort of arrested-development satyr—meets—*American Gothic.*

"Oh hi," he says. He sticks a hand out at her, examines it, and pulls it back. "Dirty hands, sorry. Pool chemicals. I'm James."

"I'm Margaret," she says, realizing as she does that he is the only person her age she has seen all week. Perhaps this, too, is part of why she feels safe in Santa Rita: There are no peers to judge herself against and find herself lacking.

"I do the pool."

"I do . . . well, right now, nothing, really," she says, vaguely embarrassed by this confession but compelled, nonetheless, to reveal it to him. She senses, somehow, that he won't care. He is, after all, a pool boy.

James smiles even wider. "Cool," he says. "Cool. I haven't seen you before."

"I'm not from here. I mean, I'm from here, but am generally not here." She considers this statement, worries that he'll think she's a spoiled local yuppie type, and revises herself. "Though really I'm not really *from* here, these days, either, if you know what I mean." She realizes that she's babbling and stops.

"Oh," he says. "I'm not either. From here. I'm actually not really from anywhere, if you know what I mean."

"Right!" Margaret senses complicity. "I mean, where is anyone *from*? 'From' is just a subjective classification anyway, a social construct of belonging. These days, we're all just digital nomads, right?" She smiles at him.

James scratches the sun spots by his left ear; his fingernails, she notices, are chewed to pieces. "Not really," he says, still smiling. "I just meant that I moved around a lot when I was a kid. But that's cool, too, what you said. So hey, I've got to get to the pool. But come back and say hello anytime."

Margaret grins to disguise the feeling that she has just made a fool of herself. "Sure," she says.

James hoists the net over his shoulder, winks at her—which just makes him look that much more like he should have little devil horns sprouting from his curls—and vanishes through the gate. Margaret sighs, watching him go, wishing that she had hung on to him for just a minute longer, had invited him for a coffee, or a drink. Or just a conversation. She turns back into the house. In the kitchen, she grabs the portable phone from the kitchen counter and bolts upstairs before her mother can intercept her and smell the smoke on her breath.

"Carly Anderson," says the woman's voice at the other end of the line. It sounds like a cell phone. "How may I help you?"

"Hi," says Margaret. "My name is Margaret Miller. I'm calling about the job?"

"Oh great!" says Carly Anderson. Her voice is so perky and bright it makes Margaret's teeth ache. "Well, I like to meet job candidates in person. So I can get a sense of, you know, personality. Would you be able to meet up for an interview? I'm interviewing candidates today, actually. Could you come in?"

"Wait a second," says Margaret. "What does the job entail?"

"Well, it would be working with animals."

"Animals?" says Margaret, suddenly wary. "Oh."

There is silence on the other end of the line. "Do you like dogs?"

"Oh, yes, of course," says Margaret, suddenly afraid that she might have scared off the *Quick cash!* and also afraid to ask more about the job lest she scare herself off. "I'd love to come in for an interview. I'm game for anything."

They arrange to meet at a café at three that afternoon, and Margaret hangs up the phone. She sits on the edge of her bed and listens to the vacuum running downstairs. Through her bedroom window she watches the top of the pool net drift into view, complete a parabola, then vanish. She feels ineffably lonely. And then, before she can stop herself, she picks up the receiver again and quickly dials Bart's cell phone number. The call goes straight to voice mail and before she's quite prepared herself she hears his voice, as laconic and damp as if he'd just climbed out of a hot tub. "Hey, it's Bart. Leave a message."

At the sound of his voice, her mouth goes dry. Oh God, she should hang up. What did she think she was going to say? Why is she even calling him? But with caller ID he'll know it was her, and if she hangs up he'll just think she's stalking him, and then she'll look like an idiot. She is still mulling over her options—to hang up or not to hang up?—when the beep comes, far too soon. "Um . . . Bart," she says, and pauses to clear her throat. "Hi. It's me. I mean, it's Margaret. I just wanted you to know . . . I'm at my parents' . . . in case you were wondering why I called. Um. My family is in the midst of a . . . a family crisis. I just wanted to tell you . . . in case of an emergency." She pauses. "Okay. That's all."

Margaret drops the phone and stares at it. "Get ahold of yourself," she mutters. It's been almost four months since they spoke; she owes him money that she can't pay back. He's dating a *movie star,* for God's sake. And yet, deep down, Margaret can't help but hope that he's sitting at home pining for her, regretting the biggest mistake of his life. What would she have said if Bart had answered, anyway? Does she want him back? Yes. No. Not really. Mostly, she wants him to want *her* back: If Bart Johnson, up-and-coming actor, star of the soon-to-be-released action film *Thruster,* still wants her, it means that she must still have a quantifiable value. And how can he beg her to come back to him if he doesn't even know that she's fled to Santa Rita?

margaret noted two things about bart the first time she saw him: the first was his penis, painted blue and on display for all to see, and the second was his British accent. Bart wasn't, in fact, British, although Bart's father, a sales executive, had dragged the family to England when Bart was a teenager, and Bart had mimicked the local accent in order to better blend in with his prep school peers and therefore avoid regular beatings by members of the school's rugby team who had issues with "focking Yanks." When he returned to the States to attend college, he discovered that an exotic accent—fake or not—was a real asset when it came to bedding college girls, and so he kept it. After a while, he conveniently forgot that the accent wasn't real.

Bart was a member of Berkeley's graduate theater program. He was starring in the school's experimental production of the play *Aristophanes in the Clouds,* a role that required him to stand onstage naked, painted a cheery shade of periwinkle, in total silence while men dressed in goat costumes feigned an orgy at his feet. Margaret met Bart at the wine-and-cheese reception after the show, on the play's opening night. It was two weeks after she'd turned in her master's thesis—"The Mother Alien: Contemporary Cinema and the Poststructuralist Feminist Cyborg"—and she'd let herself be coaxed out by her co-op roommate, Josephine, who was in search of actors for her own film school thesis short. Desperate to get away from the piles of papers and books in her room and the circuitous rhetorical arguments in her brain, Margaret had overlooked the fact that she didn't really enjoy experimental theater. *Aristophanes in the Clouds* did not turn out to be an exception; she found it pretentious and bewildering, a pointless two-hour spectacle with incoherent dialogue and no discernible plot. She wished she'd curled up at home with a Robert Altman movie instead.

The reception was in the backstage area of the theater, a warren of windowless rooms scrawled with aging theater-geek graffiti. She poured herself a Dixie cup of cheap Beaujolais and picked idly at hardened cheddar cheese cubes while Josephine disappeared in search of an actress. She felt alone, exhausted, and very, very weary of all things intellectual.

She thought of the interview she had lined up at Stanford next week with the dean of the English department—who happened to be a golf partner of her father's, which, rather than her stellar academic performance and impressive double majors, would undoubtedly be the deciding factor in why she would (and she *would*) get the assistant professorship. It was a good position, the kind of job you get and stay in forever, introducing college kids to the arcane joys of Baudrillard, writing the occasional theoretical book, living in one of the campus Victorians, and eventually marrying another professor and raising children in the easy embrace of academe. It was the kind of position she would have killed for two years before, back when she thought that going into academia—becoming part of the intellectual elite—was the most profound way to have an effect on global discourse. But after years of slogging through dense philosophical texts, growing increasingly out of touch with the world beyond the borders of her college campus, Margaret thought the job now sounded like hell.

What *did* she want? She wasn't quite sure. To have a larger audience, probably, than the dozen or so glazed-over attendees of her thesis seminar. To *Change the World,* just like her high school classmates had predicted she was *Most Likely To* do. (She could still see the yearbook photo: herself, standing behind a podium, finger wagging in rebuke.) Instead, after so much education, she sometimes felt like she herself had vanished entirely inside the circuitousness of linguistics; instead of an individual, she was merely a signifier, a rhetorical argument, a representation. (Even when she tried to masturbate these days, she couldn't lose herself in the physical sensations but would end up thinking of herself in the third person. *The woman is expressing her female-centered sexuality,* Margaret would neutrally observe; *she is rejecting binaries and entering into the Symbolic.*) She needed to ground herself in reality again. She needed to get a grip.

As she sipped the sour wine she thought of her old teenage fantasy about starting some sort of magazine; but the idea just seemed so reckless, so risky. She wouldn't even know where to start. She ate a cracker while her head throbbed.

When Bart came to the card table in search of a refill, Margaret barely recognized him. He had scrubbed off the blue paint, donned an inside-out white T-shirt (intentional) and jeans with a fist-sized hole at the crotch (also intentional). He had a mop of brown hair falling over one hooded dark eye and a silver hoop plugged through the tender flesh of his upper ear. He smiled at her as he tossed back a Dixie cup of Beaujolais.

"So what did you think?" he asked. "You're one of the few people in this room I don't know, so I trust you to give me an honest review."

Margaret wasn't sure quite what to say. Even though she hadn't a clue what the point of the performance was about—had, in fact, fallen asleep for about fifteen minutes during the second act—her graduate education had taught her that, if nothing else, that which seems bewildering is generally admirable. Just think of Alain Resnais. Long live the nonlinear, poststructural narrative, right? Plus, she had admired the sheer gutsiness that it took for someone to stand naked in front of strangers. During that long silent stretch when Bart was onstage, she hadn't been able to help but notice that he was rather well endowed, his naked body muscular and sculpted and lean. Under the periwinkle paint, she had suspected he was good-looking, in a slippery foxlike way. She was right.

Standing before him in the dingy lobby of the campus theater, she struggled to come up with something that would sound sufficiently intellectually cutting, something that a Media Studies grad student (with a secondary emphasis in Feminist Rhetoric) would say. Her brain went blank. Her eyes flitted, instead, to the crotch of his jeans and the dark shadow visible through the hole. (Was he not wearing underwear?) "Well, I can say this: It was certainly memorable," she managed, deciding that this was at least honest.

He leaned up against the card table, upsetting a raft of abandoned Dixie cups. "Well, that's good," he said. "I thought it was a crap play, myself. It didn't make any sense. I wish they'd done something classic, like *King Lear*. Or *Six Degrees of Separation*. LaBute—anything."

Margaret felt sudden gratitude and relief. "I didn't really get it," she confessed, and it was as if a burden had just been lifted from her shoulders. She smiled. "I thought that the usher had neglected to give me the Cliffs Notes. That would have helped."

"Hah," he said. "No one gets it, but no one has the balls to say it. No pun intended."

She smiled. His accent melted over her, and as she thought of him (naked!) a girlish titter slipped from her lips. Good grief. "Your performance was . . . revealing, though."

He smiled and lowered his voice. "That's one way of putting it. Anyway, I just did it to pad my résumé," he said. "I'm headed down to L.A. soon."

"To do theater?"

"Oh, bloody hell, no," he said, swishing wine between his teeth. "There's no money in theater. Film. I'm going to be the next Sean Penn or, maybe, George Clooney. Do some indie, of course, for the credibility. And then a few quality studio pictures for the money, too. Get a Coppola—Sofia, of course—or an Anderson film, P. T. or Wes." He grinned. "I'm planning to be famous by thirty."

Margaret was stunned. She couldn't recall ever having met someone so blatantly confident in his own abilities, so utterly unconcerned about appearing egotistical—except, perhaps, her own father. Her academic years had been packed with people who believed that they were the smartest thing since melted Brie but knew enough to veil their egos with socially acceptable self-deprecation. ("Oh, the genius grant? That thing? They only gave it to me because they knew they needed a female recipient this year. Really, it was a bad year for submissions.") She knew she should be repulsed by this man, with his foul mouth and crude ambition and overflowing testosterone, but instead she found herself drawn to him. She wished she had such laser-beam intention about her own carefully laid out future.

"Fame is overrated, though, right?" she asked, curious. "What about intellectual authenticity? Personal fulfillment?"

Bart shrugged. "Oh, please. That's such a bunch of shite. If you aren't *someone,* these days, it's like you don't exist at all, right? Fame is the currency of our generation. You need to be the creative genius, the next great thing, because once you are you can have anything you want. It gives you carte blanche. After you have fame, then you can pursue the authenticity and all that crap. You know? Fuck, you have to be rich to even survive nowadays, so if you're not an investment banker you best be a name."

"But by thirty? Isn't that a little idealistic?"

"Too many wunderkinds these days. Teenage superstars. Hit thirty as a nobody and you're automatically suspect."

"Oh," she found herself saying, suddenly longing to tag along in Bart's life, to let his sweeping vision whisk her away.

"What are you studying here, anyway?" Bart refilled his Dixie cup from the open bottle of wine, then leaned over and casually filled hers, too.

Margaret stared down into the liquid, freckled with floating bits of cork, searching for an iota of sex appeal in her education and coming up with none. "I'm a Media Studies grad student, with a secondary emphasis on Feminist Rhetoric. Need a Hélène Cixous quote on command? I'm your woman." She was starting to talk too loud but couldn't stop herself. "Roland Barthes? Walter Benjamin? Judith Butler? Pick one."

"A real academic, eh?" he said, doing a mock double take. "I didn't know we made those anymore. Guess I've been spending too much time with the self-involved actresses in the theater program. It must be nice to hang out with people who use their brains. What can you do with that, anyway?"

Margaret considered the table of ossified cheese cubes. She thought: *Those who can't do, teach.* Looked up and smiled—feeling suddenly light—at Bart. "I'm going to start a magazine," she said firmly. As she said it, the magazine suddenly materialized in her mind, a brilliant synthesis of her feminism, her critical theory background, and her interest in pop culture. She could see the photos, the layout, the essays, the eye-popping cover nestled in between the *New Yorker* and *Ms.* on the newsstand. Why not?

He stood back and gave her a head-to-toe examination, taking in her square plastic glasses, her clunky knee-high boots, the dyed black hair chopped into a blunt bob that she'd once thought expressed a cheerful lack of concern about the traditional trappings of femininity. Now she chewed nervously on her lower lip and wished she'd put on lipstick. "That's really cool," he said. "You should tell me about it. Perhaps over a drink."

"A drink?" She nibbled a cheese cube nervously and tried to remember the last time she'd gone on a date. It had been months.

"Cocktail," he said. "I hear even intellectual magazine editors like to drink them."

"Well," she said. "I can't say no to that, then." She chewed a bite of hardened cheese a few times and swallowed before she answered. "There's this poetry reading I was thinking of going to tomorrow night if you want to come . . ."

"Poetry? I said *cocktail*. Or we could go for a ride on my motorcycle."

She could picture it clearly: a throbbing engine between her legs, sitting behind this cocky man with her arms wrapped around him, holding on for dear life. The ultimate submissive female position. She found herself nodding so vigorously that she nearly made herself dizzy. Oh, she was weak, so weak. She needed to go home and reread her Germaine Greer.

"I'll pick you up at eight."

Margaret scribbled her address on the back of a stained playbill and bolted away to look for Josephine before she could do anything else stupid, like have sex with him right there in the middle of the lobby.

six weeks, twenty motorcycle rides, forty-one mind-blowing orgasms, and one bailed-upon interview at Stanford later Margaret found herself following Bart down to Los Angeles and renting a small one-bedroom with him near a noisy freeway on-ramp in East Hollywood. She didn't inform her parents that she was turning down the Stanford professorship until after she'd already packed her boxes; it was easier that way. They did not take it well. Margaret wasn't sure whether her mother was more upset that Margaret had embarrassed her by standing up their club friend, the dean of the English department, or that Bart hadn't bothered washing the blue paint from underneath his fingernails before meeting them for dinner at L'Étouffée. Her father had rolled his eyes and muttered something about "throwing away her potential" and the fortune they'd wasted on her education. Lizzie had eaten all five of their desserts, making herself as sick as she'd looked through the entire meal. The dinner had finally ended when her mother began to dab at her eyes. "But you're smarter than this," Janice had said, words that somehow fueled Margaret's fury. "And it's so far away."

During the entire six-hour drive down to Los Angeles, Margaret felt sick to her stomach, knowing that she had somehow betrayed her parents' faith in her and unable to totally convince herself that she didn't care. But the longer she stayed in Los Angeles with Bart, the more she felt herself lifted forward by the tsunami of their combined ambitions, imagined herself breaking free of the narrow confines of her family's bourgeois expectations and starting a revolution. Together, she and Bart would be an It Couple. Like Yoko Ono and John Lennon (before the assassination), Sofia and Spike (before the divorce). She would become the enfant terrible writer-editor, he would be the edgy film star. They would have free entry into every event in town, invitations to every movie opening, and dinner parties at the homes of internationally respected artists. The vision was intoxicating.

With Bart by her side, she threw herself into the impoverished-urban-hipster lifestyle appropriate to the as-yet-unacknowledged creative genius. She drank $2 Pabst Blue Ribbon at dodgy bars in East Los Angeles where "real locals" hung out. She went to edgy art openings in Chinatown. She consumed museum memberships like candy and learned to speak Spanish from books on tape. For the first year, life seemed to have a glittering edge. The fact that she and Bart were opposites in all ways was a powerful force of attraction; Bart referred to her in public as "my feminist love slave" and Margaret responded by calling him her "pussy-whipped chauvinist." The sex was violent and terrific. Sure, their apartment was too small and smelled like old cat piss and refried beans, and it was true that they bickered constantly about who would do the dishes and whether to watch *Charlie Rose* or *E! True Hollywood Story,* but she was infatuated, which made everything all right.

And if Margaret had to take a menial job as a bookstore clerk in order to get her magazine off the ground, it wasn't the end of the world. Her friends—Josephine, who had moved down to Los Angeles not long after Margaret did, and then Alexis, and then Claire—were all broke too, all worked day jobs as waitresses or salesclerks or production assistants on commercials. *Snatch* was growing, slowly but surely: The first issue, "The Body Issue," funded by the sale of the diamond stud earrings her parents had given her for graduation and written almost entirely by Margaret herself—including the two centerpiece editorials, "Why Women Should Pee Standing Up" and "In Praise of Obesity," and the "Deconstructing Pamela Anderson's Implants" photo spread—had sold out its entire thousand-copy run. Four months later, the second issue ("The Advertising Issue," which consisted entirely of reviews of the most offensive ads on television) garnered a glowing write-up in *Ms.* (which called *Snatch* "the bleeding edge of fourth-wave feminism") and two thousand subscribers. By the seventh issue ("The Mommy Issue"), when *Rolling Stone* mentioned her in a story about "the new zines" and a rich kid named Stuart Gelkind called her up, she had a tidy little subscriber list of twelve thousand and had gone from quarterly to bimonthly. Even though the magazine wasn't exactly making her rich or turning her into a household name, she still felt something palpable within her grasp. She pushed herself harder: wooing writers, negotiating her way onto newsstands, working through most weekends, and even putting on a suit to meet with sales reps. Despite his disapproval of her direction, she thought, her father would have been proud of her work ethic if he could have seen her.

Meanwhile, Bart was, as promised, fanatically pursuing an acting career—although Margaret hadn't quite anticipated how shallow this pursuit could be. He blew $395 on head shots, and the glossy black-and-white photos—Bart sitting backward on a chair, one palm gently cupping his cheek—spilled from every shelf and drawer. He spent his free time at the gym and wasted hours in front of the mirror trying to perfect his "signature expression." ("Pacino does the thing where he shows the whites of his eyes; Robert Redford has the bemused double take," he'd explain. "I'm thinking mine should be left-eye squint, with a matching half smile.") He memorized the Hollywood issue of *Vanity Fair,* marking photographs of influential producers and agents in case he happened to stand behind one of them at the Coffee Explosion.

His first two years were mostly a bust: a hemorrhoid-cream commercial, a stint as a dead body on *24,* a part in a straight-to-video indie. She was beginning to wonder whether he would meet his fame deadline, whether that tsunami of ambition was turning out to be merely a splash in a kiddie pool. But Bart seemed unperturbed. "Everyone starts out slow," he said as they made up yet another pot of pasta and canned spaghetti sauce. "Even Ewan McGregor got rejected by acting school and had to work at a pizza parlor, and look at him now: Obi-Wan Kenobi. It will come."

And, unfortunately, it did, in the form of a TV pilot for a prime-time soap set in Malibu called *Fahrenheit 88.* Tagline:

"Paradise Is Hotter Than You Think." Bart was cast as a surf-ing instructor with abs of steel, a heart of gold, and a sordid past as a paid assassin. Margaret read the pilot script and felt queasy—there was a gratuitous lesbian sex scene in a hot tub, a gold-digging wife scheming to murder her millionaire hus-band, and about a hundred bubbleheaded bimbettes running around in thong bikinis. She couldn't think of a sexist cliché they had missed. Her only consolation was that this anachro-nistic crap would never make it on the air, and if it did, Bart would surely beg out because his standards were higher than that.

How wrong she was. *Fahrenheit 88* was the big hit of the sea-son, beloved *because* of its very vapidity, and Bart, seemingly overnight, became a cult heartthrob. His signature expres-sion—half squint, half smile, like a particularly self-satisfied Marlboro Man—smoldered at Margaret from the side of every bus that drove by her as she trudged down to the Coffee Ex-plosion to scribble her editorials. It appeared on the cover of *Entertainment Weekly,* underneath the headline "*Fahrenheit 88:* Hot Doesn't Even Begin to Describe It." She couldn't turn on the TV without seeing commercials for his show.

"What happened to Clooney? What happened to *indie*?" Margaret begged, but Bart just shrugged.

"Hey, Clooney got his break on *Facts of Life.* You got to take an opportunity when you see it."

Margaret knew, when Bart's checks came rolling in, and he bought himself a new BMW, and then moved them into the two-bedroom bungalow in Los Feliz, and started taking her out to expensive dinners and on little weekend jaunts to Palm Springs spas, that she should have protested on principle. She should never have, say, let Bart cosign on a credit card so that she'd get a lower interest rate or loan her money ("no need to pay it back anytime soon") to cover her share of the rent. She was letting everything that was wrong with American pop culture—the most sexist show on television!—pay her bills. And yet she couldn't quite summon the strength to say no. Having money was, she was realizing, so nice. Bart was right: Fame got you not just money but power, and the truth was that she liked it when they went out to dinner and the maître d' recognized her boyfriend and brought them complimentary desserts, or when they got sent free tickets to see Radiohead, or when Nike delivered a whole box of promotional sneakers to their house (even if she did insist that they donate the shoes to charity as compensation for Nike's reliance on third-world sweatshop labor).

And yet every time she cuddled up under those five-hundred-thread-count Calvin Klein sheets Bart had brought home, right before she fell asleep the same thought would crash across her mind: *I'm selling out.*

Later, she would look back at her decision to include a story about *Fahrenheit 88* in *Snatch*'s inaugural "Television Issue" as a mistake, an obvious grab for spiritual atonement that had overwhelmed her common sense. But at the time, her rationale felt impeccable. *Fahrenheit 88* was the biggest hit on television, for the second season in a row, and ignoring it would undermine her own credibility as an editor. Her readers had come to expect her eviscerating reviews, her against-the-grain critiques, her ability to call it as it is, and would be let down if she didn't do the same here. The fact that she was living with one of the show's leads just gave her that much more critical authority. It was practically her moral imperative to say something. (And, frankly, she wondered whether a little controversy might resolve her flagging subscription rates and her increasing concerns that her moment in the limelight had already come and gone with that *Rolling Stone* mention, despite the ludicrous sums of money she was pouring into *Snatch* at Stuart Gelkind's behest.)

She titled her essay "*Fahrenheit 88*: A Sunburn on Their

Souls." She carefully didn't mention Bart by name, since her problem was not precisely with him anyway, and why rock that boat if it didn't need to be rocked? But she didn't refrain from calling the show "soft-core porn for the lowest common denominator" and "a sign of the final demise of intelligent discourse in America" and "one dangerous step toward herding women back into their cages."

The day the issue was shipped to subscribers, she left a copy of *Snatch*—open to the article—on the kitchen table for Bart to read when he got home from the set. She woke up in the middle of the night and heard him rattling around the kitchen, the liquid burp of alcohol being poured into a glass. Wrapping her robe around herself, she stumbled toward the clatter and found him standing over the kitchen table, staring down at her magazine with a tumbler of tequila dangling from his thumb and forefinger. His face was a mottled shade of purple. Suddenly, she saw what a terrible error she'd made: What did she think, that he'd be thrilled that his girlfriend was eviscerating his career in public? That he'd recognize her superior morals and bow down to her, quit the part, disavow his employers? That he would be *enlightened*?

She stood there in silence, watching Bart finish the article. When he was done, he gazed accusingly at her, his eyes bloodshot. "They wrote me off the show," he said. He fumbled in his jeans pocket for a cigarette. "They're killing off my character."

"Why? Everyone loved you!" Margaret's first horrified thought was that Bart had been fired because of her controversial editorial, and, despite her guilt, she snagged on a tiny frisson of excitement that she might have had such an immediate impact. Perhaps, despite her niggling paranoia that she should have started a blog instead, despite her fears that she was hanging on to Stuart Gelkind like a drowning man to a life vest, perhaps *Snatch* did have a vast cultural cachet belied by its modest readership. Like the *Paris Review*. Or the *Believer*.

Bart shook his head. "Ratings were slipping. They thought killing off a character would keep everyone talking."

"I'm so sorry," said Margaret. Bart's breath was rasping, and she realized that he was fighting off tears. She reached out and hugged him, tucked her head into his neck, smelled the sour liquor and sickly-sweet pancake makeup caught at his hairline. She reached for something, anything, that would make him feel better. "But in a way, this is good, right? It frees you up to do something more challenging. Something more, say, Coppola . . . ?"

Bart shrugged himself away from her with a cruel twist. "Guess what, Margaret?" he said, lighting his cigarette. "You really need to get over yourself."

"I'm just thinking of you," she said, realizing she'd made a mistake. "I want you to be happy, being the best you can be."

Bart stabbed his finger at the article on the table. "You know," he said. "I used to think it was cool that you were so smart. But what's not cool, *darling,* is the fact that you think you're so much smarter than everyone else. It's really getting tiresome. You aren't right all the time, you know. And your magazine is just shrill and joyless."

Margaret could sense that she had made some grave miscalculation and her boyfriend was slipping away from her as a result, but his words triggered her indignation. She had thrown everything else away for him, and for *Snatch*—how dare he dismiss that? "At least I have principles," she snapped before marching back to the bedroom and slamming the door closed.

He didn't break up with her immediately. Instead, he found an acting job—an action film called *Thruster* that costarred the rising starlet Ysabelle van Lumis—which required him to go to Monaco for three months. With Josephine and Alexis off hobnobbing with agents at Sundance, where their no-budget indie film had won the festival's top honors, and Claire away doing an art installation in London, Margaret had even more time to pour into her struggling magazine. But something about Bart's tirade had poisoned her enthusiasm for *Snatch,* and she found herself pounding away at it more out of habit than genuine passion. Yet Stuart Gelkind was still promising a lucrative sale, and with her mounting debts she needed that money more than ever. Besides, what else did she have going for her? It was her shot—her Sundance, her *Fahrenheit 88*—and she wasn't about to walk away.

Secretly, though, she mostly yearned for Bart to come home so they could reconcile. Instead, when he returned, tanned and boasting a very Italian haircut, he told Margaret that she needed to move out of their bungalow immediately and pay him back the more than $12,000 he had managed to lend her.

That was four months ago. Each day, she seems to miss him more. In occasional moments of searing honesty, she knows that he was right. She wasn't better than him, her morals weren't superior, and her career lust no less craven than his own. And, if anything, the failure of her magazine is now proof that he was on to something from the very beginning: Intellectual authenticity was overrated. Fame trumped everything. If he came back, she might even be willing to admit this out loud.

at two-thirty, margaret washes her face, runs a comb through her hair, and scrabbles together a presentable interview outfit of black slacks and a Prada blouse that once belonged to Claire. Her mother is doing something in the attic—it sounds like a power drill is running?—when Margaret creeps down the stairs, filches a five-dollar bill from her mother's purse, and drives to Le Chat Blanc.

The main drag of Santa Rita is an oak-lined arcade of conspicuous consumption. There's the boutique that sells chil-

dren's clothes hand-sewn by Belgian nuns and a store selling
fresh-baked croissants the size of watermelons and another
shop that specializes in hand-dipped candles. Where did the
old five-and-dime go, the one where she used to buy black
rubber bracelets and gold-foil-wrapped chocolates? (Demol-
ished to make way for Starbucks.) What happened to the coffee shop with worn leather booths that she used to hang out
in? (Replaced by a faux-retro diner called the Fountain.) It's
like an advertisement for gentrification, and Margaret, thinking of the mom-and-pop businesses that were driven out to
make way for $5 chai lattes, feels angry on their behalf (even if
she does have a weakness for chai lattes).

Le Chat Blanc is halfway down Centerview Avenue, in a
space that was once a musty thrift store where Margaret bought
the vintage housedresses her mother hated. It's a chilly café—
more of a bistro, really, the kind of restaurant with parquet
floors and framed fin de siècle Parisian liqueur posters and
wrought-iron chairs that look like torture devices for the back.
According to the menu posted by the front door, it serves up
a $16 cheese sandwich and oysters for $3 a pop.

Margaret buys a cup of coffee at the bar and turns to survey the room, looking for a woman sitting by herself. But the
only person in the room is a teenage girl with a round face,
her hair yanked back into a wispy ponytail. She is wearing a
black pencil skirt and button-front white blouse with a high
round collar and—could it be? Yes. Pearls. She has a folder in
front of her, squared neatly to the edge of the marble-topped
table. The folder says, in block letters, "Happy Tails." Margaret's heart sinks.

She goes to stand in front of the girl. The girl looks up at
her, confused.

"Are you Carly?" Margaret asks.

"Yes? Are you . . . Margaret?" She smiles, revealing
braces.

Margaret nods, reluctantly. She looks around to see if anyone is staring at them.

"Wow," Carly says, taking her in. "I don't usually get people applying who aren't, you know, my age or something."

"How old are you?" asks Margaret.

"Fifteen," says Carly.

"You're very professional for a fifteen-year-old," says Margaret, trying to swallow her humiliation, trying to ignore the fact that her presence here at all is a sign of how dismal her own professional life has become. Silently, she reminds herself: *Quick cash!*

Carly smiles. "Thanks! I'm an entrepreneur," she says. "I've been building this business for three years. I've got twenty-two different clients and enough money to buy myself a car when I turn sixteen. I figure I'm getting a jump start on my MBA."

Margaret manages a smile. Carly reminds her just a little bit of herself at this age. Not that Margaret was such a budding capitalist, but she recognizes the intensity and purpose and total self-righteousness that comes with youthful agenda. Her father would love this girl, Margaret thinks. He'd always hoped she'd be an MBA. She sighs, sits down across from Carly, and takes a slug of coffee. "So what is the job?"

Carly sits up straight and shuffles her papers in an official manner. "You would be a dog walker."

"Dog walker?" Margaret's hand jolts involuntarily, splashing coffee.

"It's a very lucrative, high-growth industry."

"Well, Carly, that's very nice, but . . ." She starts to stand up. She thinks of Bart in *Us Weekly,* of Josephine and Alexis being feted at Sundance and Claire putting on a solo show at the Gagosian in London.

"It's twenty-five dollars per hour per dog," continues Carly. "All cash. Plus tips. I'm leaving town for summer camp and need someone to cover my route for the next six weeks. The clients pay thirty dollars per dog, and I take a five-dollar fee off the top."

Margaret hesitates. She does some mental math. If she walks, say, ten dogs a day—which doesn't seem unreasonable—that would be $250 a day, or $1,250 a week, or $5,000 a month. *Quick cash!* It's not quick enough—she would have to walk, what, four thousand dogs to pay off her credit card bills entirely? Still, in one week she could have enough to pay down the balance on a card or two. It will be a fairly easy job to hide from her family; she'll just say that she's going for a walk and no one will be the wiser. And does she really have any better options at this point? (Internally, she answers her own rhetorical question: *Yes, you could just ask your parents for the money* and then *No, this way you will at least retain a little bit of your pride, even if you lose your dignity.*)

She sits back down. "Okay," says Margaret. "I'll do it."

"Well, I actually have three applicants so I can't give you the job just like that," says Carly. She pulls a sheet of paper from her folder and pushes it across the table to Margaret. "Why don't you fill this out, and we'll have you do a trial run tomorrow to see if you're a fit."

Margaret looks down at the paper. It is a universal application. "You need to know my Social Security number and college major?"

Carly reaches across the table and crosses the education section out with a black marker. "Most of my applicants leave the college part blank."

Margaret picks up the application and begins filling it out with a ballpoint pen. Name. Address. Relevant experience. She pushes it back at Carly, who studies it carefully.

"You went to Millard Fillmore High too? Wow, you graduated, like, ten years ago. Okay, and you live on Hyacinth. . . . Wait a second—are you Lizzie Miller's sister?"

Carly looks up in astonishment at Margaret, who nods reluctantly. "Wow. That's so . . . weird."

"And don't I know it," says Margaret. "Why don't you just tell me what I'm going to do for this test run."

Carly smiles vaguely and hands Margaret a sheaf of papers—profiles of four dogs and a map of Santa Rita drawn over in pink highlighter. "So, here's your route. And here are profiles of your dogs. You'll pick up the dogs in the order which I have listed. Mostly you'll just open the gate and grab the dog and go. Everyone leaves their gates unlocked. And then you just walk the dogs—I've marked the route on the map—and drop them off. I assume you know how to handle dogs?"

"Yes," says Margaret, remembering the shih tzu her family had owned when she was very young. She doesn't remember ever taking Bitsy for walks—the dog mostly puttered around the garden, systematically eating her mother's flower beds, until it died of stomach cancer from ingesting too much fertilizer. "I'm very good with animals," she lies.

Carly stands up and puts the completed application in her folder, closing it with a snap. She proffers a hand. "It was a pleasure meeting you," she says. "I'll call you tomorrow to check in after your walk. I'm sure you'll do fine."

"Thanks for the vote of confidence," says Margaret, and she can't quite stop the wry note that creeps into her voice.

"Oh, you're *welcome*," says Carly, clasping her hands before her chest in an offering of true sincerity.

on the way home, margaret drives past her old high school, Millard Fillmore High, a sprawling brick monolith with all the charm of a maximum-security prison, despite the multicultural mural of smiling Afro-Asian-Hispanic-Caucasian kids that has been daubed on the side of the gymnasium. Discarded Big Mac wrappers and abandoned term papers have blown up against the chain-link fence and flap idly in the breeze. The fields where she used to wheeze her way through gym laps are being replanted for the fall, and yellow tape marks off the fledgling turf like a crime site.

A group of cheerleaders are practicing on a grass patch on the edge of the parking lot, and she pulls over for a moment to watch them. The girls are working on some kind of elaborate routine in which, with the assistance of a pair of besweatered male yell leaders, they launch each other high in the air and turn a quick somersault before landing safely in their teammates' arms. It takes Margaret's breath away. She wonders what it feels like to jump that high, to trust that someone below will catch you as you come back down.

In high school, her own aptitude had mostly been for cerebral activities: the academic triathlon, Future Democrats of America, the Viola Society, the *Fillmore High Bugle*—she'd been an executive officer of all those clubs at one point or another. She'd had to tack on a whole extra page to her college applications. It was no wonder the yearbook had elected her "Most Likely to Change the World"; she had always thought she would, even if she was a shoo-in for the title because of her position as the yearbook editor. At high school graduation, it was Margaret who had given the class commencement speech, entitled "All We Ever Wanted Was Everything" after a Bauhaus song that, at the time, seemed to encapsulate perfectly the vast scope of the opportunity before them. Now it just sounds dreadfully naïve.

The cheerleaders are doing backflips now, flinging pom-pommed hands over their heads in victory. Watching them, Margaret feels terribly sad. She thinks of Carly Anderson, full of ambition, so sure of her path in life, and wonders where she herself got so lost en route. She wants, for just a minute, to run into the cheerleaders' midst and grab a pom-pom and get someone to teach her how to do a flip. Instead, she digs for a paper napkin in the side pocket of her car and blows her nose in it, scrubs at her eyes. Before she starts the car again, she rests her head on the steering wheel for a minute to compose herself. And then she turns the key and coughs her way up the road toward home.

margaret sets her alarm for eight-thirty the following morning, but she's awake and out of bed before it rings. Thinking of the money coming her way at last, she feels—what is it? A glimmer of hope? Optimism that the worst is over? She brushes her teeth vigorously, making sure to get even the molars she usually ignores. On her way out of the bathroom, she bumps into Lizzie, in her Speedo with goggles hanging around her neck, getting ready to go to swim camp.

"What are you doing up so early?" Lizzie asks.

"Going for a walk," Margaret says.

"Really? Can I come?"

"No!" exclaims Margaret, alarmed. Lizzie's face falls. Margaret tries to soothe her: "I need a little alone time, Lizzie. You know, to think?"

Lizzie just stands there, though, looking at her. "Margaret, is everything not okay in L.A.? Is that why you're here? Is that why you haven't gone home yet?"

Startled, Margaret considers her sister. How did she know? Should she tell her? But Lizzie's eyes shine with adoration and concern, and Margaret feels reluctant to burst her bubble with the news that her sister's life is a flop. "Don't be silly," she says. "I'm here because you said you needed me, remember?"

"Right," says Lizzie. "But you *would* tell me if things weren't good with, like, Bart? Or something? I mean, you trust me, right?"

"Of course!" Margaret tugs gently at her sister's earlobe, feeling only a tiny bit guilty at her deception, then runs down the stairs. At the bottom, she pauses to consider the FedEx package that's been sitting on the table in the front hallway for over a week now. Curiosity gets the better of Margaret, and, after glancing over her shoulder toward the kitchen, where she hears her mother cooking, she picks the package up.

It is addressed to Janice Miller, with the return address at the famous San Francisco law firm Sarmin, Anderson, Baretta, and Roth. It's obvious that these are divorce papers of some sort. Margaret hesitates, then puts the packet back down. It's her mother's problem, not hers, she reminds herself. Janice has already made it quite clear that she doesn't need any help. Especially not from Margaret. Anyway, Margaret can certainly sympathize with a reluctance to acknowledge bad news (RESTRICTED NO. flashes in Margaret's head).

She finds her mother preparing breakfast in the kitchen. The table is already set with fresh orange juice and a plate of cantaloupe cut open like a flower. Janice, with a cookbook propped in front of her, is tossing oats and grains into the Cuisinart and grinding the mixture into mulch. The food processor groans and gyrates to a halt.

"Well, look who's up!" Janice says. She glances up at the kitchen clock. "Has the earth moved? Or did my clock stop?"

"Good morning," says Margaret, feeling generous enough not to take the bait. "What are you making?"

"Muesli. Very healthy and good for the colon. Would you like some? I got the recipe from *Gourmet.*"

Margaret shakes her head. "I'm going out."

"Out!" repeats Janice. She opens the top of the Cuisinart and prods at the hamster food with a spatula. "That's a nice change. Where are you going?"

"She's going for a walk," says Lizzie, from behind Margaret.

Janice blinks. "I didn't know you . . . walked."

"What does that mean?"

"Well, you've never been much for exercise."

"I'm practically a fitness nut these days, Mom," Margaret lies, though she is pleased to realize that even her mother's usual nitpicking hasn't popped her fizzy mood.

Janice shakes a cup of raisins into the Cuisinart. She pauses to take in Margaret's outfit. "You're going to go for a walk in flip-flops? Those don't look very sturdy." Margaret gazes down at the blue plastic sandals on her feet, one of the few pairs of shoes she didn't sell back in Los Angeles. She shrugs, picks up a glass of orange juice, and drinks it in a gulp, invigorated by the shot of vitamin C. She grins wordlessly at her mother, who watches her skeptically. "Well, whatever you want to do, but *I* think they look uncomfortable," Janice murmurs, and hits the "On" button on the Cuisinart. Margaret opens the kitchen door and leaves.

The first stop on Margaret's route is two blocks away: a beagle named Skipper, owned by a family named Fincher that lives in a two-story Cape Cod. The beagle is waiting at the wooden fence when Margaret walks up the driveway, its tail wagging. She pushes open the gate and looks around for an owner. No one is there, but the leash hangs by the back door. Skipper bathes Margaret's bare toes with a rough warm tongue while she hooks the leash to his collar. Amused by the dog's indiscriminate affection, she scratches him behind the ears and sets off down the road.

As she walks, she keeps her head down, just in case one of her mother's friends might drive by and recognize her and rat her out. The morning sun filters through the oak trees, though, and the streets at this hour are quiet, so, eventually, she lifts her face toward the sky. The squirrels chatter in the trees and run along the electric lines. The sound of her flip-flops slapping against the asphalt is extraordinarily loud. Skipper trots along, stopping to splash some urine against the occasional mailbox. A few cars cruise by as she walks and their drivers even wave at her, as if she ought to know them. Margaret finds herself waving back. She thinks to herself that this isn't such a terrible way to pay off her debts.

Stop number two is four blocks away at the Brunschilds'— Margaret vaguely remembers Dr. Brunschild, the family GP, as always smelling like mentholated cough drops—where Margaret picks up a geriatric dachshund named Mr. Pibb. Stop three, a few houses down, is a hundred-pound bloodhound named Dusty, a gentle red monster of a dog with ears the size of dish towels who snuffles along with his nose pressed to the ground, as if snorting up an endlessly long line of cocaine.

The final stop is a schnauzer called Sadie, owned by a family named Gossett. Margaret goes around to the side of an older Spanish ranch house with a buckling driveway, to where the dog, sensing her presence, is flinging itself against a wrought-iron fence. Margaret unlatches the gate and steps into the backyard. "Yipyipyip," barks the dog, at an eardrum-shattering pitch.

Sadie is a little salt-and-pepper beast wearing a pink leather collar. Margaret takes an immediate dislike to her. Sadie does not seem particularly pleased to see Margaret either, and barks shrilly as Margaret tries to snap the matching pink leather leash to her collar while still holding the leashes of the three other dogs in her left hand. As she fumbles by the gate, a face appears in the kitchen window of the house, and a pale white hand shoots up in a half wave. Margaret tries to hurry, but the woman pushes the back door open and approaches across the lawn.

"Where's Carly? Is she already at camp? Are you her replacement?"

Margaret struggles with the collar, which refuses to latch. A foot away from her face, Dusty lifts a leg and releases a long stream of urine against the gate. Mr. Pibb farts audibly. "YIP. YIP. YIPYIPYIPYIP," complains Sadie. "I'm Margaret," she calls from her crouched position by the dog. "I'm subbing for Carly today."

She attaches the leash and stands up. By the time she is upright, the woman is standing right in front of her, wiping her hands on a towel. She wears beige linen trousers that skim over her thighs, and gold hoops in sagging earlobes. "Noreen Gossett," she says, offering a damp hand, which Margaret, loaded down with leashes, can't accept. Margaret dips her chin instead in what she hopes is a friendly nod. The dogs swarm around her feet.

"I'll have her back in an hour," she says.

Noreen examines Margaret, her gaze lingering on the limp dress, the plastic blue flip-flops. "Wait, aren't you . . . are you Margaret Miller? Janice's daughter?"

Margaret's heart sinks. "Yes," she says reluctantly. Dusty is snuffling in Noreen's flower beds. He selects a particularly comely blue pansy and gobbles it down. Margaret yanks his leash as hard as she can. He doesn't budge.

"I'm a friend of your mother's," Noreen Gossett says, one eye on the offended pansy bed, one eye frankly assessing Margaret. "I recognize you from the photos in the living room. You're walking dogs these days? Your mother told me you were working for . . . what was it, *Vogue*? A women's magazine, right? Am I wrong?"

"Actually, it's called . . ." Margaret begins, then stops, deflated. "Right. *Vogue*. I'm on vacation, just helping Carly out."

"How is your mother anyway? I haven't heard from her since the IPO. And, well, we've been wondering. . . . Such an unfortunate turn of events. Is she just devastated?"

Margaret, edging toward the gate, finds herself annoyed by this woman's nosy solicitousness. "Well, you should probably call and ask her yourself," she says.

Noreen Gossett purses her lips. Sadie turns and nips at Margaret's ankle. "YIPYIPYIP!" she barks. Margaret yelps and looks down at the broken pink skin on her foot. "I don't think Sadie likes you very much," observes Noreen. "She adores Carly. Carly always brings treats. You didn't happen to bring those liver cookies, did you?"

"Sorry," says Margaret. The beagle starts licking her toes again, and she pushes him aside with her foot. "I ate them all myself already."

Noreen Gossett, unblinking, follows her to the gate. "Well," she says. "Take good care of my princess. Keep her away from the oleander around the corner. It's poisonous, you know. And don't make her walk too fast, just because the other dogs are larger. She's old and has stiff joints."

Margaret smiles thinly and waggles her only free pinkie, as the dogs yank her down the driveway to the street.

Walking four dogs, she discovers, is infinitely more difficult than walking one. The dogs proceed at an uneven gait, and Margaret lurches between them. Sadie does not appear to be on good terms with Mr. Pibb or Skipper and yips at them whenever they get too close. She transfers Sadie to her right hand with Dusty, hoping that the enormous bloodhound will intimidate the schnauzer into submission. Her flip-flops smack against the asphalt. A blister quickly forms where the plastic strap rubs her big toe, rendering her mother's warning depressingly prescient.

She pauses while the dogs take turns marking their territory on a newly painted fence, leaving stains across the white surface. Having done their duty, the dogs then trot forward amiably, led by Dusty. They seem to have fallen into a manageable polyrhythmic pace. The birds chirp overhead. Margaret loops Dusty's and Sadie's leashes over her right forearm while she flexes her right hand to get the blood circulating in her palm again.

A gray squirrel chooses that exact moment to dart across their path, and before Margaret can get a good grip on the leashes, Dusty looks up. His nose flares. His ears swivel forward. He snuffles twice, emits a hair-raising howl, and then lunges toward the squirrel. Margaret's right arm is yanked from its socket and she stumbles forward, dragged along by the baying hound. She braces her feet and yanks backward. Dusty lunges again, leveraging one hundred pounds of torque against her. Mr. Pibb, in her left hand, decides to join in the fun and starts struggling against the leash. The leashes looped over her forearm slip. Margaret is jerked forward again and stumbles; the toe of her flip-flop catches against the asphalt and the plastic toepiece is yanked from its anchor. The shoe breaks in half. Her now-bare foot scrapes against the road and she screams in pain, letting go of the leashes in her right hand altogether to grab at the throbbing appendage.

Smelling freedom, Dusty bolts. He gallops across the road, the leash trailing behind him on the ground, and chases the squirrel straight up an oak tree. Sadie tears off in the opposite direction, her short legs taking her as fast as they can back around the corner toward the Gossetts' house. From her left hand, the still-jailed Mr. Pibb and Skipper bark at Dusty. Margaret hops on one foot, watching Sadie disappear down the street, trailing her pink leash behind her. Across the street, Dusty has his paws halfway up the tree trunk and his head thrown back as he bays forlornly at the upper reaches of the oak. The squirrel, safely out of reach, chatters tauntingly.

Swearing to herself, Margaret turns left to chase Sadie, who has disappeared around the corner, then decides that she should grab the bigger dog first, since Sadie won't get as far as fast. Sadie's yipping fades away into the distance. The broken flip-flop dangling off her foot, she hops across the street to grab Dusty's leash, trailing Mr. Pibb and Skipper behind her. It takes every ounce of her strength to haul the bloodhound down from the tree. She then rips the flip-flops off her feet and jogs barefoot down the asphalt after Sadie with the object-ing dogs behind her.

She turns the corner just in time to hear the screech of tires and see a cloud of dirt rising from the road. Out of the dust, Sadie comes sailing through the air in a balletic arc, turning slowly through an elegant spiral. Margaret squinches her eyes closed and opens them again as the schnauzer lands with a sick-ening *thunk* in a stand of calla lilies, just twenty feet from the Gossetts' front yard. A young woman in a pantsuit jumps out of an Audi TT, now idling in the middle of the street, and runs to stand over the inert body of the schnauzer.

The woman looks at Margaret, tears in her eyes. "The dog . . . it just came out of nowhere. My God, is it dead?"

Margaret runs forward, dragging the three dogs behind her. She crouches over Sadie, touches her fur, smells burnt rubber. The dog is breathing, but her front legs are bloody and jutting out at a decidedly unnatural angle. Margaret strokes the dog's head. Dusty snuffles at Sadie's body, and Margaret yanks him back.

"She's alive, I think," says Margaret.

An ear-piercing shriek breaks through the panting of dogs and women. Margaret stands up to see Noreen Gossett in the front yard of her house, running toward them. A purse has been abandoned in the middle of the lawn; her linen trousers ride up from the effort of her sprint. "Sadie!" she screams. "OH MY GOD what happened to my princess! *What did you do to my dog?!*"

margaret trudges up the front walk to the Miller home an hour later, having seen the hysterical Noreen Gossett and Sadie off to the animal hospital and returned the three remaining dogs to their respective homes. The ninety dollars in her pocket can't take the sting out of Noreen Gossett's parting words: "I am shocked—shocked!—by your incompetence and total lack of responsibility! I'd expect more from a woman your age!"

Margaret is inclined to agree. How could someone so smart be so stupid? Those idiotic flip-flops—why had she insisted on wearing them? And the dog—she thinks of it, bleeding on the asphalt, her fault entirely, and is sick with guilt and remorse. The episode curls her stomach, somehow even more shaming than the demise of her magazine. Credit card debt aside, she sees herself, suddenly, in a repulsive light: a failure, slipping rapidly into obscurity, incapable of contributing in even the most menial way to society. She had been so close to making it, and now it's all gone. *Is this it?* she thinks, as she picks her way, barefoot, through the gravel driveway. *Did I reach the end of my potential so soon?* Perhaps some people are meant to be great, and others aren't; and it has nothing to do with luck, or with working hard, but with innate ability. Perhaps all this time she was really meant more for mediocrity—an inadequate dog walker, an irrelevant intellectual, a dismal editor—and she just tried to achieve more than she was capable of. The problem with being told you are going to change the world, she suddenly realizes, is that anything less is certain to feel like a disappointment.

She enters the house through the front door. From the backyard, she hears her mother calling, "Margaret? Is that you?"

"Hi, Mom," she calls out. Standing in the kitchen, she considers her options. What are the odds that Noreen Gossett will call Janice and tell her about Margaret's morning? It's a possibility, of course, but perhaps a slim one? Really, she'd rather take her chances on Noreen keeping her mouth shut than tell her mother what just took place and have to confess everything. Besides, it was just a dog, and a very old and unpleasant dog at that; and it's not like the dog was killed, and she's already apologized. Any rational person would concur that it's not that big of a deal. It's hardly even a decision, really.

At the sink, she pours herself a glass of water and drinks half of it down in one breath, as if in the process of satisfying her thirst she might also somehow drown her sorrows. Through the kitchen window, she can see her mother working in the vegetable garden. Janice wears green rubber Wellingtons and a denim work shirt embroidered with pictures of gardening tools, her hair tucked up with an elastic. Margaret watches her with a mix of envy and bitterness: How can her mother look so placid when her life is falling apart? How can she be so functional? Why can't Margaret summon the same serenity?

The phone rings, and from the garden her mother lifts her head and gazes toward the house. "Margaret!" she calls. "Will you get that?"

Margaret tucks the phone receiver under her ear as she re-fills her water glass. "Hello?"

The phone blasts electric static at her, and then a woman's voice comes through. "Is this Margaret Miller?" she asks. "This is MasterCard, calling for Margaret Miller?"

How did they find her? The floor seems to give under her, and her Jell-O legs threaten to topple her over. "I'm sorry, but you have the wrong number," she says, dropping her voice several octaves so that the woman won't recognize it. *You are pathetic,* she thinks to herself.

"We were told by a Bartholomew Johnson that Margaret Miller is staying there."

"I'm sorry, but there is no one named Miller here. He must have given you a wrong number," Margaret says quickly.

"Sorry for bothering you, ma'am," the woman says, but Margaret quickly hangs up, cutting her off. *Bart.* Of course they would have tracked him down after she went missing—he had cosigned on her MasterCard. She recalls the message she left on his cell phone with horror, and realizes the magnitude of her mistake.

"Who was it?" her mother calls from the garden.

Margaret can't find the voice to shout a reply. Breathing deeply, she tries to slow down her furiously beating heart and fails miserably. How long will her lie keep them away? Not long; certainly, not long enough for her to devise a new plan for coming up with the money. *I am fucked,* she thinks. *Totally fucked.*

As she puts the water glass back down, her hands shake. Doesn't her father always keep a bottle of whiskey in his liquor cabinet in the study? She turns and stumbles toward the back of the house, thinking that what she needs to clear her mind is a good, stiff drink—maybe three—but as she passes through the hallway she comes to a halt in front of the side table. The FedEx packet is still sitting there, untouched. She stares at the orange-and-purple envelope, fat with portent, dense with disappointment and betrayal, and, without even consciously deciding to do it, tears it open.

She rifles through the sheaf of papers, absorbing their gist quickly. Her father is requesting an amicable, no-fault divorce, due to "irreconcilable differences." Janice gets the house. He will give Janice custody of Lizzie (Margaret is momentarily wounded that she isn't mentioned but then remembers that she is an adult and, therefore, in no one's custody but her own) with child support of $4,000 a month. Trusts will be set up in the children's names, which they will receive when they become adults at age thirty-five. *Thirty-five?!* Margaret stops, abruptly, at this figure, furious. She is not sure what bothers her more, the idea that her father apparently doesn't believe that she's an adult and responsible enough to handle money or the fact that the money she needs is so close and yet, as always, so very far away.

She flips ahead. A savings account will be split between her parents, along with assorted mutual funds and investments. Janice will keep her SUV. He's offering an additional $6,000 monthly alimony. Margaret spends a minute doing some mental math—$10,000 times 12 is only $120,000, a sum that might seem princely to her right now but probably won't even begin to cover her mother's Neiman's bills—before she realizes what's she's missed. There is no mention of the almost half a billion dollars in stock that her father recently made with the IPO. She flips through the pages again, scanning for a mention of stocks, before locating it at the bottom of page 32. "Due to previous agreement between petitioner and respondent, petitioner's assets from stock ownership in Applied Pharmaceuticals are exempt from these proceedings, and will continue to remain solely in his name."

She's not quite sure she understands what this means, so she reads it again, then flips back and forth through the document to make sure. The legal jargon can't disguise what's going on: Her father intends to deny her mother every single cent of the fortune he just made with the IPO. The panic and frustration Margaret has subsumed for the last few weeks suddenly alchemize and begin to bubble over as a completely new emotion: anger. She is furious, furious with her father, with her mother, with Bart and the bill collectors at MasterCard and with the entire horrible, shallow, greedy, unsympathetic, principle-free world that takes cruel advantage of the honest and heaps rewards on the undeserving.

"Mom!" Margaret yells.

Janice's voice echoes back. "I'm still in the back!"

She finds Janice in the vegetable garden surrounded by piles of weeds, which appear to be organized by type—a pile of chickweed here, a pile of bermuda grass there, a pile of nettles, and another of dandelions. Each pile is neatly stacked in a pyramid, roots at one end, stems at the other. Margaret stops and stares. Janice glances up at her but doesn't stop digging. "Someone named Carly called earlier. She said to call her back as soon as possible. Was that one of your friends from Los Angeles? She said you had her number," says Janice. She stabs at the dirt with a trowel. "I can't believe the gardener hasn't done this. I should fire him. No wonder my zucchini are looking so anemic."

"Why on earth are you organizing the weeds?" asks Margaret.

Janice looks down at the piles. "Oh," she said. "I don't know. I thought it would be useful to know what weed's been growing the most." She looks up at Margaret and smiles nervously, like a child caught picking his nose. "Your toe is bleeding. Did you hurt your foot? I told you not to go for a walk in those shoddy shoes!"

Fury rises like a red-hot balloon. Her husband is out there, sleeping with her best friend and scheming to cheat her out of every cent he can, and Janice is casually stacking weeds like nothing has happened? Margaret chokes on her anger. "Did you sign legal documents?"

It takes Janice a minute to respond. She pauses with her trowel in midair, and her face contorts, as if she's struggling to come to the surface of a deep, murky pond. "Legal documents? What kind of legal documents?"

"Something that Dad had you sign about money? And Applied Pharmaceuticals?"

Janice thinks for a minute. "Well," she begins, and there's an agitation in her face. "There's . . . we signed some financial documents a year or so back. To protect our assets. After your father started at Applied Pharmaceuticals. It was a risky endeavor, and we made some investments in the start-up, and he wanted to make sure that if the company was sued I would be legally protected. Why on earth do you want to know this? I don't think it's any of your business."

"Didn't you have a lawyer look at them?"

"Well, of course," she says. "Your father's lawyer put them together."

"Well, congratulations, Mom," says Margaret. "It looks like Dad is about to screw you out of every cent he can. You can kiss the IPO money good-bye."

Janice's face turns the color of nonfat milk. "What are you talking about?"

"I read the divorce papers. Which you, apparently, weren't interested in doing." She waves the fistful of documents at her mother. A creamy sheet of legal stationery drifts down to the dirt, and Margaret kicks at it, trying to pin it under her foot. It is lifted by the breeze and flutters off to land in the pool.

She expects Janice to jump up in a fury, but Janice only probes at the soil with her trowel, carefully unearthing a this-tle. Margaret is baffled—it's so unlike her mother, the queen of control, to allow life to slide past her. How could her mother let her father just walk all over her like this? Why doesn't she take steps to save herself? The brisk housewifely ef-ficiency that has been driving Margaret nuts since she got home now appears as what it is: a mask for a deeper denial, perhaps even chronic depression. Her anger begins to deflate; what replaces it is a bilious sort of guilt. Why is she yelling at her own victimized mother? They may have had their issues, but certainly this moment should transcend that.

"Divorce papers?" Janice echoes faintly. "Is that what was in the FedEx?"

"Yes, Mom," she says in a softer voice. She is surprised by her mother's unlikely cluelessness; she seems so out of it. "I read them."

"Oh," says Janice, her face registering dismay. "I don't re-member giving you permission to do that."

"Well, it's been sitting out all week. I thought it looked im-portant, so I opened it. Here—look for yourself." She holds the papers out to her mother. "In the asset allocation section. He says he doesn't have to share the IPO money."

Janice leafs through the papers. She picks them up, puts them down, and rubs her hands on the front of her gardening khakis. "I've been meaning to open that," Janice says. "But I kept putting it off."

"So? And?"

Janice sighs, a deep, bone-shaking sigh. "Oh, Margaret, I just don't know," she says. She takes off her sunglasses and rubs at her eyes with the back of her wrist. When she looks up at Margaret, Margaret realizes that there are deep black hollows of exhaustion under her mother's eyes. Her pupils are tiny pinpricks in the sun. "I just can't focus on the big picture right now."

"You need to get a really, really good lawyer, really, really fast."

Janice squeezes her eyes closed; she rocks just slightly, back and forth, back and forth, swaying like a baby that has only just learned how to sit up on its own. She suddenly looks quite helpless, and Margaret is overcome by an unexpected wave of sadness. Isn't this what she always wanted? For her mother to lose it for once, to crack the implacable surface and reveal that the person underneath isn't as perfect as everyone seems to think she is? But now that she has this helpless Janice before her, Margaret just feels terrible. Janice certainly doesn't deserve this. No one deserves this.

"I know. I know. I know," Janice says. "A lawyer. Luella Anderton—she got divorced last year. Call her and ask who her lawyer was."

"You want me to call her? Don't *you* want to call her?" Margaret asks.

Janice shakes her head. "No, you do it." She opens her eyes and looks at Margaret with a terror that makes Margaret's heart stop. "Please? You do it. I can't talk to anyone like this. They'll ask . . . questions."

Margaret looks at her mother, finding it hard to believe that the figure before her is Janice Miller, tennis champion, social secretary of the Forest Heights Country Club, indomitable mother of two, wife (soon to be former, but still) of an impending Fortune 500 CEO. Her mother looks as fragile as cut crystal; someone needs to step in and do something, before Janice shatters into tiny fragments. And then Margaret realizes, with a flash of revelation, that Janice seems to think that *she* is the only person who can help her. Her mother is asking *her* for help. Her? Does her mother actually still believe in a capable, productive Margaret? It seems that she does. Margaret is frozen in place by both fear and exhilaration, as the burden of her mother's future lands, unexpectedly, on her shoulders.

A long second passes. "Of course," says Margaret, and pats her mother on the shoulder before she steps back. "Don't worry, I can take care of it. I can help. I'll take care of everything, Mom."

Janice picks up the trowel and stabs at the thistle again. It won't come up. She drops the trowel and goes at the thistle with her hands instead, yanking at it with all her might. The spiky purple flower snaps off in her hand.

"Margaret?" she calls out as Margaret walks away.

Margaret pauses and looks back at her mother, who stares forlornly at the muddy weed in her hand. "Yeah?"

"Thank you," says Janice.

the safest place in the world is the bottom
of a swimming pool. Lizzie can hold her breath down here for
a whole minute and six seconds, the longest time of anyone at
swim camp. Drifting on her back at the bottom of the deep end
of the rec center pool, she is weightless, an exotic mermaid in a
green Speedo, waiting to be discovered by a dashing scuba
diver. Except maybe she would want to lose the swim cap and
goggles and nose guard first. She looks up at the sun through
the water. The light catches in the waves: Diamonds dance
above her. She reaches out in slow motion to grab one, but it
vanishes as someone swims by overhead, obscuring the sun.

She explodes to the surface, gasping for breath.

The fact that she is a good swimmer still surprises Lizzie.
She may have spent countless summers bobbing in the pool
and always figured that she was good at *floating* because of the
extra girth around her middle, but it wasn't until she joined
the swim team that she discovered that she actually had a knack

for the breaststroke. Maybe it is the extra buoyancy of her weight—she is so much more bulky than most other girls on the team, even after losing thirty-seven pounds—that helps launch her forward through the water with each sweep of her arms. Maybe it's simply because she needs the win more than they do. But when she races, she almost feels like she is flying, as if one particularly emphatic sweep of her arms might launch her right out of the water and into the air. She's convinced that if she practices hard enough this summer, she might be able to win in her division at the Junior Nationals meet this October.

She counts in her head: That's three months away. Would her dad show up for the meet? If so, would it be okay for her mom and dad to be in the same place at the same time? She has always felt sorry for those girls whose parents' conspicuous absences at school events reeked of family disaster. She wouldn't want the other girls on the team to feel sorry for her.

Lizzie does her freestyle laps automatically, keeping her head down, pleasantly oblivious to what might be going on outside the pool. Her hand hits the pebbled concrete of one end of the pool and she flips in a somersault, planting the wrinkled soles of her feet against the tile and giving herself a shove to slice back through the water. Through the gurgling in her ears, she thinks she hears the shriek of a whistle—is practice over?—but she has the rhythm now, and chooses to ignore it. Plus, if she waits a little while, she won't have to see all the other girls in the locker room; she's managed to avoid Susan Gossett for almost two weeks, by coming to practice early and leaving late.

Lizzie does eight more laps before pausing to take a breath and look around. The pool is empty except for Becky, a slight figure sitting patiently on the edge of the shallow end, splashing her heels in the water. She has already changed into a T-shirt and shorts, and her frizzy red curls are drying in the sun. Once again, Becky has forgotten her sun hat at home.

From a distance, it looks like she's blushing from chin to forehead.

Lizzie swims over and tickles Becky's toes. "Hey," Lizzie says.

"Hey," says Becky. "You make me look lazy."

"I just like swimming."

"You're getting really fast."

Lizzie smiles. "You think so?"

"Totally. Hey. Wanna go get a milkshake?"

"Totally," says Lizzie, pleased to have a reason not to race back home to the quiet house. Although this, in turn, makes her feel guilty: Will her mother be lonely if she doesn't come home right away? Or is it okay because Margaret is there? Should she call and tell them she'll be home late? She never did before, but maybe things have changed now. The rules dictating how kids with separated parents should behave are still unclear to her.

"The Fountain?" asks Becky.

"Totally," agrees Lizzie. The Fountain is her favorite: When they give you your milkshake, they also give you the extra in a metal cup, so you get two milkshakes for the price of one. Which, of course, isn't really on her diet, but whatever. She's earned it.

Lizzie changes into shorts and a tank top. They walk down the side streets to the main part of town, flipping through the pages of an *Us Weekly* and examining the flat bellies of assorted purportedly pregnant starlets. The afternoon is balmy, and Lizzie can feel her sweaty thighs sticking together as she walks.

The Fountain is mostly empty, since the lunch crowd has vanished and the dinner crowd has yet to arrive. Lizzie and Becky collapse heavily into a green leather booth in the corner, slumping so that they are practically supine. The restaurant is supposed to look like an old-fashioned soda fountain, with a long Formica counter and stools that twirl, but it opened only three years ago, so all the chrome is still shiny and most of the vintage appliances are only for show. Lizzie examines the menu. She briefly considers the Niman Ranch Meatloaf for $19.50 or the Chilean Sea Bass Burger for $28—but instead orders the $8 Valrhona chocolate milkshake.

Becky sighs, grabs a red curl of hair, and examines the split ends. She sticks it in her mouth, tastes it, and spits it out. "This summer has been so boring," she says. "If something exciting doesn't happen soon I think I'll die."

"I know what you mean," agrees Lizzie, although she realizes, with some surprise, that she is not bored at all. Her usual listless summer state has been replaced by a sense of constant agitation. Even when she sits still it feels like the world is spinning wildly around her. Maybe that's why she likes swimming so much these days. When she's in the water the chaos around her seems to slow down, like when the car you're in accelerates to pass another car on the highway, making it seem to just slide away behind you.

Becky looks at her nervously. "Have you talked to your dad yet? Since . . ."

"No," says Lizzie, wishing Becky hadn't asked this. "He's traveling, I think, for work, you know? So he couldn't call." The truth is that before he moved out, her father *always* used to call when he was on business trips, though he never talked to her, only her mom. He'd just bring home souvenirs for Lizzie— dolls in ceremonial native dresses, miniature replicas of the Empire State Building, stuffed bears dressed in T-shirts in other languages, some still wearing price tags from the duty-free store. She never knew what to do with them, so they just sat on a shelf in her bedroom, collecting dust. Will he still get her gifts, now that he's leaving? Some kids get even better gifts after their parents divorce. But that's kind of depressing to think about.

She is relieved when the milkshakes arrive, piled high with fresh whipped cream and shavings of bittersweet chocolate, so thick that Lizzie can barely get a spoon into the glass. She sucks at her plastic straw as hard as she can, until she is dizzy from the lack of oxygen and her eyes feel like they are going to pop, but the ice cream refuses to ascend the straw.

She pushes the shake away and gasps for breath. "It's harder than giving a blow job," she says.

Becky turns violet. "Lizzie!" she says. "You shouldn't say stuff like that."

"Jesus, Becky, it was only a joke." Lizzie stares down into her milkshake. She sticks her finger in the whipped cream and licks it off. "Get a sense of humor."

Becky rolls the paper from her straw into a tiny tube, then flattens it out with her thumb. "Can I ask you something, Lizzie?"

"What?"

Becky rolls the damp paper up again, wrapping it around her finger. She doesn't meet Lizzie's eyes. "Are you a virgin?"

Lizzie considers the question. She knows that Becky has only kissed a boy once, when they were playing spin the bottle in the corner of a school dance their freshman year and Johnny Franks Frenched her. The whole next week Becky informed everyone about how gross this encounter had been. It was totally juvenile. Lizzie recalls that she herself has had sex with Johnny Franks, and that Becky not only does not know this but would probably be freaked out if she did know, and she feels as if a canyon a hundred feet wide has opened between them. How did she get to be so much, well, *cooler* than Becky so quickly? She glances over at Becky, whose pancake-flat chest is concealed by the glitter unicorn on her T-shirt, and is embarrassed for her.

But she finds that she wants to tell Becky, even if Becky isn't as impressed with Lizzie's sexual exploits as she should be. It will be a relief, she thinks. She hasn't told anyone—certainly not her mother, and her sister hasn't asked yet, and who else is there? So her secret has just kind of grown inside her, and sometimes she feels like a pressure cooker that's about to explode its contents all over the walls.

"No," she says, sitting back in her seat. "I'm not."

Becky nods, still staring at the paper wrapped around her finger. "How long? I mean, how long ago did you lose it?"

"Three months ago."

Lizzie watches Becky gnaw on the inside of her cheek, which is what Becky usually does when boys talk to her at school and she gets scared. "Who did you do it with?" she asks.

Lizzie sticks her tongue into the whipped cream to delay her answer, and gets it all over her face. She licks it off before responding. "Um. Which time?"

Becky stares at her, the piece of paper in her hands frozen mid-twist. "So, it isn't a lie?"

"What do you mean?"

"What I heard." Becky's voice gets tinier and tinier until it's almost impossible to hear at all.

"What did you hear?" Lizzie is growing more nervous as she watches Becky's jaw working away, the straw paper twisting in her hands, but she's not sure why.

"Look, Lizzie," Becky says pleadingly. "I didn't want to believe Susan. You know I think she's a psychobitch. But everyone keeps saying that, you know, you're sleeping around."

"Oh," says Lizzie, with a sinking feeling. "Like, what exactly are they saying?"

Becky squirms in her seat. "I don't want to repeat it."

"No, tell me," says Lizzie, growing seriously concerned.

Becky mumbles something.

"What?" says Lizzie.

"They say that you've"—she pauses, winces, and whispers—"*done it*, with, like, fifty guys already and you've become the"—pause, wince, whisper—"*school slut* and everyone is laughing at you. And that you're trying to have sex with every guy in our class. That you'd suck any guy's"—pause, wince, whisper—

"*thingy* if they got you drunk. That all these guys are just using you for sex." Becky has tears welling up in her eyes. "And I told them that it wasn't true and they were full of shit, but then someone showed me the scorecard."

Lizzie's last sip of milkshake, descending down her throat, stops and reverses direction. She chokes and gulps at her glass of water, trying to swallow back down the horror that is rising up with the regurgitated ice cream. "What scorecard?" she manages.

"It's on the wall in the boys' locker room at school."

"What does it say?"

Becky shakes her head, and a fat tear drops from her eye and lands in her milkshake, making a crater in the whipped cream. "Maybe you should just look at it yourself," she whispers.

Lizzie slumps down until she is lying on her back on the vinyl and closes her eyes. She pretends that she is at the bottom of a swimming pool where even the thrashing of other swimmers on the surface doesn't cause a ripple. She can breathe water, like a fish, and she'll never have to come up for air again. From far away, she can hear Becky's voice, drifting over her like a current. "Lizzie? You know I don't care, right? I don't care what people say. You're my best friend. They're all lame. Lizzie?"

Lizzie says nothing. The word "slut" echoes through her head. She repeats it in her mind, punishing herself with the slippery sharp syllables that catch at the back of her tongue and threaten to spill out onto the table. For a long minute, there is no sound except for Becky slurping at her milkshake. Finally, she hears Becky speak again, very quietly.

"Lizzie? What's it like?"

"Like?"

"You know. Doing it."

"It's like . . ." She stops, and for a long time she can't think of anything to say. "It's just stupid."

． ． ．

after they part ways, lizzie walks the mile to Millard Fillmore High. Summer school is in and the doors are unlocked, so she wanders through to the gymnasium at the back of the campus. She can hear cheerleaders practicing in the distance and the squeak and thump of a basketball game out on the courts, but no one is in the halls. The smack of her sandals echoes off the polished concrete. The lockers have been freshly painted orange and blue, and the smell of the cheap paint makes her light-headed. She passes her own locker from last year and wonders whether the graffiti she wrote inside it last spring—I ♥ Justin—is still there. She hopes they've painted over it.

When she gets to the door of the boys' locker room, she pauses. Her heart pumps rapidly in her chest at the thought of getting caught in this off-limits territory. But she gathers her nerve and pushes the swinging door open with one hand, standing back so that she won't accidentally see in, just in case someone is in there.

"Hello?" she whispers hoarsely, just to double-check, prepared to run away as fast as she can if she gets a response. Her voice echoes off white tile and bounces back to her.

The boys' locker room, to her astonishment, is identical in every way to the girls', except that the bathroom area has urinals as well as toilet stalls. It even smells the same: like bleach and pink granulated hand soap. It is disappointingly, benignly unmasculine.

The graffiti is scribbled on the tiles on the wall just beside the sinks. It is her name, written in black Sharpie. "I did Lizzie Miller," it says, in handwriting that slants up the wall. Underneath that there is a list of names, written in different hands, with a date beside each one. "Justin Bellstrom 3/22," "Max

Grouper 4/17," "Johnny Franks 6/9 & 6/18," "Brian Cientela 5/24." There are ten names in all, and she stares at them, horrified: Six names she recognizes with a stab of embarrassment (Did she? Yes. Yes. Yes) and four infuriate her, because they are liars. Mark Weatherlove is in the latter group. What a faker! And she didn't have sex with Martin Simms, either.

"Shit," she says out loud, and the swear word reverberates off the tiles and fills the room, a dozen curses echoing back to rebuke her. She is not an object of desire to the boys of Fillmore High after all, she sees with a sudden sickening clarity. (How could she have missed this before? Did she know but somehow not know?) She is hardly a real girl at all, just a score. No different than a touchdown in a football game.

As she stands there in the boys' bathroom, the Lizzie she thought she had become vanishes like a soap bubble in a stiff breeze—gone just like *that*—leaving her with only the hideous feeling that the last three months, the months she thought had been the best of her entire life, were a horrible mirage.

She tears a handful of paper towels from the dispenser, pumps a cupful of granulated soap on top, and rubs at the graffiti. Brian Cientela's name, written in ballpoint pen, smears a little, but they aren't joking when they call Sharpies permanent. She moistens the towels in the sink and rubs harder, but the paper just deteriorates into pink mush in her hand. Still, she scrubs as hard as she can, until her palm is raw and soapy water runs down the wall and her arm feels like it will fall off from the effort.

when she arrives home, in the early evening, she goes straight to her room and slams the door. She grabs a lace-trimmed pillow off her bed and throws it at the mirror. It falls to the ground with an unsatisfying wheeze. She kicks it and it punts forward only about three feet. She kicks it once more, hoping to tear a hole in its side, and it bounces off the wall. She stands there in the room, looking down at the pillow, which now has a black smear in its center, trying very hard to breathe.

At her desk, she pulls out a piece of pink stationery with "Elizabeth Miller" embossed across the top. The stationery was a Christmas present from her grandmother in Connecticut four years ago. Her mother had cooed over it and proclaimed it a "very thoughtful gift." After writing a thank-you note to Grandma on one sheet of the stiff pink paper, she still has 499 sheets left.

Lizzie grabs her favorite pen, the one with the fuzzy blue troll glued to the top, and composes a letter to Mark Weather-love.

"Dear Mark," she writes, in her best cursive. "You are such a liar. How DARE you write that bullshit in the boys' locker room. I wouldn't touch you if you were the last person on earth, and you know it. And your mother is a total slut. Don't ever talk to me again. NOT yours truly, Lizzie Miller."

She seals it and, feeling much better, heads back down the stairs and out the front door. At the end of the driveway she looks both ways to see if anyone is watching—there is no one around—and thrusts the pink envelope into the mailbox.

When she returns to the house, she hears rustling in the living room and peeks around the door frame. Margaret is splayed out on the couch, legs propped up on a tower of decorative pillows. She is surrounded by computer printouts. Lizzie walks into the room and picks one up. It's from the *Legal Affairs* Web site, entitled "Post-nuptial Asset Allocation." Another one reads, "Unitary Appreciation of Nonbinding Marital Property." A third page is something torn out of *Ladies' Home Journal:* "When Divorces Get Ugly: Eleven Women Talk About the Hell They Survived!"

"Where's Mom? What's she cleaning now?" Lizzie asks, flopping down on the couch.

"Nothing, actually," says Margaret. "She went upstairs for a nap a few hours ago and asked to be left alone for a while. Honestly, she looked pretty rough. Maybe it's all the fumes from the Lysol. That stuff is toxic. She should really be buying eco-friendly cleaning supplies, considering how much she uses the stuff. What happened to the cleaning lady?"

"She fired her," Lizzie says. She chooses not to mention the fact that Guadalupe had been blamed for the vanishing booze that she herself had, in fact, been stealing from the liquor cabinet. Oops.

Lizzie picks up the *Ladies' Home Journal* article and skims the first paragraph: "When Jenny's husband fled for the Bahamas with his 23-year-old secretary, emptying their bank account and even taking their pet Chihuahua, Jenny thought things couldn't get any worse. Then she showed up in divorce court and discovered that her husband—an investment banker—was suing her—an unemployed housewife—for $8,000 a month in alimony. Jenny tried committing suicide, slitting her wrists in a bathtub, before she finally got smart and . . ."

Lizzie looks up. "Do you think Mom is going to commit suicide?"

Margaret wrinkles her nose. "I doubt it. It would make a mess of the white rugs. Unless she chose something neat, like a bottle of sleeping pills."

Lizzie, alarmed, tries to recall the insides of her mother's medicine cabinet. "Could Vicodin be a sleeping pill? Mom had some of that."

"Why does Mom have Vicodin?"

"She hurt herself playing tennis in the spring. She walked around with her arm all bandaged up for two weeks."

"Right," says Margaret. "Well, don't worry, Vicodin is harmless. You can't kill yourself with it. Not really."

"Oh," says Lizzie, but she's not convinced.

Margaret notices the look on her face and reaches over to

rub Lizzie's back. "Hey, I was only joking, Lizzie. Mom would never kill herself. She's just not the suicidal type. Besides, she's too much of a control freak to let us run amok in her house without her around to make sure we don't make a mess of things. Right?"

Lizzie puts down the papers. "Why are you reading *Ladies' Home Journal*?"

"I saw it at the supermarket, thought it sounded relevant."

"What are you doing?"

"Research. For Mom."

"They're getting divorced, right?" Lizzie asks reluctantly.

Margaret nods and flips to a new page, her eyes still focused on the tiny text. "If Dad has his way."

"Will he?" Lizzie's eyes are stinging, and she realizes that she's holding back tears. For a moment she hangs on to the hope that Margaret will say that her father won't, in fact, have his way; that their mom will convince him that he was wrong and he'll leave Beverly and come home and everything will return to normal.

"Yes," she says, dropping the sheaf of papers to her lap. "In all probability."

Lizzie blinks twice and frowns. "Oh," she says. "So are you going to help Mom?"

"Yes," Margaret says, in a loud, firm voice, and Lizzie is warmed momentarily by the assertion. Margaret always seems to have it together; if there is something good to be redeemed from the situation, Margaret will find it. She closes her eyes and feels safe in her sister's presence; if Margaret were home all the time, she thinks, it would be like having a best friend living right in the house with her. "I think I'm going to go make myself a sundae," Lizzie announces. "Do you want one?"

Margaret shakes her head and stacks the papers on the table. She aligns them with three quick raps. "Not hungry. Thanks, though."

Lizzie pauses at the doorway. "Margaret? How old were you when you lost your virginity?"

Margaret raises an eyebrow. "Wait, Lizzie. Wait until you're much, much older."

Lizzie feels her face flush and is frightened that her sister might be able to see right through her pink cheeks to the ugly truth inside. She's just a little annoyed that Margaret always seems to think that she's too young to discuss anything of importance. "C'mon, Margaret. I'm not, like, a child."

"You're only fourteen."

"Fifteen in October!" She grips the doorway.

"Seriously. Wait. For three reasons. A: Men suck, and all you have to do is look at what's going on with Mom and Dad to see this in action. B: Teenage boys, especially, suck. C: Teenage boys suck especially in bed. You won't enjoy it; they don't know the clitoris from the clavicle." She gives Lizzie a Very Serious look, the one with accordion eyebrows and flared nostrils that says Margaret Means Business. "More importantly, though, Lizzie, is that it's risky, both physically and emotionally. As long as you can postpone the kind of grief that comes with sex, you should. I know life sometimes seems hard now, but it gets even harder later, once you start factoring love and sex into the equation. If you really want to explore sex, let's talk about vibrators."

Lizzie, taking this in, feels sick. It's too late, she thinks, as she sees this miserable future spreading out before her. Surely, she thinks, Margaret must have some hope for her? "But it's not like that with Bart, right?"

Margaret barks a small little laugh and wrinkles her nose. "No. Bart is an angel."

Lizzie smiles bravely. "I'm sure he is," she says. "You're so lucky."

The kitchen is sparkling and smells like bleach. Janice has left a casserole on the countertop that's labeled with a stickie note: "Dinner. 350 degrees for 30 minutes." Lizzie peels back the aluminum foil and probes it with her finger, breaking through a filo dough crust to a layer of spinach: spanakopita. Lizzie hates spinach. Just once, she wishes her mother would make something like mac-n-cheese from a box. Maybe she can convince Margaret to go out to dinner.

She finds the freezer well stocked with ice cream and mango sorbet—the latter probably intended for her, but she makes herself a mocha toffee almond fudge sundae anyway, sneaking a few big bites before she goes back to the other room so that Margaret won't see what a pig she's being.

The ice cream is hard and icy, and Lizzie eats it slowly, putting a spoonful at a time in her mouth and letting it melt on her tongue as long as she can bear it, before her teeth freeze and she has to swallow. Margaret watches her and sighs; a long, hot puff of air. "I really need a cigarette," Margaret says, but she doesn't move from the couch. Lizzie looks at the rose arrangement on the sideboard, the neatly stacked pile of coffee-table books—*Golf Courses of the World, Mediterranean Castles,* and *The Gardens of Manet*—and her mother's weird French magazines that no one reads and the collection of antique boxes on the display shelves. She thinks, again, of the writing on the wall in the boys' locker room—of her whole secret life exposed for everyone in school to see, of all the boys who pretended to like her when it turned out they didn't care at all, of the boys who scribbled their names on the wall even though she never touched them, the liars. (Mark! Mark Weatherlove! What a creep!) She wants to sweep everything to the floor, to crunch the porcelain under her heels, tear the books in half, make a mess of the house. She has the crawling sensation that she is being watched and that there is some impending doom before her. She puts the sundae down and sinks back into the beige velvet cushions, letting the voluminous couch cocoon her. Maybe she'll slip into the cracks between the cushions and disappear forever.

Out in the front yard, the gravel crunches and Lizzie hears the whir of an engine idling to a stop. A car has pulled into the driveway. Margaret looks at Lizzie, looks at the living room window, and jumps up to pull the curtains aside.

"Who is that?" Margaret asks, as she peers out.

Lizzie follows her and peers out too. A woman in a fuchsia drop-waist cocktail dress is climbing out of the driver's seat of a Mercedes station wagon, carefully placing one black heel before the other as she navigates the gravel of the driveway. She carries a woven basket filled with silver tissue paper in one hand and uses the other to tug her panty hose into place in the back. She looks up at the house, glances down at her watch, and then begins to walk resolutely toward the front door.

"That's Barbara Bint," says Lizzie. "She's a friend of Mom's, from the club."

"Why is she here?" Margaret asks.

Lizzie shrugs. "No idea."

The sisters stand transfixed in the window, watching Barbara pick her way through the gravel and then vanish out of their view. The doorbell rings.

Margaret heads for the front door. Lizzie stays frozen at the living room window, watching the evening light sparkle in the gravel, catching on bits of mica trapped in the rocks. She can hear the murmur of Margaret talking to Barbara Bint in the foyer. She wills time to stop, so that she is forever standing in this window, watching the setting sun, staving off whatever danger or embarrassment lies behind the closed doors of this reassuringly beige room.

Mrs. Bint bursts into the living room just as Lizzie turns around.

"Am I the first person here? I'm always the first person," Barbara Bint wails. "Such a terrible habit I have, but don't you think that promptness has just gone the way of etiquette and good manners these days? I really think it should be revived. If an invitation says seven o'clock, then I say, be there at seven o'clock. I can't stand it when I throw a party myself and everyone is late and the canapés get dried out in the oven while you wait! Give this to your mother, Lizzie? Home-baked carrot muffins!" She flourishes the basket, sweeps over to Lizzie, and leans in to kiss her on the cheek. She smells like baby powder and jasmine, and up close, Lizzie can see the droplets of dried hairspray that shellac her hair into perfectly symmetrical wings.

Mrs. Bint stands back, holding Lizzie at arm's length with one hand. "Let me look at you. It's been so long since I've seen you, Lizzie, and I can really see what your mother was saying about your weight loss. You look marvelous! Though I don't understand why kids these days don't feel the need to dress up. My own Zeke never wants to wear shoes either, and his feet get so filthy!" Lizzie looks down at her bare feet, her cutoffs and tank top—with dripping brown stains from her afternoon milkshake and evening sundae down the front—and blushes.

Mrs. Bint continues: "And it looks like I'm so early that your mother isn't even dressed yet? Well, that will give us some time to catch up while she gets ready. Tell me, Lizzie, how are you? How's school? I hear you're quite the swimmer."

As she babbles, Lizzie looks around wildly for Margaret and sees her standing in the doorway. Margaret mouths something incomprehensible at Lizzie, her lips churning around exaggerated silent vowels. Lizzie, alarmed, shakes her head in incomprehension. Margaret points dramatically at the ceiling and then circles a finger beside her head, seemingly suggesting that someone—herself? Barbara Bint?—has gone cuckoo.

"I'm good," Lizzie begins, as through the window she sees another car arrive in the driveway. The doorbell rings once more. Margaret vanishes again.

"Where's the caterer?" Still holding the basket out, Mrs. Bint looks around, as if a waiter might pop up from behind the couch or erupt out of the sideboard. "I'd love something to drink. Some sparkling water, maybe. With lime. Is there a bar somewhere?"

"I'll get you some," Lizzie says, seizing the opportunity to escape. She thumps out of the living room, passing Margaret, who is standing in the foyer taking coats from Martha and Steven Grouper, parents of her classmate Max. Max, the third person she slept with. On April 17, according to the bathroom scorecard. Oh, God, she thinks. They are the last people she feels capable of facing right now. She dodges them with a quick "hello" over her shoulder and trips into the kitchen.

Lizzie grabs a plastic tumbler from the kitchen cabinet, stops, and puts it back. Her mother would be appalled if she served guests with the cheap glasses. Instead, she climbs up onto the kitchen counter so that she can reach the top shelf, where the wedding crystal is kept. She grabs as many glasses as she can balance in one arm and drops back down to the ground. A glass tumbles from the crook of her elbow and explodes on the tile floor, leaving a million shards of crystal glittering on the floor.

Margaret runs into the kitchen, banging through the swinging door so quickly that it slams against the wall. She has sweat beading up on her forehead.

"What's going on?" Lizzie asks, but she already knows. She remembers her mother clipping recipes from *Gourmet* magazine in preparation, and the pile of invitations that Lizzie mailed for her mother a month ago, just a week before her father vanished with Beverly Weatherlove.

"Mom forgot about her cocktail party," Margaret says.

"She did!" Lizzie finds this hard to fathom. It's like Santa forgetting about Christmas. Like her math teacher Mr. Nimroy forgetting the algebra final. It explodes the natural laws of science. "What do we do?"

"Run upstairs and get her out of bed. Quick, before these people eat us alive. I'll man the door."

"But Barbara Bint wants some sparkling water."

"I'll get it," Margaret says. "Do we have anything to feed them? Some cheese and crackers? Any mini-quiches in the freezer?"

"There's spanakopita that Mom made. I could make some spaghetti."

Margaret makes a face. "Don't think that will fly. I'm sure Mom has something she can whip together. Go get her!"

"But she said not to disturb her, right?"

"I'm serious. Go!" whispers Margaret, already slamming mineral water and ice into a glass. "Don't leave me alone for long."

Lizzie takes the stairs two at a time, catching sight of herself in the full-length gilt mirror that stands at the top of the landing. She is red-faced and makeup-free—she didn't put on any after getting out of the pool—and strings dangle from where she chopped the bottom off her cutoffs.

The door to her mother's room is closed, and Lizzie stands outside it for a minute, pressing her ear to its surface. Is her mother still napping, with all this noise? All she can hear through the door is the air echoing through her own eardrum. Lizzie taps on the wood with a knuckle and presses her ear to the door again. Nothing. She knocks louder. Still nothing.

She screws up her courage and opens the door, just a hair so that she can peek in. It takes her a minute to adjust to the dark of the room and see her mother lying on her side on the bed, wrapped in a silk bathrobe, her back to the door.

"Mom?" Lizzie asks. "You awake?"

Janice doesn't move. Lizzie pushes the door all the way open and enters, then clicks the door gently closed behind her. The thick carpet muffles the sound of the party downstairs, so that only an occasional distant high-pitched squeal wafts up from the living room. Lizzie tiptoes over to the bed, lifts a pile of pillows out of the way, and sits down on the edge beside her mother. Janice's eyes are open. She stares vacantly at the silk curtains that are pulled closed against the evening sunset.

"Lizzie," she says, in a croak so shallow that Lizzie has to lean in to understand her. "Is someone here?"

"Yeah," Lizzie begins. "It's. Well."

"Is it James?" Janice pushes herself up on an elbow. "Has James come yet?"

Lizzie is taken aback. "James?"

"The pool boy," says Janice.

"No," says Lizzie. "But Mrs. Bint is here."

"Oh, no," says Janice, and rolls heavily onto her back. She presses a palm to her forehead and leaves it there, her eyes closed. "What is she doing here? Make her go away. Tell her I can't make it to her church meeting this week."

"She's here for a cocktail party," Lizzie says. "So are the Groupers. And I think some other people. Were you supposed to have a party?"

Janice sits up quickly and exhales a sharp breath. "Oh!" she whispers. "I totally forgot. How could I forget?"

"Do you want me to run you a bath or something?"

Janice presses her index fingers into the corners of her eyes, as if she's trying to pin them closed. There is a long silence. "No," she says. "I can't do it. Not right now."

"Can't do it?" Lizzie is alarmed; this is the first time she has ever heard her mother say that she can't do something.

"I can't go down there," says Janice, shaking her head. She lies back down and closes her eyes. "Stupid. Stupid stupid stupid. Your mother is an imbecile, Lizzie."

"No, you're not, Mom," Lizzie says, about to totally freak out. What is going on? "I forget stuff all the time. I forgot to take out the garbage just the other day, remember?"

But Janice is shaking her head back and forth against the pillow and, to Lizzie's alarm, her eyes are filling up with tears. "I can't face them," she says. "I'm a wreck."

And Lizzie has to agree that her mother does not, in fact, look her best. She has crescents of old mascara under her eyes, and her hair is dark with oil around her hairline. A tiny red sprinkling of rash has materialized under her nose, and the skin around her eye sockets looks bruised. The last time she saw her mother look this bad was when she got a nasty case of salmonella from a bad batch of oysters a few years back and almost died. She spent a week in bed with a 103-degree fever, unable to eat anything but Gatorade and Wonder bread, which Paul had to drive two towns over to find. Lizzie remembers the terror she felt then—the shock at how fragile her mother could be, taken down by just one bite of a spoiled mollusk. "All you need is a little fresh mascara," Lizzie says hopefully.

"Don't lie," says Janice. "I look ghastly." But she pushes herself upright again anyway, clutching her robe with one hand so that it doesn't gape open. Instead of stopping when she's vertical, though, she continues in a 180-degree arc until her forehead is touching her knees. She gulps at the air.

"Oh God," Janice says. "I think I might throw up." She lurches out of bed, stumbling over the hem of her robe as she bolts for the bathroom. In a few seconds, Lizzie hears the sound of her mother's heaving retches. By the time Lizzie makes it to the bathroom door, her mother is draped over the toilet, wiping her mouth with a pink square of tissue paper. Little brown flecks of bile spot the white tile.

Lizzie is flooded with understanding—it's just the flu. "Oh," she says. "Do you have the stomach flu or something?"

Janice smiles wanly. "Right," she says. "Something like that."

"Want me to call the doctor?"

"No!" Janice says. "There's no need."

"Okay," says Lizzie. "But what should I do about the guests?"

"Just tell them I have the flu. No, tell them it's terribly contagious. Tell them it's a bacterial virus."

"Okay," whispers Lizzie conspiratorially, pleased to be on the planning committee of a secret's formation. She is also faintly relieved that her mother won't be coming downstairs after all; Lizzie's not at all sure she could handle seeing her mother talk to the Groupers right now. "I'll tell them your doctor told you not to move out of bed."

"That's my baby," says Janice, and puts her hand out so that Lizzie can help her up from the tile. She is surprisingly light, and when her robe accidentally gapes open, Lizzie can see her mother's breasts. She averts her eyes from the blue-veined flesh, tucks Janice back into the bed, and moves a wastebasket within arm's reach—just in case Janice vomits again—before slipping back downstairs.

there is a crowd in the living room now; lizzie counts at least two dozen couples, including the Groupers, the Gossetts, Luella Anderton and Barbara Bint, the Maxfields, and Dr. Brunschild from around the corner. To her alarm, the Bellstroms (parents of Justin) and the Franks (parents of Johnny, 6/9 and 6/18) have also arrived. It's almost as if her mother invited only the parents of classmates Lizzie had sex with—what a terrifying thought! She looks around at the faces of her classmates' parents, faces she has seen at endless summer barbecues and holiday cookie-decorating parties and Labor Day pool parties and winter ice-skating weekends and more birthday galas than she can count, since she was old enough to walk—and reads nothing but burning condemnation in their gazes even as they smile and wave at her. How can they not know about her reputation? The *whole school* knows!

The room is warm despite the air-conditioning, and the volume keeps rising as the guests attempt to outtalk one another. A jazz CD plays on the stereo. She can hear the rich clink of jewelry against stemware. Margaret has raided their parents' wine cellar, and a half dozen dusty bottles of Château Lafite are sitting on the sideboard beside the crystal. A plate of olives is arranged next to the wine, along with a bowl of peanuts and a plate with pita bread cut into triangles and a tub of hummus. Lizzie admires her sister's industriousness: *She* would have just made spaghetti.

Margaret is backed up against a wall with Steven Bellstrom on one side and Barbara Bint on the other, her nose buried in a glass of wine. She has an expression on her face that reminds Lizzie of a stray dog that's been cornered by county animal services. Lizzie can hear only bits and pieces of their conversation from across the room—"academic pursuits" and "the age of affluence" and "potential in wireless networking."

Margaret catches her eye from across the room, and Lizzie shrugs. "Sick," she mouths at her sister. "The flu." Margaret narrows one eye and nods, without stopping her conversation.

Lizzie feels a hand on her arm and looks up to see the Franks, Linda and Jeffrey, standing right next to her. The Franks. She recoils, but there's nowhere to run. Linda Franks reaches over and pats her on the head. Lizzie thinks she might pee her pants.

"So *good* to see you, Lizzie," says Mrs. Franks. "I hear you've joined the swim team! Good for you. I'm sure your mom is very proud."

"Right," says Lizzie warily. "I got third place at the last meet. Sort of."

"Good for you!" continues Mrs. Franks. "You heard that Johnny won the all-league MVP for soccer this year, right?"

Lizzie remembers this fact vividly, since she let Johnny talk her into giving him a blow job in the Franks' guest bathroom one evening as a "celebratory gift," when the Franks were at the opera in San Francisco. She nods, unable to trust her voice.

"Well, *of course* you probably knew, didn't you. I actually heard—through the grapevine, since Johnny never tells me *anything* anymore, such a *boy* he is—that you have been spending some time with Johnny lately." She sips from her wineglass. "My neighbor saw you going into the house a few weeks ago—and Johnny *knows* he's not supposed to have friends over when we're out, but when I heard that it was you I forgave him. I know your mother has raised you as a proper little lady, but next time, only when we're home, okay?" She shakes a finger in mock admonishment. "You know, you kids are almost getting to the age where we need to worry about you. I keep forgetting you're not in junior high anymore."

"Oh, Linda," says Jeffrey Franks. He pokes his wife in the arm. "Leave Lizzie alone. I'm sure she doesn't want to talk about her social life with her friends' parents. I don't think the kids would think that's cool, would they, Lizzie?"

"Um," says Lizzie. "I'm not sure what the kids think."

Linda Franks keeps smiling while she shakes her head. Lizzie is struck by her resemblance to a polished hazelnut: brown skin stretched so high and tight over her cheekbones that it looks like it might crack if she smiled. Mrs. Franks tucks a strand of hair behind her ear. "Jeffrey, you have no idea," she says. "I'm sure that Lizzie doesn't mind talking about Johnny. I'm sure she's popular with *all* the boys these days."

"Popular!" says a voice right near Lizzie's ear. She looks over her shoulder in alarm and thinks her heart might thud straight out of her chest when she sees that it is Joannie Cientela, mother of Brian. Brian, 5/24. Brian, a pale boy, blond to the point of albino, has a crooked ballpoint-ink tattoo of a snake on his hip that he carefully re-inks every night before he goes to bed. He showed Lizzie this tattoo and swore her to secrecy before he got her stoned for the first time a few weeks before school got out. They had done it twice, once in his parents' bathroom, which Lizzie doesn't think counts because Brian ejaculated prematurely in the sink, and once in his bedroom, which had *Star Wars* sheets on the bed. He told her he thought she was really nice, and she thought that meant he wanted her to be his girlfriend, but then he never spoke to her again. *Slut.*

Joannie Cientela leans over and gives Linda Franks an air kiss, then grips Lizzie's upper arm with a tight fist. "It sounds like Lizzie is just fighting them off," she says. "Aren't you, Lizzie."

Lizzie stands stock-still, petrified, as Mrs. Cientela's wedding ring digs into her shoulder blade. "Um, fighting? Not really," she mumbles.

But Joannie Cientela isn't listening. "Just look at her!" She pushes Lizzie a few inches forward. "Cute as a button. You finally grew into your own, sweetie, and you're such a darling thing, it's no wonder all the boys have crushes on you. Your mother must be so proud. Where is your mother, sweetie? So good of her to have the party—keeping up her spirits despite everything. It's *nice* to see. Anyway, let's not talk about that. How is school? I hear you're doing well?" She turns to the Franks. "Brian told me Lizzie was tutoring him after school a few weeks ago—his Spanish is terrible, and this one here"—she jiggles Lizzie's shoulder—"has apparently been helping him out after school. Lizzie, you know you left a barrette in the bathroom? I should have thought to bring it."

Linda Franks turns to Lizzie. "You tutor! Your mother never told me. Johnny needs Spanish help too."

Lizzie's vocal cords have frozen, so she nods instead. In fact, she is getting a C in Spanish, but she decides this probably shouldn't be mentioned. She sees Justin Bellstrom's mother, Cecile, walking their way. Oh God. She hates herself! These parents, they are all so nice and trusting and they have no idea that they are talking to the *school slut.* What if her mother found out? Would she throw Lizzie out of the house? How could Lizzie have been *so stupid*? She thought they *liked* her when all they liked was her . . . Lizzie thinks of a vile word and then erases it from her mind. She tenses up into a hard little knot of muscle and thinks that if she lets her muscles relax she might just melt into a puddle, like the Wicked Witch of the West. Her nether regions tingle from the need to pee.

The doorbell rings again and Lizzie sees her opportunity to escape. "Gottagetdoor," she mumbles, slipping out from under Mrs. Cientela's grasp.

As she pushes her way through the living room, Noreen Gossett appears in Lizzie's path. Her patrician nostrils flare like a rearing horse's and she purses her peach-lacquered lips with displeasure. "Where is your sister," Mrs. Gossett says, articulating every syllable. Is. Yer. Sis. Ter. "Your sister, Margaret. I need to speak with her. I am *very* upset." Lizzie shakes her head. Noreen Gossett cranes her neck to survey the room and spies Margaret by the sideboard, guzzling a glass of wine with her eyes rolled back in her head while Mr. Bellstrom, on her left side, pontificates at the empty air. Margaret lowers her glass and makes eye contact just as Noreen Gossett locks in on her target.

"Excuse me," says Mrs. Gossett, sweeping past Lizzie. Margaret drains the wine in one gulp, drops her glass on the sideboard, and makes a beeline for the kitchen, Noreen Gossett in pursuit.

The doorbell rings again—*BA bum BA bum ba bum be ba bum*—and Lizzie flees to the foyer. She squeezes her eyes shut as she pulls on the handle to the front door, not sure who else might arrive on the doorstep but convinced that there must be still more punishment waiting for her. The Liverbachs, maybe? When it swings open, she sees James, the pool boy, standing on the front step. He is not dressed in party attire, at least not unless he considers party attire to be a wife-beater tank top paired with shorts held up by a belt of brown yarn.

James hooks a thumb over his shoulder and gestures at the cars. "Are you having a party or something?" he asks.

"What are you doing here?" she says. "I thought you already came today?"

"Special delivery for your mom. Where is she?"

"She's upstairs," says Lizzie. "But she's sick. She isn't seeing anybody."

"Oh, don't worry. She definitely wants to see me." He steps through the doorway and heads straight up the stairs, taking the steps two at a time. Lizzie follows him to the bottom of the staircase and watches him vanish in the upstairs hallway. His presence baffles her. Maybe her mother forgot to pay him?

She lingers for a minute with her hand on the balustrade, listening to the din in the living room and wondering if anyone would notice if she just slipped out the front door and left. Would Margaret be mad? Maybe Lizzie could go back down to the Fountain and get a hamburger and fries and by the time she returned everyone would be gone. She turns around, preparing to bolt, and runs smack into Barbara Bint, who has materialized behind her in the foyer.

Barbara plants her pump on the first stair. "I just thought I'd chat with your mother while she gets ready. See how she's doing. Catch up."

"Catch up about what?" says Lizzie, thinking of her mother wrapped around the toilet, and stalling.

"There are *lots* of things to talk about," she says. There is a slithery quality to this statement, something decidedly ominous—and pointed? From her elevated position on the step, Barbara gazes down her nose at Lizzie, her face cast in shadows by the overhead chandelier. Lizzie panics.

"You shouldn't go up there," she says. She lurches forward and, as Barbara climbs up the stairs, grabs Barbara's fuchsia dress by the hem. In the process, she accidentally gets a glimpse of control-top panty hose stretched tight over Barbara Bint's thighs. "She's really sick."

"Sick?" says Mrs. Bint. She reaches down and gently unpeels Lizzie's hand from its grip on her dress, then smooths the skirt back over her thighs. "How awful. Why didn't she cancel the party? If I'd known I would have brought a pot of soup. I'll go see what she needs."

"No, that's a really bad idea. She has bac . . . bad . . ." She can't remember the phrase, though, and struggles to retrieve another medical-sounding illness. "Melanoma. It's really contagious."

"Melanoma?" Mrs. Bint says. "She has skin cancer?"

"Um, I mean. Food poisoning?"

Mrs. Bint looks at her suspiciously. "Are you being honest, young lady?" Lizzie tries to smile but fails and can feel her face flush pink. "You know, Jesus pities a liar. That's the Ninth Commandment! 'Thou shalt not bear false witness.' "

Lizzie feels the weight of yet another screwup piling up on her and slumps under the added burden. "Is it?"

"Lizzie! Everyone should know the commandments."

A figure appears at the top of the stairs, and both Lizzie and Barbara look up. It is James, who hurtles down and past them. He pauses at the front door, winks, and vanishes, slamming the door closed behind him. Barbara watches him go with a cocked head.

"Who is that?" she asks.

"James," says Lizzie, relieved that her failings are no longer the topic of conversation. "The pool boy."

"Oh," says Barbara, sounding puzzled. But then her hand jets forward to clutch Lizzie's forearm. "To finish what I was saying. . . . Maybe—and I'm just saying this because I feel a lot of compassion for you—maybe you should consider going to church more often, Elizabeth. I have heard things from my son Zeke, things that he's heard about your behavior—very disturbing things that I don't plan on repeating right now, but I think you know what I'm talking about. And I know you haven't had a whole lot of good role models lately, what with your father's behavior. And I know your mother is having a terrible time of it—the poor thing—but that doesn't give you license to do . . . the things you're doing. Your body is a sacred temple, Lizzie. It belongs to Jesus Christ! Didn't you know that?"

Lizzie is definitely going to pee her pants. She squeezes her legs together until they burn. Barbara stares at her, and Lizzie realizes that she is waiting for an answer. She can't remember the question. "Yes?" she says tentatively.

"Well, then you should know better than to desecrate that temple, Lizzie! Lizzie, listen to me." She leans in closer, using Lizzie's forearm as leverage. She whispers, "Jesus forgives all sinners. His love is boundless, and if you come to Him and pledge your devotion He will show you the path to eternal grace. He will bless you with happiness."

"He will?" Lizzie whispers back. She senses that she is being told a profound secret and lets herself be pulled in close. Barbara Bint is warm, practically steaming, and in the hot nimbus of this holy righteousness Lizzie is helpless. She feels herself being sucked into a dizzying vortex.

"Yes, Lizzie. And you should experience the joy of taking the Lord into your heart and being cleansed of sin. God loves you, Lizzie! Loves you! You should come with us to River of Life Church. Thursday nights are introductory nights for new members. We can give you a ride—it's en route anyway. I'll pick you up next Thursday at seven and Zeke can introduce you around."

The vortex pulls her in and tosses her gently about. Jesus loves her. Really? She isn't quite sure what this means, but it compels her. There seems to be no alternative but to go to church and see for herself. Lizzie closes her eyes and succumbs. She unclenches every muscle in her body and is relieved to realize that she isn't actually going to pee on herself after all.

"Okay," she says, still in a whisper.

Barbara steps back. "I'll be praying for you," she says. She looks up past Lizzie's head, and her face, already glowing from the effort of her religious prostrations, brightens further. Lizzie turns to see Janice standing at the top of the stairs, her face freshly washed and her hair yanked back into a bun. She has traded in the bathrobe for a simple black dress. She has even put on panty hose. She looks pale, but she exudes a nervous buzz, as if every little pore on her body is pulsing with pent-up energy.

Janice bounds down the stairs, her manicured nails reinforcing each step with a tap on the balustrade, and stops to air-kiss Barbara at the bottom step. "I am so *sorry* to be so late to my own party," Janice says to Barbara. "I hope my daughters entertained everyone while I got dressed."

"Lizzie said you were very sick."

"Sick?" Janice looks amused at the very idea. Lizzie is confused. How could she have recovered so fast? Wasn't she just puking a few minutes ago? "No. Nothing serious. Just a little upset stomach. I hope you weren't too concerned."

"Well, I figured it couldn't be all that bad, because you had a visitor up there—who was that young man?" Barbara's face twitches, as if she's battling her own curiosity and losing. "What a strange-looking boy. He could use a real belt, couldn't he."

Janice doesn't blink. "Just the pool boy, Barbara. I owed him his salary."

"Well, don't you worry yourself about being late," says Barbara. "I've just been catching up with Lizzie. We've had a good chat, haven't we Lizzie?" She winks at Lizzie. Lizzie blanches.

"Good good good!" cheers Janice. She steers Barbara back toward the living room. Lizzie follows behind, unsure if the vast sense of relief she feels has to do with her mother's rapid recovery or with the bargain she senses she has just made with

Barbara Bint. Janice comes to a halt just before the door to the living room, reaches up and smooths an invisible strand of misplaced hair, then wades right into the party as if she was never missing in the first place.

Heads turns. Hands are thrown up in mock-surprise pleasure. Faces register their delight. Her mother is swallowed up in the melee. Lizzie watches Janice, in the middle of the room, the Groupers on one side and Luella Anderton on the other; she talks animatedly, refilling drained wineglasses with one hand, grasping welcoming handshakes and peppering the air with kisses. Lizzie is struck by her mother's efficiency, not for the first time. Only her mother could be a vomiting wreck one minute and a gracious hostess the next. Watching Janice, Lizzie believes in her heart that she will never be that capable. She has already messed up everything in her own life in a way that feels so ghastly and permanent that she knows she will never be anything like that pretty, perfect woman in the center of the room. Even if Jesus does forgive her.

Lizzie backs out of the living room very slowly, so that no one will notice her retreat. She goes upstairs to her room and lies down on her bed. She stares at the ceiling without blinking until her eyeballs burn with pain, and then she closes them and slips off into oblivion, lulled to sleep by the rising and falling of the tides of conversation downstairs.

james doesn't return until his regular tues-
day, a full four days after the cocktail party. He hasn't responded to the six messages Janice left on his cell phone,
begging him to come sooner. When Janice hears his truck rattle to a stop in the driveway, in the early afternoon, she springs
from the bed, where she has been lying all morning in a black
funk—hair greasy, calves stubbly, face unwashed—and bolts for
the door on legs that wobble like a newborn calf's.

She trips down the stairs at double speed, trying to ignore
what her eagerness suggests. Even after two-and-a-half weeks
of using the white powder in the little plastic baggie, she still
reasons that her behavior is no different from that of any person taking a prescription drug. After all, a few years back she
had voted to legalize marijuana as medication for the termi-
nally ill—after reading the scientific research, of course, and
deciding it was cruel to deny pain relief to suffering cancer pa-
tients—and really, what is so different about It? Just like pot or

Vicodin or Valium, It is a simple chemical that serves a utilitarian purpose: to help her feel better in a difficult time. A time that will, she tells herself, eventually pass, at which point she will no longer need pharmaceutical aid.

And there are *so many* beneficial side effects to It. There's the weight loss, of course (James was right about that), but also the productivity! She has filled the refrigerator with casseroles, put up twenty jars of fresh lemon curd, and distilled five batches of veal stock for the freezer. She's hand-embroidered a set of kitchen towels and designed a cunning series of origami boxes to hold her paper clips and rubber bands. She can clean for hours and only much later feel the satisfying ache in her fingers from scrubbing away the ancient black stain at the bottom of her roasting pan, the cramp in her shoulders from reaching up to wax the curtain rods in the living room. With It in her veins, no task feels too menial, as if by scrubbing a little bit harder, stirring the pot that much faster, she will be granted a glimpse of nirvana.

Sleep is no longer a necessity for her, but a concept from which she's grown increasingly distant. In the blank hours of the early morning, when it's so quiet that she can almost hear the snails crawling through the dew-dampened lawn, she feels reborn, as if anything is possible. Cleaning out the attic, she recently came across her old French textbooks, and sometimes she reads them when her daughters are asleep. It's surprising how quickly it all comes back. *La fille regarde par la fenêtre. Le jardin est ensoleillé.* Practicing her *verbes transitifs et intransitifs* as the sun rises, she senses an expansion inside herself, a potential she has neglected for all these decades. In these moments, she doesn't miss Paul at all.

And yet. Her reasoning that this is a temporary and ultimately benign experiment is sometimes difficult to sustain. For starters, the indignity of how she must consume It makes her cringe: It would be one thing if it came in a pill form, but it seems so tacky to inhale powder up one's nose using a twenty-dollar bill, no matter how many times one's laundered and ironed it. She avoids looking at herself in the mirror while she does it, afraid to see herself cramped over the plate, a hunchback hoovering up miracle dust. And God only knows what germs she's sucking into her nasal passages.

By this point, too, she has done her reading on the Internet. Just before dawn after one totally sleepless night, as Lizzie and Margaret slept upstairs, Janice crept into the study and typed the words "crystal" and "drug" into a search engine. The top result was the home page of the U.S. Department of Justice. Yes, she had sensed all along that no matter what this crystalline miracle powder was, it surely couldn't be legal, but as she sat there in the dark she cursed herself for looking it up, because now she couldn't pretend not to know. Methamphetamine, the DOJ called it. Scientific name: N, alpha-dimethylbenzeneethanamine. Schedule II drug. Possession punishable by one year in prison.

She read on: "Also known as meth, poor man's cocaine, jib, crank, ice, glass, tina, speed, zip." She articulated these words out loud: "Jib. Meth. Crank." The colloquialisms were blunt and unpleasant on her tongue; in her mind, crystal had always been simply It, a generic sort of term with no unattractive subtext at all. She read on: "Extremely addictive. Long-term effects include psychotic behavior, paranoia, and permanent brain damage." She winced. "Overt signs of problem use include insomnia, repetitive behavior, anxiety, lack of control, and a chronic inability to focus."

Her left hand, she noticed, was rapping out an agitated rendition of the William Tell Overture, her fingernails articulating the chorus with gusto. She willed her fingers to still themselves, and her palm flattened against the surface of the desk. She felt a twinge of satisfaction. Clearly, she could still control her body. And focus? Surely, the fact that she had made coq au vin yesterday—a five-hour ordeal from braise to garnish, using Julia Child's original recipe!—proved that she had focus to spare. Satisfied, she poked the computer monitor's "Off" button and listened to the screen whine down to an electronic sleep. She reassured herself that she had been using the drug for only a few weeks—which hardly seemed enough time to get hooked on the stuff. How ridiculous to think that she could become a drug addict overnight!

But there *is* an ugliness that she can sense growing deep inside her, a sort of ulcerous beast with gnashing teeth and bleeding gums. There are moments when she simply *craves* It, in an even more all-consuming way than she craved fried chicken when she was pregnant with Lizzie. (She would wake in the middle of the night and make Paul drive her to a filthy fast-food chicken joint, where she would eat and eat and never get her fill.) Sometimes, she can feel the need devouring her, as if that insatiable gremlin inside her has taken over her body with its drooling lust for more more more.

And then there are days like today, when the high from It has worn off entirely, and she is left waiting for James to replenish her stash. The descent from Its heights is precipitous: She plummets very low, as if she has been chained inside a pitch-black safe and thrown to the bottom of a cold river. Before, her sober thoughts of Paul and Beverly were red and furious; now they are dark and hopeless. And even though she has never been the type to consider suicide, when she slips into that bleak and empty place she finds herself considering what a relief it would be to fall asleep and never wake. Only another dose of It can lift her out again.

And she has been without It, now, for two days. Two days in which she has not cleaned, has not cooked, has not done an errand or studied her French or even gotten dressed. Days in which she has done nothing but sit in her room in her bathrobe, exhausted, watching television. Her brain is as lumpy and formless as a bowl of oatmeal. She cannot even muster the energy to cry. If she concentrates, she thinks she can feel her muscles atrophy as she lies there, moving only her index finger to change the channels. Her daughters tiptoe through the house, going about their lives without her. Margaret (who still hasn't mentioned when she plans to return to L.A.) has taken to answering the phone when it rings, which is fine, because Janice has no interest in talking to anyone at all. There are never any messages. It is devastating, if a vague relief, to discover that the world does not seem to need her anymore.

So when James returns, on Tuesday afternoon, Janice thrills to the sound of his truck on the gravel. As she runs down the stairs, she thinks of those old television advertisements for Alka-Seltzer: "Get Speedy Alka-Seltzer, for fast relief, you bet!" Her nose burns in anticipation. Alka-Seltzer to the rescue.

But by the time she gets downstairs, James is already packing up his truck, heaving the chemicals into the bed as fast as he can. When he sees her standing at the garden gate, watching him, he freezes.

"Are you in a hurry?" asks Janice. She folds her arms in front of her, then unfolds them and clasps them behind her to hide the anticipatory twitching of her fingers.

"Not much to do today," he says. He heaves the last bottle of chlorine into the pickup and slams the tailgate shut.

"Did you get my messages?"

"Sure," he says.

"And?" She hopes to sound casual, but she can hear that her voice is as thin and piercing as the needles in her sewing kit.

"I didn't bring any," he says. He pauses. "I don't have any."

"I don't understand."

James shrugs. "Sorry."

"I mean it, James. I need you to get me some more," she says insistently. "You keep giving me such small amounts, I used up the last one in two days. So this time, I'd like three times as much, if you please."

"I don't know if that's such a great idea. That stuff isn't so good for you."

"You said it wasn't any different from Vicodin," she points out.

"Well, Vicodin isn't exactly a walk in the park either."

"I think that's beside the point, James. I mean, really. I hardly need you to tell me what I should and shouldn't do. I'm not sure that's your place anyway."

James leans against the back of his truck, sticks a finger in his mouth, and proceeds to tear at a hangnail contemplatively. Janice finds this a disgusting habit (and what of the pool chemicals on his hands?), but she says nothing. "I don't feel good doing this," he says. "You're way too into it. I probably shouldn't have even gotten it for you in the first place."

"Nonsense," she says, as alarm bells go off in her head. Where else will she get it if not from him? Ask Margaret or Lizzie? God, no. Could there be more than one drug dealer in Santa Rita? It seems unfathomable. Buying it here, inside the gates of her home, feels safe, but if she had to journey into the streets. . . . Where would she go? And what if she were caught? . . . A Schedule II drug! A year in jail! She can't, can't let James cut her off. "I'm doing much better *because* of it."

"Not at the rate you're going through this stuff," he says. "You should stop."

"And *you* should stop selling it," she says. "You're hardly in a position to judge. Anyway, it's none of your business. Just get me some more. Can you get it for me by the end of the day?"

"No," says James.

"Yes," she insists. "Yes!" She feels all self-control fleeing as her oncoming need roars in. She will repeat "Yes" until it just happens, until he concedes that she is right. He is just the pool boy, after all. He has to give in eventually. "You must."

"Sorry," he says.

"If you don't . . . I'll, I'll . . ." She reaches for something, anything. "I'll have to fire you," she says, heated by her indignant fury. "And I'll tell everyone you stole from me. I could even report you to the police as a drug dealer!"

"Jesus," says James. He rubs the back of his neck with damp fingers. "Jesus, Janice. Mrs. Miller. Janice. Why would you do that?"

"I'm sorry." Her courage vanishes, almost immediately. She feels compelled to grab his hand and just beg. My God, she *is* acting like a drug addict, she thinks. "I'm just a little worked up."

He looks down at her, a good three inches shorter than him, as she stands there in the driveway. And she sees pity in his eyes, an intent, moist gaze. Somehow, this is the worst thing. It makes her want to turn her head away so that he can't see her face. He sighs. "I guess it's been a pretty rough month for you, hasn't it."

"Yes," she says weakly, staring away at the house, wondering how he knows the details of her personal life. She has never felt so humiliated. She has never begged or threatened anyone in her life, let alone a boy her own daughter's age. She wants to cry for the self she has lost, for the rational Janice, the Janice who had it all together, the Janice she thought she was preserving by doing It in the first place. "Just do it, please?"

"Oh, fine," he says. He opens the door of his truck and unlatches the glove box. Janice gets a glimpse of a stack of baggies, rubber-banded together, before he palms a folded plastic bag into her hand. "It's your life. Not mine."

Relief pours through her. She cups the little plastic baggie in her hand and is amazed that she can find such immediate comfort in something so light and insubstantial. She can almost taste the chemical drip in the back of her throat. The gritty crunch of the crystals rubbing against one another in her palm, the slip of the plastic warming against her flesh erase the mortification of having just prostrated herself before a twenty-six-year-old boy for drugs. Of having behaved like a depraved zombie. No, now that she has It in hand, she revises that scenario and reframes it: She was merely an employer asking her employee to provide the goods and services he had previously promised her. (Their legality is irrelevant.) She is forty-nine and a mother of two, the wife of an almost-billionaire-on-paper, a respected member of her community; and who is he? A pot-smoking kid, a slacker, a drug dealer. This baggie is simply her due. Shame on him for making her feel anything but that. He certainly doesn't have the moral upper hand.

"That's right," she says, tucking the bag into her pocket. "It's not your life at all."

lewis grosser, esquire, is a porcine man, shorter than even Lizzie, with shiny pink skin that stretches across well-fed cheeks. Janice has always thought of short, fat men as jolly by nature, having compensated in some way for their diminutive stature by cultivating excessively genial demeanors. But Lewis Grosser is all business, no pleasantries, as befits a divorce lawyer.

"Let's get straight to the point, Mrs. Miller," he says, as he sits down on her living room couch. The couch emits an audible cotton fart as his ample rear end makes contact. "We're in a tough situation. You signed a postnuptial agreement, more formally known as a transmutation agreement, which transfers community property in a marriage into separate property. There is a signature, your signature, on a document that cedes all your rights to any Applied Pharmaceuticals assets. To wit, the document you signed a year ago." He reaches for his suitcase and whips out a thick sheaf of papers. "Blah blah blah. . . . Here we are. Page 243. Janice Miller hereby and herein agrees to fully relinquish her marital rights to any assets accrued by Paul Miller via any public offering of Applied Pharmaceutical stock, as listed in Exhibit C."

Janice twists her hands in her lap. The clock on the living room wall ticks away the seconds—three minutes past noon. She has not slept since James's visit: *It* kept her buzzing all night long, all day long. Last night, she made an attempt to go to bed, around two in the morning, but could only lie stiffly on her back, staring at the molding on the ceiling, until she got up and began working on a set of hand-painted flowerpots instead. She spent the predawn hours watching cooking-show reruns on the Food Network, intently studying how the Barefoot Contessa braised a chicken as the light outside turned gray and then yellow and then white, until at last she rose from the couch, showered before the girls woke up, and made waffles for breakfast.

Today, she feels like a simulacrum of herself, a Janice doll, shiny and varnished on the outside, hollow on the inside. She had promised herself she wouldn't take any It before the meeting; it somehow didn't seem right to meet with a lawyer in that condition. But at the last minute, she changed her mind and decided that she could use the extra jolt, the clarity. She took just a *tiny* bump. She hopes that the lawyer won't wonder why her left leg is jittering so uncontrollably.

Margaret sits besides Janice on the couch, in her new capacity as her mother's legal assistant. On her lap she's placed a folder of clippings and a notepad. Janice is soothed by Margaret's presence. This is an unfamiliar sensation, quite the opposite of the pins and needles she typically feels when Margaret is around. Since the day in the vegetable garden, some tension between them has been relieved, although Janice worries that this is only because she essentially gave her daughter the upper hand by requesting her assistance. Still, Janice feels the pressure of Margaret's weight on the couch beside her and lets the depression from their rears on the sofa slide them slightly toward each other. She smiles to herself.

"Well, I didn't know," she says to Grosser. "That wasn't at all what I was led to believe the documents contained." Her left foot jitterbugs across the carpet and back, describing a four-inch circle.

"Did you *read* the documents?" says Grosser. He cocks his head at her. She can hear his breath wheezing in his nostrils, a soft liquid sound. He shifts his behind and settles even more deeply into the couch. "Because unfortunately it's very clear if you read it. To a lawyer, at least."

"It was just a few sentences on page 243. Page 243, in a 411-page document!" she says. Is he implying that she's stupid? She grows even more indignant: "Even if I did read through the whole thing I would have needed a magnifying glass to catch that. It was *obviously* a trick!" She points at the paper with a finger that, she notices with dismay, is vibrating. She reels the finger back into her lap and grips her hands together.

"Of course, of course. I'm not disagreeing. I'm being the devil's advocate here, just pointing out what the other side is going to argue. Though I am going to give you some advice for the future, not useful now of course, but. . . . Always, I repeat, *always* read every word of every legal document put in front of you," says Grosser. He folds his arms across his chest and shakes his head gravely.

Janice stretches her mind back to the day she signed the papers, over a year ago. She was racing to San Francisco for a luncheon, and Paul had asked her to stop in at his office en route to sign a few papers regarding their investment in Applied Pharmaceuticals. There was an accident on the 101—a

Hummer had driven clean over a Miata, setting the coupe on fire and shutting the whole freeway down—and she sat, idling, in dead-stopped traffic for nearly an hour, late to both her appointments.

When she arrived, Paul shoved a three-inch stack of paper toward her and flipped to the pages she needed to sign, one after another, at least three dozen in all. "Just legal arcana," he said. "Limits our personal liability should Applied Pharmaceuticals ever be sued, stuff about stock options and executive compensation. Just sign here . . . and here." She remembers that Paul's lawyer, Milt, sat in the corner of the office that afternoon, flipping through a magazine, nattering on about his recent golf trip—to Palm Springs? Or Taos? And that was it. Over in two minutes. Just like that.

Now, in hindsight, she can see the deliberate deception in Paul's actions that day. The liar! It strikes her, suddenly, that he must have been planning that moment in his office for months—perhaps even for years. Was he already sleeping with Beverly at that point? Was Milt in on it too? Did *everyone* but her know that Paul was betraying his wife so completely? The implications of this are dizzying. She gazes down at the document, at her signature in that goddamn green ink, and feels sick to her stomach. How long had their marriage been over, in Paul's mind, before he had come up with his ruse for cutting her out of his fortune? He had taken her to a weekend spa in Colorado not long before she signed the papers. They had even (she feels faint) had sex in their room's vast Jacuzzi overlooking the Rocky Mountains, complete with candles and jazz music. Was that supposed to be his last hurrah? Some kind of consolation prize for her? She glimpses herself as he must have seen her: a pathetic chump.

She can't remember the expression on Paul's face as she signed the papers. If she had looked at him, really taken a moment to pay attention, would she have noticed any guilt flickering across his face? Would she have suspected that Milt's babbling was intended to distract her from the content of the document? If she had known she was signing away her future, would she have noticed the little details that revealed that, in Paul's mind, their marriage was already over?

Her leg bounces faster, venting her anger. "I had to sit in traffic," says Janice. "There was an accident on the 101—I was late. I was agitated. I didn't know it was anything important."

"I take it you didn't hire your own counsel to review it?"

"Why would I have hired my own lawyer? He was my husband. Marriage is a partnership built on trust." Janice hears herself protesting and realizes how shallow this must sound to Grosser. It sounds shallow even to her, considering the position she is now in. Trust—apparently that had gone out the window years ago. Too bad she hadn't noticed its departure. She adds, as explanation: "He'd just taken me on a romantic vacation."

"What does that have to do with anything?" Grosser leans back. "I am continually amazed how many marriages end with one party devastated because their spouse looked out for themselves first while they didn't. It's human nature, Mrs. Miller. Everyone's watching out for number one. Then they let the lawyers sort out the rest."

"Well, *I* don't like to subscribe to such a pessimistic worldview," she says. "Look—I'm not an idiot. He said it was an asset protection plan. My God, he even put that on the cover of the document. I had no reason not to believe him."

"I know, I know. Well, unfortunately for us, it's not the cover of the book but the contents that count," says Grosser. He shakes his head again. He picks up the document and flips through it.

Janice feels something on her leg and looks down to see that Margaret has put her hand on Janice's knee. Margaret leans in and whispers in Janice's ear: "Your leg's shaking,

Mom. Don't worry. You'll be fine. Just take a deep breath and relax." Margaret leans forward, clears her throat. "Mr. Grosser, are you planning on referring to *Havell*?" she asks.

"*Havell*?"

"*Havell v. Islam.* You know—if someone's behavior 'shocks the conscience' then they shouldn't have a right to any property in a divorce? In my opinion, it's fairly shocking to the conscience to coerce your wife into signing all her assets away." Margaret smiles triumphantly, and Janice is taken aback. When did Margaret learn so much about the law? Could her daughter have a secret propensity for a legal career? She sees, suddenly, an alternate life for Margaret. Stanford Law School, a legal practice in something Margaret-like and liberal, like environmental law. It's not too late. Janice nods in encouraging agreement, despite having no idea what her daughter is talking about.

Grosser regards Margaret with bleary eyes and sighs. "Right. You've done your homework. But it's not at all relevant in this case: 'Shocking' behavior means beating your wife with a barbell, not coaxing her to sign documents. Look, young lady, why don't you let me do my job. I've got quite a bit of experience in this matter—more than you're going to get from reading a few back issues of *Legal Affairs*." Janice can feel Margaret stiffening beside her.

Grosser begins stuffing papers back in his briefcase and closes the clasp with a decisive snap. "Well. We're going to have to get creative here, Mrs. Miller, but we have options. I can argue undue influence. Or go with forensic evidence, proving you were incapable of sound decision. Maybe a handwriting expert who can show that this document was signed under duress."

"Really? Handwriting will show that?" asks Janice.

"The wonder of our legal system is that you can prove almost anything, no matter how insane it seems. Pay an expert enough, he'll say anything you want him to." He pauses.

"There's one more matter I need to discuss with you, Mrs. Miller." He looks at Margaret and raises his eyebrows. "In private."

Margaret remains seated, clutching her notebook, until Janice turns and gestures for her to leave. Janice is disappointed to see her go. Grosser waits until the sound of Margaret's footsteps fades before continuing in a low voice.

"This is a sensitive subject, Janice. I received a call from your husband's counsel at SAB&R this morning. They told me that they have testimony from a reliable source that you have been having . . . relations . . . with one James Court. A pool cleaner."

Janice freezes, her toe halting mid-tap. "Relations?"

Grosser pinches his lips together. "Of the sexual variety, Janice. Now, I'm not passing judgment. But are you aware that this young man is a known felon? Because SAB&R's lawyers have apparently done their homework and they let me know that Mr. Court was arrested last year for possession of drugs with intent to sell. He had two ounces of marijuana and twenty pills of MDMA, better known as Ecstasy."

"I was not aware," says Janice, struggling to keep her voice calm, moderated, professional, rather than guilt-ridden or hysterical. This is not easy.

"Far be it from me to get involved in my clients' love lives—"

"I'm not having an affair with him," Janice insists. "He's just my employee. He's the pool boy."

"As you say. But your husband's lawyers say they have testimony that you have been associating with this young man. And they plan to use it as leverage to get you to drop your lawsuit."

"How do they plan to do that?"

"Well, for one, they could argue that fraternizing with a known drug dealer invalidates your claim for child custody."

The knee has now taken up a high-speed jig. "Lizzie?!"

Janice blurts, horrified. "But he can't do that, can he? Paul's having an affair, too. I mean, no. Let me rephrase that: I'm *not* having an affair. And he *is*. Definitely. He doesn't even want custody. It doesn't make sense!"

Grosser shrugs. "I'm not saying it's fair. They may not even have real evidence. Keep in mind that custody of your daughter is most likely not their goal. All they are trying to do is intimidate you into dropping your demands for your husband's IPO money. It's a scare tactic. But it could get dragged into court. I would suggest that you cut off all contact with this young man, immediately."

Janice's jaw tightens. Cut off her supply of It? Now? When she needs it most? She couldn't possibly. How much does she have? Four days' supply? A week's? The sparkling enriched blood courses through her veins, and in the rapid beat of her heart she hears Its seductive coo: *Yes. Yes. Yes. YES YES YES YES.* The jig picks up its pace until she thinks her leg might just detach itself from her body and dance right on out the door.

"I will not let my husband dictate whom I see or don't see," she tells her lawyer through gritted teeth. "He has no right. No right at all."

"As you say," Grosser says. "I'm just offering my counsel on this matter." He pushes himself up from the couch, tottering slightly to regain his balance. The cushions exhale a relieved sigh.

Janice rises with him, pausing to whack the pillows back into shape before escorting Grosser to the door. "Thank you for coming," she says. "I'll be in touch."

janice seethes, the subcutaneous fury and humiliation bubbling up to a dangerously high boil. She seethes as she strips all the beds in the house and hauls the sweat-fragrant sheets downstairs to the laundry room. She seethes as she opens the windows and lets the summer air freshen up the living room. She seethes as she prepares a lemon-rosemary roast chicken and toasts pine nuts for a salad. And she seethes as she taps out two more lines, just before dinner, and sniffs them back with a sharp inhalation. The baggie is already upsettingly light.

The family—*sans* paterfamilias—sits down for dinner at six.

"Oooh, chicken," says Lizzie. She sits down at the table and flaps open her napkin with a flourish. "Looks really good, Mom." Janice smiles faintly, finding herself irked by the false brightness in her daughter's voice. It reminds her of the way kindergarten teachers encouragingly address the shy and stupid children in the back of the classroom.

Margaret works her away around her plate methodically. A bite of chicken, a bite of basmati rice, a bite of spinach salad. She has always eaten as if it is a task to be completed, with none of her sister's gorge-as-if-there's-no-tomorrow enthusiasm. She might as well be consuming cardboard with glue sauce.

Janice looks at her own plate, at the withered lemon slices plastered to the china and the shreds of white meat she has pushed around with her fork. She has had no appetite for weeks. It satisfies her to drain herself, as if by siphoning away her hunger, her flesh, she might also cast off all earthly needs. Famished, she feels as light and heavenly as a saint, just a pound or two away from floating off to somewhere far more interesting than where she is right now.

While Margaret and Lizzie eat their chicken, Janice sits at the head of the table and lets her speeding mind tussle with the question that has bothered her since Grosser's visit. Who could have told Paul that she was having an affair with James, and what on earth did she do to give them that impression? Is someone intentionally lying? And even though they clearly can't prove that she is having an affair with him, could they find out about It? And would that be enough to take Lizzie away?

It is Margaret who breaks the silence. "So, Lewis Grosser wasn't so bad, was he?" She smiles at her mother, confident in their newly minted camaraderie. "I mean, considering he's a divorce lawyer. I can't imagine why anyone would *choose* to do that for a living."

Janice smiles thinly, only half conscious of what her daughter is saying. It's almost unbearable to keep sitting motionless at the table. For just a moment, she almost hates her daughters, as if they've pinned her to this chair like a butterfly in a specimen cage. "Yes, yes, I'm sure he'll be fine," she says, peeling the skin from the flesh of a chicken thigh and carefully shredding it into strips. "He better be, for what he charges."

"You've just got to stay optimistic, Mom. We'll win."

Janice, with a knot in her stomach, takes a small bite of her chicken and quells the impulse to spit the greasy meat right back out onto the plate. Margaret's use of the word "we" should be comforting, but it is not. She thinks of the horrifying information that Grosser conveyed, and feels terribly terribly alone. She looks up to see Lizzie staring at her with her Bambi eyes and forces a reassuring smile. "I *am* optimistic," she says, already feeling guilty about her thoughts of just a moment before. *Remember,* she thinks, *your daughters are all you have. You love them.* It disturbs her that she even has to remind herself of this. What is *wrong* with her?

Mercifully, a car honks from the driveway, releasing her from the strain of conversation. Lizzie jumps up from her chair. "I gotta go," she mumbles. Only now does Janice notice that Lizzie is wearing a skirt, one that actually reaches as far south as her knees, and shoes that don't involve platforms, glitter, or cork.

"Where are you going?"

"Um," Lizzie says, "church?"

"Church?" Janice is not quite sure she's heard this correctly.

"Yeah."

"What kind of church?"

"I dunno," says Lizzie. "River of Life Church. Evangelical, I think?"

"Evangelical?" Margaret says. "You know, Lizzie, you might want to keep in mind that there's some pretty backward thinking in that movement, especially when it comes to women's roles in the family. Woman as subordinate to man and all that. We did a story about it in 'The God Issue.' Didn't you read it?"

"Oh," says Lizzie, pausing to consider this information. "I'm not sure?"

"Lizzie, don't listen to your sister," says Janice. "You can explore any religion you want. Within reason. Who are you going to church with?"

Lizzie edges toward the door. "Zeke Bint," she says. "His mom is driving."

"Barbara?" says Janice, spitting the name off her tongue as she abruptly recalls the tableau of the cocktail party and Barbara Bint at the bottom of the stairs; she would have had a direct view of James leaving Janice's bedroom. She remembers Barbara's curious eyes, scrutinizing Janice after James's departure. Of course Barbara would have interpreted it in the ugliest way possible. And of course she would have talked.

"Stop!" she tells Lizzie. She pushes herself back from the table, folding her napkin over the congealed chicken. "I need to discuss something with Barbara first. You wait here."

Janice marches past Lizzie and out to the Mercedes station wagon that idles in the driveway. She knocks on the driver's window. Barbara rolls it down and smiles the priggish smile of the saved. Her skin, Janice notes, is sunburned and dry, the tiny veins in her cheeks bursting from heat. "Hello, Janice!" Barbara chirps. "I assume you don't mind that we're taking your daughter to church? Would you like to join us?"

"We need to talk," says Janice.

"What about?"

Janice eyes Zeke, who sits in the back seat of the car. White headphone cords snake from his ears down to the iPod in his lap; even outside the car Janice can hear the thump of rock music that is blasting holes in the boy's eardrums. Zeke gazes at Janice with as much interest as he would regard a lump of boiled liver, then looks away, out the window.

"I think," whispers Janice, "that you may have gotten the wrong impression. About a young man in my employ. I think you know who I mean. And I have to tell you that I deeply, deeply resent you calling my husband, of all people, and filling his head with this . . . this *nonsense*. I'm shocked that someone who describes herself as a Christian would do such a deeply uncharitable thing."

Barbara bites one lobstered cheek. "I'm sorry, Janice," she says, looking confused. "But I really don't know what you're talking about."

Janice again glances at Zeke, who has completely tuned out their presence, and drops her voice to a whisper. "You told Paul that I was having an *affair*! An affair with the pool boy!"

Barbara's face contorts itself into obtuse angles, struggling to conjure up a memory. "An affair?!" she says. "No. That wasn't me. I've never spoken to Paul. I wasn't aware you *were* having an affair. I'm not sure how. . . . But wait, I *did* mention to Noreen Gossett that I saw James coming out of your bedroom at the cocktail party last week. Maybe she jumped to conclusions?" Janice, watching Barbara, can see the disingenuousness in her neighbor's eyes—that sanctimonious hypocrite may pretend to be a Christian, but at heart she's a lying gossip!—and Barbara clearly reads Janice's suspicions in return because she stammers as she flounders on. "I just mentioned it to Noreen because she was wondering why you were so late coming down. Noreen wasn't being very *nice* about it, so I

thought, just to explain . . ." She wrinkles her nose with concern. "Why? Janice, are you really involved with your pool
boy? I would never have said anything. . . . I'm sorry!"

"No!" Janice barks, but she backs off and straightens up as
she does it, recognizing that Barbara may be a gossip but she's
not overtly cruel enough to go to Paul with her suspicions.
Noreen Gossett. It must have been her. But why? What on
earth could Noreen have against her? Janice has always been
nothing but nice to her, even after Noreen's daughter, Susan,
invited everyone in her class *except* Lizzie to her ninth birthday
party. And yet—Janice suddenly remembers Noreen's snub in
the parking lot the day of the IPO, and the pieces begin to fall
into place. She sees Lizzie peering at them from the front
door and waves her daughter out to the car, ready to escape
this conversation.

"What's going on?" Barbara repeats.

Janice moves back toward the house as Lizzie approaches.
"Nothing," she mutters. "Nothing at all. Forget I said anything. My mistake."

Barbara fixes a smile back on her face as Lizzie climbs into
the back seat of the Mercedes. "I'm sorry to hear that you're
having a hard time, Janice. I'm here for you if you need moral
support. You know that, of course. Just a reminder!"

Next to Lizzie, Zeke turns up the volume on his iPod and
hurls himself tightly against the car door, as if proximity to
Lizzie might afflict him with a contagious disease. Janice feels
a stab of remorse for her daughter, wondering what on earth
could have driven her to go sit in church with these people.
Janice can't back away fast enough as the station wagon pulls
slowly, maddeningly slowly, into the street and toward the
arms of a pitiless God.

.   .   .

the gossetts' house is five blocks away, and although Janice normally drives the distance between their homes when she visits Noreen, this evening she decides it will do her good to walk instead. Her body, replenished with one more *tiny* line of It, relishes the exercise. She moves with detached, stiff-legged purpose, her limbs propelling themselves forward and up and around and back again as if they are the cogs in a well-oiled engine. Fragments of long-forgotten pop tunes from her college years flicker through her subconscious—the hummed chorus from the Rolling Stones' "Miss You," which segues into a rolling bass line from Earth Wind & Fire and lands her at "Stayin' Alive," so popular at parties when she was younger. She is a disco queen, now if never before. Her ballet flats ricochet rhythmically off the asphalt, impossibly loud.

The lights blink on in the houses of her neighborhood. Picture windows illuminate idyllic tableaux: Ellen Fern at her kitchen sink, washing the dishes. The Brunschilds and their three children sitting around their living room table, glimpsed in slices through the lowered venetian blinds. The blue light of the television reflecting off the ceiling of the Franks' den; four heads silhouetted by the screen. She wonders whether the Miller house still looks this placid and safe from the street or if its taint is detectable to passersby.

As she walks the few blocks to the Gossetts', the stars begin to materialize in the evening sky. The temperature drops, and Janice wishes she had brought a cardigan to throw over her top. At the Gossetts' ranch home every room is lit up, and Janice can hear the faint thrum of some teenybopper boy band from Susan's room in the back. She pulls at the decorative lion's-head knocker and lets it fall heavily on the door, waits a quarter second, and rings the bell. The tones echo off the Spanish tile of the hallway.

Inside, the Gossetts' dog begins to yelp. "Yipyipyip," it

barks. There is a scrape and a thump, and a silence before the dog starts in again. "Yipyipyip." *Scrape. Thump.* Janice peers through the window and sees Noreen's geriatric schnauzer, Sadie, coming down the hallway toward the door. The dog's front legs have been completely swathed in plaster, and its efforts to run to the door are being thwarted by the Gossetts' tile floors, worn slick from use. "Yipyipyip," barks the dog as it lunges forward. Its front legs skitter for purchase on the tile, scrape sideways, and collapse. The dog, momentarily stunned, struggles to get up, its front end fishtailing helplessly across the hall. As Janice watches, Noreen comes up behind the dog, swoops it under her arm, and traipses to the front door.

Noreen smiles thinly when she sees Janice. "Hello," she says, snapping at the syllables like a turtle. Sadie, under Noreen's arm, continues to yip at the intruder.

"What happened to Sadie?" blurts Janice.

Noreen scratches the fur at the back of Sadie's neck. "Yipyipyip," goes the dog. "Shhhh," Noreen says, ineffectively, and looks up at Janice. "You don't know?"

"Should I?"

"*Your* daughter nearly killed my dog," Noreen says. "And she didn't seem in the least bit concerned about it. Nor, for that matter, do you."

"Lizzie hurt Sadie?" repeats Janice.

"Not Lizzie, *Margaret.*"

"Margaret? Really? How? Did Margaret run over your dog?"

"Everything but. She let Sadie run away and get hit by a car while she was walking her."

"Why was Margaret walking your dog?" It's all terribly confusing. Sadie starts to yip again, and the piercing noise makes Janice want to shake the dog until it shuts up. "Yipyipyipyip."

Noreen looks at Janice with a wounded expression. "Maybe you should ask Margaret that question. I assumed that was why you were here. Honestly, Janice, considering all the years we've been neighbors, I was really hurt that you didn't even bother to call. You know how much Sadie means to my family—she's practically Susan's sibling. We've had her thirteen years! And now you don't even call when your daughter nearly kills my dog? Janice, I'm trying to be sympathetic because I know the last few weeks haven't been easy on you, but I expected better." Noreen pauses, as if she's finished with her speech, then bursts out: "I mean, really. Your husband makes a billion dollars and now you can't even pick up the phone to talk to your old friends anymore? Maybe Greg and I aren't in your social bracket these days, maybe you're off with your private-jet friends now and you wouldn't deign to spend time with a plain old struggling orthodontist and his wife anymore—and God knows we've seen enough of that in recent years in this town—but really, I thought you'd still have common courtesy . . ."

Janice, flabbergasted by the outburst, shakes her head, hoping to shake off this digression and get back to her purpose. The movement makes her slightly dizzy. Her foot bumps forcefully against the Gossetts' doorjamb. "Well, Noreen, I'm truly sorry. Really, I am. I've not been calling *anyone*. It's not you. Or about dentists, or jets or anything like that. I mean, I *don't* care." As she talks, her mind meanders to the Gossetts' finances, wondering for the first time how much an orthodontist *does* make and whether keeping Millard Fillmore High in braces would readily cover the cost of the BMW in their driveway and Susan's private tutors and the roof that really needs new tiles. "And I'm sorry about Sadie. She's a wonderful dog. I'll talk to Margaret, really. This has nothing to do with braces. No . . ." She pauses, realizing It has grabbed hold of her tongue and is turning her into a blathering idiot. She tries vainly to focus herself. "No—but that has nothing to do with why I'm here. I need you to tell me, truthfully, Noreen, whether you said something to Paul about me having, having . . . this is hard to even say, it's so ridiculous . . . about me having an affair with our pool caretaker?"

In Noreen's narrowed eyes, Janice reads distaste. She wants to choke back her words, rewind the journey to this house, rewind the last few weeks to a time when she had never imagined humiliation like this. But it's too late—she has no choice, at this point, but to grovel in front of her neighbor. Noreen, with whom she cohosts the neighborhood gift exchange every December, with whom she has attended PTA meetings for years, a woman whom, to be honest, she has had to tolerate for the airs that she puts on despite the fact that her own background (a mailman's daughter, for goodness' sake) is no better than Janice's. She feels herself withering under Noreen's contemptuous glare. Noreen edges back. She raises her chin. "I didn't say anything to Paul. But I may have mentioned something to Beverly when we played bridge on Monday."

"But why, Noreen? Surely you know that's just not true. He is a twenty-six-year-old boy! Why? And to Beverly, of all people? I have to assume you know that my husband and she are . . . are . . ." She can't even bring herself to finish this sentence. It doesn't matter, she realizes. The dirty laundry is already hanging there, in her front yard, for everyone to see. They have been looking at it for weeks now. They have seen the streak marks and the grass stains and the yellowed armpits and have judged her accordingly. It is too late. "Why?"

Noreen doesn't answer immediately but instead lifts Sadie up, dangling the furry schnauzer right in front of her face, and kisses it right on the nose. The dog shuts up for a second while it licks Noreen's face with a frenzied tongue. Noreen lowers the dog. "Well, Janice, I'm sorry. I don't really know what got into me."

"Yip. Yipyipyip."

Is that what this is all about? Her entire life and reputation and *family* put on the line as revenge for a nasty mutt's broken leg? For financial jealousy? Janice finds herself wishing that Margaret had killed the damn dog. The next time she sees the yapping runt in the street, Janice plans to kick it.

"I think you do," Janice says.

Noreen looks contrite, which Janice doesn't find reassuring. "I suppose I was just overcome with emotion after spending two days at the animal hospital, wondering if Sadie would live. And then, of course, there was the matter of the twenty-two-hundred-dollar veterinary bill, which may be nothing to *you* but for us is still quite a bit of money. I guess I was just so traumatized that I didn't know what was coming out of my mouth."

Janice stiffly reaches for her purse and pulls out a checkbook. "Did you say twenty-two hundred dollars?" she says.

"Twenty-two-oh-eight fifty-two, actually. Plus the matter of a new collar, because Sadie's old one was stained with blood."

"Lets just make it an even three thousand," says Janice. She remembers now that Noreen once confessed to her that her daughter, Susan, was bulimic, and that Noreen had to monitor her after meals so that she wouldn't go to the bathroom to vomit. Janice had never breathed a word of this shame to anyone. And this is how Noreen rewards her discretion. What a betrayal.

She grips the pen tightly as she writes out her bribe. Janice Miller has never coerced anyone into giving her anything in her life, she thinks, and now she has stooped to doing just that twice in three days. She feels utterly impotent. Even the check has Paul's name on it, reminding her that she is a second-class citizen: half of a disgraced couple, a scandalously discarded wife whose older child is apparently the talk of the neighborhood. She scribbles the figure on a check from their joint checking account, taking what grim satisfaction she can from the fact that Paul will be paying half of this bribe, too, and places it in Noreen's waiting hand. Writing the check feels like writing Noreen off forever.

Inside her head, where random crystal thoughts ping-pong off the walls of her brain, Janice flails about, looking for someone to blame for this latest ignominy. Paul? Beverly? James? Herself? She lands on Margaret. What on earth was Margaret doing walking the neighbors' dog? A job for children! And behind Janice's back, too—making Janice look like a fool and, worse, a bad mother. Maybe Margaret should have just stayed in Los Angeles, Janice thinks. Her presence in Santa Rita hasn't made anything easier.

The dog sniffs the check twice and then sneezes all over it. "Well, this is very generous of you," says Noreen, though the flatness of her voice suggests otherwise.

"I'd appreciate it," Janice says through clenched teeth, "if you would mention to . . . Beverly . . . that your information was very wrong."

Noreen puts a palm against the door and begins to push it slowly closed. "Of course. I'm playing a golf foursome with Beverly at the club tomorrow. I'll be sure to tell her that I was mistaken."

"That would be greatly appreciated," says Janice, suspecting that it's already too late.

"Anything for a neighbor," says Noreen, as the door swings shut before her. Janice is left staring at the ornamental knocker a few inches from her face, the brass tarnished on the head of the carved lion, which bares its teeth at Janice as if preparing to tear out her heart and eat it raw for dinner.

eight

july marches through santa rita, hot and
hazy. By ten A.M. on the last Friday of the month the brass
thermometer by the back door registers ninety-five, an uncharacteristically high temperature for this time of the year.
The streets are quiet, the neighbors having closed their windows to the world and turned on their air conditioners. The
grass in the backyard is brown and crisp around the edges, like
burnt toast. The news reports that a forest fire is raging in the
inland hills, and a yellowish scrim hovers along the horizon.

Margaret pours herself a glass of her mother's homemade
lemonade, fixes a bowl of cornflakes, and carries them both
out to the pool, balanced on top of a pile of law books from
the local library. The flat gray stones of the patio scorch the
bottom of her feet. She wears a swimsuit that belongs to
Lizzie—a faded black Speedo, two sizes too big, with fraying
elastic at the leg holes. Crammed in the crook of her elbow is
the portable phone, which has not left her side in over a week.

Since that first call, two other collection agencies have tracked her down here; both times, she answered the telephone before her mother or sister could get to it. Both times, she convinced the collection agency that they had the wrong number. How long will they believe it? She can feel an itching inevitability of the crash to come: It's just a matter of time before the process servers show up on the doorstep of her parents' house to slap her with a court order. And yet, for the first time in her life, her focus has completely deserted her; instead, she's overcome by a profound and inexplicable inertia. Since the dog-walking fiasco, she's been incapable of conceiving a solution to her financial woes, even a vague plan. She'll sit down at the computer, intending to research debt relief, then wake up from a fugue state an hour later having accomplished nothing, almost as if she'd been hypnotized by staring at the swinging ticking watch of her crisis.

The only thing that *does* seem to motivate her is her mother's divorce case. Whatever energy she has failed to pour into her credit fiasco is instead being spent on research into California divorce law, as if her winning this lawsuit for her mother will somehow make everything else fall into place. Today, she sits on one of the half dozen teak chaises surrounding the pool and deposits her pile of books on a matching side table. The first title on the pile is *The Valuation Expert in Divorce Litigation*, which is proving to be as tedious as its formidable title. The law books, which she checked out last week in preparation for Lewis Grosser's visit, read like ciphers, as if the authors of these pages intentionally set out to eliminate the clarity of the English language—all those "heretofore"s and "forthwith"s and "wherewithal"s make her jaw hurt. The overachiever in her, though, finds it all a challenge; this same impulse also leads her to believe (yes, perhaps naïvely) that she might unearth some arcane case, some legal loophole, that the lawyer has missed.

Besides, every time she throws down a law book to eye the

latest *New Yorker,* which sits folded on the tray next to the cornflakes, she recalls her mother's wan, exhausted face in that meeting with Lewis Grosser and the jittering leg that betrayed her
stress. After twenty-eight years, her mother has finally opened a
window to her weakness, and damned if Margaret isn't going to
take the opportunity to prove herself her mother's savior.

Margaret takes a bite of soggy cornflakes and washes the
mush down with lemonade, an unfortunate combination that
makes her tongue pucker. The truth is that she feels a twinge
of guilt for having so quickly aligned herself with her mother.
Would it have been wiser to take a neutral position in the family debacle? In a not-so-distant past, her first assumption
would have been that her father was probably right. And yet
her instinct now is that her mother is the more clearly offended party in this situation and the one with fewer resources
at her disposal. The *Snatch* in Margaret has raised the alarm of
gender inequity. Anyway, her father has made the decision
easy: He hasn't called his daughters, hasn't e-mailed, and
Margaret doesn't particularly enjoy feeling forgotten. His absence just strengthens her resolve.

There are more than a few parallels between critical theory
and law, she realizes as she settles into her book. Both are a
collection of secret codes that can be manipulated in any
number of ways to make a point. She has to admire the law's
quality of the infinite—there is really no established right and
wrong, merely a series of endless evolving calculations, a mu-
table collection of moral codes and cut-and-paste rules that
have been artfully assembled and reassembled over time.

Her father is a master of this art. As she combs through the
divorce papers and the documents Paul had Janice sign last
year, she can sense the web that he's been weaving ever since he
hatched his plan. (What triggered it? Was it Beverly? Or
something else entirely?) On a purely aesthetic level, she admires his design; it is intricate and calculating and yet so very

subtle as to be almost undetectable unless you know what to look for. Still, the callousness of his strategy makes her shiver.

Regardless of how they might have grown distant over the years, she recognizes that she has always thought of her father as a benchmark against which she could measure her own success in the world, even if her path was so different from his, even if her path was in fact a distinctly *opposite* reaction to his. Her father, like her, had always seemed to have an expansive view of the world, especially compared to her mother's tunnel vision of life in Santa Rita. Paul was the one who'd encouraged Margaret to start a lemonade stand when she was eight ("to learn the value of money"), who had insisted on an Ivy League over a state school ("Don't kid yourself, brand names count"), who had given her a copy of *The Seven Habits of Highly Effective People* when she graduated from college ("A must-read," he'd told her, though, of course, she hadn't). And even if she had eventually turned on him—by majoring in liberal arts instead of business or premed; by starting *Snatch* rather than working for the *Wall Street Journal;* by advocating homeopathic remedies while he sold overpriced and probably toxic chemicals—she still felt, all these years on, that she shared with him a respect for ambition. A passion for the pursuit of something bigger.

She recalls an office he'd once had, on the forty-eighth floor of a modern high-rise in downtown San Francisco. She visited once, when she was in grammar school, and had to dare herself to look down at the solid building lobby racing away from her as she rocketed up in the glass elevator, higher than she'd ever been. Pressing herself against the pane, she stared at the view of downtown San Francisco below her, the streets laid out like a puzzle, and as she rose above the city she understood for the first time what the phrase being "on the top of the world" really meant.

And yet her father has decided to reside there, on the top floor with the grand view, all by himself. It seems a cold, lonely place to be. Then again, she reminds herself, he's got Beverly in the elevator with him. So weird. She sighs and busies herself with *The Valuation Expert* and doesn't look up until she is startled by the sound of metal clattering on stone; James has arrived with his pool-cleaning supplies. He drops a net and a gallon of chlorine at the foot of her chaise. The jug topples over with a glug and rolls toward the pool.

"Hi again," he says. "Hot, huh?" His black curls are damp with sweat, and his white T-shirt is soaked in a triangle from his neck to his belly button. He is wearing faded madras shorts—pleated front, like an old man's, but held up with a string tied through the belt loops—and she can't help noticing that he has almost no butt at all. His attire is odd, and yet there is something weirdly attractive about him. Something about him—those big dark eyes—reminds her of a Keane painting.

"Like Dante's inferno," says Margaret. "I can practically hear my skin sizzle."

"You wearing sunscreen?"

"No," says Margaret.

He reaches into his bag and pulls out a sticky-looking tube of SPF 45. "You should. You're really pale. You don't want to end up with skin cancer."

Margaret is strangely touched by this gesture. She takes the tube from him and gingerly squirts lotion on her arms and legs, smearing it in with a sweaty palm, aware, the whole time, of his curious eyes observing her.

"Don't forget your back," he says. She reaches an arm behind and swipes vaguely at her shoulder as he watches. "Here, let me do it."

Margaret lets him take the tube from her. When his hand touches her back, the rough skin of his fingers tickles. His palm is warm against her flesh and unexpectedly intimate through the sticky lotion. She breaks out in goose bumps. Embarrassed, she pulls away.

"That's fine," she says. "I'm going to lie on my back anyway."

She lies down, expecting James to go on with his pool cleaning, but he sits on the end of her chaise and lazily chews on a fingernail. Unsure what to say, she picks up her book, but even with it held up in front of her face she can feel him watching her. Acutely conscious that Lizzie's oversized swimsuit droops in an unflattering way around her breasts, she tries unobtrusively to press her chest forward, then feels shallow for being so vain. Finally she gives up and drops the book in her sticky lap, staining the leather cover with sunscreen.

"So . . . ?" she asks, cocking a friendly eyebrow. "What's up?"

"Just curious."

"About?"

"What's your deal anyway?"

"What do you mean?"

James shrugs and examines his other hand for hangnails. "I don't see a whole lot of people our age around here. It's all soccer moms and little kids. Are you just on vacation, or did you move back home?"

"I'm taking time off from capitalism. Which, it turns out, is pretty hard to do. It finds you, wherever you are." She offers a wry smile, vaguely concerned that she might have shown her cards too soon.

"Your mom says you're a successful writer."

"My mother tends toward hyperbole. Don't trust her."

James shrugs. "I don't know about that. Your mom is pretty cool. She's always friendly. Makes me lemonade and cookies and stuff."

"Yeah, that's her specialty. One could say, her purpose in life."

James sucks at the tip of his finger and shades his face from the sun. "Wanna smoke some weed?" he asks. "I've got some killer Humboldt."

This is not what Margaret expected to hear. Surprised, she sits upright and instinctively glances at the house to check if her mother is standing in the window, policing against such a grave infraction of house rules. No one is there. Margaret turns back to James and smiles. "Absolutely," she says. "Here?"

"We can go in the pool shed," he says. "No one ever goes in there but me."

Margaret follows James along the path behind the rhododendron bushes to the shack at the back of the garden. The shed is long and narrow, like a walk-in closet—if she opens her arms, she can touch both walls at once—and built from whitewashed concrete. It is cool in here, a haven for the spiders that have taken up residence in the corners. Margaret plops down on a pool raft that has been inflated and placed in the center of the room, next to the water heater and pump. The smell of chlorine reminds her of summers as a child, days when she spent so much time in the pool she could still smell the chemicals on her skin when she lay in bed at night listening to the cicadas in the garden.

James settles in next to her on the raft, kicking aside a couple of bottles of pool chemicals to make room for his legs. She watches as he pulls a hand-blown glass pipe and a plastic baggie from his shorts pocket. He holds the pipe close to his face as he loads it, scrutinizing the pot, pinching out the fattest buds. He hands her the pipe and leans over to light it for her. She is aware, as she inhales the sweet, sticky smoke, of his hand hovering just inches away from her nose. James holds the lighter steadily, cupping it with his other hand to keep the flame from singeing her.

The pot flows through her like a long sigh. "God, that's good," she says and leans backward until she is flat on the raft. She closes her eyes and listens to James flicking at the lighter, hears the rush of his breath as he exhales a plume of smoke. Behind her, the pool pump emits its electric heartbeat.

"So," says James. "Why are you hiding out?"

"How could you tell I'm hiding out?"

"It's not hard to figure out."

"Well, let's just say that I've run into a little trouble with the nice people at Visa," she says. "And MasterCard, actually. And one or two collection agencies."

James sparks up the pipe again and inhales deeply before responding. "When I lived in New York I knew a guy who lived in the subway tunnels. He was totally broke," he says. "He made these crazy-ass sculptures out of broken bicycle locks. Apparently there are lots of broken bicycle locks in New York. Anyway, this guy lives in a tunnel where the only light at all is from his flashlight and he sleeps on a sleeping bag on top of a row of orange crates and he can hear the rats squeaking away underneath the crates at night. And he lives down there in the dark for, like, six months while he builds these insane sculptures that look like the digestive tract of some kind of mutant monster. And somehow this guy, who smells like rat piss and garbage, wanders into some trendy gallery and convinces the owner to come down into the tunnel and look at his work. This art-dealer guy proclaims him a genius and carts all the sculptures away and sells them for a goddamn fortune. And now the guy is living in a loft in SoHo for, like, five grand a month. He hangs out with Chloë Sevigny."

Margaret tries to follow the relevance of this story to her own life, but she's grown too hazy to capture the intent of his narrative. "Is this some follow-your-dreams morality tale?"

James is quiet for a moment. "No point, really," he says. "Just felt like telling you. Happiest guy I ever met."

"Now that he's rich and successful?"

"Well, yeah," James says, looking contemplative. "I guess."

"Oh," says Margaret, disappointed. She rolls on her side on the mattress, bobbing gently on her cushion of air. "Why were you living in New York?"

"I was getting my PhD at Columbia," he says.

Margaret tries to sit up and almost falls over. "A PhD in what?"

"Chemistry. I dropped out."

"Why?"

"Too much work," he says. "It was stressing me out. I never got enough sleep and I'd wake up in the morning with a dry mouth and a headache and need to drink six cups of coffee to get out of bed. And then I'd spend the whole day feeling like I was twelve steps behind where I should be. I'd kill myself for these tight-assed professors who were overloading us with work to see how much they could make us endure before they gave us some totally arbitrary grade. And I realized that this is what it would be like for the rest of my life and I decided that that kind of life sucks. So I moved here."

"Why Santa Rita?"

James shrugs. "Rich people always have lots of money to spend."

"And you became a pool boy?"

"Well, you know, it's still chemistry."

"It's indentured slavery. You can't possibly be making more than eight dollars an hour."

"Twenty," he says. "And I've got other sources of income. I'm saving up to move to Puerto Escondido, this surf town down in Mexico. I think I might open a bar on the beach. Sell surfboards."

"Huh," says Margaret, as she reaches for the pipe. "You surf?"

"No," he says. "But I could."

"Right," says Margaret. And after taking another hit she closes her eyes. She can vividly see Mexico: the immaculate white-sand beaches, the stolidly proletariat Mexican fishermen, sunsets on the beach and cold Coronas. Chilled coconuts and carnitas tacos. Serapes hand-woven by indigenous artisans. "I've always wanted to learn to surf," she says and, surprisingly, means it. Four years in L.A. and she only went to the beach twice; she'd spent all her time working on *Snatch* instead. *What a waste,* she thinks.

"I gotta get to work," says James. He stands up and wipes his hands on his shorts. "Got two more houses today."

"Thanks," says Margaret. "It was nice talking. And thanks for the pot."

James pauses at the door of the pool shed and chews on a thumbnail. He looks out at the garden and then back at her. "By the way," he says. "I think your mom might have a problem."

"Yeah?" says Margaret, surprised. "You know about the divorce? I wouldn't have thought she'd tell you."

James swallows, his Adam's apple bobbing in the sun. "Aw, forget it. I don't know what I'm saying. I'm stoned."

Margaret tries to focus her eyes on him, but her head is wobbling too much. "Don't worry, I'm helping her out," she says.

"Good," says James, and disappears.

When Margaret gathers the energy to rise up off the air mattress, a few minutes later, James is already gone. She goes back to her chaise and stares down at the law books. She shouldn't have gotten stoned. Now she won't be able to understand anything in them. The day stretches before her, empty and hot and blurry.

She gathers up her books, puts her sundress back on, and moves to the cool darkness of her father's abandoned study. The house is silent—her mother is napping, her sister off at swim camp. Blearily, Margaret turns on the computer to check her e-mail. Josephine has e-mailed her twice, asking where she's disappeared to, why her phone is turned off, demanding to know if she's okay. Claire has invited her to her latest art opening, and Alexis has even sent an e-mail from Tokyo, where she is on location, that reads, simply, "????" Margaret absorbs their concern but can't quite summon a cogent (or honest) response—not now. Not yet. Instead, she types one line to all three of them. "Hi guys, Home taking care of my mother. Will write more soon. XO M." She clicks "Send," satisfied that she's put them off for a while.

As the computer chugs away, retrieving a pile of spam, the telephone rings once, and Margaret automatically picks it up and hangs it right back up again, cutting it off without even checking to see who is on the other side. The words of the e-mails blur, then come back into focus, then split again into a kaleidoscope of meaningless letters. Squinting hard, she stops abruptly at the sight of her father's name on an e-mail dated five days earlier. For a minute, she thinks she's hallucinating it, but when she blinks and looks again it's still there: Paul Miller <miller@appliedpharm.com>.

"Margaret," it reads, "I've been trying to reach you but it seems your phone (phones?) has been cut off. I have something urgent to discuss with you. Please call me as soon as possible. Love, Dad."

Margaret stares at the message, trying to decipher what it means, but her brain spins in lazy circles and doesn't deliver a clue. She registers a sense of alarm, however—this mystery must be resolved immediately. Could it have something to do with the IPO? The divorce? *Urgent!* She picks up the phone and begins to dial her father's office number, but the sound of Janice moving around in the hall above her causes her to stop. What if Janice walks in on her while she's on the phone with her dad? She sits there, the phone warming in her hand, and vacantly reflects on the catastrophe that might ensue. Talking to her father from within the sacred confines of Janice's home would be, in a way, like an infidelity, akin to Paul having sex with Beverly in Janice's bed. And what if Janice picked up the phone by mistake and heard them talking? *Cruel!* She stares at the keypad of the phone and suddenly even the sound of her breath seems very loud in the quiet house. There's absolutely no way she can call him without Janice overhearing her. And she doesn't even have a cell phone any-more.

Urgent! The word triggers an ache in Margaret both animal and instinctive—made worse because she's stoned. What can she do? The only logical thing, Margaret puzzles out, from this deliciously dulled state, would be to get in her car and drive to see her father in person. She might even serve as a sort of ambassador or emissary for her mother, the white flag of neutrality flying behind her as she leaves home turf and enters enemy territory. (Or would that be the demilitarized zone?) Janice wouldn't have to know about her visit until Margaret returned home with Paul's surrender in hand. Or a truce, at the minimum. It's possible, right?

Deep inside, somewhere near her spleen, a warning signal tells her this is a *very bad idea.* It would be wiser to just stay at home, ignore the e-mail, and avoid any sort of conflict. Is there really anything to be gained? (*Almost a half billion dollars!* She pushes this thought away before it can fully form.) But the embarrassing truth, which even her marijuana high can't quite obscure, is that the novelty of finally being sought out by her father is something Margaret is unable to resist.

traffic on the 101 is light, which is a relief, be-cause Margaret is aware that her faculties are blunted. She drives behind a gardener's truck that spills a cloud of grass clippings onto the hood of her car. Her air-conditioning unit splutters and hisses out an anemic stream of tepid air. She rolls down the window, and the crosswind whips her hair into a wild nest. The tape deck grinds through a warped PJ Harvey cassette, then reverses direction to play the other side.

By the time she reaches the office park, she has sobered up enough to wonder whether this is a good idea and can't quite recall what she planned to say to her father in the first place.

She stares up at the black glass facade—a forbidding blank monolith designed to ensure that outsiders mind their own damn business—and then smooths her hair, wipes her face with the hem of her skirt, and examines herself in the broken rearview mirror. She wishes she had thought to change out of the tired orange terry-cloth sundress. Sweat trickles down between her breasts. She feels dizzy.

The lobby of Applied Pharmaceuticals is blindingly white. The walls are painted white. The floors are white marble. The couches are white leather, sitting on a white shag rug. On the walls hang framed photographs of the apple-green Coifex pills, blown up to three hundred times their actual size. The Coifex logo has also been enlarged and rendered in green neon. Sitting in its eerie glow is the receptionist, an attractive young Asian woman with her hair pulled up into a tight bun and trendy black geek glasses perched on the end of her nose. She is wearing green, too: green shirtdress, green shoes, green clip in her hair. Margaret wonders whether this has been mandated by upper management or whether she chose the color out of allegiance to her employers. Either way, it strikes Margaret as a depressing display of corporate fealty. Then again, she probably has stock options.

"I'm here to see Paul Miller," she informs the receptionist.

The woman lifts the receiver and holds it six inches from her head. "And who may I say is here?"

"His daughter," says Margaret.

The receptionist dials and then leans over, cupping her hand around the phone so that Margaret can't hear her, and holds a brief conversation with someone on the other end of the line.

She sits up again. "He wants to know which one?"

"What?"

"Which daughter are you?"

"His firstborn."

After a brief conference, Margaret is pointed in the direction of the elevator and instructed to ride to the fourth floor. When the elevator opens, Paul's assistant, Evan, is waiting for her. "Well, hi!" he says, patting her on the shoulder. She shrugs away. He guides her through a warren of cubicles toward the back of the vast room, where a bank of tall wooden doors screen the more important members of the Coifex family from the hoi polloi. "So good to see you again. How are you? And your sister?"

"Surviving," says Margaret, remembering the last time she saw him, marching out their front door with three suitcases. "Considering."

Evan blanches. "Right." They reach the last office and he knocks twice, gently, before tipping open the door and gesturing her in with a grandiose sweep of his hand. She takes a deep breath, chasing away the last cobwebs of her marijuana high with a blast of air-conditioned oxygen. She rubs her arms and walks in.

Paul's office is so silent that she can hear the whine of the fluorescent lights overhead. Her father is sitting behind a vast mahogany desk, staring at a point on the floor. He glances up at her, winks, and holds one finger aloft in the air. It's only then that she notices the wireless earpiece plugged into his left ear.

She comes to a halt just inside the door. He has gained a bit of weight around his middle, and the wide expanse of his forehead reflects the lighting overhead. Everything about her father is solid—jowls that are fleshy and tanned from weekends on the golf course, a muscular neck that battles against the collar of his button-down shirt—except for his mouth, which is pink and delicate and reveals sharp but tiny white teeth. It's the mouth of a girl. He wears trim wire-framed glasses and a pinstriped suit with a green satin tie the exact color of the Coifex logo, and looks carnivorous and powerfully self-entitled, as if he is about to savor a twelve-course meal cooked just for him. Money suits him.

"That's great, great," he says into the earpiece. "Look, tell them the report is due any day now and send them a gift basket, okay? . . . No, not the doctors, the VCs."

Hanging up, he stands and comes around to the front of his desk. There is an awkward moment as he leans forward and places his arms around Margaret's shoulders in a bear hug. Margaret, taken aback, puts her hand on the wide part of his back, feeling the expensive Italian wool under her palms. They both pull away quickly.

"Margaret," Paul says. "This is a surprise. Why didn't you call me?" He gestures at the armchair in front of his desk, and Margaret sinks down into its soft leathery depths. Her nose is barely eye level with his grand mahogany desk. She suddenly realizes what a terrible mistake she has made. Here, surrounded by the smell of leather—buttery and slightly fecund, the aroma of money itself—she is both very weak and very small, totally out of her element. The bracing distaste for her father she felt just hours ago fades and she feels, instead, like a small child who has been granted a rare visit with the king.

"I just got your e-mail," she says.

"You did? I was wondering why you hadn't responded—well, we'll get to that. First, though, how are you? When did you get into town?" He frowns slightly, as if hurt. "You could have called to let me know you'd come home."

"Kind of the way you called me and Lizzie to tell us that you'd left Mom? Or that you'd made a fortune with Applied Pharmaceuticals?"

"Your phone was disconnected, as you might recall. Besides, I e-mailed you about the divorce. You didn't e-mail me back."

"Oh. Right." Margaret's indignation withers and becomes a vague and unwelcome shame. Naughty, naughty Margaret. She hates her father for doing this to her—turning her into a little girl who longs for a lollipop and a gold star. She looks at the contents of his desk, a few inches from her nose: an amber paperweight with a fly trapped inside, a titanium laptop, and a neat stack of papers. A very old framed photo of her and Lizzie—a fourteen-year-old Margaret in braces propping a baby Lizzie on her lap like a doll, the nervous smile revealing her terror of accidentally dropping her sister—is turned out just so, so that visitors can see it (*Paul Miller, Family Man, a Man You Can Trust!*) even if he can't. The photo, for some reason, makes her very sad. There is no picture of her mother. She is relieved that there are no pictures of Beverly either. Yet.

"How is everyone holding up?" Paul asks. One hand is in his pocket, fiddling compulsively with some unseen item; he seems nervous, and Margaret, for a brief moment, is touched by this.

"Fine, I guess. Lizzie's always off swimming. Mom's . . ." Margaret doesn't know quite what to say that won't betray her mother. "Well, as you would expect, I suppose."

"Right," says Paul. "Look, I'm sorry I've been so absent, but the situation has been, well, more than a little awkward, as you might imagine. I hope you and your sister know that this has nothing to do with you. I promise you'll be seeing more of me soon."

"Awesome!" Before the word is out of her mouth Margaret is already regretting her sarcasm. She looks at her hands, overcome with discomfort, then glances back up to see her father assessing her with a tightened brow.

"Anyway, there's something I want to talk to you about," Paul says. He sits on the edge of his desk in front of Margaret, pinching the fold in his pants with one hand to prevent it from wrinkling. "I've been getting some phone calls, Margaret. From collection agencies. I understand that you owe them quite a bit of money."

So this is it, Margaret thinks. *He finally knows.* The relief that surges through her—*Daddy's going to fix everything, make it all better;* is that what she was secretly hoping when she drove up here?—is quickly replaced by nausea. He knows, and she is going to be

ill. She is going to vomit on the floor right there in front her
father, right on the green Coifex logo that has been woven
into the center of the rug. Her failures exposed, she feels like
a bug under a microscope; no, worse, inside out, as if someone had reached inside and grabbed her entrails and yanked
them out for her father to see. She half-expects him to turn
away in disgust at the sight.

And yet. Her father is smiling at her, a warm smile of pa-
ternal forbearance that is—she grows perplexed—totally unexpected. What happened to the lecture about living up to her
potential? About making wise financial decisions? About how
she should have gotten an MBA instead of a string of useless
degrees? About how other people her age have made something of themselves and how she has instead thrown her life
away on some obscure magazine that's put her in debt?

"You know," her father continues. "I'm not exactly hurting for money right now. I'd like to help you out financially,
if that's what you need."

Margaret swallows. Here it is: Daddy bailing her out. It
should hurt, but as Margaret looks for a bruise, a tender purple blemish on her conscience, she realizes that what she is experiencing, instead, is the glory of reprieve. The solution to
her problem has magically arrived, the one she didn't have the
guts to admit she wanted—*the one, let's be honest, that compelled me
north to Santa Rita,* she thinks—and she didn't even have to ask
him outright. And if this is selling out—no better, possibly
worse, than letting Bart support her back in Los Angeles—well,
honestly, she just doesn't care anymore. As long as the phone
stops ringing. As long as she can start her life over again without debt looming over her head. She finds that she is practically beaming at her father. It's this easy?

Paul continues. ". . . And I think it would probably make
sense to give you a little extra, too, just to get you back on your
feet again."

Something about this makes Margaret hesitate. This is not the father she grew up with, the father who always said that children should learn self-sufficiency, who required her to get an after-school job at a local bank in order to better appreciate the value of money. Watching him smile at her, it dawns on her that this is what divorced parents do—they bribe their children to love them more than the other parent. Gifts—money—in lieu of time and affection. Lizzie is probably getting a check, too.

"I'm stunned," she says slowly, trying to gauge how she feels, as her father walks behind his desk and pulls a checkbook from a drawer.

He signs the check with an illegible scribble and tears it off, handing it to Margaret without folding it so that she can see the sum written on it: $200,000. Her jaw works silently around the figure. *Trust-fund kid,* she accuses herself. *Taking the easy route, letting Daddy solve your problems.* But that passes quickly. *Two hundred thousand dollars!* Her mind fixes on the number and repeats it, like a mantra. *Two hundred thousand dollars!* It's almost twice as much as he's giving her mother each year for alimony. She digests this fact about as comfortably as she would a handful of tacks, but eventually pure childish excitement takes over again. Horizons unfold before her, too vast to even grasp. She could pay her bills, find a new apartment, maybe even start up *Snatch* again, if she wanted to. She rubs the check slowly between her thumb and forefinger, just to see what that much money feels like, and looks up at her father. "That's . . . really generous, Dad," she says, aware of how inadequate her words seem in this context.

"Well, I have a favor I have to ask of you, too," Paul says. He picks up the paperweight and fondles it, staring at the ancient fly trapped in its depths, then looks at Margaret. "You are aware, I imagine, of the fact that your mother and I are arguing over the proceeds of Applied Pharmaceuticals."

Margaret freezes. "Yes," she says slowly.

"Well, you probably know that this is going to end up in

court, then," he says. "And I'm pretty sure you know what that will mean. What I was hoping was that you would be willing to testify on my behalf. Nothing's certain yet, but I suspect that your mother has been behaving poorly, and if things got ugly it would help me tremendously if you were willing to testify for me. Maybe about some of what you've been witnessing around the house."

Margaret looks down at the check. She stares at it for a very long minute, until the zeros start blurring together, and wants to cry. "Oh," she says. There is nothing else she can think of to say. She waits for an answer to come to her, but her mind is a void. Could she do it? She grows aware that a tear has spilled out from her left eye and left a moist trail down her cheek.

"Hey, there," says Paul. He puts a hand on her shoulder and wobbles it gently, sending tremors down her torso. "Don't get like that. It's really not that big of a deal, Margaret."

Not a big deal? She sees, suddenly, how completely divorced from empathy her father really is—a moral relativist, using people only to advance his own needs. She realizes that his is the endgame of all ambition: Success at any expense. And she is, abruptly, furious. Furious that her father would put her in this position, furious that she ever identified with him, furious that he saw her as someone who could be bought off, and even more furious that—despite everything she has worked for, stood for, and believed in—he was almost right. How could she have considered taking his money? Was she really that weak? That easily seduced by a bunch of zeros? What happened to self-sufficiency?

She puts the check down on the desk and hoists herself out of the chair. "You've got to be kidding." Immediately, she is buoyed up by the strength of her moral position—she had forgotten how good that felt! Better than money! Standing, she is face-to-face with her father, who sits on the edge of the desk. He looks down at his trousers, suddenly fascinated by a fleck of dirt on his knee, and she is granted a rare close-up of the top of his head, where only the faintest sliver of pink scalp peeks through his graying brown hair. "You're screwing over my mother and you don't think it's a big deal to ask me to help you do it?"

The muscles in Paul's cheek twitch, but his expression remains blank. He stands up and moves away from Margaret, behind the safety of his desk. "Don't be melodramatic, Margaret. It's a divorce. People get divorced all the time. It may seem abrupt and clinical, but there's no room for sentimentality in this kind of situation. It's like taking off a Band-Aid—it hurts less if you do it quicker."

"This isn't a business transaction," Margaret says. "This is your *wife*, Dad! How could you be so mercenary? I mean, half a billion dollars? You really need all that to yourself, so much so that you'll lie to and then sue your wife? How can you even *spend* all that money? *That's* what makes you a total prick in this situation."

"I'm not a prick, Margaret," he says. "I'm a libertarian." He sees the incredulity on Margaret's face and seems to think that she doesn't understand. "That means I believe in personal responsibility and rational self-interest. I'm just owning my own happiness. Honestly, I'm doing the *right thing*, Margaret. For myself, and probably for your mother too."

"I know what a libertarian is," Margaret spits. "I read Ayn Rand in *grammar* school, Dad. And no. You really are a prick. You think that throwing Mom to the wolves is doing the right thing for her? The woman who has spent her entire life taking care of your home and driving your children to school so that you could kiss the asses of your investors over business breakfasts without worrying about our poopy diapers? Wow." She walks to the door and stands there, too furious to even leave. "Yeah, you're a prick. *And* an idiot for thinking that I'd sell myself out for a measly two hundred thousand. Really, I'm offended you didn't at least try to bribe me with a million. God knows you have it."

Her father looks at her critically. "Well, Margaret, what did you expect? Look at you. You'll be twenty-nine this fall, and what are you doing with your life? As far as I can tell, throwing it out the window." There is a soft knock on the office door, which Paul ignores. "I can't even *fathom* how you managed to get yourself a hundred thousand in debt. I never knew you could piddle that much away just playing around with magazines."

The words feel like a fist to the stomach, but they are a swing Margaret has seen coming for years, and instead of crying she mostly feels compelled to punch her father in the face. "Dad, I really could care less about your approval," she says. "I don't believe that success is a measure of how much money you have, or whether you're so powerful that others feel the need to kiss your ass, or whether your name shows up in the *New York Times*." As she says this, she questions whether or not she does, in fact, believe this, and decides that yes, for the moment anyway, she actually does. It feels marvelously liberating. "In fact," she continues, "if you think I'm failing then I'm glad, because it means that I haven't bought into your fucked-up value system."

With that, she throws the door open, revealing Evan. "Paul," says Evan, avoiding looking at Margaret. "You're going to miss your three o'clock."

"Margaret," says Paul. "Someday you're going to realize how wrong you really are and you're going to call me and apologize."

Margaret stands for a minute in the doorway, trying not to look back at the check on the desk, reminding herself that she is aligning herself with the *right* side in this argument. "Fuck you, Dad," she says, loud enough for the entire Applied Pharmaceuticals staff to hear, loud enough to make her father wince and Evan recoil. "I should have taken French."

With that she wheels around and marches out of the office.

it is nearly dusk when margaret arrives back at the house, still flush with adrenaline from her confrontation. Maybe she didn't return bearing the flag of surrender as she'd naïvely imagined, but she feels like she's won some kind of victory, one she is eager to share with her mother. She imagines Janice's grateful surprise at her loyalty, and the moments of tender approbation that will follow. Her stomach churns with acid. Margaret thinks it's excitement until she realizes that she has not eaten a thing since the bowl of cornflakes she had for breakfast.

"Mom?" she calls out as she walks through the side door and into the kitchen. There is no response. Margaret opens the refrigerator and confronts a wall of Tupperware containers. Each translucent brick is labeled with masking tape in her mother's spiky hand: "Carrot-Ginger Soup 7/25," "Smoked Salmon Frittata 7/23," "Lemon Chicken 7/26," "Shrimp Fra Diavola 7/24."

Margaret removes the containers of chicken and soup and turns to deposit them on the kitchen counter. She slams right into Janice, who has materialized just a few inches behind her. The soup container clatters to the floor.

"God, you scared me," Margaret blurts as she retrieves the Tupperware. In the white glow from the refrigerator's light she can see that the emotional trauma of the last month has taken a real toll on her mother. Janice's skin is pasty, her face thin, her eyes bloodshot and feline. There are red channels on her forearms that look like fingernail marks. "Mom, you look terrible. Are you even sleeping at all anymore? Have you considered taking Ambien or something?"

"We need to talk," says Janice.

"Can I tell you about my afternoon first?" says Margaret. She peels back the lid of a container, removes a chicken leg, and takes a bite, smearing cold, fatty meat across her chin. She feels like the conquering warrior, marching in to claim the hand of the princess. She turned down $200,000! Sacrificed her own well-being for her mother, in the ultimate display of filial love! Margaret radiates warmth toward her mom—*the two of them against the world*—and turns her face up as if to catch that love reflected back at her. Together they will solve all their problems—Janice's *and* Margaret's!

"Not now," says Janice. She reaches out and takes the chicken leg from Margaret's hand, marches over to the kitchen cabinet, and deposits the meat on a plate. She walks back to where Margaret stands, puts the plate down on the kitchen counter, and hands Margaret a fork and napkin. "I was at the Gossetts' last night. And I saw what happened to Sadie."

Margaret again sees the floppy gray dog arcing through the air, and closes her eyes against the image. "Oh," she says. "Yes. That."

"I don't think you understand," says Janice. She takes a wobbly breath and claws at the skin of her forearm with a stiff hand. "I don't think you understand what you have done. The magnitude of it."

Margaret wipes the grease off her chin with the napkin, nervous—*the cat out of the bag*—but also confused by her mother's histrionics. "The magnitude? Aren't you being a little melodramatic? I took a temporary job doing some dog walking, to make a little cash. The dog got in a small accident. I felt terrible about it, but there wasn't much I could do."

"You don't understand," says Janice, and Margaret recoils from the fury in her mother's voice. "You nearly killed the neighbors' dog. Noreen Gossett's dog. You have no idea how much Noreen loves that dog. And you didn't tell me! Everything would have been fine if you'd told me! I would have dealt with it earlier and everything would have been okay. How could you be so irresponsible?"

Margaret tries to make sense of the encounter she is having, but can't. It's just a *dog,* she thinks. Her mother doesn't even *like* dogs. She crumples the napkin in her hand and heaves it toward the garbage can. It lands in the middle of the kitchen floor. "You're not making any sense, Mother. The dog is fine. Just a few broken bones. There's no need to act like I just triggered Armageddon. I apologized to Noreen Gossett. What else could I do? I wasn't the one driving the car."

Janice marches over, picks the discarded napkin up off the floor, and examines it, as if it is evidence, before placing it carefully in the can. "I'll have you know that I had to write Noreen Gossett a three-thousand-dollar check to pay for that dog's hospital bills."

"Three thousand dollars? For a vet bill? God, that's insane. That's more than my rent for two months," Margaret says, but internally she is wincing: She's been bailed out by her mommy? She thought she'd already battled that mortification today, stared it in the face and won, but this time it's too late. It's done, and her humiliation is complete. The recognition of her own incompetence chokes her, like the tight pink leather collar on that horrid half-dead dog. "Is that what this is about? Because I will reimburse you."

"Why did you take a job walking the Gossetts' dog?"

"Does that really matter?"

"Honestly, I have the feeling that you don't have enough money to pay for even a decent pair of clean underwear. But how would I ever know?"

Margaret impulsively lifts the skirt of her dress, revealing a wall of white panty with blue lace trim. Janice quickly turns her head away, clearly terrified that she is about to glimpse a flash of her daughter's raw pubes. The sight of her mother's distaste makes Margaret feel sick. "They're clean," she says bitterly. "Don't worry about me getting in any traffic accidents."

"That's not the point."

"What *is* the point, Mother? What difference does it make to you whether I have money or not?"

"The point is that you never tell me *anything*! I'm your *mother*!"

Margaret looks at her shrieking mother, whose cheeks have erupted in hot red spots of fury, and finally lets petulance get the better of her. "You really want to know?" she asks, bristling under her mother's completely unfathomable—*unfair!*—attack. "Okay. *Fine.* I'm behind on some credit card payments, Mom. I owe some money and I'm trying to find a way to pay it back and I thought getting a job while I'm here would help." She watches her mother's face as it flickers rapidly with surprise and then concern and then dismay. "*Snatch* didn't exactly work out the way I thought it would. Is that what you wanted to hear? Does that make you happy?"

Apparently not. Janice has narrowed her eyes and is shaking her head furiously, as if by refusing the truth she might make it go away entirely. Her fingernails sink deeply into her own flesh. "Oh, God, Margaret," she says. "Not now. Why?"

"*Why?* You think I did this on purpose?"

"You blame me, Margaret, but it's you. You. Yes, you." Janice points her finger at Margaret, jabs it forward with each "you." The finger wobbles in midair. "You spoiled it. This entire . . . *mess,* it's your fault. With Lizzie, and James, and Noreen. With *everything.*" Margaret listens, baffled, to her mother's incoherent babbling. Lizzie? James? What the hell do they have to do with anything? Janice stops suddenly and takes a breath, as if to calm herself. And then she blurts, as her eyes fill with tears: "And you weren't even *sorry.*" Janice blinks rapidly, then turns and flees the kitchen.

Margaret stares at the chicken leg, lying forlornly in the middle of a dinner plate. She is too upset to move. What mess is her mother talking about? The lawsuit? The credit card debt? The *divorce*? Does she really believe that Margaret is somehow at fault for that? For a moment, she considers chasing her mother down to tell her about her confrontation with Paul—*I gave it all up, for you!*—just to see the stunned look of guilt on Janice's face. *No,* she thinks. *Let her find out on her own, and then she'll* really *feel terrible.* Mostly, she wishes she could erase the whole afternoon, regrets that she ever defended her mother to her father, regrets that she ever offered to help her mother in the first place. What was she thinking? She should have taken her father's $200,000, paid off her bills, and just left town so that her parents could duke it out by themselves. Despite the divorce, she thinks bitterly, her parents still have this in common: Nothing she does will ever be good enough for either of them. To hell with them both.

Margaret walks the chicken to the sink, dumps it down the garbage disposal, and hits the switch. The disposal clatters and grinds to a halt as the chicken bones destroy the rotor. Then she turns, grabs her purse, and walks straight back out the kitchen door.

In the driveway she passes Lizzie, returning home from God-knows-where. Lizzie pivots around and follows Margaret toward her car. "Where are you going?" she pleads. "Can I come? Puhleeeze?"

"No!" Margaret snaps. As she marches past her sister, she gets a glimpse of Lizzie's wounded face and knows that she's hurt her feelings, but she's just not in the mood to deal with her needy sister. The engine of her Honda is still warm when she climbs in the front seat and putters back out the driveway.

margaret can remember when the cineplex 13 was built on the main street of downtown Santa Rita, when she was in junior high school. It had seemed to her an adolescent Xanadu. Parents dropped their kids off here on the weekend, secure in the fact that they would be safe within its concrete confines. They weren't aware that the college dropouts running the ticket counter would happily sell R-rated movie tickets to PG-age kids, for a two-dollar bribe. Or that Captain Cork's, across the street, sold booze to underaged kids, who snuck it into the theater in their backpacks. On Friday nights, at the café tables, preteen girls would bat their eyelashes from behind their extra-large Diet Cokes (spiked with spiced rum) at boys who blithely ignored them, enraptured instead by the stand of video games just off the reception. The last row of Theater II was where, it was rumored, half of her class had gone to second base.

The Thirteen has not aged well. The lobby is dark and cavernous and smells like rancid grease. Spiders suck flies dry in dusty corners. The rug dates the place, with its eighties-era pattern of green triangles and pink squiggles now mottled by years of dirty sneakers and spilled soda to a uniform shade of gray-brown. The neon letters spelling out the names of the beverages for sale—Sprite, Coke, Jolt Cola—flicker erratically. The Frogger video game she once played while waiting for her mother to pick her up has been replaced by a game called Death Metal: Blood Match that screeches and hiccups in the corner of the lobby.

"Whamoovee," says the teenage girl from behind the glass of the ticket counter. Margaret looks up at the marquee, ready to pick a film at random. Anything that will keep her away from the house and her mother for a few hours. Hell, maybe she'll spend the rest of the summer here, slipping from movie to movie, sleeping through the matinees, living on salted popcorn, hiding out from the collection agencies.

She scans the list of titles, considering the dismal offerings, and then freezes. There, in Theater II, is *Thruster.* For a minute, she thinks she must be hallucinating it. It's out already? She turns around to look at the movie posters lining the wall, and her heart begins to palpitate. There is Bart's face, three times its normal size, staring back at Margaret. He is wearing wraparound sunglasses with a Ferrari reflected in the lenses and is wielding a subatomic machine gun. "One man. One machine. One bloody road to revenge," reads the caption.

"Whamoovee," repeats the girl in the glass box, as the people in line behind Margaret begin to grumble.

"Thruster," blurts Margaret, before she can think better of it.

"Starts in ten minutes." Margaret takes the ticket and stares at it. Then she looks across the street to the Captain Cork's liquor store. She knows what she'll need to make it through.

eleven minutes later, margaret settles into one of the last seats in the theater just as the opening credits roll, a pint of tequila wedged in her purse. She sits between a bearded man who looks to have slept there since the last showing and a college-age couple feeding each other popcorn from a bucket the size of a spaghetti pot. The springs in the seat are broken, and the velvet has worn down to the netting underneath, but Margaret is already too absorbed in what she sees on the screen to really notice. There he is, staring back at her, twenty feet high. He sits behind the wheel of a jet-black Ferrari, racing through a desert landscape, a barely legal blond vixen—Ysabelle van Lumis—in the passenger seat. She can see every pore on his nose.

"Jesus," she whispers at the screen, just to vent some of the pressure that is building up inside her.

"Sssssshhhh," says the woman sitting next to her.

Margaret pulls the bottle of tequila out of her purse. She takes a swig, not even bothering to hide it. It makes her eyes water. The woman sitting next to her clicks her tongue loudly.

"Jesus Christ," Margaret says again, just because it feels so good to be losing it in public, and takes another swig.

The plot is, as always with these movies, not the point. Bart, a former truck driver—poet turned undercover FBI agent, must infiltrate a ring of European jewel thieves by competing in the Le Mans and in the process falls in love with a gorgeous Frenchwoman (Ysabelle, with a deplorable accent) who turns out to be the ringleader of the thieves. In between, abundant car crashes, countless gun battles, five fistfights, and one exploding skyscraper. Of course, Ysabelle has to be saved three times, usually while wearing scraps of lingerie. Is it less offensive than *Fahrenheit 88*? Only marginally. In her head, Margaret composes a screed against it, a *Snatch* editorial about the absence of strong female action heroes.

This, at least, is what Margaret does between swigs of tequila. Mostly she fixates on Bart's face, noticing that the "look" he was practicing in front of the mirror all those years—left-eye squint, combined with contemplative smile—is, actually, quite effective. He comes off as simultaneously fuckable and totally unapproachable. She thinks of jumping up and pointing at the screen and screaming, "Look! That was my boyfriend. *My* boyfriend!" Why did they break up again? She can't remember. It must have been something trivial, something silly. It was the biggest mistake of her life. Her heart thumps in time to the gunfire pulsing from the end of Bart's AK-47.

When Bart kisses Ysabelle on-screen, she closes her eyes and feels hot all over, remembering what it felt like to hang on to him as she rode on his motorcycle. The second time he kisses Ysabelle, though, the back of her throat tightens unpleasantly as she fights off a tear. The third time, when the two of them shed their clothes (Ysabelle's breasts are phenomenal) and hop into bed, she is just pissed. The asshole probably cheated on her while he was on location, she realizes belatedly; that's why he came back and dumped her.

"Fucker," she says to the screen as Ysabelle emits a banshee cry, her blond hair flying wildly around her bucking body. She drinks again. "You weren't *that* great a lay."

The woman sitting next to her shifts to the far side of her seat.

"Shut the hell up," says the man on her other side, who is now leaning forward, examining all four yards of Ysabelle van Lumis's exposed mammaries.

On the screen, Bart seems unreal, as distant to her as a glossy two-dimensional picture of a celebrity in a magazine. The icon he had always wanted to be. How did he *do* that? What did he have that she didn't? What was the intangible *thing* all her friends—Josephine, Alexis, Claire, even her father—embodied that had somehow allowed them to find success so quickly, whereas she had not? They made it look so *easy*. She finds it hard to imagine that they wanted it more than she did, or that they worked harder, or sacrificed more, or were that much more talented than she was. (Or were they?) Perhaps, instead of caring so much about principles, about credibility, about being *right*, she should have put Paris Hilton on the cover of *Snatch* and started a shopping column.

Maybe the only way to make it anymore is to give up and sell out.

As she sits in the dark, this new consciousness makes her terribly anxious, as if a prior awareness of this fact might somehow have made a profound difference in her life. Because the truth is, as disposable as Bart's movie is, she knows she is jealous that he has made it and she has not; that he has achieved his dream and that she doesn't even *know* what her dream is anymore. What if she had taken the $200,000? Would she really have started *Snatch* again? She thinks of the last issue—*vibrator reviews*, for God's sake—and suddenly sees how insular and shrill and single-minded her magazine had become. How, in a word, tiresome.

By the time the movie ends Margaret is emotionally depleted and very tipsy. She stumbles out of the theater, thinking that maybe she will just take a nap in the back seat of her car before she drives home. Stopping at the water fountain, she slurps greedily at the tepid water, trying to ignore the pale green lump of gum stuck to the drain. The water tastes of rust, but she's so thirsty she doesn't care.

"Margaret?" she hears a voice behind her say. "Is that you, Margaret Miller?"

She turns to see a small round woman in track pants and a yellow polo shirt, hair cut in a matronly shag that frames a squat pug nose. The woman has the pink plump cheeks of the well fed and manicured and shampooed. Behind her is an equally small man in penny loafers and a "Sand Hill Cart Races Runner Up" sweatshirt that doesn't quite disguise his premature paunch.

The woman places herself just inches from Margaret's face and beams, her expression not wavering from its pure child-like joy even as Margaret continues to wrinkle her brow in confusion. "Remember me? Kelly Maxfield? From your class at Millard Fillmore?"

"Oh," says Margaret weakly. Her first thought is that she can't believe that this woman is her age. Has Kelly aged prematurely or is Margaret simply stunted? Margaret has a dim recollection of a plump girl in her class who matched the color of her shoelaces to her socks. Pleasant if forgettable. The same girl, she now recalls, that her mother has been nagging her to get in touch with for the last month. "Wow."

"I can't believe it's been ten years! We missed you at the reunion, you know," Kelly says. She grabs the arm of the man standing next to her, who smiles vaguely. "This is my husband, Duncan. Duncan, this is Margaret; she was—I'm serious here—the *smartest girl* in my high school. Everyone used to try to cheat off her tests." She looks at Margaret with bright eyes and laughs. "Of course, *I* never did. Which is probably why I ended up at San Jose State instead of Stanford."

Margaret smiles faintly. "So, what are you doing these days, Kelly?"

"I'm a publicist. Do you know of Maxfield & Associates?

Of course you wouldn't have unless you were in the industry. But anyway, that's me. High-tech PR. Mostly I do social networking and wireless and big pharma." She grimaces. "Oh! I should have said before, great news about your father's IPO! I've been tracking it. You must be thrilled."

This is not the word Margaret would have chosen, but she holds her tongue. Despite her mother's tirade this afternoon, Margaret is silenced by an understanding of how much it would mortify Janice if the family drama ended up in the paper. And publicists aren't to be trusted with discretion. Los Angeles was lousy with publicists, pretty young celebrity parasites with their botoxed brows and carb-free diets who made their living lying to the papers. Bart had a publicist, a girl named Bunny who called Margaret "Meredith" and specialized in getting items planted in *Teen People*.

"Absolutely," Margaret lies. "We're just thrilled."

"Tell him I say hello. I saw him at a conference this spring," Kelly continues. "Though I'm actually on maternity leave right now. We just had our first baby—Audrey, four months old. Pretty difficult to think about the wi-fi market when I've got a baby grabbing for my boob—pardon me, but it's the truth—every twenty minutes. Thank God we found a nanny so that we could get out and have some mommy-daddy time, isn't that right?" She squeezes Duncan's hand and Duncan shakes his head briefly, as if trying to focus, and smiles again. He looks like he hasn't slept in months. "We were dying to see a movie. Didn't you love it? *Thruster*?"

"It was great," manages Margaret.

"I'm such a fan of Ysabelle van Lumis. And that guy Bartholomew Whatshisface? What a hunk. I'm a sucker for a British accent. Sorry, Duncan!" She pokes him in the ribs with a French-manicured finger. Duncan doesn't seem to notice; he looks like he's sleeping standing upright.

"Actually," says Margaret. And then—the words seem to fall

out of her mouth without her even thinking about it—"Bart's my boyfriend."

"Ha ha—no, he's mine! I called him first!" Kelly says. Then, seeing the pained expression on Margaret's face: "You're serious?"

"Oh, it's nothing," she belatedly demurs.

Kelly's eyes go big. "I mean . . . wow, Margaret. That's just amazing. I had no idea. You're dating a movie star!"

"Yeah, well," says Margaret awkwardly. She eyes the exit behind Kelly's shoulder, wondering if she can make a run for it without looking like a total moron.

"Look at you, living the glamorous life! I'd *heard* you were in L.A. And here I was just going on and on about myself. So sorry; I do that sometimes, you know? They say it's such a bad thing for a publicist to do. We're supposed to be zip-lipped. Wow. Bartholomew Whatshisface. I swear—Duncan, everyone always said that Margaret was going to *be* someone, and we were right. . . . But, wait, why are you seeing the movie here? You must have seen it before, right? Oh, gosh—did you go to the premiere?"

"Um . . ." Kelly stands there waiting for Margaret to say something. Margaret, backed into a corner, hopes that if she says nothing, Kelly will shut up and move on.

Kelly has no such plans. "I want to hear all about what the *interesting* people do in L.A. I mean, what are *you* doing? I recall that my mom said that your mom had told her you were some kind of famous writer or something? You were working for some women's magazine, right? Was it *Vogue*? *Elle*? I'm so sorry, I can't remember."

"Well," begins Margaret. She sees an entire alternate reality materialize in her imagination: the award-winning magazine leading to a six-figure book deal; the fulsome profile in the pages of the *New York Times Magazine*; the couture dress worn on the red carpet of the Golden Globes, Bart on her arm; the sleek midcentury modern home in the Hills; the breezy, happy family vacations on St. Bart's, to which she is able to treat her adoring parents and sister as a Christmas present. It's suddenly too exhausting to contemplate lying anymore.

"Oh, Christ," she says, realizing belatedly that she is actually very drunk after all. "Here's the deal. Bart dumped me months ago, and I owe him twelve thousand dollars. My magazine—which, let's face it, was an outdated idea even when I started it—just went under, and never had more than fifteen thousand readers anyway. I'm a failed feminist academic, which I realize is something of a redundancy, and I've got a half dozen credit card companies after me. Did I mention I had to move back in with my parents? My father just called me a loser and tried to bribe me to testify against my mother, who, in turn, disapproves of everything I do. The only remaining person with the slightest modicum of respect for me is my fourteen-year-old sister, who doesn't know any better. Yet."

"Oh," says Kelly, and her hand clutches at her chest in a little spasm of surprise. "I'm so sorry. That's just terrible."

"Hey, that's why God invented alcohol," says Margaret, waggling the tequila bottle, which juts from her purse. She suddenly feels totally unencumbered, as if she's been carrying a boulder in her shoulder bag and only now thought to remove it. She laughs aloud, feeling the lightness—or is that hysteria?—in her throat. Why didn't she come clean sooner? It will feel *good* to become the object of Kelly's contempt. She sees the headlines Kelly will surely plant in tomorrow's tabloids: "Margaret Miller, Best in Class, Turns Loser Boozer!"

She thought she'd hit bottom already, but in fact here it is now. And it's exhilarating. She just doesn't care about what anyone thinks of her anymore—not the lactating good-girl classmate before her, not her judgmental parents, not Bart, not her semifamous peers, no one. She lifts the tequila bottle and gulps down a slug of amber heat. It lights her up like a 100-watt lightbulb. Fuck yeah.

Margaret defiantly waits for Kelly to retreat backward into the protective aura of her husband, who has just focused his eyes on Margaret for the first time. But to Margaret's disbelief, Kelly just inches in closer to her. She puts a hand out and touches her arm, leaning in so that Duncan can't hear what she's saying. "Hey, I've been there myself. Thank God for Percocet," she whispers, her dimples vanishing and her chin hardening.

Before Margaret has time to register her shock, Kelly steps back quickly and raises her voice back into its original brisk chirp. "We should go for a drink sometime and really catch up. I'll leave the baby with Duncan so we can have a girls' night. That okay, Dunc? Anyway, what I'm saying is give me a call, I'm happy to talk." She fishes in her purse and comes out with a business card, which she presses into Margaret's hand with an affirming squeeze. "Anything you need, I'm here. I mean it."

Margaret stands, turning the business card in her hand, as Kelly disappears from the neon-lit lobby into the darkness of the night, her shag bouncing, her weary husband trailing just a half step behind her. Echoes of booze burn in Margaret's throat.

She fingers the embossed lettering—"Kelly Maxfield, Public Relations Specialist"—before shoving the card into her purse, where it glues itself to the tequila bottle, which has spilled the last of its contents into an odoriferous puddle that drips slowly through the leather as she makes for the exit.

"smash!" this is what the sign at the front of the room says, and Lizzie can't help thinking that it's a weird name for the Friday night youth group at River of Life, but maybe she's missing something. Maybe God will smash you over the head if you sin? The Bible will smash your toes if you drop it on your foot by mistake?

The Bible Lizzie was given last week when she visited River of Life does not, however, look like a book that would smash much of anything, despite its heft. It is pink, for starters. With a photograph of three girls on the cover, girls in pastel sweaters who look like they just stepped out of a Noxema ad. They are laughing at something they have just read in the Bible (Lizzie flipped through quickly but has yet to find anything that makes her laugh out loud). Or perhaps they are just in a state of bliss. This, after all, is the name of the Bible: *The Bliss! Bible:* "A Bible for teens like you, written in language you'll totally understand!" Exclamation points feature large in the world of teen Christianity, Lizzie is learning.

The Bliss! Bible has not yet made Lizzie feel blissful, but she's hopeful. She kind of wishes the Bible didn't come with an ostentatious pink faux-alligator carrying case; but since the other girls display theirs as proudly as they would a Prada purse, she tucks hers under her arm rather than hiding it in her book bag. (The boys' version is blue; it features three white boys in hip-hop gear on the cover and is conveniently sized to fit in the rear pocket of a pair of baggy jeans.)

Smash! is held in a meeting room at the back of the church complex. There are no pews, nor are there chairs. Instead, the room is lined with acres of blue industrial carpeting and lit by fluorescent lights, and rather than a pulpit, at the front of the room, is a neon sign that says "Smash!" and a mural of a smiling Jesus—in a Roy Lichtenstein pointillism style—painted on the wall below it. A gold glitter drum kit is set up in the corner. On the opposite wall, a graffiti artist has rendered the phrase "God is Love" in bubble letters.

About a hundred teens sit cross-legged on the floor. Lizzie pauses in the doorway and considers where to deposit herself. Zeke Bint, who has begrudgingly obeyed his mother's orders and escorted Lizzie to Smash!, squeezes in past her and bolts for the front of the room. "Don't even think of sitting next to me, Miller," he whispers in her ear as he moves past. "I know all about you. Whore of Babylon."

"I wouldn't want to sit next to you if you were the last guy on earth," she says to the cowlick at the back of his greasy head. "You smell like dog turds." She is not disappointed by his lack of interest in being her church friend; she recognizes him as one of the losers who lurk lower than her on the social food chain. He is a mama's boy with halitosis whose companionship could immediately doom her ability to meet anyone of interest here. Especially if he tells them about her reputation.

When Lizzie first visited River of Life, last Thursday, she had half-anticipated a disaster, despite Barbara Bint's promises of abundant love. Zeke Bint, a class pariah for as long as Lizzie can remember, hadn't exactly been a promising introduction to the world of Christianity. In the car, she tried to distract herself from her growing dread by counting the number of times Zeke scratched his dandruff-covered scalp (twelve) before they arrived. The "introductory" meeting at the church was only half full and almost entirely composed of middle-aged women like Barbara Bint, who, from her position between Zeke and Lizzie, perched on the edge of the pew and underlined key phrases ("all of God's little creatures," "redeemed in His eyes") in the hymnbook with her index finger as she sang along. But there was free apple cider and cupcakes decorated with little crosses, and everyone seemed delighted to meet her.

The sermon was titled "Is God Forgiveness, or Is Forgiveness Godly?" "The forgiven who give their sinful lives over to God will be lifted up to heaven," the priest explained. And Lizzie envisioned herself rising, on some kind of ethereal elevator, up to a puffy little cloud in the sky. In a little white dress, maybe, with wings. Though she'd probably have to die first, wouldn't she? Would she still have to diet in heaven to be skinny? Probably not. It sounded pretty good.

But what clinched her return was when the priest mentioned the Friday night youth group, Smash! "I'd like to encourage the young members new to our congregation to attend," he said. "It's a real groovy time, lots of young people who love to make new friends, celebrating Christ's love. There's music, dancing, singing, movies."

Lizzie had imagined walking into a room of smiling faces— *new* faces, faces that weren't already familiar from Fillmore High. Faces of girls who would want to play makeover with her and go shopping and talk about boys, and faces of boys who would ask her out on real dates, dates where they picked her up in a car and took her to a restaurant and paid for her meal and didn't expect a blow job in return. Cute, stylish faces who wouldn't know that Lizzie had ever been fat, or unpopular, or the school slut.

Before Barbara Bint even suggested that Zeke take Lizzie to Smash!, Lizzie decided she would go.

But reality doesn't quite match her vision. There is no heraldic music greeting her when the doors to Smash! open, no new friends rushing to shake her hand. In fact, no one seems to notice her at all as she worms her way through the crowd. The teens are fixated on the front of the room, clutching their Bibles, whispering under their breaths ("Dylan is so . . ." "He says that Jesus . . ." ". . . heard he once hung out with Bono . . .") as they stare at the empty space below the neon sign. The air is crackling and bright with anticipation. Lizzie plunks down on a square of industrial carpet located inauspiciously in front of the drum set.

The buzz in the room stops abruptly when the music starts, a swell of hip-hop beats that thump the walls and vibrate the floor. "Yo, dawg, it's the dogma, rising up to teach ya, God is gonna love ya, Jesus gonna greet ya." The song rises to a bumping chorus that has a hundred heads moving in time— "Lift the Lord's name on High, He'll forgive ya 'fore you die!"—just as Pastor Dylan steps to the front of the room. He is wearing an Abercrombie & Fitch T-shirt with jeans and flip-flops, topped off with a trucker hat that reads "Come to Jesus" on the front. He's also wearing a hands-free microphone over his ear, and his hair, under the cap, is frosted blond. He holds up a hand, and the room bursts into cheers. The booming bass crescendos.

The pastor jumps up and down three times and pumps his hand in the air. "Are we feeling joy today?" he yells.

"Yes!" the room screams in unison, and Lizzie feels a bolt

of excitement piston through the center of her body. The scream echoes throughout the room. Her own peers didn't even seem this excited when Millard Fillmore High won the homecoming football game last year. She looks at the expressions of rapture on the kids seated beside her and sits up to pay closer attention.

All around her she sees beatific faces, other kids looking so *happy,* so *well adjusted*—like they'd ingested a quart of Wellbu-whateveritscalled before walking into the room. They gaze with serene smiles at the pastor, close their eyes in ecstasy as they listen to him; some even lift their palms up to the sky, as if M&M's are about to fall from the ceiling and right into their hot little hands. *I want that,* she thinks. *How do I get it?*

"Do we have God in our hearts?" Pastor Dylan continues.

"Yes!" the room thunders.

"Are we going to *smash* the obstacles that keep us away from God?"

"Yes!" Lizzie shouts with the teens all around her, picking up on the momentum. She longs desperately to feel what they are feeling, and as she screams at the top of her lungs she thinks she might be experiencing some of the elation she sees around her. A kind of giddy sensation. Or maybe it's just hyperventilation.

The pastor smiles and pumps his fist over his head. The teens in the room burst into whoops, which sounds like one of those African rain chants from the documentaries Lizzie sometimes watches on public television. They fall quickly silent when Pastor Dylan lifts a finger to his lips.

A pretty blond girl sitting next to Lizzie glances over at her and smiles. She wears tight jeans and a T-shirt that reads, in glitter letters, "Jesus Is My Sugar Daddy." She points her finger up at the ceiling, then gives the thumbs-up to Lizzie. Lizzie, thrilled to have been noticed, jerks her own thumb aloft in response, although she's not a hundred percent sure what she is approving. But she is feeling something, definitely, a warm fuzzy tingling in her nose. Maybe that's God.

Pastor Dylan waits until the hushing stops to begin his sermon. "Today, my friends, we're gonna talk about secrets," he says. "We all have them. Look in your hearts. You have secrets. You have these awful, terrible things that burn away at you, day in and day out, and won't let you sleep. And you think that if you just keep hiding them, they'll go away. But that's not going to happen. They'll just keep on eating you up, from the inside out, until someday in the future you will be as unattractive on the outside as you feel on the inside."

The pastor lifts his hand and points a remote at the back of the room. A screen comes down behind him, and the room goes black.

"Oooh!" the kids gasp, and begin to applaud.

Lizzie hears herself oohing along with them, letting herself dissolve into the unity of the crowd. She is one with them. Yes. God is smiling down upon all of them, her included. She claps her hands even louder.

The screen lights up with a projection from the back of the room. It's a montage of faces—black, white, Asian, Latino, unified in the fact that they all look totally fucked up. There's a photograph of a woman passed out in her own vomit; a young man missing his front teeth; a teenage girl with crossed eyes holding a crying baby; a young woman in a tawdry pink micromini with pustules all over her face; a teenage boy slumped in a wheelchair, drooling. The room gasps at each picture. The U2 song "I Still Haven't Found What I'm Looking For," plays over the film.

Pastor Dylan's disembodied voice calls out from the dark. "See these faces? These are the faces of the lost. Drug addicts. Criminals. Prostitutes. Gang members. They are people with terrible secrets that they keep bottled up inside. Sinners who haven't come to God. People who never acknowledged that

God's Son died for them in order to wipe their slates clean. And look what it did to them! See how ugly it makes them, how it rots not just the inside of their minds but their bodies too? Their secrets destroy them. They are lost."

He lifts his voice: "But you don't need to be like these people. It's not too late. God forgives all sins. You just need to make him your best friend. Tell him all your secrets, even the horrible, humiliating ones that sting. The stuff you would never, ever tell your mother. And you know what? If you promise never to do it again and start to lead a clean, good, Christian life, God will forgive you. He will *live inside you.* He will teach you the *power of love.* He will help you *never sin again.* And you can live a life of beauty, inside and out. Because guess what? He knows all your secrets anyway. He just wants you to come clean with him." Pastor Dylan pauses, and the room rustles quietly as the kids attentively absorb his words. Lizzie leans forward in anticipation. "Otherwise," the pastor says, pointing a finger at the audience and giving a beatific smile that reveals rows of perfect white teeth, "he's perfectly happy just sending you to hell. Up or down, guys. Heaven or hell. It's your choice."

The lights flicker back on and Lizzie blinks in the glow, puzzling through Pastor Dylan's words. She can't decide if they are ominous or promising. Does this mean she'll be ugly if she doesn't confess everything to God? Or that she'll be prettier if she does? If she confesses all the terrible things she did, will she, like, lose ten pounds? That would be awesome.

The pastor smiles, exposing even white teeth. "Okay!" he says. "Time to do some reading. Let's all open our Bibles to page 223, and we'll read James 5:15. It says: 'If you pretend that you're, like, totally sin-free, you're full of b.s. and God knows it. But if you go ahead and confess your sins, God will prove to be one righteous dude: He'll forgive you for screwing up and scrub all that nasty shizzle out of you.' "

The pastor stops and looks up. "Time for free prayer. Five minutes. Go for it!"

Lizzie glances around and observes a sea of bowed heads and twitching lips. The sibilant hisses of whispered prayers make it sound like she's sitting in a snake pit. She bows her head and stares at a small brown stain on the patch of industrial carpet in front of her and tries to focus. She wants to feel redeemed so badly, it almost hurts. It seems somehow too easy, just ask God for forgiveness, and she'll be happy and pretty for the rest of her life, and all her mistakes will disappear and everyone will love her. But how does she know if she's done it right? She concentrates very hard.

"Dear God," Lizzie whispers under her breath. She pauses. This does not sound right. It sounds like she's writing a letter. She tries again. "Hi, God," she says. This, she decides, is far too chummy. Who is she to consider God a buddy? After all, they have been acquainted for only a few minutes.

Still, that's what Pastor Dylan said she should do: "Think of Jesus as your best friend," the pastor had said. She closes her eyes, tries to imagine Jesus as a teenager she'd hang out with, but instead comes up with a cute blond guy who looks kind of like Justin, which is a little distracting. And so far, Jesus hasn't actually spoken to her, which makes it even harder to imagine him as a friend. Doesn't a friend need to, you know, actually hold up his end of the conversation? she wonders.

But she's willing to put these doubts aside if working really hard to be God's friend means that you get forgiven for everything and stop being a social leper. It would, she thinks, be a relief to know that someone knows everything about her and doesn't really mind how much she's fucked up.

The truth is that she has never really thought much about God. If anything, he—or, rather, He—has always seemed like some distant historical figure—like Alexander the Great or Attila the Hun—who existed only in musty old stories. The Bible read much like her Western Civ textbook, a dry listing of irrelevant old battles and pointless vendettas. When her mother dragged her to church on Christmas or Easter, she never bothered listening to the sermon. Instead, she would spend the hour filling in all the *e*'s and *o*'s in her songbook with a ballpoint pen.

This, she now recognizes, is a sin. And God doesn't really want to be best friends with a sinner. Or does He? It's all so very confusing. She'll have to go back to church on Sunday to get clearer on some of these details.

"God." No. "Lord." Yes, that's better; conveys a certain sort of respect for His authority. But saying it out loud seems awkward. She feels like she is talking to the carpet. She hates the scratchy sound of her own voice. And what if the blond girl sitting next to her hears her secrets? She glances over to see the girl bowed over, her glossed lips moving frantically.

She decides she will speak to God in her head. She tries again. *Lord. Hi, Lord.* Yes. That's better. *Your Lordness. I've done some really stupid things. I slept with a guy who I wasn't married to. Actually, a lot of guys. And I guess that makes me a fornicator. And I called Susan Gossett a bitch behind her back. I guess I'm supposed to love her, because You say I should love my enemies, but the fact of the matter is she's really hard to love. She's really hard to even like. I don't really understand why you—sorry, You—would love someone who is such a bitch, but whatever, if You say that I should like her, I guess I'll try.* She pauses. Should she have used the word "bitch"? Maybe she should take it back. But wait, if God can read her thoughts, then won't He know what she's thinking right now? This is harder than she'd thought. *So, I guess what I want to say is that I'm afraid that no one is going to like me ever again. So can You make people love me, please? I mean, maybe not Zeke Bint or Susan Gossett, but, You know, just a few cool people. Like the girl sitting next to me, maybe?* She pauses, concentrates very hard. Yes, she thinks, the tingling sensation in her belly is *definitely* God, hanging out inside her, waiting to hear what she has to say before He decides to take up residence. Or wait, is that her stomach growling?

And God? There's one more, kind of important thing . . .

The pastor claps his hands. "Okay, time's up. Now it's time for some friendship healing. Let's everyone go and make a new friend in Christ tonight. Then we'll rock out with some singing and finish up the night with chastity pledges. Okay?"

There is an audible rustling of denim as the teens in the room get up and begin to mingle. Lizzie stands and turns to the left, but the blond girl sitting beside her is already absorbed with the girl on *her* left. She looks to her right and sees a small Asian boy with metal headgear clamped around his head.

"Hi," she says, but the boy shakes his head frantically. She decides to try again. "My name is Lizzie," she says. "What's yours?" But the boy keeps shaking his head. He points at the headgear and rolls his eyes and grunts.

Lizzie hears a voice behind her. "His jaw was wired shut last week," the voice says. "He had this freaky underbite. They had to break his entire jaw and, like, weld it back into place."

Lizzie turns to see Mark Weatherlove standing right behind her, his hands shoved into the pocket of his hooded sweatshirt and his shoulders hunched forward protectively, as if anticipating a fist in his face. "Hi," he says. His voice somehow manages to catch on that one simple syllable and crack, a nails-on-chalkboard sound that makes Lizzie wince. Mark looks quickly down at the industrial carpet.

"Are you still mad at me?" he asks.

Lizzie's pulse quickens. "I'm not talking to you," she says.

"What are you doing here?" he replies.

She straightens her back and discovers that from her towering position on her platform sandals, Mark is fully two inches shorter than her, which means that she can actually look down her nose at him. "Learning about the power of prayer," she says. "Learning what it means to be a *good Christian.* If you know what I mean. Though I think you don't. What are *you* doing here?"

Mark shoves his hands deeper into his pocket. "I dunno," he says. "My parents make me come. They say it's a good place to make friends." He scowls.

"Well, you're not going to make one here," she retorts. "You're a total liar. I never . . . *did it* with you. Why did you write that on the wall in the locker room? Did you think it made you, like, cool to do that? 'Cuz it didn't."

"I'm sorry," he says. "I don't know why I did it."

"Yeah, well, considering that your mom's a lying bitch who stole my dad and ruined my mom's life, I guess it's not surprising that you're so lame. It must run in the family." Lizzie is thrilled by the acidity in her voice; she didn't realize she was this capable of cruelty.

"Yeah," Mark croaks. "I guess." He rubs at the corner of his right eye with the sleeve of his sweatshirt, but a tear slides out of the other and lands on the front of his sweatshirt.

Lizzie watches him for a moment, trying hard to sustain her self-righteous anger—why should she feel bad when *he's* the one who was such a jerk? But it mostly just feels terrible to watch him cry. Cruelty, she realizes belatedly, is not a very godly trait. *Sorry, God,* she thinks. Her stomach turns over in response. And suddenly she thinks she can *feel* everything Pastor Dylan was talking about, all that stuff about forgiveness, and how when God lives inside you He lets you experience love in a way that you never could before. Because there is something purple and swirling inside her, something like empathy, and she sees that she has the power to make the boy standing before her *feel better.* And it feels pretty good.

Thanks, God, she thinks. And as she says this to Him she realizes what should have been obvious to her weeks ago: Mark's mother has run off with her father, which means that he, too, has a broken home right now. Did Beverly move out of the house, like her dad did? Who is Mark living with? Who's taking care of him? *Who's doing the cooking?*

All of the pain of her own family situation comes flooding back. She swallows, hard, to keep tears from erupting. "Yeah, well, my dad's a bastard, too, I guess. Fuck them both."

Mark looks at her for a long minute, his nostrils flaring as he gulps down shaky puffs of breath. "Yeah," he says. "Parents suck. Who fuckin' needs them anyway."

Lizzie wants to give Mark a hug—he looks so sad and forlorn. She considers the other teens around them, who all seem so simply happy, like they don't have any problems at all, and then she looks back at Mark. He is probably the only person in the world who could possibly understand how weird her family is right now, and at that thought her own eyes spill over with salty, hot tears. Mark takes a half step toward her, and Lizzie manages a tiny smile.

"Okay," yells the pastor. Once again, the buzz of activity in the room ceases. "Before we move on, I want you to turn to your new friend in Christ and tell them one thing that you really like about them."

The spell is broken. Lizzie looks at Mark. "We don't really have to do this, do we?" she asks.

Mark shuffles backward again and shoves his hands deeper in his sweatshirt pocket. "I dunno," he says. "God might be mad if we don't."

Lizzie sighs. "Okay." She pauses and looks Mark up and down. Mark's acne has cleared up a lot, she observes, and when he looks up to meet her gaze, she notices, for the first time, that his eyes are the cool green color of the algae that sometimes grows in the neighbor's ornamental koi pond. "Okay. I like the color of your eyes," she blurts. She is surprised to see bright pink flares erupt on Mark's cheeks.

"Thanks," he mumbles. He stares at her and says nothing.

"Okay, it's your turn," she prompts him.

Mark puts one arm in front of his face and speaks into his sleeve. "Dinkaroolakootanlekulot."

"What'd you say?" Lizzie asks, instantly on guard. Was that some kind of insult? Did he call her a coot? A slut?

"Um," he says and steps backward again, so that there is a full arm span between them. His eyes dart around wildly, he clenches and unclenches his fist and then closes his eyes. "Ithinkyou're-reallycuteandIlikeyoualot," he whispers. And then he turns and bolts for the other side of the room.

Lizzie freezes, unable to move as she watches him flee. When the drums start up, just a few inches from her face, she feels like the hollow pounding is coming from inside her head. She tries to sing along with the band as they belt out a rousing rendition of a song called "Pumpin' Da Passion" but finds that she can't focus on the words. She completely tunes out the pastor's final sermon as Mark's words run through her head in a loop. "I like you a lot." No one has ever said that to her before.

When the chastity pledges are passed out, she considers the paper, which promises that she will never have sex again until she gets married. Her skin crawls as she remembers the surprising intimacy of flesh pressed up against flesh. The way boys looked at her in the kitchen. Can she really give this up forever? But then she remembers the electricity in this room around her, the potential of blond girls who smile at you (blond girls who would probably never approve of you having sex with six guys) and God (also not a fan) hanging out in your belly, making it feel warm and gurgly, and boys who tell you that you are cute, and she scrawls her signature. It seems a fair enough trade.

And she only barely remembers, before she leaves for the night, that she came here tonight with something on her mind that she really needed to bring up with God. As the kids around her begin to gather their backpacks and Bibles, and parents congregate outside the door to pick their children up, Lizzie bows her head again and hastily offers up one last prayer.

Hi again, your Lordness, she prays. *I got interrupted before—there's one more thing. Could you please make sure I get my period soon? It was due three days ago, and I haven't gotten it yet. Actually, I didn't have it last month either. I thought that maybe it was because I lost all that weight, I read on the Internet that that happens sometimes, but I'm not losing weight anymore—actually, I'm putting weight back on again. So I'm kind of getting kind of freaked out now. Can you, like, do something? I promise never to have sex again, seriously. Okay, thanks, God.*

With that taken care of, Lizzie jams her *Bliss! Bible* under her arm and goes out to the front steps of the church to wait for Zeke and Barbara Bint.

"i'm quitting swim camp," lizzie announces at breakfast the next day. She turns the page of the comics section and peeks out the corner of her eye in order to gauge her mother's response.

Janice is on delayed-reaction time. She stands at the stove, poking absently at an egg-white omelet in which she has just deposited a handful of what looks like weeds but which Janice has assured Lizzie are actually *herbes de Provence* and will be very tasty. With the other hand, she holds open a copy of *Paris Match,* silently mouthing words to herself as she stirs the coagulating mess. Lizzie wasn't aware that her mom ever *read* those stupid French magazines, which always have lame celebrities like Celine Dion on the cover and no pictures of Paris Hilton at all.

"Mom?" Lizzie says.

Janice starts. "What?"

"I'm quitting swim camp," she says again.

Janice turns and focuses on Lizzie, her eyes wide. "Now,

why would you want to do that?" she asks. She drops the magazine by the stove and sits down in the chair next to Lizzie, spatula still in hand. She cups her hand underneath the spatula to ensure that the eggy bits that cling to it won't fall. Her foot taps at the floor. "You love swimming. You're such a *good* swimmer."

Lizzie shrugs. "I'm bored," she says.

This is not entirely a lie, because Lizzie *is* utterly bored. But her boredom has nothing to do with swimming, because she hasn't actually been to swim camp in well over two weeks, not since she discovered the graffiti in the locker room. She has, instead, gone to the public library every morning to sit in the beanbags in the corner of the children's book section, devouring Danielle Steel novels and Snickers bars until it's three in the afternoon and time to go home. In this fashion, she has worked her way through *To Love Again* and *Toxic Bachelors* and *Second Chance* and a half dozen others, learning at least fourteen different euphemisms for the male anatomy (her favorite so far: "tumescent member," which aptly describes the way Max Grouper's fat little thing had appeared when they had sex in the guest bedroom while his parents were in Kauai). Sometimes she just sleeps in the beanbag all day; she seems to be exhausted all the time.

At first she thought that her absence from the swim team would be a temporary thing, that she was just skipping a day or two while she worked up her nerve to face Susan Gossett and the rest of the girls again. The day after she found the graffiti, she walked all the way to the front gate of the rec center before losing her nerve and fleeing. The next day she made it only to the end of her street before changing direction. The more she thought about it, the more terrified she became of facing a hostile group of classmates. After all, she had slept with some of their ex-boyfriends, and she could see clearly, now, the contempt they must have felt for her for the last few months.

She would hate her, too, if she were them. No wonder Susan Gossett had been so eager to share the news of her father's affair.

When Becky called a few days ago, asking why she was absent, Lizzie told her that she had come down with a bacterial virus and had been instructed to stay in bed for the rest of the summer. "I'm really contagious," she told Becky when Becky offered to visit, and thereby sealed her solitary fate. When Becky mailed her a stash of old *People* magazines and DVDs of Brad Pitt's entire filmography as a "get well soon" present, Lizzie was miserable. She wasn't just a slut; she was a liar and a bad friend, too. She prayed to God and asked forgiveness, but that didn't seem to help much either. Maybe you have to reach a certain threshold of prayer—kind of like a minimum balance in your checking account—before God starts responding?

Her initial plan was to just hide out in the library until the summer ended. But she's already worked her way through every Danielle Steel novel in the library's collection and the thought of starting on Judith Krantz brings up waves of ennui. She is getting bored of heaving bosoms and throbbing manhoods. (Would God approve of Judith Krantz? Should she be reading the Bible instead?) Her back is stiff from the beanbag. Whatever her mother might say about being a quitter couldn't be worse than spending another day in the children's reading room, which smells like dirty diapers and pea soup.

"Well," Janice says now. She jumps back up to shake the omelet aggressively. "Do you want to do ballet again instead? I could see if they'll take you even though the summer courses are half over."

"I hated ballet," says Lizzie.

"Ballroom dancing? Language camp?" asks Janice. She pokes and scrapes and jiggles.

Lizzie sighs. She knew this wouldn't be easy. She realizes, with sudden terror, that if she's not careful she'll end up back in elocution and etiquette courses, doomed to a summer with the dread Mrs. Grimley, discussing whether "buffet" is properly pronounced "boo-fay" or "buf-fay." She shivers.

"Actually," says Lizzie, "I really want to focus on SAT prep. I picked up some workbooks in the library. You know, if I'm going to get into a good college, I have to start studying the SATs now. To make up for my grades last quarter."

Janice leaves the stove and presses a warm palm against Lizzie's forehead. "Well, you don't have a fever," she says. "Is this my Lizzie, offering to do extra SAT prep? I didn't realize you were already so focused. Isn't it a little soon? Though I'm not going to stop you. Do you want to start visiting colleges? Your father and I could take . . ." Janice's jaw freezes. "I mean, maybe your sister and I could help you plan a research trip for this fall."

"Sure," says Lizzie, feeling guilty about yet another lie. She hasn't thought about college at all. "That would be nice." But the mention of her father seems to have already brought the discussion to a halt. Janice turns the spatula in her hand for a moment, staring at it as if it were a mysterious alien object, and then, with a jolt, jumps up again to check the omelet.

"Shoot," she says. She pokes at the browned eggy mess. "I didn't turn it in time. It's ruined. I'll make you another."

"That's okay," says Lizzie. "Can I have bacon instead?"

Janice looks at her strangely. "What about your diet?"

"I'm quitting my diet, too," says Lizzie, emboldened by her victory. And it is to Janice's credit that she opens her mouth but pauses, and says nothing, before she shuts it again and yanks open the freezer door to retrieve a slab of bacon.

there isn't all that much more to do at home than there is at the library. Up in her room, Lizzie sits on the lavender pile rug with a pair of tweezers and plucks the hairs, one by one, out of her legs. Today she is focusing on a patch just below her knee, one where the hair has begun to grow back in after its last plucking. She tugs at the baby-fine brown hairs, eyes watering slightly at the pain. A good one is one that comes out with the root still encased in a gooey rim of flesh.

Until last year, this was her favorite pastime, though she dropped the habit once she took up swim team. Now that she has endless hours to fill, it seems a good enough way to kill the day. She knows that this self-abusive hobby would cause assorted school psychiatrists no end of alarm, but she has always found it meditative. Here, with the door closed and her stereo cranked to top volume ("You told me you loved me. . . . How could I break your pretty little heart?" croons Bobby Masterston, her favorite singer), she can empty her head of the abstract dramas that have no tangible resolution—the fact that her period has yet to arrive, the graffiti that's still on the wall of the boys' locker room, the increasingly manic mother in a domestic frenzy downstairs, and the father who seems to have vanished off the face of the earth. The fine point of loneliness that needles at the center of her chest. Each hair extracted is a step toward a finite accomplishment: total denudation. And then it will grow back, so she can do it all over again.

Her bedroom is purple, a half dozen shades of it, from the deep purple velvet curtains over the windows to the purple striped bedspread to the artfully coordinated floral pillows printed with lavender blooms. Lizzie hates purple. Unfortunately, she did not hate purple when she was seven and requested this as the color of her bedroom in their new house. Her mother obliged, and now Lizzie's *House & Garden* bedroom thwarts her every attempt to assert her personality upon it. She cannot tape her Brad Pitt posters on the walls, because this might make marks on the purple floral wallpaper. Pushpins are strictly forbidden. Books and CDs are artfully arranged on the bookcases—any errant tomes are reordered every time her mother comes in to clean—and nestle next to the bowl of dried lavender blooms and the unopened SAT prep booklets (just in case her mother checks).

Lizzie is torpid in the grapy maw, so listless that she can't muster the energy to do anything but pluck the hair from her body. She feels, for the first time in months, fat and lazy—the combination of quitting the team and her secret Snickers habit seems to already have had an effect on the size of her stomach, which is once again creeping over the waistband of her shorts. At least, she hopes that's why she's getting fat. The thought that pregnant women also put on weight flickers across her brain. She sucks in her stomach, making the roll of flesh vanish, then tugs a particularly thick black hair out of her knee and examines it. She scrapes at the bits of flesh still attached to the root, then wipes it off on the bedspread. The skin on her knee is pink and raw-looking.

She thinks of Mark Weatherlove. Should she call him? She wants to call him. But why? What would she say? What did that mean anyway—"I think you're really cute?" Does he mean it in an "I'd like to date you" kind of way or was it more of a polite, friendly kind of thing? More to the point: Does *she* think *he's* cute? She has never really thought about it. He has never really seemed to be the kind of guy to think about. She has known Mark Weatherlove since they were both at Mrs. Kraus's nursery school together, but they have never been friends. He was always part of the game geek squad, those scrawny boys who sit on the lawn at lunchtime and read video-game magazines and brag about how they've jacked the video cards on their desktop setups in order to increase their respawn rates in Half-Life 2. At the obligatory neighborhood barbecues, Mark would usually just sit inside and fiddle with his Game Boy, no matter how much his mother nagged him to come out and play. Once, Lizzie recalls, he tried to show her how to play Super Mario 4, but she was more interested in the contents of the buffet table than in saving a digital princess from a bunch of gorillas.

She used to think that Mark Weatherlove was an antisocial dork; now she wonders if perhaps he was just shy. She thinks again of the way he turned bright pink when he told her she was cute. She's never made a boy blush before. She didn't even know boys *could* blush. Maybe she will call him, to apologize for calling his mom a bitch.

Lizzie puts down the tweezers and picks up *Us Weekly.* She devours the glossy photographs of the "Stars Are *Just* Like You!" pages—her favorite section, which shows teen starlets with pimply skin pumping their own gas and buying Dr. Scholl's foot powder—and lands on the gossip section. Halfway down the page, she stops abruptly. She examines the photo, reads the caption, and then examines the photo again. It shows Lizzie's favorite star, Ysabelle van Lumis, exiting a white Bentley outside a Hollywood restaurant. In one hand she is clutching a gold Fendi purse; her other hand reaches behind her to grasp the hand of a gruff-looking man, cigarette hanging from his teeth, who peers out from the depths of the Bentley's back seat. The picture is blurry, but Lizzie recognizes him instantly: It's Bart.

"Ysabelle van Lumis has a hot new man," the story reads,

> in Brit Bartholomew Johnson, former *Fahrenheit 88* hunk
> and her costar in the new action thriller *Thruster.* Our
> Hollywood spies have seen the happy couple canoodling at
> My Pilates Body and buying nonfat green tea Blended
> Freezies at the Coffee Explosion. . . . Word is that Johnson
> has even moved into Yzzie's six-bedroom mansion in
> Malibu! Is the new 5-carat pink diamond on her right hand
> a gift from her new love? "I wouldn't be surprised if it's an
> engagement ring," says an insider. "It's a whirlwind
> romance!"

Lizzie is outraged. Poor Margaret—here she is, home taking care of her family in a time of crisis, and Bart is cheating on her. The jerk.

She hesitates for only a minute before deciding that Margaret needs to know—*this second*—exactly what's going on behind her back. Margaret will show Bart a thing or two. Maybe she'll get on a plane and go kick his ass. Lizzie envisions her sister driving to Malibu with a righteous fury, screeching to a halt in front of Ysabelle van Lumis's Greek Revival mansion, and storming up the steps. And then she'll walk in on Bart and Ysabelle drinking Cristal half naked in bed, and she'll throw a bucket of ice water over the both of them, and stalk out. Ysabelle's hair will get soggy and she'll scream like a baby. And then Bart will realize that Margaret is such a badass that he never should have fooled around on her and he'll race after her. There will be a high-speed chase through the hills of Malibu until Margaret comes screeching to a halt—maybe because there are sheep in the road?—giving Bart a chance to catch up. And then he'll fall to his knees and apologize and they'll kiss under the setting sun and then Margaret will bring Bart up to Santa Rita to see her family and they'll all go out to dinner at the Fountain. And everyone in town will marvel.

As Lizzie bounds down the hall to Margaret's room, the *Us Weekly* rolled tightly in her fist, she admits to herself that she thinks it's pretty cool that her sister's boyfriend would cheat on her with a huge Hollywood star. It makes Margaret seem even cooler. Someday, Lizzie thinks, she'd like to date someone who also dates huge celebrities.

She throws open the door to her sister's room to find Margaret dead asleep on her bed in the middle of the day. An open book—it appears to be Lizzie's freshman English copy of *The Catcher in the Rye*—lies on the bed beside her. Lizzie sighs. Margaret has spent the better part of the last week sleeping and drinking beer. She barely leaves her room at all except to eat, and even then she never has dinner with Janice or Lizzie anymore. She just eats in the living room by herself, in front of the TV. Lizzie wonders if Margaret is sad—maybe she has already heard the gossip?—and, for a minute, considers whether this is such a good idea.

No. Margaret needs to know. And Lizzie will be there to console her. She slams the bedroom door shut, waking Margaret up. Her sister jolts upright in bed.

"Wha?" she says. "Lizzie, I was sleeping."

"I have some bad news," Lizzie says, as gravely as she can. She throws the open *Us Weekly* onto the bed, letting her hand linger in the air for dramatic flair. "Look."

Margaret grinds bits of sleep from the corners of her eye with the edge of her thumb. "Jennifer Lopez is pregnant?" she asks.

"No," says Lizzie impatiently. "Below that."

Margaret stares at the page in silence. She slumps in her wrinkled sundress. "Oh," she says. "Right."

"That's your Bart!" points out Lizzie.

"I know," says Margaret. "He's dating Ysabelle van Lumis." She tosses the magazine down on the floor and falls back into the pillows. She yawns.

Lizzie is appalled by her sister's lack of vindictive fury. Isn't Margaret supposed to be jumping from the bed, screaming and yelling and wailing in rage? "He's cheating on you, Margaret," Lizzie points out gently, just in case Margaret doesn't get it.

"He's not cheating on me," says Margaret. "We broke up months ago."

"Oh," says Lizzie. She looks down at the page again and watches her romantic revenge movie fade to black. No credits, not even a blooper reel. "Why did you pretend you hadn't?"

Margaret sighs and screws up her shoulders. "Oh, you

know. I didn't want everyone to make a big deal about it. Our mother, in particular, would have gloated."

"But you could trust me, Margaret! You could tell me anything! Maybe I could have helped you work things out with him!"

"That's sweet, Lizzie. But you're fourteen. I'm not sure you would have had a whole lot of context on the situation."

Lizzie stares at Margaret uncomprehendingly, wondering who on earth this cynical stranger sleeping in her sister's bed might be. What has she even been *doing* here for the last month, anyway? She views her sister in a completely new light, as if someone has just flipped the world upside down: Her sister is not enviable, living a fast-paced glamorous life in a city far away; she is not the savior who is going to help fix their family; she is not even that good of a friend. She is actually (Lizzie sees now) a seemingly underemployed, secretive know-it-all who never includes Lizzie in anything. It feels like the air in the room is hissing out, leaving Lizzie deflated and flat. She looks down at the pink raw skin on her legs. "I'm not a *child,* Margaret. You don't need to act so *superior.*"

"Aw, Lizzie," says Margaret. She reaches out from the bed and pats Lizzie on the shoulder. "It wasn't anything to do with you. I just didn't feel like talking about it. I needed to go through my own internal grieving process first, you know?"

"No, you lied," says Lizzie, and yanks her arm away from her sister's patronizing touch, finding herself unexpectedly quite angry. "You know what you are? You're a total faker, Margaret. And you know what? I don't even like your magazine."

"Oh, Christ," says Margaret, flopping back down on the bed. The *Us Weekly* riffles in the breeze from the open window. She talks to the ceiling: "I can't believe that even my little sister hates me now. It's just all too hilarious." But she doesn't sound amused at all.

"Don't take the Lord's name in vain," Lizzie says, already feeling guilty about having been so mean to her sister, despite how pissy Margaret is being. She thinks of M&M's pouring from the ceiling into outstretched palms—that's what she wants. "You should pray to God. That might make you feel better. Or I could lend you my Bible."

Margaret stares at Lizzie in disbelief. "You're kidding, right? Your Bible?" She opens her mouth to say something, then stops. "You know what, I don't even have the energy to ask."

Lizzie watches her sister lying on the bed for a long while, feeling decidedly queasy. She thinks of Pastor Dylan and the way he stood there, so confident, at the front of the room, dispensing grace and mercy and love to his gathered masses. She squinches her eyes tight and focuses very hard, trying to feel the God light in her belly. There. There it is. A hot little spot beneath her belly button. When she opens her eyes again, she is dizzy. The room seems to spin slowly around her and her sister, who still lies there on the bed as motionless as a corpse; it's as if the entire universe is rotating around just the two of them.

"I'll pray for your soul," Lizzie says. "Even though you totally suck."

the invitation for the annual summer silent auction at the golf club arrives on a sticky August morning, only four days before the actual event. Janice stands in her spotless hallway fingering the embossed envelope, feeling strangely jolted by this message from beyond her walls. She hasn't been to the club in almost six weeks. Ensconsed as she's been in the house, she has forgotten all about the party, usually the highlight of her summer. So it is only now that she realizes that she wasn't asked to be the auction host, for the first time in six years, and feels it like a slap to the face. *Une gifle en pleine figure.* Perhaps it was just an assumption on the part of the club's social committee, a delicate maneuver around her perceived grief, but Janice can't help suspicion from settling in. Is she being publicly ostracized? Did Noreen's rumor about James spread even further?

She will not let it deter her; Janice feels invincible. Just a quick visit to the ladies' room is all it takes to conquer another six hours (actually, more recently, four; sometimes three). She's even started to run out of household projects—having already given the wedding silver a really thorough polish, organized the books in the study by color and genre, ironed every napkin in the linen closet—and now, sometimes, she itches to do something beyond the boundaries of her home. The boundaries of Santa Rita, even. The other night, she looked up airline prices to Morocco after reading a story in *Departures,* although she didn't go so far as to purchase a ticket. It was enough just to know that she had considered it.

James continues to arrive on Tuesdays and Fridays, his glove compartment a treasure trove of clear plastic baggies. He says nothing more about cutting her off, and she, in turn, brushes away any further thoughts of firing him. Yes, yes, his presence on her property is risky—*Lizzie,* she remembers sometimes, *they could take Lizzie*—but she cannot seem to let James go. Where else would she get It? She fantasizes about buying a year's supply all at once and then sending him off until a less hazardous time, but this is implausible. (The cash outlay would be far too large, at least until she wins her case against Paul, and what if they are monitoring her bank account?) Her blood surges at the sound of his truck in the driveway; a whiff of chlorine makes her light-headed with anticipation. She is so *alive,* which just goes to show how dead she had been for so many years without realizing it.

Still, Janice senses the wolves outside, circling her house, waiting for her to make a fatal mistake: the lawyers, and Paul, and, now, the credit card companies pursuing her daughter. The phone rings constantly with collection agencies calling for Margaret, who has stopped answering the phone entirely. Instead, Janice takes down alarming messages in all capitals that she hopes convey to Margaret the urgency of the situation. She leaves these on Margaret's bed or tucks them under her door:

"MASTERCARD TWICE—WOULD LIKE YOU TO CALL THEM BACK IMMEDIATELY"; "COLLECTION AGENCY/VISA: WANT TO TALK SETTLEMENT"; "AMEX: HAVE YOU CONSIDERED CREDIT RATING? 1 WEEK TO PAY MINIMUM BALANCE, THEN THEY WILL PURSUE LEGAL REMEDY."

When Margaret first told Janice that she was behind on her credit card payments, Janice assumed it was a manageable sum. Ten thousand dollars, maybe—nothing insurmountable. But then Janice answered the first call, and the second, and the fifth. She has done the math, by this point, and has totaled up a sum of over a hundred thousand dollars. The figure seems implausible. Margaret had mentioned financial problems with *Snatch* but this, *this* feels so much bigger. She is horrified by her daughter's situation—hadn't they always told Margaret to pay her balance off immediately?—but the clawing avarice of the collection agencies also brings out Janice's most protective instincts. How could her straight-A daughter have gotten herself into so much trouble? Janice knows that she should feel the helium lift of victory—she was right, right about the prospects of that magazine, right about Margaret's misdirected career path, probably even right about Bart too—and yet she can't derive any satisfaction from this knowledge. Is her daughter's irresponsibility a result of her own failings as a parent? She is aghast that her daughter would have concealed her situation, would have put herself at the mercy of these sharks rather than turning to her own mother for help. This wounding realization—that her daughter didn't want her around in a time of crisis—is what deters Janice from just outright offering to help Margaret pay off her debts; that, and the fact that unless the lawsuit is settled in her favor, she doesn't have a hundred thousand dollars in cash to give Margaret anyway. Yes, she could pay off the minimum balances to keep the collection agencies at bay—but would Margaret even let her do that?

Somehow, she doubts it. Otherwise, what can she do? Nothing except take down the messages, each one noted in slightly larger letters than the last.

Margaret appears to be doing nothing to address her situation, either. Since their fight about the Gossetts' dog, Margaret has been downright petulant—drinking beer in the middle of the day, spending hours in her bedroom with the door closed and the music loud, reading Lizzie's trashy magazines out in the garden. The only person her elder daughter speaks to anymore is James, which causes Janice no end of concern. Sometimes, Janice spies on them through the blinds as they chat by the pool. Once, Janice was convinced that she saw Margaret follow James back toward the pool shed. Could he be giving Margaret It, too? The thought appalls her, but she can tell from Margaret's behavior that this is not the case. If anything, Margaret seems to be sleeping even more than she did at the beginning of the summer.

There are so many questions Janice wants to ask Margaret: What happened to *Snatch*? How did she end up so deeply in debt? Does the fact that Bart hasn't called once mean they've broken up? What is she doing out there in the shed with James? But Margaret's confession about her poverty and Janice's residual anger about the dog-walking mess have, together, broken apart some tenuous peace, so that Janice is now left distant, watching her daughter drift away on an invisible tide. Margaret no longer talks about assisting Janice with her lawsuit. In fact, she no longer talks to Janice at all, whereas Janice communicates through stiff, inch-high capitals.

And now this, from Janice's friends at the club. She looks down at the invitation and realizes that it has been addressed solely to "Mrs. Janice Miller." It should hurt to see that but, oddly, it doesn't. Yes, she feels more utterly alone than ever before in her life, but is it so bad? No, not at all. In fact, her fortress of solitude is what makes her feel safe, untouchable, removed from the grasping fingers of useless emotion. She is fine as long as she has *It,* the icy bright powder that lights up inside of her brain.

Of course she will go to the party, she thinks. She will prove to everyone that she is doing just fine on her own. *Better* than fine. She's terrific.

on the evening of the party, janice sets aside three hours to gird herself. She takes an hour-long soak in champagne bath salts and moisturizes with cardamom cream. She unsheathes a black Diane von Furstenberg silk wrap dress from a bag hanging in the cedar storage closet and freshens it up with a spritz of Evian spray. The special-occasion crystal-encrusted Ferragamo pumps are exhumed from their tissue-lined tomb on the closet shelf. From the safe in the floor of the linen closet Janice lifts the Tiffany necklace from its velvet box, a Christmas gift from Paul a few years back, and clasps the cold circlet of diamonds around her throat.

Standing before the mirror, she is pleased with her armor; the dress hangs on her a bit more than she remembers—well, she has lost weight!—but it shows off just the right amount of leg and cleavage. The wreaths of black exhaustion under her eyes are another matter; they require two coats of foundation to conceal. Her pupils have shrunk to pinpoints; the irises around them are enormous pools of fierce, furious blue. As she brushes on her mascara, her hand jitters so much from It that she has to reapply the black goo three times. There is nothing she can do about the red welts on her forearms from her fingernails, but the sleeves cover those. When she examines the result in the mirror, she is satisfied. She does not look like a retiring divorcée. In fact, she looks better than she has in years. In the mirror she sees sharp angles, lean lines, a point to her chin that lets the world know she is not to be taken lightly.

Before she goes downstairs she pauses in her bathroom to do a quick line of It for extra fortification, tilting her head back to enjoy the tickle in her throat, and stashes the baggie in the lining of her Judith Leiber clutch, just in case.

as she enters the kitchen, she sees lizzie sitting at the island eating a bowl of Corn Pops for dinner. Lizzie is clearly once again losing her battle with obesity, and Janice's first impulse is to blame Paul for this, for upsetting a kind of precarious balance in their daughter's metabolism. One step farther into the kitchen and she realizes that a boy is perched on the bar stool next to Lizzie. Janice stops, mid-stride, as his face comes into focus. It is none other than Mark Weatherlove, Beverly's son, eating a bowl of sugary cereal with a spoon—the good wedding silver, the handles engraved with the Miller family initials. The logic of this stumps her: her best friend gone, and yet her son inexplicably here.

She stands there, taking in his alien presence in her kitchen, trying to grasp what it might portend. Lizzie and Mark have never been particularly friendly, a fact that she and Beverly delicately used to avoid mentioning, each convinced it was *her* child that was shunning the other's less socially apt one. Now she wonders whether Beverly has sent Mark as a spy. Is he here to find out whether Janice is still consorting with James, information that he will pass on to his mother, who will deliver it to Paul? (*Wolves! The wolves are in the house!*) Or perhaps he's looking for legal documents? She glances around the room, trying to locate any legal papers she might have left sitting around, but the counters are still sparkling and bare from her cleaning last night. The paperwork is all filed in a drawer in the study.

She examines Mark, taking in the dirty sweatshirt and the

scuffed tennis shoes. He sees her staring at him and jumps up from his seat.

"Hi, Mrs. Miller," he says. He grips the spoon in a fist.

The sanctity of her cloister has been disrupted; she feels his unwanted presence in every pore of her body. How can she get him out? He is here as Lizzie's guest. It would be rude to eject him—and word would surely get back to Paul and Beverly about that, too. Her limbs vibrate with tension. She longs to scratch at her tingling forearms, but the dress sleeves are in the way.

"Mark," she says, and her voice comes out chillier than she intended. "How are you."

This question seems to petrify Mark, who says nothing. Next to him, Lizzie shovels the last bite of cereal into her mouth and wipes the milk from her lips with the back of a hand. "Maphhffphhf," she says.

"I can't understand you with your mouth full," Janice says. She watches Mark lick a dribble of milk off the handle of his spoon—tongue running slowly across the embossed initials— and quivers with fury. "Why are you using the good silver, Lizzie?"

Lizzie stares down at her spoon. "Oh. It was sitting out."

"I was polishing it," says Janice. She shifts nervously forward and backward in her already uncomfortable heels. She yearns to snatch the spoon right out of Mark's sticky little fist. Mark just stands by the stool, as animated as a clod of dirt.

Lizzie puts the spoon down and finishes her cereal by tilting the bowl up to her lips and gulping down the syrupy milk. "We gotta go. We're going to smash," she says.

"Smash what?" Janice says, alarmed. Smash? The china? She looks around her for breakables.

"Smash, the church youth group thingy," continues Lizzie. Janice is only momentarily relieved. Church? When she let

Lizzie go to church with Barbara Bint's son she had imagined
that it could be a healthy social environment where her daughter might make some friends. She had not imagined that those
friends would include Mark Weatherlove. Maybe the whole
thing was a conspiracy on the part of her enemies? Barbara
and Beverly and Paul and Noreen colluding together to drag
Lizzie to church, where Mark would befriend her and infiltrate the family? Did hapless Lizzie fall right into a trap? Or,
God forbid, has Paul brought her in on his plot?

She shakes her head. No. Of course that's not it. Mark is
just a boy. A child, like Lizzie. He is probably just as nervous
seeing her as she is seeing him. She remembers his bleary face
at the door of the Weatherloves' house the day Paul left her and
feels a pinch of remorse. Surely, this hasn't been easy for him
either, poor boy. She gazes at Lizzie and wonders whether she
will someday be buying Lizzie self-help books so she can
"process" the divorce. But if Lizzie is traumatized, she is hiding it well—there have been no tears. Janice wants to believe
that through sheer will, she has held her household tenuously
together. She looks back at Mark and forces a cheerful smile.
And yet, the niggling voice at the back of her head says. *And yet.*

"Church. Well," she says. "You kids say hello to God for
me, okay?"

Lizzie looks Janice up and down. "You look pretty," she
says. "Why are you so dressed up?"

"I'm going to the silent auction at the club," she replies.
Mark Weatherlove drops his spoon with a clatter. The piercing
ring of silver hitting tile makes Janice's teeth hurt. There will
be a dent. Mark scrambles to pick up the spoon, stands up,
and avoids Janice's gaze. He carefully wipes the spoon on his
jeans leg and examines it.

"The party at the country club?" he says.

"Yes," replies Janice.

"Oh," says Mark. He looks green.

Janice wants to tear herself away, but remains rooted in place. Mark has inside information, she realizes. Her mind reels with the questions she wants to ask him: Is your mother still living at home? Has she moved into the Four Seasons with Paul? Do you see Paul a lot? At all? How is your father taking it? What does your mother say about me? Does anyone say anything about me at all? Do I even exist anymore, or have I vanished entirely into an imaginary world of my own design?

But she says nothing.

There is the sound of footsteps behind her. Janice turns just as Margaret marches into the room, an *Us Weekly* under her arm. Janice watches as her daughter walks to the fridge, opens it, takes out a beer, twists the top off, and blithely pours the whole thing down her throat without even pausing for a breath. When she's done, Margaret drops the bottle into the garbage with an alarming crack, then takes another from the fridge. She turns toward Mark. "Wow, a visitor," she says. "We haven't had those in a while. Are you a friend of Lizzie's?"

Her daughter speaks! She moves! Janice is gratified by the temporary détente, but her relief is undermined by Margaret's strangely aggressive behavior and bedraggled appearance. Two beers? Is her daughter becoming an alcoholic? She longs to say something about that, but the weight of Margaret's question is still hanging heavily in the room. Lizzie shifts in her seat. "This is Mark," she says.

Margaret looks at Mark again and then recognition dawns on her face. "Mark *Weatherlove*?" she asks, her eyes darkening with animation.

Janice wants to blurt out *Yes! And using the good silver!* but she realizes that if she remains quiet and just watches she might glean valuable information. Lizzie and Mark look at each other, each waiting for the other to respond. Mark seems incapable of movement. Lizzie manages a cautious nod.

No one says anything. The only sound is a rapid tapping;

it takes a minute for Janice to realize that this staccato sound is coming from her own shoe, her bobbing foot having apparently become the one outlet for her body's pent-up energy. Margaret is still wearing that ridiculous dress, Janice notes. Her apparent inability to change outfits has gone beyond the merely unpleasant to the pathological. Is it a pointed message intended for Janice? Some kind of rebellion against her mother's standards of hygiene? A vengeful response to their fight? Probably all of the above.

Margaret glances at Janice, then shakes her head. "Hey, Mark, can you give us a minute? Family stuff," says Margaret, as Janice intently examines the texture of the Spanish tile floor. As she watches, it bows alarmingly, then flattens itself out again. She shakes her head slightly to clear her vision.

Mark nods and slides sideways toward the door. "I'll get the bikes, Lizzie," he says, vanishing into the front drive.

Margaret waits until the door has clicked shut before she speaks. "Jesus, Lizzie. If Mom's not going to say it, I will. Are you *insane*?"

"What?" Lizzie says, wide-eyed.

"Don't you realize there is a lawsuit going on here? That he is the son of"—she glances at Janice and lowers her voice—"*the woman our father left us for*? Didn't you think how it would make Mom feel?" She looks over at Janice and furrows her brow. "Are you okay, Mom?"

"I'm fine, Margaret," Janice demurs, vaguely annoyed by her daughter's infantalization but also surprised by her protectiveness. "It's fine."

In the meantime, Lizzie's face has turned purple. "Oh," she says. She looks at Janice, and the kicked-puppy expression in her eyes makes Janice wince. *Poor Lizzie,* she thinks reflexively, forgetting that just a minute ago she, too, had wanted to throw Mark out. "I didn't think it was an issue."

"Not an issue?" says Margaret. "Wow, Lizzie, you are just incredibly naïve."

Lizzie is on the verge of tears, and Janice can stand it no longer. "It's okay, Lizzie, we know you didn't do it intentionally," she begins.

"I didn't think he really cared about all that," says Lizzie. "I just wanted to make a new friend."

Margaret shakes her head. "Whatever you say, but don't you think the timing is a bit odd? I mean, what if Mark is taking information back? There's a lot of money at stake here, Lizzie. You have to consider how that affects people."

Janice is stunned by this validation of her own concerns and feels a moment of unexpected closeness with Margaret— is there a reconciliation on the horizon?—which is broken when Lizzie explodes from her chair in a tantrum.

"He's *not* doing that," she shrieks. "He *likes* me. God, Margaret, you're so mean. Not everyone in the world is out to get you. Don't you even want me to have, like, one friend? Or do you just want everyone to be as miserable as *you* are?" She trips as she gets up, sending the stool bouncing across the floor, and bolts out the kitchen door. It slams shut behind her. The wedding silver, lined up along the velvet cloth on the kitchen counter, shivers.

"Someone clearly hasn't experienced the ugly side of human nature yet," Margaret observes. "Oh well. Whatever." She shrugs, a blasé gesture that seems intended for no one but herself, and turns around to go back upstairs.

Janice is left standing in the echoing kitchen by herself, and despite everything she longs to call after Margaret. They can examine the collusions against Janice, parse this web of suspicious entanglements, discuss solutions to her daughter's financial problems. Perhaps Janice was too harsh with Margaret about the dog mishap; she'll gladly apologize, so that

Margaret will stay with her a minute longer . . . but Margaret is gone.

What does it all mean? Alone, her children scattered, she feels like she has lost her grasp on what, just a few minutes earlier, seemed perfectly aligned. It feels like too much, far too much, to even consider walking out to her car now, let alone drive it all the way across town and then spend three hours in the company of two hundred friends and acquaintances. Only now does it occur to her that Paul might attend this party too. With Beverly, even, judging by Mark's green face. But surely they wouldn't dare be so public, not so soon? She looks at the granite countertop, the silver stacked along its edge, and reaches out to straighten a few forks that have gone askew. She can see her face, reflected upside down, in a serving spoon. It looks like a Halloween mask, ghoulishly stretched, her mouth a gaping gash, her eyes smears of black. Shaken, she drops the spoon back to the counter. And then, quickly (before Margaret comes back downstairs) and furtively (ducking low, just in case Lizzie and Mark are loitering in the driveway), Janice snapes open her clutch. She extracts the baggie, taps a pile of powder down on her clean kitchen countertop, and uses a butter knife from the good silver to cut it up into a neat little line. As she sniffs it up, she can smell the Pledge she used earlier that morning to buff the granite to a shine.

She closes her eyes and visualizes the crystals floating through her bloodstream, tiny chemical hexagons of strength and vitality. She breathes deeply, a breath so clear and enriched that she can picture it filling her lungs, and then she opens her eyes, straightens her dress, and clicks firmly on Ferragamo'd heels out to the Porsche.

.   .   .

by the time she arrives there is already a pa-
rade of cars making their way down the oak-lined driveway that
leads to the club. The club parking lot looks like a luxury au-
tomotive dealer: Mercedeses, BMWs, Audis, Escalades, and
Navigators lined up in neat rows—even a Bentley, parked in
the corner far from the other cars lest someone dent it with an
errant door. She hands off her SUV to the valet.

Tonight, the old granite staircase leading to the front
doors of the club has been decorated with floral arrangements
of cabbage leaves and carrots in big woven baskets. The party's
theme is "Peter Rabbit," and the recipient of the money raised
by the auction will be a rabbit rescue organization. Janice
pauses by the door to read the placard: "Each year, millions of
bunnies are abandoned not long after Easter when families
discover that their new pets require as much work as dogs or
cats and don't lick or purr. Tonight, we raise money to help
rescue animals like Munchkin, a six-month-old French Lop
who was found in the trash, and Binky, an English Spot with
one eye who was recently mauled by a pit bull."

In the gardens behind the clubhouse, the adoption agency
has set up a white picket fence. Rabbits hop freely inside the
enclosure, tended by an elderly man dressed as Mr. McGregor; he wears overalls and carries a pitchfork. A hand-painted
sign hangs from the gate: "Adopt us!"

The party is already in full swing. Janice accepts a Garden
Shower—a green martini, tasting of kiwi—from a passing
waiter. She walks to the windows to look out at the display on
the lawn, smiling and nodding and exchanging pleasantries
with assorted club members along the way. No one seems dis-
turbed by her presence—in fact, quite the opposite. Noreen
Gossett courteously waggles her fingers at Janice from across
the room, where she's holding court with the Groupers, and
Janice manages a congenial nod in return. Joannie Cientela,

from her school fund-raising committee, waves at her from the grand piano. It's as if the events of the last six weeks had never happened, and for a moment, Janice wonders if maybe this summer has all been a fever dream.

She recognizes club members from golf foursomes, PTA meetings, tennis tournaments, the swimming pool. The room is thick with grace and manners, and Janice, relaxing, feels the synchronicity deep in her bones. To the manor born—she thinks of this phrase and is conscious that none of those around her were, and yet they all inhabit this room as comfortably as if they had been birthed in the back row of a Gulfstream. How quickly it becomes normal to own a house with a special room just for wrapping presents. How easy it is. And she's earned it as much as anyone.

The crowd seems to dance before her as she wanders through the room, each person in her path waltzing out of the way to allow her through. It is like flying through a cloud. The club president, Jim Rittenberg, grasps her elbow as she walks by and whispers in her ear, "You look fantastic, Janice. So glad you came. Hope you don't mind that we gave Noreen a shot at hosting this year. She's been begging to do it for years, and I thought you'd appreciate the break."

"Very thoughtful of you," says Janice, as she is borne away by the crowd. There is so much stimulation she barely knows where to look. She has been away for so long, too long. Why has she been hiding away at home? She sails through conversations, words sliding easily from her mouth as if she had never stopped socializing in the first place. The crystal seems to speed everything up, making her tongue capricious and spry; sometimes It speaks without stopping to confer with her brain first, and yet nothing inappropriate falls from her lips. She can turn her mind off completely.

She drains the last of her cocktail and takes another from a passing waiter as she chats with Steven Bellstrom about the new gymnasium planned for Millard Fillmore High. Partway through the second Garden Shower, though, she begins to feel flushed, perhaps a little too high, her voice a little too loud. She grows acutely aware of the glass in her hand. Every nerve in her fingers is conscious of the heft of the crystal, the moist condensation on the crown, the cramped position of her hand holding the narrow stem.

Janice excuses herself and goes to stand by the open balcony door, swallowing down the evening air. Her crystal clarity is vanishing, she realizes, replaced by an alcohol muddle. She breathes with an open mouth, hoping to get more oxygen into her cottony head. The evening air is balmy, not refreshing at all. Her ankle itches horribly, and she reaches down to scratch it, but that just seems to make it worse. The thought of another conversation about tennis camp or the last city council meeting or property values on the east side of town is suddenly unbearable. It hits her that she could leave right now—just walk out into the warm night without even telling anyone she's going—and she is shocked when this thought fills her with relief.

But she stays anyway, unable to take that leap. As she steadies herself against the doorjamb, she spots Barbara Bint making a beeline for her from across the room and braces herself.

Barbara arrives at her side in a nimbus of Trésor-scented poppy silk and swoops in for an air kiss, accidentally making contact and leaving a smear of her lipstick on Janice's cheekbone. Janice removes it with the palm of her hand.

"So good to see you here, Janice," says Barbara, leaning in to touch Janice's wrist. "I feel like I've been seeing more of your daughter lately than I've seen of you!"

The feeling of Barbara's hand on Janice's wrist is unbearable, like pins and needles. Janice takes a sip of her cocktail, dislodging Barbara's hand. "Right," she says. "The church. Well, she seems to find it interesting."

"You should be very proud. She's really devoted herself to

the youth group and so quickly!" Barbara leans in conspiratorially. "I think it's so important for our children to have spiritual lives. Kids these days are so . . . lost on their own, don't you think? What with all the terrible influences in contemporary culture. You know, I'm thinking of homeschooling Zeke next year. He needs to learn his morals along with his algebra. And maybe this is none of my business, but if we're going to be honest, so does your Lizzie."

"Lizzie's morals are just fine," says Janice. She glances out to the golf course and sees that the rabbits have somehow escaped their hutch. Dozens of bunnies are dispersing across the manicured green, hopping straight through the sand trap and toward the third hole. Mr. McGregor has thrown his useless pitchfork aside and is trying to herd the stray rabbits back into the enclosure. Noreen Gossett and a handful of women in cocktail dresses trip along after him, trying to help, but their heels sink into the grass. Noreen, her hair coming loose from its elaborate coiffure, lurches after a small gray bunny and falls on her knee in the grass, muddying her dress. Janice lifts her glass to her lips to conceal the smile at the thought of Noreen hosting the auction in a grass-stained frock. The bunnies vanish into the bushes.

"Well, I think you should consider it, at least. Have a talk with your daughter," Barbara says and straightens her shoulders. A queer expression slides across Barbara's face. Janice sees that Barbara is staring over her shoulder and, as black premonition prickles across her back, resists the urge to turn around. Barbara quaffs the rest of her mineral water.

"Hi, Beverly," Barbara says, her voice an octave too high.

The gracious smile on Beverly's face has frozen into a rictus of horror by the time Janice turns around. The two women are face-to-face, inches away from each other. Barbara has managed to melt away.

"Oh," says Beverly. "I didn't realize that was you, Janice. What a surprise."

"Hello, Beverly." Janice speaks before she is even aware what's coming out of her mouth, and wishes she had spent more time preparing for the inevitability of this moment. She doesn't have a clue what she might say.

Beverly recovers quickly, readjusting her face with a series of twitches until it settles back into a cordial mien. "I wasn't sure whether you'd come," she says, infuriatingly casual. "Considering."

The two women shift in their stilettos. Beverly looks devastating. Janice takes in, with dismay, Beverly's new hair color— a flattering golden brown—and fresh pageboy cut, the trim periwinkle cocktail suit that shows that Beverly has managed to lose a bit of weight, the blush of a tan, as if she just returned from a relaxing Mediterranean vacation. But something about Beverly feels foreign, as if she's just a caricature of the woman Janice used to know so well, not the real thing at all. She wonders if the Beverly who was her good friend—the person who brought Janice home-brined olives for her birthday, who watered her herb garden when they went on vacation, who was Janice's confidante about her distress when Margaret abruptly moved to L.A.—was ever a real person at all or just a serious misperception on Janice's part. And then, all at once, Janice is furious. It is marvelously freeing.

"You thought I would melt away and disappear, making it convenient for you to just take over my life?" says Janice. Beverly's chilling presence seems to have jerked Janice back from her muddled inebriation; she is sharp, focused. "Think again." The words snap like freshly starched linens, and Janice thrills to see Beverly flinch. Janice has never enjoyed fights, the way they seem to pry you open and expose your biggest weaknesses and most irrational impulses. She rarely fought with Paul. Their arguments were more of the passive-aggressive seething variety—her frustration revealing itself through nagging, a clawing desperation that she recognized in herself and hated, and his through total absence and workaholism. But now she itches for a good battle. She must have It to thank for this.

"I didn't intend to hurt you. You must know that," says Beverly, widening her eyes and blinking pleadingly. Janice wants to kick her.

"I don't know anything, Beverly," says Janice. "You didn't bother to call and tell me, after all."

Beverly pinches the bridge of her nose, a habit Janice recognizes from the tennis court—it is what Beverly does when she is concentrating on her game strategy. "You know I was having issues with Louis," Beverly continues, in lowered voice, "and then Paul and I were paired up for that golf tournament when you were in Indiana at your mother's funeral last summer, and it just happened. I couldn't bear to tell you, and of course I had no idea that it would be anything more than that week. But then, there were these *feelings*. . . . And I knew you weren't exactly in a happy state . . ."

Janice remembers, miserably, a conversation she and Beverly had not long before Paul left her, right here at the club after a tennis game. Beverly told her that sex with Louis had grown tedious, and Janice, flush with this confidence, described a recent night when she'd heard Paul masturbating in bed, right next to her, when he thought she was asleep. She assumed Beverly would share her disgust at the disconcerting fact that he would rather masturbate than wake her up to have sex and that he blithely *did it in the bed,* totally unconcerned about whether Janice would notice, but the look on Beverly's face was one of pity. Janice believed, at the time, that Beverly was pitying her, but now she wonders whether that pity was directed

toward Paul instead. And, worse, whether Paul had been thinking of Beverly.

"So," Janice says, "what you're saying is, you decided my
supposed unhappiness was an excuse to make me even less
happy?"

"Well," says Beverly, "I think you'd agree that something
had to change. To help you escape your claustrophobia."

"Claustrophobia?" The word throws Janice off, the phrase
triggering some sort of déjà vu she can't quite place. It hits
her, then, out of nowhere: "Escape this claustrophobia" is the
phrase Paul used in the letter he wrote to divorce her. God—
did Beverly help him write it? Or did he show her what he
wrote? The thought sickens her. Either way, it is incontro-
vertible evidence of their affair, of the fact of their *relationship,*
and for this she hates Beverly.

"I hardly think you're in a position to tell me what I need,"
Janice says, her voice rising. She can sense a stillness in the
ballroom, as if everyone is straining their ears to hear what
they know is a juicy conversation. The people within a few feet
of them are studiously looking away.

"I don't blame you for being angry," Beverly says, "I know
what I did, what we did"—Janice recoils at Beverly's use of
"we"—"is horrible. And I don't expect we'll ever be friends
again, but I do hope that we can be civil. For everyone's
sake . . ." She steps in a little closer and rests her hand on
Janice's forearm and Janice realizes that Beverly has actually
been anticipating this moment—that this is actually a *catharsis*
for her. Janice knows, without a doubt, that Beverly has been
practicing this speech in her head for two months, waiting for
the inevitable moment when they would run into each other at
Whole Foods or Neiman's. She jerks her arm away.

"Oh, can it with the sappy clichés, Beverly," she snaps. "I
have no intention of being civil to you and making you feel

better about yourself. I have no interest in you at all. I just hope that when Paul discards you like a past-due carton of yogurt, the way he dumped me, you won't come crying at my door, because I won't be feeling charitable."

Beverly attempts a furrowed expression of compassionate concern, but her frozen forehead—shot full of Botox—merely buckles peculiarly around the eyebrows. Janice thinks she can see Beverly mentally running through her lines, like an actor who has forgotten the sequence of his monologue. Janice looks around at the stiff backs of her club friends, who have been rendered motionless in their effort to pretend they haven't been listening. She is aware of the sweat beading up on her forehead, the burning itch that has blossomed on her other ankle, too. She doesn't feel centered at all. All she can think about is getting another line of It in her system.

"I'm done with this conversation," Janice says. She turns to make a beeline for the bathroom, but stops short and circles back to where Beverly still stands, looking lost.

"He's here, isn't he," she says.

Beverly opens her mouth, then closes it and nods. "He's in the Club Room," she says, her voice as flat as a spatula.

the only sound in the bathroom is the hum of the air conditioner. The room smells like lilies of the valley and clean cotton. Janice washes her trembling hands under the tap, presses her palms against the cool marble countertop, and then holds them to her hot cheeks. She is, she realizes, more than a little bit drunk. She envisions herself as the wobbly line that a child might draw with a sticky crayon. The thought of seeing Paul makes her queasy. Again she considers just giving up and slipping out the back door of the party.

But her racing pulse propels her forward. The metallic taste of victory is at the back of her throat. She has conquered

Beverly already, has channeled her self-righteous anger into a dangerous weapon, and now she feels ready to turn it against her husband. If she somehow perseveres and makes it through this evening, she will have proven something, although she can't put a name to what, exactly, that something might be. The alternative is simply to fade away and vanish, and she is not prepared to go out with a whimper. She is glad that she didn't flee earlier. She lifts a foot and scratches at her ankle furiously.

She double-checks that the door to the ladies' room is locked, then fishes in her purse for the plastic bag. A line of powder goes down on the marble. She pauses, taps at the baggie with a lacquered fingernail, and considers the wisdom of doing two lines. It is more than she usually takes, but just this one time it shouldn't hurt. Yes. If she is going to face Paul, she needs the extra boost to properly straighten out that wobble. She taps another fat line of powder out, nearly depleting the baggie. She will need to get some more. Tomorrow. Maybe after that she will finally fire James.

There is a knock at the door just as she's sniffed back the first dose. Janice nearly jumps out of her skin. "It's occupied!" she barks.

She flushes the toilet to mask the whoosh of air as she sucks the second dose up into her nostril, then runs the tap to complete the charade. The second line of It makes her eyes water and the tender linings of her nostrils burn, and then, within seconds, she can feel the room lift as if elevated on hydraulic springs, the previously imperceptible hum of lights rushing into a roar, the throb of the blood beginning to pump its furious circuit through her limbs. It makes her feel so alive—so *bright*—that it almost hurts. Christ, how could she ever give this up? *Nevernevernever,* her veins pulse in answer.

Janice studies herself in the mirror, looking for any visible flecks that might have clung to the inside of her nose, then flings the door to the bathroom open with such gusto that she accidentally knocks over the woman who is standing behind it, waiting her turn for the toilet. "Sorry!" she sings, barely registering the woman's astonished face, before she makes her way down the hallway toward the Club Room.

The Club Room was, at one point, the mansion's vast library, with fourteen-foot-high ceilings and a mahogany frieze carved with cherubim. Deep leather chairs and a red pile carpet fill the room. One wall of books has been removed to make way for a long polished brass bar; another went to make room for the cigar humidor. As Janice arrives at the door she can see a low cloud of blue-gray smoke drifting just over the heads of the club members.

Halfway into the room she realizes that the itching in her ankles has vanished; in fact, she can no longer feel her feet. She wonders whether the second line of It was, perhaps, a bit too much. Her mouth is sour, and she takes another one of those green martinis from a passing tray in order to wash it away. Janice can feel herself vibrating with intention. She sees herself at the center of the room, sending out waves of energy. *Nevernevernever,* her body throbs furiously. The faces of those standing around her shift in and out of focus. She can zero in on only one: Paul's. He stands directly across the room with a snifter of scotch in his hand, looking straight at her.

It seems to take ten minutes to cross the room to him, and yet she sees her journey only in flashes, as if lit by a strobe. There: Her hand grazes the back of a chair, hard, leaving her knuckles bruised and raw. There: Her hip knocks against Dr. Brunschild, who turns his head with alarm and then vanishes from her peripheral vision as she is propelled forward. There: the hand of the bartender, who rattles a silver martini shaker in time with the racing pulse in her temples. She can feel the symmetry of everything around her, each molecule in the room recognizing the larger purpose in her journey.

Paul watches her approach, his wary gaze like a beam, pulling her in. It isn't until she comes to a wobbly halt in front of him that she realizes she has no idea what she is going to say. She stands before him, hating him with such all-consuming rage that she cannot even form words to describe what she feels. And yet, at the same time, she is compelled to reach up and touch his face, feel the familiar papery patches of skin with her fingertips, touch the prickly hair on his earlobes that she knows so well. He stands only a few inches away, his shoulder close enough to rest her chin on, and she feels that if she were to break the barrier and reach out and touch him, somehow the physical contact might bring a melting end to all this incivility and ugliness. She tips forward, just slightly, in anticipation of this movement. But he takes a half step back, and in that motion she sees that it's far too late; he is already gone. That, in fact, he has been gone for longer than she can remember. And the momentary hope vanishes, leaving behind only the deep ache of loss.

She clenches and unclenches her fist, unsure if she will use it to punch him in the face or clutch at his blazer and weep. She had not anticipated that the purifying fury she experienced with Beverly would, with Paul, be so tainted by grief and remorse.

Paul speaks first. "Janice," he says, his voice strained and thin. "I thought you'd be here. Beverly said you wouldn't, but I knew you wouldn't miss it."

"Well, I'm so very pleased that after twenty-nine years of marriage you know me better than your new mistress does," she spits, involuntarily thinking of Beverly blithely using the term "we." Janice shudders.

Paul's broad chest rises and falls as he takes a long, deep breath. "How are the girls?" he says, maddeningly calm. "I saw Margaret last week—she was a mess. Someone needs to have a talk with her. I tried, but she wouldn't listen."

Janice is momentarily unmoored by the revelation of her

daughter's infidelity; the vista before her shifts as new alle-
giances and fresh betrayals spring up to block her view. She
can't get a clear grasp on the situation anymore—certainly not
on her apparently duplicitous daughter.

"Why are you pretending you care?" It takes a concentrated
effort to get the words out; she hears her own voice as if it is
coming from the end of a tunnel, echoed and diffuse. "Your
children seem to have fallen to the bottom of your priority list,
somewhere below getting your suits dry-cleaned and screwing
my tennis partner and attempting to blackmail me with custody threats."

Paul glances around him and lowers his voice to a near
whisper. "Janice, can we not? Please. This is not the time or
place. I see that you're upset, but can't you just be civil? I
highly doubt you want our friends and neighbors getting into
our personal affairs."

"I don't really give a damn," says Janice. She raises her
voice to make it that much more of a weapon. "*I* don't have
anything to be ashamed about. *I* did nothing wrong."

"Do I need to bring up the pool boy?" whispers Paul.

"You know that's baseless," she whispers back. (*Nevernevernever* she hears in the back of her head.) "Noreen won't back
that up. She lied. You have no proof. No. Proof."

Paul looks at her critically. "You're drunk," he says. "We
shouldn't be having this conversation. Let's leave this for the
lawyers."

"No," she says loudly, furious that he would try to push her
off, like a pest best removed by the professionals. "To hell with
the lawyers. I can't believe that in six weeks you haven't picked
up the phone to explain to me why you're throwing our marriage down the toilet. And I really can't believe that you would
try to screw me out of everything we built together and then
expect me to be decorous about it." The words are beautiful
and vicious as diamonds, but she can barely hear her voice

through the rush of blood in her ears. Her heart is beating much, much too fast. *NEVERNEVERNEVER,* it pounds. Sweat trickles down the side of her face and drips off her chin. The itching on her ankles is back with a vengeance. She has lost a critical sense of balance.

Paul winces, then glances casually around with a tiny smile flickering across his lips in a blatant bid to look natural. People are staring nakedly at them. "You're really going to regret this tomorrow unless you just take a breath and calm down."

"I am calm," she says, lying. In fact, she feels quite panicky, and she's finding it increasingly hard to string words together in a way that makes any sense. "But why should I be? It's everything we have. You are taking. It all."

Paul sighs. "You're exaggerating," he says. "The only thing I'm not giving you is Applied Pharmaceuticals, which I built without any input from you anyway."

"You never could have done it without me," she spits at him. "You think I enjoyed making small talk with the dull wives of your Japanese investors? You think I enjoyed playing the gracious hostess to boors like"—she glances around the room, picks out a venture capitalist who once told her a filthy joke at her own cocktail party, and points a furious finger— "like Mitch Villardi? No. My entire life was about supporting. Supporting yours. Who do you think packed your bags? Bags for your travels? And picked up your passport and did your laundry and coordinated your social calendar? And shopping and cleaning and the house and kids? All me."

"You *wanted* to do that," he says. "You *wanted* to be a wife and mother—you chose this life for us from the start. I never asked you to do anything."

"Like hell you didn't," she says. "That's just an excuse. It wasn't like that at all."

"Look, let's not retread the past," he says, pressing his temples with one hand as if trying to press away a headache.

"I'm sorry, but I can't help it that things changed for us. Finding someone else wasn't intentional on my part. But you're resourceful, Janice. You're going to be fine. Really, you are. It will probably be better for you in the long run."

She sees Beverly appear in the doorway of the Club Room, pause, then walk intently toward them. Her ankles threaten to give out altogether, and out of the blue she feels very cold. She clutches at her cocktail and tries to focus on the liquid in the glass. It changes colors as she stares at it, from green to blue to lavender. When she looks up at the people standing around her, the faces distort, like a blurry photograph. She slips to one side as one heel gives out under her foot.

"Are you okay?" Paul asks, looking concerned. He grabs her arm to pull her upright.

"You hypocrite," she slurs, wrenching herself away. In the electric space that opens up between them, for one fleeting instant, she sees her passage out toward a different world, one that is cruel and furious in its liberation. She pauses, struggling to come up with words that might express this feeling, but her mouth is numb and void.

"I think you've had enough to drink," Paul says, and reaches for the glass in her hand.

"I've had enough of everything," she says, and lifts her nearly empty glass to her lips. She tilts her head back to get the last drop and then, inexplicably, her head seems to keep tipping, and her torso follows it backward and then she's falling slowly through space. She seems to fall forever, long enough to feel the blot of numbness spreading like spilled paint through her head and body and limbs (*neverneverneverne*) and to wonder where the black came from, before she feels the pile of the rug scratching her bare neck and she passes out.

. . . .

later, janice will remember only static moments, like video postcards.

Dr. Brunschild, kneeling over her, peeling her eyelid back.
His fingers are cold and damp from his cocktail. "Passed out,"
she hears him say, as fragments of his sentences bounce in and
out. "Dehydrated, with a wild pulse . . ." She feels his hand
cradling the back of her head, cold water being poured down
her throat, and she chokes.

Paul and Beverly stand behind him, their faces blending
together into one; an audience of familiar faces behind theirs,
standing, gawking, mouths agape in wide O's. Their faces
swirl, wildly, as if painted by van Gogh. They whisper words,
the Greek chorus narrating her fate: ". . . spectacle of herself . . ." whispers Noreen Gossett, a delighted look of concern on her face; ". . . erratic behavior . . ." says Joannie
Cientela, clutching the pearls around her neck; ". . . drank at
least *four* . . . maybe *five* . . ." says Jim Rittenberg, brushing away
the broken martini glass with a toe; ". . . totally incoherent . . ." says Beverly Weatherlove, hanging on to Paul. Who
says nothing. His brow forked with fissures, his eyes fixed on
some point just beyond her body.

". . . needs help," says Barbara Bint, veering into view.
She bends over, takes Janice's hand. Janice feels the soft unex-
pected weight of Barbara's palm in hers, unbearably intimate.
"Someone help her. Poor Janice."

Dr. Brunschild waves them back with an impatient arm,
and they inch out of her periphery. Barbara's hand slips away,
leaving behind an impression of warm flesh.

It is easier to pass out again than to bear this pain.

when she awakens next, she is on her back in a
shower in the women's locker room, cold water raining down
on her from the adjustable-pressure showerhead. Needle-

sharp water hits her face. Someone is dumping a bucket of ice on her chest, which causes her to shudder in shock. She is still in her silk dress, which is drenched through, and the wrap has come half open, exposing her bra.

Dr. Brunschild's bearded face zooms into her field of vision and she hears his voice, bouncing off the white tile of the shower and hitting her from a thousand directions. "Janice, can you hear me? Are you awake? Can you speak?"

Her purse is open beside her, the silk lining stained by water drops. Dr. Brunschild holds up the nearly empty baggie, white powder clinging to the plastic. "I found this in your purse, Janice," he says. "You need to tell me what it is, so I can help you. What is it?"

She can't make the words come out right. "It," she says, strangely relieved by the confession. "It's It."

"What is it? Is it cocaine? Heroin? Methamphetamine?"

Blinking from the water in her eyes, her dress pooled around her hips, she can't think of anything to say in response except "It, It," before rolling over and vomiting down the shower drain.

social discretion is all that saves her from a trip to the hospital and the requisite visit from a policeman. The value of a club membership might be adversely affected if the weekly police reports—printed every Wednesday in the *Santa Rita Crier*—revealed that someone had overdosed on Schedule II drugs in the Club Room. But it is difficult for her to see the providence in this as she arrives home near midnight, bloated from drinking a gallon of water, still dizzy, still cold, still damp, in the passenger seat of Dr. Brunschild's Mercedes.

The wagons have circled round, yes, but she knows that they are not around her.

Janice and Dr. Brunschild don't speak until he pulls into

her driveway and comes to a halt. He turns the ignition off and they listen to the ticking of the engine as it cools. She looks up at the dark facade of her home. The tall double doors are shadowed by the pilasters; they look like they might swallow her whole. She imagines herself entering, and the ivy that grows up the front of the house creeping in the night to cover the doors and windows, sewing her up inside its twisted green vines.

Upstairs, a light is still on in Lizzie's room, and through the living room windows downstairs she can see the flickering blue of the television set. The girls are still up. What will she tell them?

Dr. Brunschild fingers his beard. "Why don't you call me at my office tomorrow," he says. "We'll talk about how best to deal with this." She can feel him watching her, hoping to catch her eye. Janice stares resolutely ahead at the house.

"Thank you, but I'll be fine," she says. "It's not really a problem. Just too many drinks on an empty stomach."

He clears his throat. "I'm a doctor, Janice. I can tell the difference between alcohol and stimulants. You're taking methamphetamine—am I right?" He examines Janice's face intently for a sign, but Janice stares out the windshield, even though his gaze feels like tiny needles pricking her cheek. "Look, I know the last few weeks have probably been horrible, and I certainly don't judge you for whatever you might turn to as a coping mechanism. God knows where you're getting it, Janice, but in case you aren't aware, this stuff is very, *very* addictive." She says nothing, considering his words. He continues, gently: "You need to get professional help. Check in to a clinic."

Janice jerks upright in her seat. "No!" she blurts, imagining herself incarcerated in some horrible clinic in the desert for weeks on end and what that would mean. Everybody would know. The lawyers would have a field day with it. They would take away Lizzie. "That's not a possibility. I'm in the middle of a lawsuit."

Dr. Brunschild sit silently for a minute, contemplating this as he stares out into the midnight gloom. "I see. It doesn't necessarily have to get out, if that's what you're worried about." He turns to her reassuringly. "You could deal with a local clinic. But you really shouldn't try to deal with this alone."

The house sits twenty feet away. In the dark it is an oasis. And her daughters. They are hers. If nothing else, if Paul takes everything else away, if she has crashed and burned and lost everything she once believed she had, she at least has the girls who sleep inside the sturdy walls of her home. They alone are worth giving It up for. Because if she doesn't, she sees now, she will surely lose them, more than she already has. She will drift away until she is totally gone, so lost in It that she can't find her way back. And then the lawyers will expose her, and IPO money will be the least of her concerns. Paul will get custody of Lizzie, Margaret will hate her, and then where will she be? It will all have been for nothing, all of it. It might already be too late, she worries, thinking of Paul's and Beverly's faces, of the new "we" that has aligned against her and is just waiting for her to slip up. The wolves are on the prowl.

She puts a weak hand on the door handle and struggles to push it open. "I won't," she says. "I can do this on my own." And with her pumps in hand, her bare feet pierced by the gravel, she is able to stay upright during the long march toward home.

eleven

when margaret was in third grade, her
teacher jotted a note in the margin of her report card. "Margaret shows exceptional promise," she wrote, in a perfect cursive hand. "She can be a bit of a know-it-all, but that is, of
course, the hallmark of a bright mind and a strong leader.
Have you considered having her skip a grade?" Margaret
rereads this line in the dim light of the upstairs attic. The au-
thoritative red ink has faded to an anemic pink, the tissue-thin
paper nearly disintegrates in her hands. She marvels that even
at eight years old, her personality had already so clearly
formed—*know-it-all!*—which raises the question of whether she
had actually sprung from Janice's womb already convinced that
she had nothing left to learn. And yet, how wrong her teacher
had been. *Strong leader!* she snorts. She'd had them all fooled,
even before she'd outgrown her Barbies.

She tosses the report card at her feet, where it comes to rest
on top of a growing pile of yellowing papers: report cards

from thirteen years of grammar, grade, and high school; marked-up essays, each emblazoned with a capital A (often, an A+) on the title page; her high school transcript, with its implausible 4.3 GPA; her high school graduation cap, its flattened rayon top enthusiastically inked with the name of her upcoming alma mater, CORNELL; her twin senior theses, one for each college major, two forty-page tomes that she had composed during marathon sessions in the campus library; her admittance letter to grad school and a pixilated photo of her in the local paper for having made Phi Beta Kappa. The archive ends there, abruptly, at age twenty-four, when she left for Los Angeles, as if she'd fallen off the map and been written off for dead.

She rifles farther back in the file cabinet that her mother has carefully marked, on labels decorated with an ivy motif, MARGARET. (The file cabinet next to it is LIZZIE, with a daisy motif; another one, next to it, is curiously labeled ARCHIVE: FRANCE TRIP). Her entire childhood is here, carefully organized in color-coded files: PAPERS (ENGLISH); a whole series of ARTWORK folders organized by medium (CRAYON and PENCIL and WATERCOLOR); ARTICLES: ⁵LLMORE BUGLE; SANTA WISH LISTS; and CORRESPONDENCE: SENT. At age twelve, Margaret had written the president a letter, addressing her concern about ocean pollution: "Our earth's heritage lies in the depths of the ocean—home to the humbling humpback, the dancing dolphins, the tenacious tortoises—and we must strive to preserve that habitat for them and for ourselves," she had written. "Mr. President, I appreciate you taking the time to consider my proposed legislation." The president—or, rather, some White House mailroom intern—had sent back only a form letter with a rubber-stamped signature, thanking her for her support. She remembers throwing the letter away in disgust, but now here it is, saved by her mother, the wrinkles smoothed out with an iron, and filed away under CORRESPONDENCE: RE-

CEIVED. She crumples it and tosses it into the pile, too, with only the slightest twinge of guilt about undoing her mother's careful work.

The attic is unexpectedly bright and clean. So this is what her mother was doing up here—mopping and organizing and washing the windows, so that the room smells equally of mothballs and Windex. Margaret has to duck among the wooden rafters, but even these have been dusted, with only one lonely spider attempting to refashion its web between boxes marked CHRISTMAS ORNAMENTS (GLASS) and TABLE CENTERPIECES (FORMAL). A half-drained beer by Margaret's side is leaving damp astonished O's on her SAT scores: 1560, the best in her graduating class, enough to get her into Harvard, though she'd preferred Cornell for its more liberal curriculum. A clay bowl she made in first grade—she remembers giving the malformed lump to her mother for Christmas—serves as an ashtray for the cigarette she is smoking, unconcernedly, indoors.

Her mother has saved all this, the record of her accomplished youth, and looking at the hill of paper, at years of achievements so numerous that she'd forgotten half of them, Margaret can only think, *Why?* She wants to rid herself of this precocious kid who excelled in everything she did, who got A's without even cracking a book, whose vocabulary at age six rivaled that of many high schoolers. If Margaret could only find just one F among the report cards and essays, just one glimpse of the failure that she would become . . . but there is nothing, just a uniformly optimistic series of A's and 100's and *"Well done!"*s. They had all lied to her—all those authority figures, encouraging her, telling her that if she worked hard the world would be her oyster, and she'd blindly believed them, believed in that entire American Dream sham. She tosses a blue ribbon from her junior year debate team championships on the top of the pile and the precarious mountain collapses, sliding in every direction across the attic floor. With one bare foot, she kicks the heap even farther, sending papers skittering fearfully away from her toward the corners. What a burden achievement is. She is glad to be done with all that! All hail Margaret, the failure! Her new mantra: *Fuck it!*

Having emptied the file cabinet of its contents, she gathers papers up in a crumpled lump at her chest. Leaving a trail of perfect scores fluttering down behind her, she descends the attic stairs and marches past her sister's room (the door shut firmly against any intrusion), down the grand staircase to the living room, and to the fireplace, where she tosses in the lot. One match and the papers flicker into flame, the fire gaining strength so quickly that she has to step back so that she doesn't singe her eyelashes. Magnificent! In just a minute all that is left of her past is smoldering ashes, dancing up the chimney and away.

Back up the stairs she marches for another armful—next, she thinks, she'll burn her yearbooks, and her high school photo albums and then the trophies in her bedroom! Will the burning plastic be carcinogenic? Who cares! She laughs out loud as she ascends the staircase, feeling as light as the ashes now lifting off into the Santa Rita air.

The last couple of weeks, since she hit rock bottom, have been a revelation: She just doesn't care, about anyone or anything, as if she had woken up one day and discovered that she no longer had nerves to feel pain and was therefore liberated from fear. On Tuesdays and Fridays, she gets stoned with James, sitting on the inflatable mattress in the pool shed and talking about nothing she can later remember. (Books? Movies? Eastern philosophy? Somehow it all fades into a blur.) She reads Lizzie's back issues of *Us Weekly* (fascinated, now, rather than repelled, as if she's an acolyte studying at the feet of the new despot). She sleeps, for ten or twelve hours at a time, and otherwise, she happily does nothing. *Nothing!* She waits for someone to notice and say something, but for the past week the Millers have been studiously avoiding each other. Her mother spends her days in her own bedroom, watching television. Her sister floats in the pool on an inflatable lounge chair, her iPod perched in the beverage holder, bulbous head-phones clamped over her head, like a frog sunning itself on a lily pad. Meanwhile, the phone rings and rings. Margaret can hear it from her bedroom, where she often lies for hours at a time just staring at the plaster frieze on the ceiling while lis-tening to musty old albums by Nirvana and Dinosaur Jr., but now instead of an electric charge the ringing triggers no re-sponse in her at all. She reads the messages her mother shoves under her door with a total lack of interest, almost as if they were intended for a stranger. *Let the credit card companies come for me!* she thinks. What could they possibly do to her?

In the upstairs hallway, near the attic stairs, Margaret bumps into her sister returning from the bathroom. Lizzie averts her eyes and tries to pass, but Margaret blocks her path. "What are you doing?" she asks, feeling cheerfully belligerent. Some nameless disappointment has been hanging in the air between them for the past week, something bad that Margaret recognizes she herself has brought about, though she doesn't exactly know what it is. It reminds her unhappily of a time when, as a freshman in college, she was entrusted with the care and feeding of a friend's pet rabbit while the friend was visit-ing her sick grandmother for the weekend. Margaret spent the weekend at the library pulling all-nighters as she studied for her final exams and completely forgot about the rabbit. When she finally remembered, two days into her friend's absence, she discovered the bunny lying on its side—eyes glazed over, its breathing labored, nearly dead from dehydration. Looking at the suffering animal, Margaret felt a horrible shame. She spent the rest of the day tending the rabbit, feeding it water with an eye dropper and bits of lettuce leaves from the dorm cafeteria, so that by the time her friend returned the animal was as good as new—but still, Margaret couldn't look her in the eye for a month. She was, she had discovered, a selfish person, thoughtless in her single-minded intent, and it made her feel ill. And although she can't put her finger, this very minute, on how she might have wronged Lizzie, she notes that same sickening sense of having failed someone horribly. Only now, she reminds herself, she's not going to let it bother her anymore. *Fuck it!*

"Nothing," says Lizzie, and squeezes past Margaret. "I'm not talking to you."

"Why are you not talking to me?" Margaret calls to Lizzie's back. But Lizzie has already scuttled back into her room, leaving only the faint smell of bubble gum in her wake. The door to Lizzie's room shuts quietly—even when angry, Margaret notes, Lizzie doesn't really have the inner rage required to give a door a satisfying slam. She feels a protective stab of love for her baby sister, who seems so naïve and so utterly incapable of handling the ugliness of the world outside these walls.

When Lizzie was born, Margaret was almost fourteen, and she still remembers how light and vulnerable Lizzie was when Janice allowed Margaret to hold her. The infant Lizzie seemed as fragile as a porcelain teacup, something to put on a shelf and carefully dust but never expose to the dangers of actual use. They slipped into natural roles from the first day: Margaret, the knower and protector, and Lizzie, the eager acolyte, always wanting to know what Margaret was doing, wearing, eating. Lizzie was only five when Margaret left for college. The summer before she left, Margaret read her sister to sleep most nights from Kerouac's *On the Road,* Margaret's favorite book at the time. She would lie under Lizzie's covers with a flashlight, crushed between her sister's stuffed bears and plastic-faced dolls, carefully skipping over the swear words and the sex. "Are you sure you want to read this?" she would ask. "We could always read one of yours." But Lizzie, drowsy and warm, would just hum and nod and cuddle up closer until her skin buzzed with sleep. Margaret left the book with Lizzie when she went to college; she wonders if her sister has rediscovered it yet.

Being the older sister has always been an ego boost—that flattering mimicry, that blind adoration—and Margaret has learned to count on it. In fact, she has probably taken their dynamic for granted; and only now does she realize that Lizzie's adoration is palpably absent. Her sister feels distant, a stranger, and probably Margaret feels the same to her. She's so much older, she's been gone from the house so long, and absence doesn't ensure eternal idolatry. Maybe it's only natural that Lizzie has become disenchanted with her, just part of the growing-up process. Kids get older, grow jaded, and discard their well-worshipped heroes. It happens. Especially when they discover, as Lizzie recently has, that those heroes were just dumped by their boyfriends and currently have no form of gainful employment. Margaret shrugs—*Fuck it!*

Margaret collects a second batch of papers, shuttles them down to the fireplace, and is en route to the attic for a third when she is startled by the sight of her mother standing in the doorway of her bedroom. Margaret comes to a dead halt. For a moment, she thinks she's seeing a ghost. Her mother, in her gauzy white nightgown, hair hanging uncharacteristically loose, black circles under her eyes, looks ethereal, as if Margaret might be able to push a hand right through her. Her ribs are visible through the nightgown.

"Do I smell smoke?" Janice asks, her voice phlegmy and ragged. She clutches the doorway with one hand and peers past Margaret, as if there might be flames erupting behind her.

Margaret hasn't seen her mother in five days, not since Janice was chauffeured home from the summer country club gala by Dr. Brunschild. Janice stumbled in, gave a startled Margaret a moist, clutching hug that smelled of vodka and violets and lasted about five seconds longer than Margaret felt comfortable with, and then vanished upstairs to administer the same to Lizzie before retiring to her bedroom and shutting the door. Since then, Janice has stayed in her bed, watching the Food Network in her bathrobe and coming out, only occasionally, for a mug of herbal tea. She has stopped cleaning and cooking and gardening; the preternatural energy she's exhibited all summer has vanished, and the house is quickly descending into chaos.

Lizzie and Margaret had been unable to elicit any details from their mother about why she'd arrived home bedraggled and damp and in someone else's passenger seat, other than the fact that Janice had had "a bit too much to drink." But Margaret senses that something critical has happened—her mother, falling-down drunk! She can't remember the last time that happened, if ever, and this, combined with the sudden decline in her mother's housekeeping skills, would alarm her if she hadn't already decided to stop caring about everything.

"I'm just burning some old papers," Margaret says, coming closer, until she is standing a foot away. Her mother's blue eyes are gray and oddly flat, like a pond reflecting an approaching storm, and as Margaret looks into them her triumphantly aggressive apathy vanishes abruptly. Something is terribly, terribly wrong. This wraith is not Janice Miller. Margaret is paralyzed by the sensation that the mother she has known all her life has vanished, leaving behind this desiccated husk. The hair on her arms stands on end.

"Oh," says Janice flatly. "Well, I hope you remembered to open the flue." Behind her, the television is on, and Mario Batali is braising a shank of lamb in a Dutch oven. Janice turns back to watch him and then gestures vaguely toward the bed. "I'm learning how to make lamb crostata. It's a kind of savory pie. Maybe I'll make it for us for dinner tomorrow night?" She looks at Margaret and straightens, forces a small smile across her face.

Despite her smile, Janice's expression is somnambulant, as if she were looking out from inside the gates of death. And something else is off. Margaret watches for a minute and realizes what it is: Janice is strangely still. It occurs to Margaret that her mother has seemed unwell for the better part of the summer—gaunt, moody, jittery as a Tilt-A-Whirl—and Margaret has written it off as a postbreakup/predivorce case of anxiety. But now, watching her mother retreat into her bedroom, walking with an unbalanced gait back toward the unmade bed, Margaret wonders if something more is at work. Her mother reminds her of a crashed-out drug addict, the kind of emaciated half-dead junkie you might see propped against a liquor store in downtown Los Angeles. She recalls, with a start, James's mention of her mother's "problem"—perhaps he wasn't talking about the divorce at all. Could he have been insinuating that her mother is taking pills or, or . . . ?

Pills? It's impossible to fathom. And yet. She recalls her Betty Friedan, the legacy of the suburban housewife hooked on tranquilizers—back then it was quaaludes and Valium and ephedrine-packed diet pills (that would explain Janice's weight loss). God—could her mother, who Margaret has seen cry only a half dozen times in her life, really be *so* down that she's turned to tranquilizers? She remembers that Lizzie found a Vicodin bottle in the cabinet—empty. Vicodin? It seems implausible that Janice Miller could be addicted to something—and yet there is the bruised skin around her mother's eyes, her drawn expression, the near emaciation. Not to mention the erratic behavior.

Her mother is climbing back into bed when Margaret finally blurts, "Are you taking something?" Instantly, she wishes she could take it back: *She doesn't want to know.* And yet she has to know—she can help!

Startled, Janice turns, and sits on the edge of the mattress. She swallows tightly. "What do you mean?" she asks. She gesticulates toward a notebook, where she has been transcribing the chef's instructions. "I'm taking notes—recipes?"

"You know. Like . . . have you been taking Vicodin?" She watches her mother carefully.

"I can't believe you would think that," says Janice. Her voice is a tense wire, high and tight.

"I'm sorry," says Margaret, backpedaling from an accusation that already sounds preposterous. "But, well. You just look like death. And you've been in bed all week."

Janice's mouth twitches. "Like death, huh?" she says, sinking back into the pillows. "That's very flattering, Margaret. Well, I'm glad you're worried about me. But I'm going to be fine. I've just been a little under the weather. I'm actually feeling much better today. And I'm not taking Vicodin."

"Right." Margaret feels stupid for even bringing it up. This is idiotic, she thinks. Her mother is just depressed, and no wonder. Depressed people often take to their beds and stop eating and act erratic, as Margaret knows from personal experience. The thought that her mother—*Janice Miller!*—would abuse some sort of drug really is so unlikely it's almost funny.

And yet, the first step of addiction is denial. Or is that the second stage of grief? "Well, you know that if you're having a problem, you can always talk to me," Margaret says, aware of how impotent this sounds.

"Margaret, I'm fine," says Janice.

Margaret lingers in the doorway, not sure what else to say. She feels the cloudy murk of that *indefinably wrong thing* hanging in the house, and tries to remember that she doesn't care anymore. It's the first time they've really spoken since their fight, and the malignant anger that once hovered over the house has finally vanished, replaced by something Margaret can't identify. Janice looks at her, her mouth slightly parted, as if a question is forming on her tongue that she can't quite verbalize; and Margaret stares back at her, wondering whether she should finally tell her about the meeting with Paul. But it feels like such ancient history now, not worth the emotional chaos that might ensue. *Fuck it.*

After an awkward moment, Janice reaches over to her nightstand and picks up an envelope. "Actually, I could use one thing from you. I want to talk to you about James," she says.

"James?" repeats Margaret, taken aback. She realizes, with consternation, that Janice must have figured out that he's been getting Margaret stoned. How? Margaret calculates the distance across the garden from pool shed to bedroom window, the trajectory of summer winds, the half-life of marijuana smoke molecules.

"I need you to do something for me," Janice continues. She holds out the envelope. "He's due here any minute. Will you tell him I have to let him go? And give him this check as a thank-you bonus? I'm not feeling up to doing it myself."

"Why are you firing him?"

"Summer's almost over," Janice says, but she doesn't meet Margaret's gaze. "We'll be covering up the pool soon."

"It's the middle of August. Is this a money issue? From the divorce?"

"No, that's not it," says Janice. She fingers the envelope, crisping the creases with her nail. "It's just . . . I'm not satisfied with his work. Although you don't need to tell him that."

Margaret's mind races. How on earth did her mother figure out what they were doing in the shed? Does she have spy cameras in the garden? James will lose his job and, if her mother talks, will probably be forced out of the neighborhood, poor guy. And it will all be her fault, too. She wants to cringe. "You should know," she says slowly. "It isn't his fault, what I think you're firing him for."

Janice tilts her head. "I'm aware of that," she says, but her tone is cautious.

Damn, Margaret thinks. *She does know.* "In fact, if you're firing him for what I think you're firing him for, then you're being really closed-minded, Mother," she soldiers on, unable to stop herself. "It's got legitimate medical uses, more so than a lot of prescription drugs. We even legalized it for that purpose in California a few years back, remember?"

Janice is looking more than a little confused. "Oh," she says. "I wasn't aware of that. Legal? Are you positive?"

Margaret feels like her head is about to explode. "What are we talking about?"

"I'm not entirely sure," Janice says, carefully watching Margaret's expression.

"I'm not either," says Margaret. "Can we just forget it?"

"Certainly," says Janice, with obvious relief. She sits up straight again and smooths the bedspread over her legs. She brandishes the envelope at Margaret. "Just give him the check and let him know that he has been a very good employee but we need to let him go because of circumstances beyond my control. Tell him . . . that I appreciate what he has done for us and that I would be happy to give him a recommendation, but it's best that he take his services elsewhere."

"Sure," Margaret says, realizing that she is going to lose her only friend here. She reluctantly takes the envelope from her mother's hand and weighs it in her palm.

Her mother turns back to the television as Mario Batali comes back on the screen, holding a duck carcass in one hand. "In Italy," he says, "they call this recipe *carpaccio d'anatra affumicata,* but I like to just call it delicious . . ."

"so it goes," james says, and leans back on the air mattress. He holds the check over his head—Margaret cranes her neck to read the number her mother has written, but she is too stoned. They recline in silence on the air mat-

tress, the smoke still gathered in clouds at the bottom of the
bong. She can hear the hum of the water heater behind her,
and in her wasted state experiences it as not one note but a
harmonic convergence of atonal pitches.

"I'm really sorry," says Margaret, her tongue thick and
numb. She props herself upright, looking down at his supine
body. "I think she fired you because she knew you were getting
me stoned."

"I don't think it was that," James says.

"Why else?"

He sits upright too and slides down the mattress closer to
her. He gives her a consoling pat on her bare shoulder, just
next to her sundress strap. His touch leaves her skin tingling
for a minute after he pulls his hand away. He is wearing overalls over a gray T-shirt riddled with holes, and his curls are
pushed back with a faded red bandanna. "It doesn't matter,"
he says. "Don't feel bad. It's not like doing pool work is my
driving ambition anyway. It's just a way to get from here to
there."

"Are you talking about Mexico again?" she asks.

"Yeah, sure, Mexico," he says. "For now. I don't plan. I
like to think of life as a wave that I'm riding, just seeing where
it takes me. I can't control it. I just need to keep my eyes ahead
and learn to accept wherever I wash ashore."

"I thought believing in destiny went out with the Greeks."

"Not destiny. I believe in life."

"And that means . . . what?" says Margaret. "I think what
you're really doing is just relinquishing agency."

"Relinquishing agency? What the hell does that mean?" He
tugs at a piece of her hair. She can feel his denimed thigh
squishing against hers as the weight of their combined bodies
depresses the air mattress. "Get your head out of a thesaurus
and think about it: Life never hands you what you really want
anyway, so why bother fighting it?"

"I see your point," she says. "Trying hard hasn't gotten me anything but a whole heap of debt. Did I tell you about my new mantra? *Fuck it.*"

"That's great. See? Instead of struggling against life and letting it make you miserable, you should roll with it. Enjoy what the world has handed you."

"I'm trying to believe that it's that easy."

"It is. You'll see when you come to Mexico with me," says James. He leans backward on the raft until he's flat, folds his hands behind his head, and smiles up at her like a particularly pleased cat.

It takes her a minute to realize what he's suggesting. "Don't mess with me," she says, slapping his thigh.

"I could use the company for the drive. And it's not like there's anything holding you here. Unless you want to hang out and wait for the credit card assholes to haul you off to jail?"

She looks down at her arms bracing her upright on the mattress and realizes that he's right: There is nothing tying her down. She has no job, no commitments, no possessions except for a half-dead Honda. Could the collection agencies find her in Mexico? Probably not. The thought makes her smile inadvertently. *Fuck it!* Finally, the potential of the vulgar phrase opens up before her: Mexico!

It's not like she's happy here, or even necessary. She's here only as a cop-out, and any delusions she might have had about helping her family have long since vanished. Her mother not only doesn't require Margaret's assistance but doesn't want it. Lizzie isn't speaking to her. She thinks of her mother's words: "I don't need anything." She considers her sister's petulance, her father's dismissiveness. James is right. She could slip out of town as easily as she arrived. There isn't even anything to pack.

Moving to Mexico. Yes. It seems inevitable, the end point of her slow, inexorable decline into oblivion. This is where her life will come to a halt: on a beach in Mexico, letting her brain grow mold while she serves up two-for-one margaritas to college kids on *Let's Go* world tours. Margaret Miller, voted most likely to change the world, shacking up with a stoner in a third-world country. Her friends in L.A. will roll their eyes and promptly forget her. Her parents, she thinks, will die of mortification.

"Sure," Margaret says. "I'll come with you. Why not?"

James smiles. "We'll leave tomorrow."

"Tomorrow?" Margaret counts the days until her mother's court date—ten days—and has to swallow hard. She'll miss it. And yet, did she really think she would somehow march into court when the trial started and bolster her mother's case, her argument based on reading a couple of law books and watching a summer's worth of *Law & Order* reruns? "You sure you don't want to wait a week or two? Give notice at the other pools?" she asks.

"Nope," says James. He examines the check again. "I think this was a sign, today, that it's time to go."

She calms herself and focuses on his words: riding life like a wave. Underneath the ten-cent sophistry his metaphor is not that far removed from the Zen philosophy she studied as part of her World Religions requirement in college. If Buddha were a surfer, that's what he'd say. Why not? She's always been curious about Buddhism.

"Okay," she says. She could be that kind of person—the worldly traveler, migrating through remote countries and accumulating new varieties of knowledge, intimate with obscure third-world customs and expert in lost languages. Serene, calm, at one with her surroundings wherever they might be, uninterested in material success. She would be a *better person.* Maybe she'd even pick up yoga.

James smiles. "I'll come get you at ten A.M. We'll be over the border before dark."

He sits up and leans over, and at first she thinks he's coming in for a handshake, but he keeps leaning until he is just in front of her, his breath in her face smelling like marijuana and mint gum, and, without ceremony, kisses her. She flinches backward with surprise, startled by the sheer physical proximity of his face. But after she feels his mouth sliding into hers, as if latching into a groove, she realizes that this is not a surprise at all, that of course all along she's been wondering what this might feel like, and she closes her eyes and lets herself vanish into the moment.

As if of their own accord, her hands float up to the gap in his overalls where his T-shirt has bunched up, and slide underneath his T-shirt. The texture of his skin, under her palm, is pebbly and dry—she can *feel* his tan. Without moving his lips from hers, he unsnaps his overalls, and they fall down and pool around his hips. She moves her palm farther up his chest, which is hairless and smooth. One of his hands inches the hem of her sundress toward her upper thigh, while the other deftly flicks the strap off her shoulder, and she feels his warm fingers on her chest. With her eyes closed, with the fog of pot enveloping her in dreamy cotton clouds, she forgets where she is, who she's with. The further they continue forward—his overalls kicked off onto the floor (her eyes fly open with the discovery that he is not wearing underwear), her dress hoisted over her shoulders, her panties tangled around her ankles— the more a sense of unreality envelopes her. Who has she become? This is not any Margaret Miller she recognizes.

He pushes her back and before she has time to think, he's inside her. For a moment she watches him hovering naked above her. She closes her eyes again, feeling as if the air in the mattress below is buffeting her upward. As they finish, she is distracted by the sudden, insistent fear that when this is all over, she will just vanish into the ether, as if she never was born at all, and thinks, with a start, that she should never have burned her childhood papers, erasing any proof of her existence.

When she peels her eyes open again, though, she is still there. It takes a minute to adjust to the watery light in the shed. James is already standing up, hoisting his T-shirt back over his shoulders. His eyes are red-rimmed and glazed. As she looks up at him, trying to shake off a peculiar crawling sensation— like ants, climbing all over her naked body—the door to the pool shed is flung open, flooding the room with sunshine. Margaret grabs at her sundress, lying on the floor beside her, and scrambles to cover herself. By the time she has it over her head she can see that it is Lizzie—not, thank God, her mother— who stands in the doorway, staring at them, her Speedo damp from the pool.

Margaret struggles to get up off the air mattress but can't quite manage the traction to heave herself upright. Sprawled and floundering, she smiles foolishly up at her little sister. But Lizzie just stares at her, flicking her eyes from Margaret to James and back again. In her twitching face, Margaret reads disgust. She can suddenly see herself as Lizzie must now, no longer her hero or mentor or role model but an unemployed slacker having drugged sex with the pool boy. The last vestige of Lizzie's worship—worse, of her *respect*—vanishes before her, and Margaret is surprised to realize how distressing this is to her. She tries to summon back her new mantra, but this time her indifference rings hollow. Instead, she feels like the last star has just winked out in the night sky, leaving her alone in the pitch black.

"I smelled pot." Lizzie's hands are on her hips. Water drips down her thighs.

"You want some?" asks James.

Margaret whacks at his leg with her hand. "She's fourteen years old!"

Lizzie stares at the sundress wrapped around Margaret's

waist, the unbuttoned overalls, and blurts: "You were having *sex!*"

"No! No," says Margaret, just as James says, "That's okay, it's no big deal."

Lizzie stares at Margaret and then at James and then back at Margaret again. She swallows. "You know, in Smash! they tell us that's a sin," she says. "Timothy 2:22. 'Run away from anything that makes you feel horny and instead pursue stuff that makes you want to be a good person.' I signed a chastity pledge, you know."

"Oh, Jesus Christ, Lizzie," says Margaret.

"Don't take God's name in vain or else He'll get mad at you," says Lizzie, before turning on a pruned heel and disappearing back into the garden, toward the house. In the distance, they hear Lizzie slam the French doors.

"Crap," says Margaret.

"I didn't know your sister was a religious nut," says James.

"She wasn't last month."

James shrugs. "Fuck this place," he says. "It makes people weird. Just think—by this time tomorrow, we'll be drinking dollar Coronas in Tijuana."

Margaret knows that an enthusiastic response is appropriate, but her mouth is too dry and gummy to form words. She swallows twice and offers him a weak smile instead.

After James leaves, she stays in the pool shed for a half hour, trying to sober up. Eventually, she rouses herself to go inside and dig through the refrigerator. The house is quiet except for the high-pitched buzz of the downstairs television. En route to the kitchen, she pauses at the door to the family room: Lizzie is curled up at one end of the couch, eating a candy bar. At the opposite end of the couch, a half mile away, is Mark Weatherlove, wearing a blue windbreaker. They are intently taking in something on the television screen, but from where she stands Margaret can't see what show it is. She takes a step forward into the room, causing Lizzie and Mark to turn their heads in unison. They gape at her with identical expressions of alarm, and Lizzie frantically jabs at the remote with her thumb. The television snaps off.

"What show . . . ?" begins Margaret, hoping somehow to patch things up with Lizzie, but she is interrupted by her sister, who emits a hysterical shriek: "Close the door!"

Margaret pauses, then shrugs and leaves, pulling the door closed behind her. Curiosity about what they could be watching drifts through her head, but she's too exhausted from her own afternoon to really care. She feels ill, her hands shake, and she is very, very thirsty. Dehydration from the pot, probably. She stands at the kitchen sink and drinks three glasses of water in a row. It is only after the third that she remembers that she never asked James whether he knew what was wrong with her mother.

margaret finishes off the day with a long, unsettled nap. When she wakes up it is dusk. She lies in bed, naked except for a tattered pair of panties, overcome by the memory of the events of the afternoon. Just a few hours ago she was having sex. Sex. For the first time in—God, five months? Has it been that long since Bart broke up with her? Bart had been an aggressive lover—there was something jolting and abrasive about having sex with him that always left Margaret feeling bruised. Sex with James, by comparison, was kind of like swimming in the Caribbean, warm and liquid.

She closes her eyes and sees the azure sea. The white sand. The hot yellow purifying sun, high in the sky, unimpeded by smog. And her new lover. Her new lover who she is going to Mexico with. Her new lover, a stoner slacker who is hauling her to Mexico to grow dreadlocks and live as a minimum-wage barmaid. No, Margaret thinks—that's the old mode of thinking. She's going with her new lover, a free spirit unfettered by bourgeois mores, to live in that yellow sunshine, far from the excesses of American culture, free from the judgments of Western civilization, out of sight of the collection agencies. It's all so much, so fast. The enormousness of her afternoon washes over her, and she isn't sure if her quickened pulse is the result of excitement or panic.

The house is silent. Stretching, Margaret forces herself to rise out of bed. She stumbles to the window for fresh air. Her left foot tingles from sleep.

She looks out the window over the backyard. The summer fog has finally arrived, creeping in from the ocean in the late afternoon, bringing with it gray sky and temperatures that hover just below comfortable. The garden looks unappealing in the flat light, the roses past their bloom, the flower beds on their last legs. Tabloid magazines sprawl in disarray on the patio furniture, and a Snickers bar wrapper lies abandoned in the middle of the lawn.

She gazes out farther, to the pool, and stops, not quite sure what she's seeing. She squints through the evening gloom and then freezes.

Lizzie floats facedown in the center of the pool, arms spread-eagled to the sides, her legs sinking slightly. Her body drifts slowly across the surface of the water, generating tiny shock waves in the otherwise still surface. She clearly hasn't moved in some minutes.

Margaret's heart seizes. She fumbles with the window latch, pushes the screen aside, and screams, "Lizzie!"

Lizzie doesn't show any sign of life.

Margaret is out the door before she can stop to realize that she is wearing only her panties. She takes the stairs three at a time and runs out into the cool evening air, imagining Lizzie's head cracked open by a shallow-end dive, an accidental overdose on the pills in the medicine cabinet (Vicodin?), a freak brain hemorrhage. Suicide? Margaret stubs her toe on the paving stones, emits a garbled screech of pain, hops the final ten feet to the edge of the pool on one leg, and plunges in. The pool is bathwater warm from a long summer. She feels the friction from her dive tug at the stretched elastic band of her old cotton underwear. She paddles frantically toward the deep end, gulping down water as she tries to keep her head in the air.

Blinking from the chlorine in her eyes, Margaret struggles to see Lizzie's floating body as she swims, looking for bubbles coming from her mouth. She realizes that there is something strange about Lizzie's head, something bulbous and distorted. When she is just a few feet away, her sister's body moves. Lizzie rights herself and looks at Margaret, an expression of astonishment on her face.

It is only now that Margaret can see that Lizzie is wearing a swim mask. They stare at each other through a filter of thick plastic.

Lizzie unpeels the mask with a moist thunk and pushes it up to the top of her head. She has a purple ring across her forehead from the pressure of the plastic, and her lashes are clumped together with water. She gazes at Margaret and wipes spit from the sides of her mouth. Dizzy and near hyperventilation, the chemical-laden water burning her nose, Margaret stops swimming but continues floating toward her sister from sheer momentum. She is overwhelmed with relief and, for a moment, fears that she might start sobbing.

"You're not wearing a shirt," Lizzie observes, with an infuriatingly blasé expression on her face. "Or a bathing suit. Better hope James doesn't show up or he'll see your boobs. Oh wait, he's already seen them."

"I thought you were *dead*," splutters Margaret, her sympathy waning in the face of her sister's antipathy. Did Lizzie miss that there was a heroic rescue taking place?

"Nope, not dead," says Lizzie. "I'm surprised you even care, anyway."

"Christ, Lizzie. You scared me to death," says Margaret, hearing the plaintiveness in her own voice and struggling to re-capture her composure. But her heart still palpitates wildly, stuck on the thought of her sister dead in the deep end. "Don't do that again, okay?" she insists, her voice a little too forceful. "Mom would have had a heart attack if she'd seen you like that."

Lizzie pouts. "You don't need to get so bossy about it."

Margaret paddles to the edge of the deep end and hangs on to the tiled rim, trying to catch her breath. "You spend too much time in the pool, anyway. Your fingers are probably about to rot off from all the chemicals in here."

Lizzie rolls her eyes. "You know, if you close your eyes and just float on your stomach it kind of feels like you're sus-pended in space," she says. She treads water in the middle of the pool, waggling her arms back and forth to keep her head above water. "Did you know that they have these things called sensory deprivation chambers and they charge you, like, a hundred dollars to climb in these crazy dark water tanks and just float in there? You can't see or hear or feel anything. I saw it on TV. People, like, freak out in them and go insane. They say it's like being dead."

"What's *the matter* with you?" says Margaret, her breath fi-nally slowing down. "You're fourteen, for God's sake. Stop being so morbid, you're too young."

"Just because Bart dumped you for Ysabelle van Lumis doesn't give you the right to tell everyone what to do. Or *lie* to them about everything."

"He didn't dump me for Ysabelle. It was more complicated than that."

"Whatever," says Lizzie. She swims toward Margaret and stops just out of arm's reach. "I didn't see *your* picture in *Us Weekly*. But the point is, my life sucks, too, you know."

"It can't be that bad."

"You have no idea."

"Lay it on me."

Lizzie looks at her balefully, her eyes rimmed in pink from the chlorine, her lower lip quivering. It's almost painful to watch her trying to stay afloat; her waterlogged skin is as puckered and plump as an infant's. Lizzie's chin dips below the surface, and she spits out a mouthful of water. "I'm pregnant," she says, and then she bursts into tears.

In Margaret's head, the hot yellow purifying sun of Mexico sets swiftly, unexpectedly, plummeting into that azure ocean and vanishing completely out of sight. In the pool, the fingers of fog have blotted out the last of the day's light. Margaret finds herself instinctively reaching forward, gathering her hysterical baby sister's soft body into her protective embrace.

"Don't worry," says Margaret to the top of Lizzie's soaked head, as they cling to the edge of the pool. "I'll help you." Lizzie nuzzles into her sister's clavicle, snuffling as her sobs subside, and Margaret, still stunned, thinks that she has never before felt so old.

twelve

lizzie sits in her swimsuit, at the lavender
lacquered desk in the corner of her bedroom. On her right-
hand side lies her *Bliss! Bible,* looking a bit chewed around the
edges, its pages warped from a dried slick of spilled Coke, a
chunk of Snickers bar gluing the pages of Mark and Luke
together. On her left sits the dog-eared pamphlet she found
shoved under her bedroom door when she woke up this
morning, presumably by Margaret. On the front, in inch-
high pink letters, it reads, "Choice: It's a Womyn's Right."
Below is the cartoon face of a girl with a ponytail, her ears
decorated with enormous hoop earrings, one hand raised defiantly in a fist.

Lizzie flips open the pamphlet and reads the top paragraph: "77 percent of anti-choice leaders are men; 100
percent of them will never be pregnant. The government has
no right to meddle in a womyn's womb any more than it dic-
tates what a man can and can't do with his penis." She turns

the page: "It's your choice. For thirty years, the United States Supreme Court has defended the right of a womyn to decide what to do with her own body. Don't let the anti-choice propagandists distract you from this fact with their lies." And farther down: "Abortion is one of the safest medical procedures provided in the United States today, no more dangerous than getting a tooth pulled." Below is a picture of a smiling doctor with a stethoscope around her neck.

Lizzie drops the pamphlet and picks up her *Bliss! Bible.* She flips to the appendix at the back of the tome. At the top of the page it reads, "What does God think about . . . ?" Below it lists a series of hot-button issues: "Premarital sex?" "Masturbation?" "Cheating on math tests?" "Being rude to your mom?" and "Swearing?" For each, it denotes the Bible passages where you can glean God's personal point of view on these matters.

The word "Abortion" is right at the top of the page, and only one passage is listed underneath: Exodus 20:13, page 133. She flips to page 133 and reads the verse: "Don't kill!!!" This sentence is underlined in red.

It makes her head hurt. Lizzie gives up and picks up her tweezers, focusing her attention today on the hair that grows on her toes, hair that is promisingly coarse and bristly. She yanks out one hair, and it feels like someone just jabbed a needle into her big toe. Her eyes water. The offended follicle turns bright pink and swells satisfyingly. She yanks another, and watery mucus starts to drip from her nose. A peacefulness descends. The only sensation she can feel is the burning in her foot. Thoughts about the fate of her pregnancy drift away; so, too, does the unpleasant memory of the video she watched with Mark the day before, images from which flashed in Lizzie's head all morning despite her best efforts to push them out, until she wasn't sure whether she felt so peculiarly swimmy because of what's growing in her belly or because of the flickering movie in her mind.

She finishes the first foot and is beginning on the second when there is a knock at the door. Lizzie drops the tweezers into a drawer and limps to open it. Margaret is standing there. Her terry-cloth dress is fraying around the bottom, and the fabric that was traffic-cone orange at the beginning of the summer is now a blotchy and inoffensive peach. She clutches a dog-eared book under her arm. Lizzie twists sideways to read the spine: *Your Body, Your Life: A Feminist's Guide to Reproduction Rights.*

Lizzie has never really understood Margaret's whole feminist thing—like, what's really the big deal? Even the word "feminism" has a certain musty quality to it, more of a vocabulary word from a history test than a term applicable to Lizzie's own life. As far as she can tell, women have it pretty good in the world; they get to wear cuter clothes than men, for example. She doesn't mind if boys open the door for her every once in a while. She actually kind of wishes they would.

Margaret marches into the room, pushes Lizzie's crumpled comforter aside, and arranges herself on the edge of the mattress. She leans forward and folds her hands together over her knees. "So," she says. "Let's talk."

"Okay," says Lizzie with trepidation, as she sits beside her sister on the bed. She can see, in the brightness of Margaret's eyes, a lecture coming on. Lectures mean expectations that Lizzie will need to live up to, and Lizzie is not at all sure that she is in a position to please anyone right now. Let alone her sister, who has been acting like a total bossy, lying bitch all summer.

"I want to say, first, that I know I've been a pretty rotten sister. I've been preoccupied with my own issues, totally self-absorbed, and clearly wasn't paying enough attention to what was going on with you. And I know that I lied to you about what was going on in my life, and that was unfair of me. And it wasn't right to attack you about Mark Weatherlove, either.

He's your friend, and I should have trusted your judgment. What can I say except that I'm really sorry?"

"That's okay," says Lizzie and manages a tiny smile. A ray of hope cuts through the murk of confusion. She hadn't expected an apology. Margaret doesn't often apologize, a fact that she had always interpreted to mean that Margaret was always right but lately has reinterpreted to mean that Margaret doesn't like to be wrong. Maybe, she thinks, Margaret *will* be able to help her figure everything out. "I mean, you've had Bart to deal with and all that," she says, feeling generous.

"Forget Bart," says Margaret, waving a hand as if to shoo him out of the room. "Let's talk about you. I assume you got the pamphlet I left for you?"

"It was kind of . . . I don't know. Harsh?"

Margaret waves a hand again. "Yeah, it's outdated rhetoric: 'woman' with a *y* and all that. But you get the point. First of all, you understand that you aren't in this alone, right? I bet you feel really alone, but there are legions of women standing behind you."

"There are?" says Lizzie, unsure about the meaning of the word "legions" but beginning to suspect that this is not going to be an objective discussion after all.

"They have paved the way so that this situation you are in shouldn't have to be traumatic," says Margaret.

"Oh," says Lizzie. "Do I know them?"

"Well, no," says Margaret.

"How can they be behind me then?" asks Lizzie, aware that she is being difficult but unable to resist. Pretending to be dumb is the only way she knows to torture her sister.

Margaret sighs with exasperation. "Okay, bad metaphor. Forget it. I'm just saying that you've got a whole sisterhood out to help you here. I assume the father isn't taking any responsibility for this, right? Who *is* the father? Is it Mark?"

"No," says Lizzie.

"Then . . . ?"

Lizzie pauses. "Well, I'm not really sure."

Margaret's eyes widen. "Wow," she says. "I mean, *wow*. Lizzie, I had no idea."

Lizzie flushes with unexpected pride as she recognizes that she has, somehow, impressed her sister with this fact. She thinks of Margaret in the shed, her dress pooled around her waist, James standing over her, and blushes at the shared knowledge that this implies. Yes, of course, Margaret would get it.

But the pink Bible sitting on her desk, a foot away, catches her eye, and the wave of mortification washes over her again. "But it's a sin," she reminds herself out loud. "It's nothing to be all *wow* about."

Margaret grimaces. "Who told you it was a *sin*? Please. Desire is a perfectly natural human instinct. You shouldn't be embarrassed about your sexual awakening. We've normalized sex for boys and taught girls that if they express a healthy sexual curiosity they are sluts. It's a double standard, and you really shouldn't fall victim to it, okay? If there was one thing we tried to convey at *Snatch,* that was it."

"Okay," says Lizzie, feeling vaguely assuaged by her sister's support, even if she's not entirely sure she understands what Margaret is trying to say.

"You know, I lost my virginity in high school, too," Margaret says, reaching out to rub Lizzie's shoulder. "My senior year. I lost it to a guy from Modesto during the spring debate conference in Los Angeles. He won the silver medal for his speech on radical eco-activism. The sex was pretty unmemorable—actually, it was pretty bad—but I didn't feel ashamed about it, and neither should you."

Lizzie *wants* this revelation to make her feel better about her own slutty behavior, but it just sounds so *benign* compared to what she has done. She suspects that if Margaret knew the truth, she wouldn't be quite as understanding. Lizzie is quiet for a minute while Margaret's sympathetic hand warms the middle of her back, but finally she can stand the deception no more. "I slept with six people," she blurts. "In less than three months."

Margaret's eyes look like they might just pop right out of her head and onto the carpet. "Jesus," she explodes, and her involuntary outburst makes Lizzie want to crawl under the bedspread and never come out again. She was right. Margaret swallows hard and lowers her voice. "I mean, this is not in any way a judgment, anything but, but boy, Lizzie, you really took ownership of your sexuality."

"Thanks, I guess," says Lizzie, still stuck on Margaret's outburst.

"Didn't you use condoms?"

"Sort of," says Lizzie. "But I kinda forgot a couple times."

"Well, I guess it's a case of lessons learned the hard way. In the future, no condoms, no sex, okay? Do you want me to talk to you about STDs, too?"

"No, that's okay," says Lizzie, not eager for another lecture. It's not like she didn't take sex ed, she just kind of ignored it. She looks over at her sister. Margaret is perching erect on the edge of the mattress, the way Goody Two-shoes Alice Schumacher always sits in English class when she's about to raise her hand with the answer. A deep furrow is pressed into Margaret's brow, and yet her sister looks almost *happy*. Her cheeks are flushed, her shoulders square. It dawns on Lizzie that Margaret is more involved in some dialogue going on in her own head than anything Lizzie is actually saying. Margaret needs to see herself as some kind of a hero in this situation, like a wise-older-sister figure, Lizzie realizes. And as much as she feels the familiar tug of admiration for her sister returning, there is something sad about Margaret's behavior. Is her life so boring that this sermon is all she has to get excited about?

"Well, I'll have to take you up to Good Vibrations one of these days and get you set up with a condom starter kit so this doesn't happen again. But in the meantime, let's talk about what we're going to do now. One of my old classmates runs the Planned Parenthood clinic up in San Francisco; I talked to her this morning and she said she could slot you in for an appointment as early as tomorrow. You really shouldn't wait any longer. The sooner you do it, the easier it is."

"Easier what is?" Lizzie suspects she already knows the answer, and it makes her queasy.

"An abortion, of course."

Lizzie stiffens. She sensed this was coming, but the force of her sister's assurance is nonetheless like a nuclear blast, eradicating any of Lizzie's own will. "Actually, I hadn't really decided on an abortion," she says. Her voice sounds very small.

"Oh," says Margaret, taken aback. She looks down at the palm of her hand, as if crib notes might be written there. "Well. Be real, Lizzie—is there really any other decision to be made? You are *fourteen,* for God's sake, and that's just far too young to have a baby. What are you going to do? Drop out of school to take care of it? Take your SAT tests with a baby in a sling on your back? What about college? What about a career? You don't want to jeopardize your entire future for a baby."

Her sister's prediction sounds like one of those awful after-school TV specials, and Lizzie reels from the vision of herself as its protagonist. College? SATs? Jobs? She hadn't even *thought* about where she wanted to go to college yet, though it always *sounded* like fun. Parties. Boys. No parents. For a brief second, she is inclined to conform to her sister's plan. Still, something holds her back. "But," she says.

"But what?"

"But God says abortion is murder. And that I'll go to hell."

"Oh, Lizzie," says Margaret, shaking her head. "I don't even know where to start with that."

"What?"

"It's all propaganda," Margaret says. "The religious right has just imposed its own twisted idea of morality on this situation—morality, by the way, that is based on fictional tales that were written by politicians two thousand years ago in order to suit their own political needs, not by some"—she jerks two fingers through the air as quote marks—"all-knowing 'God.' They want to convince you to sacrifice your own life in honor of something that right now is an unviable cell cluster about the size of a pistachio nut. Abortion is not murder, any more than taking out your tonsils is. The people at that church of yours have just guilted you into calling it a sin, in order to give themselves the moral upper hand."

Lizzie isn't convinced. She thinks of nice Pastor Dylan and is compelled to defend her church friends. "They haven't guilted me. They love me."

"They love you?" says Margaret. "They hardly *know* you. You've been to church, what, four times? Five? And you'll take their advice over your sister's?"

"But *I* think it's bad. To kill the baby."

Margaret sits back and rubs her temples. "It's not a baby yet. Didn't you read . . . ? You know what? Forget it. Let's bypass the partisan arguments and just talk this through logically. What will you do? You'll have the baby? Raise it yourself? Without even the father around to help you?"

Lizzie thinks about babies. She doesn't really know any babies. The only infant she can remember meeting is her cousin's on her father's side, who visited a few years back. The baby was very soft and quiet and it just slept in its car seat the whole time they visited and it was wearing a pink dress of the softest cashmere that her cousin had knitted herself. Lizzie mostly remembers the baby's feet, though—tiny and velvety and perfect, like a doll's. She fondled those feet for hours.

"I dunno," she says. "Maybe. I'm sure Mom would help. Mom loves babies."

"Mom loves babies that don't belong to her teenage daughter."

Lizzie closes her eyes and a vision of her future swims before her: a rocking chair, a sweet-smelling warm little baby girl who needs nothing but her. She would have to leave Millard Fillmore High, like her sister warned, but the truth is she wouldn't mind never stepping foot on school grounds again anyway. Maybe she'll just skip the end of high school and head straight to adulthood. She can move into an apartment somewhere and raise the baby on her own. It'll be just like the *Gilmore Girls*—they'll be best friends. Maybe Mark Weatherlove will want to come live with them. And Becky will babysit.

Would it be bad for the baby not to have a father? She considers her own father, thinking, oddly, of his old golf shoes, which she found the other day in the hall closet, abandoned, dusty, and smelling like mold; suddenly, with a pang, she feels like crying, she wants his love so much. But if she hadn't known him in the first place there would be nothing to be upset about now, right? Following this logic, this baby will never feel disappointed or abandoned by her father because the father will never exist. So that will actually be a good thing. Of course, maybe if it's a boy she'll need to have a man around to be a male role model, but someone else could do that. Like Mark.

She wants to be good, she thinks. And it seems so clear that a baby is a *good* thing, something pure and perfect that's the antidote to everything awful she's gone through in her entire life. It would be a miniature version of her, only without her flaws. And it would be her responsibility to protect the baby, hers alone, and no one—not even her mom or her sister, be-cause what do they really know about parenting anyway?—could tell her what to do with it. She'd be in charge. Just the two of them. She would love her baby so much. And it would love her back.

When Lizzie opens her mouth again, she speaks slowly and carefully, knowing that the wrong words will make her sister upset. "I've pretty much done everything wrong that I possibly could," she says. "I mean, I've broken almost *all* the Ten Com-mandments. I've fornicated and I've coveted and I've lied and I've stolen. I can't remember the rest, but I've probably done them, too. I've got, like, only two friends in the whole world and I think Dad hates me, probably Mom, too. But, Margaret, this is something that I could do right. I mean, I can make something *live*. Like, how bad could that be?"

Margaret just stares at her, her face collapsing. It looks like she might cry. "Lizzie, you are far too hard on yourself," she says. "You're a *great* kid. Please don't doubt yourself like that. You're amazing. It's far too soon in your life to hate yourself."

Normally this is the kind of thing Lizzie loves to hear, but she has already worked herself up into a crescendo of repen-tantly miserable righteousness. "No," she says gravely. "I need redemption."

"You think you'll find redemption by giving birth to a baby?" Margaret says. "That's just naïve. I *know* you're smarter than that."

Lizzie sits up straighter, picks up the Bible, and puts it on her lap. She presses a palm against its pebbled cover and tries to draw the strength of His Lordness into her innermost be-ing. She thinks she can feel a white light in her belly, a faint gnawing where the baby is growing. She must resist her sister's cynical worldview. "No. I'm not having an abortion," she says, in as strong a voice as she can muster. It is surprisingly easy.

Margaret breathes sharply through her nose, a tight sigh.

"Okay, well, we can look into adoption options then. There are thousands of people who would kill for a healthy white baby."

"No, Margaret. You don't get it. *I* want the baby."

Margaret rubs the back of her neck with her fingers and stares at the floor. A long minute passes. She speaks slowly, her voice rough and low: "Look, I'm pressuring you, and that's not fair. I realize that. It's all about you being able to choose for yourself, right? The right to choose. Not the right to choose abortion. Right. That's what feminism is all about. So, okay. Just do me a favor, Lizzie? Don't decide now. Just think about it. I'll move the date with Planned Parenthood back and I'll get you some more stuff to read. And maybe we can talk again when we're both a little calmer."

Lizzie watches her sister carefully, realizing that the purple spots on her sister's cheeks and the strained cords in her neck aren't about being a self-righteous know-it-all anymore but are a sign that her sister is actually really upset. She has won this battle, Lizzie understands, and for a moment, this fact makes her feel beatific and powerful. Who knew she could defeat indomitable Margaret so easily? But the miserable expression on her sister's face also makes Lizzie want to surrender to her entirely just so she will look happy again.

She resists this impulse. *Think of the baby,* she reminds herself. She pictures again the pink foot in her hand. "Don't bother," she says. "I've decided."

Margaret loses her composure altogether. She bolts up from the bed as if propelled by an electric shock, her arms sticking stiffly out at thirty-degree angles. Her eyes are moist, though it's not clear whether these are tears of anger or frustration. Margaret's hands have balled up into tight fists, and she looks like she wants to punch someone—Lizzie?—in the face. Lizzie flinches. "Lizzie! You can't let them do this to you!" Margaret squeaks.

For the first time ever, Lizzie is terrified of her sister. She touches her belly protectively, feeling the thick belt of flesh under her swimsuit, and wonders if the raw curling sensation in her belly is the baby moving.

"It's my decision." Lizzie can hear the heavy thumping of her own heart. *Blam blam blam* it rattles her rib cage. Her heart beats so loud that the windows vibrate in their frames. *Blam blam blam.* And then she realizes, just as Margaret does, that the sound comes from downstairs, where someone is banging on the back door. The doorbell rings, there's a brief moment of quiet, and then the banging starts again.

"Go away!" calls Margaret, not moving, her hands still curled into little coils of fury.

"Who is it?" Lizzie asks her.

Margaret says nothing, but her face pinches tight as the banging continues. It is clear that Margaret doesn't want Lizzie to answer the door—why? Lizzie's fear of being socked by her sister is abruptly replaced by curiosity, but with a dollop of power. Lizzie is dominant: She has made her own choice, stood her sister down, and Margaret is just frustrated that Lizzie didn't simply go along with whatever she was told to do. Knowing this, Lizzie's impulse is to run for the door, just to spite her sister. Because she can.

"Aren't you going to go answer it?" she asks.

"Mom can get it."

"Mom doesn't get anything these days." Lizzie stares her sister down, enjoying this strange new sense of authority.

But Margaret continues to stand there. "I'm not moving until you agree to be more open-minded about this. Just *talk* to Planned Parenthood, that's all."

"Fine, I'll get it," says Lizzie. She turns and bolts for the staircase, taking the stairs as fast as she can, running her hand along the smooth banister. She hears Margaret call "Don't!" behind her but ignores it. She hits the landing with a thud that makes her stomach twist.

Behind her, Margaret leaps down the stairs, losing her footing a few steps down and tripping unevenly through the rest. Lizzie breaks into a run. The sisters sprint through the house, bare feet slamming against floorboards that haven't been swept in a week, leaving hot toe-shaped imprints in the accumulating dust at the edges. Lizzie collides with the frame of the kitchen door, winces, thinks of the baby. Margaret grabs at the straps of her bathing suit, stretching the fabric tight, but then loses her grip. The elastic snaps back, stinging Lizzie's skin.

"Ouch!" yells Lizzie.

"Leave the door alone!" Margaret pleads.

"What's your problem?" Lizzie skids around the kitchen island, which is stacked with dirty dishes and the crusts of a three-day-old pizza. She knocks a half-empty carton of spoiled orange juice to the floor with a flying hand, and the fetid contents splatter against the cabinets.

Lizzie reaches the back door first, by a matter of seconds, and flings it open. James stands on the doormat. A moldy-looking souvenir sombrero is pushed back on his head.

"*Hola,*" he says. "Is Margaret there?"

"Oh, it's you," Lizzie says. She's not sure who, exactly, she had hoped to find behind the door—Bart? Ysabelle van Lumis? Her father?—but it certainly wasn't him. The presence of James—who she last saw with his pants undone in the pool shed—makes her blush. He doesn't seem very embarrassed about it, though. "It's just your *boyfriend,*" Lizzie says to Margaret, who has come panting to a halt behind her. "What's the big deal?"

James looks over Lizzie's shoulder at Margaret. "*Hola,* Margarita. Where's your suitcase? You ready to go?"

Lizzie looks at James and then Margaret, who seems decidedly nervous. "Where are you going, Margaret?"

James adjusts the sombrero on his head, lowering it so that Lizzie can read the yarn stitching. LA VIDA LOCA SPRING BREAK

'01, it reads. "I'm absconding with your sister to Mexico," James says. "Didn't she tell you?"

"Mexico?" says Lizzie.

"Mexico?" echoes another voice. Janice stands with her hand clutching at the kitchen island, a satin bathrobe belted tightly around her waist. Three bodies pivot, as if on cue, to stare at her. Lizzie struggles to remember the last time she saw her mother in an upright position. It's been at least five days. In fact, Lizzie has not seen her at all in at least two, choosing instead to tiptoe past the closed bedroom door. *You are a bad daughter,* Lizzie thinks to herself. *You don't pay enough attention to your mother. That's another reason you need to keep the baby.*

Janice gestures at the open door. "I heard the door. Someone was banging and banging . . . ?" She focuses her gaze on their visitor, pauses, and turns to Margaret. "What's James doing here? Margaret, didn't you tell him? What's this about Mexico?"

"It's nothing," says Margaret. She turns to James. "Look, can we talk in private?"

"We're going expat," says James, talking over Margaret's shoulder at Janice and Lizzie. "We're moving to Puerto Escondido."

Lizzie lets this fact sink in. Her sister is going away? Her sister is abandoning her? Her innards, steely with victory just a few minutes ago, now melt into a wobbly pool of lime Jell-O. She doesn't want to be left alone with the baby *yet.* How could Margaret just leave her?

Her lower lip quivers, but before she can say anything, Janice speaks. "You can't go to Mexico with him," her mother says, her voice a razor.

"I'm not," insists Margaret. She turns to James. "Really. I changed my mind. They need me here."

"I mean it. I don't like you spending time with him," Janice says, as if she hasn't heard anything Margaret just said.

Margaret swings her gaze over to their mother. "Why not?"

"You just can't," Janice urges. She comes up behind Margaret and clutches at her daughter's shoulders. "Because I said so. And I'm your mother."

Margaret twists out of Janice's grip. The strap of her dress snaps under Janice's hands, and Margaret grabs at it to keep the dress from falling down. "What the hell? Is this some kind of classist thing? You don't want your daughter spending time with the hired help? Is that it? Christ, Mom, this is the same thing you pulled when I left with Bart—he wasn't 'good enough' for me, he was a 'bad influence' on me because he wasn't a Harvard grad or a lawyer-in-training. Well, you know what I think? I think you're just scared that your daughter might be the real failure. I think you're scared that I'm proof that all the social constructs that you've always believed in, that have defined your entire life, are actually empty, and that neither you nor I are any better than anyone else." Her words get more and more choked as the speech goes on.

Lizzie glances down at her arms and sees that she's broken into goose pimples, not from cold but from anxiety. She parses her sister's speech and comes to the nugget of truth at the center: Her mother cares too much about what other people think. But doesn't Margaret care too much, too? Otherwise, why would she always be working so hard to be the smartest person in the room? A new understanding makes Lizzie shudder. It's as if a cord has drawn her and her sister and mother tightly together, all three of them trying so hard to please and yet always failing to live up to some unspoken expectations. Poor Margaret. Poor Lizzie. Poor all of them.

But Janice looks confused. "That's not it at all," she says, her voice strangled.

"Actually," says James, "my dad is a pediatrician. In Great Neck. Not working-class."

As James speaks, Lizzie has a revelation: If Margaret has been planning to leave for Mexico today, that means that she was never planning to go with Lizzie to get an abortion anyway. "I can't believe you didn't tell me you're moving to Mexico," Lizzie says, now imagining a different future in which she *did* go to the clinic with her sister, and her sister held her hand while the doctors in their blue paper suits put her to sleep, and after she woke up Margaret fed Lizzie chicken noodle soup and chocolate ice cream in bed until she felt better. Inside, she aches for the loss of this future, which she now realizes wouldn't have been so bad after all. "What about that appointment you set up for me? You were going to make me go by myself?"

Margaret whirls around. "No, Lizzie, I am *not going to Mexico.* I told you. I'm staying here to help you."

"Oh," says Lizzie, still too lost in her melancholy vision to digest this properly.

"What appointment?" asks Janice.

"You're not going?" says James. He leans against the door frame, takes off the hat with exaggerated disappointment, and clutches it to his chest. "You're bailing on me?"

"No! I am not going! Not! Going! For God's sake, is no one listening?" shouts Margaret. She smacks her temples with the palms of her hands, *hard,* a gesture that startles Lizzie. "I was going to go, Lizzie, and then when I found out about your situation I decided to stay. To *help.* To *do something.*" She seems to be talking to herself. The strap of Margaret's dress tumbles, exposing the top of one pale white breast. Lizzie wonders if she is aware that they can almost see her nipple. She wants everyone to just be quiet—all the yelling is making her stomach hurt. The scene in this room is so *wrong,* she doesn't even know how to start fixing it. She wishes there were a "Rewind" button on life, so she could reverse everything until they got to a point where life at home was normal again. They might have to rewind all the way back to the beginning, but wouldn't they do it all better this time?

"But I still don't want you spending time with *him*," Janice repeats.

Margaret turns around furiously and yanks the dress back up. "And why not? It somehow offends you that your darling Ivy League daughter is fucking the pool boy? Did you know he went to Columbia?"

"You were . . . ?" Janice seems unable to finish the sentence. She stabilizes herself on the granite edge of the kitchen island. "You are . . . ?"

James's calm seems finally to desert him. He jams the sombrero back on his head. "Dammit, Margaret. That has nothing to do with it. She doesn't want you hanging out with me because I'm her drug dealer, that's why."

Lizzie's first thought is *James, a drug dealer?* She's never seen a drug dealer before, but she certainly didn't think they looked like him. And then, as she analyzes his sentence and realizes that this implies that her mother has *bought drugs* from him, she grows light-headed with confusion. What? No. Huh? Her brain churns up half thoughts. Apparently, she is not the only person in the room who is stopped cold by James's statement. The room has grown so quiet that she can hear the finches splashing in the garden fountain, an airplane flying by overhead. Both Lizzie and her sister turn to stare at their mother, who seems to sway slightly from the impact of their gaze. As Lizzie watches, Janice feels behind herself for a stool and collapses down onto it.

"Drug dealer?" says Lizzie, turning back to look at James, who is now edging away from the doorway, toward his car. Her head feels like it is about to explode. Does not compute. Alert. Alert. "You're kidding. Mom does drugs?" She turns to Margaret, then back to James, somehow incapable of looking at her mother for the answer. "Like, what? Pot?"

"Look. I tried to tell you, Margaret. Your mom's a meth addict, and you should probably get her some help," says James. Lizzie is unsure what exactly meth is, but the word "addict" makes her feel even dizzier, as she thinks of the slide show at Smash! and the pictures of toothless crack whores with empty eyes. She looks at her mom again, who maybe doesn't look her best but certainly doesn't look like *that.* It just doesn't make any sense.

"Oh, James," says Janice, her head in her hands. "Did you really need to do that? You were supposed to just *leave.*"

"Meth?" says Margaret. She is frozen. "You gave her *meth*?"

"Is meth like crack?" asks Lizzie, feeling left out and utterly confused about absolutely everything. No one answers.

James shrugs. "She begged for it," he says. "I was just trying to make some cash. It's what's selling these days. And then I tried to stop her, but she threatened me."

"You studied to be a *chemist,*" Margaret says. "That crap *kills* people. I thought—but, meth! And—you!"

"Don't be a hypocrite, Margaret. You've been smoking pot with me all summer." This new revelation is anticlimactic, and doesn't come totally as a surprise to Lizzie, who smelled the evidence in the pool shed yesterday. But as she considers it all together she realizes that a whole other world has existed at this house all summer, one where her sister and mother secretly did drugs and had sex and Lizzie was lying around in the pool without a clue. As usual. She feels like crying.

"That's different," Margaret continues. "Meth is *addictive.*"

"You'd be surprised how many people around here do it. At least a quarter of my pools."

"I already stopped, Margaret," protests Janice. "I quit almost a week ago. After the club party. I'm fine. That's why I fired James. That's why I've been such a wreck all week, if you really need to know. But it's all *fine* now." She reaches a hand toward Margaret, who stands, stunned, on the other side of the kitchen island. "I stopped taking it."

Lizzie senses that she has grown invisible, just an anonymous audience member of the theater performance taking place before her. Nothing seems quite real at all, except the lurching in her stomach. "I think I'm going to be sick," she announces, but no one pays attention.

Janice turns toward Lizzie. "Lizzie . . ." she says, then stops, lost.

"Get out of the house, James, please," says Margaret. "Really, just leave now, before I forget that I have conscientious objections to California's drug laws and feel compelled to pick up the phone and let the police know that a meth dealer is running off to Mexico. I'm sure they'll love that."

James hesitates. He looks at Janice, who is now pressing her forehead to the granite countertop between her arms. "Mrs. Miller . . ." he begins.

Janice lifts her head just a few inches off the granite, then drops it again. She groans loudly.

"Just go," says Margaret.

James sighs and throws up his hands. Before he can say anything else, Margaret slams the door in his face, so hard that the entire house shakes. A glass perched on the edge of the counter jitters, tips, and falls into the sink. It rocks back and forth in the stainless tub, miraculously unbroken.

Lizzie looks out the window as James walks slowly away. When he reaches the truck he takes the sombrero off and throws it in the bed, alongside a suitcase, a guitar, a few cardboard boxes. She imagines Margaret in the front seat with him, the back of her head receding into the distance, and wonders whether it wouldn't have been for the best if Margaret had gone with him, after all. Her mother, too. If all of them just *left,* James and Janice and Margaret, she could be all alone with just her baby and the Lordness light. It would be simpler.

When James's truck pulls out of the driveway, Margaret speaks. She is apparently talking to the orange juice splotch on the floor. "Jesus, Mom. Crystal? I mean, wow. Honestly, I can't believe I didn't see it earlier. I mean, the whole cleaning thing should have been a giveaway . . ." Janice doesn't respond; her face remains planted on the granite. Margaret grips two fistfuls of hair at her temples, tugging the skin tightly back. "Anything else you want to tell us, Mom? Any other deepest, darkest secrets you feel like sharing?"

Janice lifts her head from the counter. "Oh *can it,* Margaret. You have no right to speak to me like that. If you want to talk about lies, how about your little visit to your father while you were supposedly helping me sue him? Were you ever planning on mentioning that? And what about this little jaunt to Mexico with the pool boy? Please drop the Saint Margaret act."

Margaret gives her hair another tug, grimacing. "It's unbelievable . . ." she continues, as if Janice hadn't spoken at all. "I mean, really. It's almost too much to take. My mom is a meth addict—"

"What's meth?" interrupts Lizzie again, sensing that something is spiraling quickly out of control, hoping to steer this exchange back to facts, figures, *information.*

Margaret talks right over her: "—and my father abandoned his family, and my sister is a born-again teen-pregnancy statistic, and I'm bankrupt and homeless without a boyfriend or a job. Where do we live, the Ozarks or something? It just blows my mind. It's all such a . . . mess."

The resolute Margaret from Lizzie's bedroom is gone. This Margaret looks petrified, with tears in her eyes, and the torn dress sliding off her body makes her look so young. Lizzie senses that if she were to go over and give her a hug, this

Margaret might stop talking and start crying instead. Lizzie twitches as the light in her belly glows back on and feels a saintly desire to fix everything. Could she do that?

But Janice has finally sat up and is staring at Lizzie as if she's a visitor from Pluto that has just materialized in the pantry. Lizzie can see that her mother has been weeping, and there are pizza crumbs from the countertop trapped in the tears on her face. Lizzie belatedly realizes what her sister has just revealed, and she turns away so that her mother can't see her face. She hadn't even considered how to tell Mom yet.

"A pregnancy statistic?" Janice asks. She wipes a crumb from her lip. "Somebody please tell me that doesn't mean what I think it means."

"Nothing," says Lizzie quickly. "It's nothing."

"It's *not* nothing, Lizzie," Margaret barks. "Mom: Lizzie's pregnant. I tried to convince her not to have it, but she won't listen. She's going to have the baby, because *God told her to.*" Margaret covers her face with a hand, then mutters, "And I don't think she *ever* read *Snatch.*"

Janice turns from Lizzie to Margaret and back again, uncomprehending. Lizzie can't bear her gaze. "What's meth?" she whispers one last time, as if the answer to this question might somehow explain away all the other chaos and confusion in the room. And then, as her stomach rises up in protest, she runs to the sink to dry-heave.

"Pregnant?" echoes Janice, behind her. "No. Margaret, that's really not funny. Not—Lizzie? Oh, Christ. Is this true? Lizzie?"

Lizzie watches her distorted reflection in the stainless steel of the sink, a blur of brown hair and pink flesh dipping and bobbing as she struggles to regurgitate the sour knot in the bottom of her stomach. But nothing comes up. In her belly, the Lordness light has vanished and left behind a coiling pain, as if someone were grabbing her intestines and twisting. She turns slowly back to face her mother.

"Yes," she says, and in her mother's horrified gaze Lizzie sees reflected all the disappointments Lizzie has ever delivered upon her, all the failed elocution lessons and late-night ice-cream binges and date-free Saturday nights. Lizzie squares her shoulders and aligns her spine, just as she learned in her ballet classes. She places one hand on her navel, feeling the worn elastic of her bathing suit stretched tight over her belly. She conjures up the love of God—she tries very, very hard to feel that warm solace again—and speaks. "I'm gonna have a baby," she says. "Isn't that great? Mom?"

"A baby . . ." Janice echoes. Her hands float uselessly in the air before her, shaking visibly.

There is a silence. Lizzie watches her mother's sharp nasal breaths; they start slow, like sighs, and then come faster and faster. It looks like she is hyperventilating. Lizzie is transfixed, afraid to move. The walls of the kitchen seem to press inward.

Janice's hands flutter back down to clench the rims of her bathrobe pockets. "I can't do this anymore," she says. Her voice is faint, and Lizzie and Margaret glance at each other, both unsure what this means. Janice looks out the kitchen window to the front yard with dark eyes. Her voice rises an octave and threatens to snap. "I can't. I can't! I give up. Do you hear me, girls? I GIVE UP!"

And Lizzie helplessly watches her mother cinch the belt of the bathrobe around her waist, take her purse from where it sits on a chair, and walk right out the kitchen door. She hears the tires of the Porsche squeaking in the gravel and turns to watch, through the kitchen window, as her mother peels out of the driveway and into the street, leaving a thick layer of black rubber behind. To Lizzie, her face pale and drawn in the window's reflection, it looks like her mother is leaving forever.

. . .

the pool is august warm, and peaceful. floating on her back, a half hour later, Lizzie closes her eyes and sees the inside of her eyelids, pink in the sun. She squeezes her eyes closed even tighter and watches the starbursts of sunlight exploding into her darkness. When this fails to distract her from the cramping in her stomach, she rolls over and hugs her knees to her chest. Her head bobs, half submerged. The water that leaks into her mouth and ears tastes gritty. She wonders if she could sink to the bottom of the pool and disappear forever.

When she rolls over onto her back again, she hears Margaret's bare feet on the patio, slapping as she jogs across the hot stones to the cooler tile by the edge of the pool. Lizzie doesn't look up but registers wrinkled toes gripping the tile, a dab of chipped red nail polish.

"Lizzie," says Margaret. Her voice is garbled through the water in Lizzie's ears. "We need to talk."

Lizzie takes a deep breath and descends below the surface. Under the water, drifting down toward the rough cement, all she can hear is the hollow ringing inside her head; when she looks up, she sees only the mirrored surface of the water, magnifying the light of the sun into shimmering shafts. Tiny bubbles cling to her brown limbs, which float loosely from her sides as if they weren't even attached to her. She makes small gestures in the water to keep herself there, down at the bottom of the pool, curled up like a sea horse, counting. When she gets to thirty-seven, her lungs force her back to the surface. She is above water long enough to hear Margaret shout, "Please, Lizzie, stop . . ." before gulping in another deep breath and propelling her body back down to the bottom of the pool.

Surfacing. ". . . don't be angry at me for . . ."

For. "Mom needs us to . . ."

More. ". . . a family, dammit, despite . . ."

Air. ". . . are you doing?!"

On Lizzie's sixth trip to the surface, Margaret is gone. Lizzie gasps in the summer air, breathing deep into her belly, hoping that this will make the pain go away. The knot there tightens and tightens, and she wonders whether God is punishing her. She is going to die here in the pool.

Your Lordness, she thinks. *Tell me what to do. Am I a sinner? Am I going to hell? What do I have to do to be happy again? What do I have to do to make everything in my family right? How can I be loved? How can I be good?* She recalls the photograph in her Bible of Mary, virtuous Mother of God, a beam of yellow light illuminating her from heaven, her face suffused with the joy of righteousness. Suffused with the forgiving love of Jesus. *Please Lord,* she thinks. *Give me a sign. Show me what to do.*

She opens her eyes and looks around. The pool water slaps against the tile. A dead dragonfly floats by her. Overhead, in the sky, there is no heavenly shaft of light, just a feathering white plume of exhaust trailing a private jet. She swims toward the air mattress, which bumps uselessly against the wall in the deep end like a prisoner with no chance of escape.

Halfway there, the knot in her stomach convulses and contracts. It feels as if someone has stabbed her. Lizzie chokes on the pain and closes her eyes. She paddles frantically toward the edge of the pool with one hand, the other clutching at her belly. Water churns and roils and splashes up her nose and she thinks she might drown.

Behind her, a trail of dark blood inks and spreads, marking her path through the water.

thirteen

janice feels the crunch of the gravel through
the thin rubber of her slippers, the slap of the purse against
her satin bathrobe as she jogs toward the car, the dimple of the
remote lock under her finger. She is behind the wheel of her
SUV and then—just like that—she is out the driveway. Her
pulse races, almost as fast as when she took too much It, but
this is just adrenaline. She presses the pedal to the floor, the
Porsche leaping forward like a thoroughbred released from the
gate (zero to sixty in 4.8 seconds, the salesman had told her,
but she'd never considered trying), and skids out as she
rounds the corner down the street, crushing some poor azalea
bushes in the Upadhyays' front yard.

Who had made the decision to leave? It was as if some invisible hand had jerked her forward, propelled her out and
away from her house. She passes the Gossetts' home and the
Brunschilds', drives past Lizzie's old nursery school and
toward downtown, before she realizes that she doesn't have a

destination. *It,* she thinks. *I want It.* And she has none. She should never have let James leave like that, a drastic mistake. Could she chase him down?

Reeling the car around—a U-turn, right in the middle of the street, nearly taking out a Porta Potti that sits in front of a freshly bulldozed home—Janice turns back toward her neighborhood. James was headed to Mexico, which means that he must be making his way toward the highway. She accelerates along the streets, keeping her eyes peeled for a red truck. He already has a fifteen-minute head start, but perhaps he stopped for gas or coffee? She can still catch him. She'll buy the entire contents of his glove compartment and maybe even talk him into sticking around for a while longer.

Lizzie is pregnant. Her initial shock and dismay has given way to anger. Lizzie is *pregnant.* How could her daughter have been so foolish? Was this somehow Margaret's influence, that magazine filling Lizzie's mind with sex talk and propaganda about vibrators? Was it Paul's fault, for never having given Lizzie the attention she deserved? Was it her own? What did she do wrong? She imagines her daughter, her swollen watermelon belly, waddling down Centerview Avenue, and swallows down the horror of it all—her poor baby girl will be shunned, her life will be ruined. And Janice, Janice too will be judged. A middle-aged woman abandoned by her rich husband, with one daughter in debt and living back at home and a second one pregnant before she even has a driver's license. Janice knows this town well enough to understand that they will see her at the center of all this disaster and find her somehow lacking. It is always the mother's fault, isn't it? It is *not fair.*

It. She needs It. Janice had worked so hard to give It up, had locked herself in her own bedroom like a patient in a lunatic asylum, a cell padded with silk wallpaper and wall-to-wall pile carpeting but a cell just the same. She had persevered through the most difficult week of her life—a week of sweaty nightmares in which she was chased by faceless monsters with grasping claws, an excruciating week of insomnia and nausea and anxiety so overwhelming that she thought she would suffocate, a week in which she was finally and totally consumed by her own failed marriage. She'd committed herself to quitting with the same perseverance with which she'd tackled a six-course dinner party, and she had succeeded despite what she now knew were impossible odds. When she woke up this morning without that feeling of *want*, she knew she had somehow kicked It, but this moment wasn't as victorious as she'd imagined it would be. Instead, it was as if she had committed murder, killing off the better version of herself—the more spirited, more interesting, more adventurous self—that she had only recently met. But that was all right; she had done it because she'd thought she had to.

Now, though, she wonders why she'd bothered to go through that hell. She had relinquished the one thing that had brought her relief, and why? For her ungrateful, deceitful, irresponsible children? For some sense of obligation to a community that's rejecting her despite everything she's done to earn a place in it? For fear of being found out by her philandering, deceitful, soon-to-be ex-husband? It was an *unjustifiable* homicide, and she is thankful now for the chance for resurrection.

Affixed to the sun visor is a laminated photograph of her family, a picture snapped three years ago during a Christmas vacation in Hawaii, the last they'd all taken together. She'd always loved the photo: They sit in a foursquare formation on a ledge overlooking the ocean with leis around their necks, squinting into the sun, the sea impossibly turquoise behind them, and, for once, everyone is smiling. The Millers in paradise. And yet. She remembers, now, the awkward dinners, during which Janice and Margaret bickered about whether the luxury resort Janice had so carefully selected was causing some local ecological disaster, and Lizzie took five trips to the sundae bar, and Paul left the table before dessert to call the office back home. Janice sees now that she had invented the whole thing—the solid marriage, the happy children, the cozy family unit. None of it had ever existed. Instead, it was all just a horrible mistake. Janice yanks the photo down and tosses it in the back seat's footwell.

"To hell with them," she says out loud, just to clear the ringing in her ears. Then she yells, even louder, "To hell with them!" It sounds marvelous, and huge. She loosens the bathrobe, letting it slip down her shoulders to expose the straps of her nightgown. She is giddy with the madness of it all—driving recklessly through town in her pajamas, hunting for drugs, not even wearing a seat belt! It is insane, and she shivers as she realizes that this pleases her. Could she let it all go, once and for all? All the control and the stability and the need to do *the best thing*? Why not?

But first she must find It. She can feel a residual surge in her veins, a faint lift, compelling her forward. She drives by the gas station, but James's truck is not there, and it's not parked in the Starbucks parking lot. By the time she arrives at the highway she realizes that he is surely well on his way, headed south toward the border. The on-ramp looms ahead, and she has to choose whether to merge with the accelerating cars and let their momentum carry her onto the interstate or to turn around. For a moment, she is tempted: Onward, toward James—she can still overtake him! But already this is starting to feel like a wild-goose chase, and that is what ultimately causes her to brake and turn right, back toward town. Is she really going to pursue him all the way to Mexico in her nightgown?

Besides, surely James isn't the only drug dealer in Santa Rita! Doesn't one find such a thing at a bus depot (this is the first faint vision that pops into her head) or in a dark alley . . .

and yet there are neither in the tidy streets of this town. Perhaps the train station? She turns sharply to the right—driving straight through a stop sign without slowing down—and backtracks toward the center of town, where the commuter trains stop every thirty minutes during rush hour. She pulls into the parking lot, lined with late-model German luxury sedans waiting for their owners to return on the 6:10 express, and peers into the tiny brick shelter that serves as a station. It is deserted, just a copy of the *Wall Street Journal* on an empty bench, riffling in a faint breeze.

What now? She starts the car and turns it back toward the east side of town, toward Millard Fillmore High. She has a hunch that this is where drug dealers would likely be lurking, where their customer base is most concentrated. The irony is not lost on her that she and Paul had moved to this town precisely because it *didn't* have drug dealers, because it seemed a nice, safe, wholesome community in which to raise a family. And yet of course they'd been deluded; no town is really safe anymore, is it? The insidious creep of social decay has reached here anyway, has breached the fortress walls, because otherwise how could Lizzie have ended up pregnant, how could Paul have left her for another woman, how could Janice herself have ended up hunting for a drug dealer on an overcast August afternoon?

The high school comes up on her right, and she circles the block, surveying it from every angle as she considers her options. Summer school has ended, the parking lot is empty, the grounds deserted. She drives through the front gate, under the LED display sign that reads, CONGRATS SENIORS! SCHOOL STARTS SEPTEMBER 3 and past the auditorium, prepped for the fall term with a coat of fresh paint. A teacher exits the door of the main building, carrying an empty fish tank, and scurries across the parking lot toward one lonely green Passat with a dent in the front passenger door. Worried about appearing conspicuous, Janice drives away, circling back around the school toward the athletic fields.

There, on the edge of the freshly reseeded turf, she sees what she's come for. Two teenage boys are sitting on the edge of the field, their feet in the dust of the track, smoking. The boys are black and—she hates herself for the racial profiling but isn't there some truth in all that? don't the stereotypes exist for a reason?—they look faintly dangerous, their hair worming tight against their skulls in cornrows, their baggy jeans hanging so low that she can see the dimpled crescents of their behinds, like bruised fruit, rising over their belts. They hunch under the weight of their own arrogant attitudes, against the chill of the fog coming in over the foothills, and pass the cigarette back and forth. Janice suspects that if she were to roll down the window, she would smell the now-familiar reek of marijuana. If anyone in Santa Rita knows where to get *It,* she recognizes, it would be them.

Janice parks at the far end of the lot, just on the other side of the chain-link fence, and watches the boys' backs. One of them glances up, registers the presence of her SUV, and leans over to say something to his friend, who immediately cups the joint out of view inside his palm. Janice tightens the robe around herself and pulls her purse into her lap in preparation. Her pulse has accelerated until she can hear it in her ears, a high-pitched rush like the sound of wind screaming against an airplane. What will she say? What will they think? It doesn't matter. She can feel herself forsaking everything—her family, her identity, the entire life she used to want so badly—and she is relieved to finally relinquish that tight grip, to unpeel her fingers and just slip away forever.

She thinks of van Gogh, of the exploding fury of his starry night sky—hinting at some entirely new, enraptured reality—and remembers that in the end, he cut his ear off and then shot himself. Is that the endgame of her own madness? And yet she can't quite let go of her grip on the door handle. If she can open it, she thinks, and walk toward the boys, she will somehow be free of all this. Freedom. She has never *really* had it, she has walked away from it every time it presented itself, and it finally sits right there, so close at hand, with so many possibilities. Can she surrender to its thrall, and give herself up as a selfish mother who just doesn't care anymore? Can she walk away entirely, leave her lost children to fend for themselves, leave Santa Rita altogether and start a new life somewhere else? Paris, all these years later!

She pushes the door open and looks down from her driver's-seat perch. The asphalt seems two miles away, and she is suddenly dizzy, as if she were about to step off a precipice. She is rejecting everything she's ever worked for, is risking her children's lives and her own, but instead of feeling like she's falling into a void, when she finally does swing her legs around and slip down—her satin robe sliding against the leather of the seat, the key in the ignition emitting a warning, *ding ding ding*—she instead senses that she is being lifted safely up, as if by a current of warm air. No, she *doesn't* care anymore. She doesn't care! A low laugh erupts from the back of her throat.

Janice steps out onto the field, the fresh turf giving slightly under her slippers, her purse hugged in tight against her side. The boys are just yards away, and from here she can definitely smell the marijuana smoke, the tang of unwashed bodies and fresh sweat. She walks eagerly toward them. But the sound of her car door slamming has startled them, and, without turning around, they are standing up and wiping the dust off their jeans, preparing to walk away. The shorter boy tosses the joint on the ground and grinds it under a white basketball shoe the size of a loaf of bread, then pulls the hood of his black sweatshirt over his hair, as if to avoid being identified.

She sees herself suddenly as they must—a middle-aged white woman in a fancy car, not their usual customer, surely.

They are avoiding her. And she hurries to close the gap between them, too intent on catching up to consider what she is going to do when she does. The boys start to walk down the track, and she picks up her pace, perspiring with the effort despite the chill in the air. She trips on her slippers in the tall grass and falls on one knee, but she bounces back up immediately, too focused on her goal to pay attention to the pain that flares out from her hip.

Finally, the two boys break into a run, and she realizes that she is about to lose them. She chases after them, the purse knocking against her side, the robe falling open to expose her nightgown. "It's okay!" she calls at their backs, growing panicked. "It's okay! Don't run!"

At the sound of her voice, the shorter of the two boys turns his head and looks back at her. Their eyes meet and when they do, she cannot breathe. He is astonishingly young—Lizzie's age, maybe even younger, his features still softened by baby fat, his skin as yet unscarred by adolescent acne. She recognizes the fear in his wide eyes before he turns back around and runs even faster, thin adolescent limbs pumping frantically inside oversized jeans. He is not yet a hardened criminal—perhaps not a criminal at all, just someone's child, smoking pot in the afternoon—and this, for some reason, breaks her heart. She looks at him and sees Lizzie, sees Margaret too, young and lost and afraid.

She stops abruptly and watches the boys run away, scaling the chain-link fence and tumbling out toward the street, and she begins to cry. She cries because despite everything, despite all the years of obediently following the rules and trying her hardest to be the wife and mother she had chosen to be, she has not been able to protect her children. They are sad, they feel pain, they rail against the world and come up short and it *hurts.* She has failed. She hasn't even been able to protect herself. Her tears begin as a sniffle and then turn into a wail, mucus dripping out of her nose and crawling, thick and salty, over her upper lip, rivulets of tears collecting in the crease of her nose before darting down to her chin, a pool of moisture collecting in her nightgown cleavage.

She stands, weeping, in the center of the open field, the tender new turf spreading out in every direction, the dull gray sky low above her. She is unable to move, unable to walk away, unable even to fall to her knees in the grass. For a moment, she thinks that time has stopped altogether and she will remain here for all eternity, in this field, exposed and alone.

It takes a few moments for her to realize that her cell phone is ringing. She reaches blindly for it, digging into the purse that she still has clutched to her side. When she flips the phone open, she is surprised to see that the caller ID has identified her own phone number. HOME, it flashes. For a minute, Janice is confused, as if she has been split in two, leaving one Janice at home to call the other. She lifts the phone to her ear and waits to see what she is going to say to herself.

But it is Margaret on the other end. Her voice is high-pitched, and even though she is trying to speak slowly, Janice can hear the fear in her daughter's words. Instinctively, Janice's heart lurches.

"Mom," says Margaret, "I just found Lizzie bleeding in the pool."

"Bleeding?" Janice echoes. Her throat, already constricted with phlegm, closes further until she can hardly breathe. She looks out at the street. The boys have vanished completely, and now all she can see is the afternoon traffic, driving slowly by. "Did she hurt herself?"

"I don't know," Margaret says. "There's a lot of blood. She says she's got terrible cramps, too. She's freaking out!"

Janice experiences an electric shock of memory—herself, hunched over a toilet, screaming with the pain. "It's a miscarriage," she says, remembering. "Lizzie's having a miscarriage."

She takes a deep breath and turns back toward her car, parked at the edge of the field. She feels a curious sense of relief as the possibilities that lay before her only minutes ago fly away, one by one, until there is only one option before her. As she jogs back to the parking lot, she is surprised by her own calm. She can see exactly what needs to be done, each act—summon the ambulance, retrieve the insurance card from her desk, call Dr. Brunschild, pack Lizzie's nightgown—flashing in sequence before her.

"A miscarriage?" Margaret sounds hysterical. "What should I do?"

"This is what we're going to do, Margaret," she says. "It's going to be all right, honey—I'm right here, I'm only a few blocks away. I'm coming home."

the hospital waiting room needs to be re-decorated. The two rows of facing seats are plastic and orange and discolored from decades of spilled coffee and runny noses. Margaret slumps in a chair across from Janice, several feet of worn linoleum separating them, and reads a dog-eared copy of *Sunset* magazine. Janice watches CNN on a grainy television bolted to the wall. The sound is off, so she reads the news ticker. The Nasdaq is down 30 points. A suicide bombing in the Middle East killed fourteen. The president went fishing with the secretary of defense at his ranch and caught a sturgeon. An endangered panda bear in the zoo has given birth. These facts soothe her: Outside, the world continues as normal. People die. People live. People fish.

In the lap of her sweatsuit, Janice holds the bloody beach towel she'd wrapped Lizzie in for the ride, now folded neatly into a square so the stains don't show. Lizzie is in the examining room. Janice wonders whether Lizzie's sudden and—yes, thank God—convenient miscarriage is her reward for not finally succumbing to It. When she stopped, out in the middle of the field, was it her maternal instinct, still there despite it all, wresting control? Did she sense, as she neared the precipice, that Lizzie was bleeding in the pool and that she needed to turn back? Yes, she decides. She likes this idea.

Janice examines Margaret, who has put on weight since her return home; a softness has returned to her bony frame, something about the roundness of her shoulders and a touch of flesh under the chin. Margaret studies her magazine intently, as if truly absorbed by *Sunset*'s spring planting tips, but Janice sees that her eyes are not moving at all but boring holes through the center of the page. It strikes Janice that she has wasted the last six weeks scrubbing the kitchen in a drugged frenzy when she should have been finding out why her older daughter is so unhappy, just as she should have noticed that her younger daughter was no longer a virgin.

Margaret looks up and catches Janice staring at her. She lets the magazine sag. "Can a miscarriage cause permanent damage?" she asks. "It looked so horrible. All that blood."

"She'll be fine," says Janice.

"Are you just being optimistic or do you know something I don't?" asks Margaret.

"I had three of them myself," says Janice. "So yes, I know."

The magazine drops to Margaret's lap. "I didn't know you'd had a miscarriage. Let alone three? Three miscarriages?"

"They told me I might not be able to have another baby, after you," says Janice. "When I gave birth to you, I ruptured my uterus. I couldn't carry a baby to term, so eventually we stopped trying. Lizzie was a happy accident. I thought you knew."

"You never told me."

"Oh. I'm sorry." Janice knows that she never told her daughter—she never told anyone, not even her mother. Somehow the miscarriages had always seemed a failure on her part, a weakness she didn't want the world to share. But now they feel irrelevant, such ancient history that they might have happened to another person.

"How much does a miscarriage hurt? Relatively speaking, of course."

Janice remembers a violent smear of pain, a melancholic sense of inevitability. "It was horrible," she says.

"I've never been pregnant," says Margaret thoughtfully.

"I certainly hope not," says Janice.

Margaret picks the magazine up, reads a line, then puts it down again. "Are you going through withdrawal? From the . . ." She looks around the empty room. "You know."

"Withdrawal?" Janice thinks of the boys in the field, the one cupping the joint in his palm. "No, I went through all that already, I think," she says, hoping that this will be true.

Margaret smiles thinly. "I guess I should commend you for at least being adventurous with your choice of substances. I wouldn't have thought it of you."

Janice looks at Margaret, sitting across from her, and wonders if this is a backhanded compliment. But there isn't any judgment in her daughter's face, just a faraway look of bemused wonder. Janice lets her daughter's strange—if misplaced—admiration settle in, feeling a bit like a prizefighter showing off her bruises. "Well," she says wryly. "Had I known it was so addictive I wouldn't have."

"I can't believe you didn't know what it was," says Margaret. She pauses. "Actually, come to think of it, I can."

"Honestly, Margaret. I can't believe I'm having this conversation with you." But secretly Janice is pleased that her daughter can joke about it. In place of judgment, she sees the possibility of an unexpected closeness.

Margaret raises her eyebrows. "Well, it's better than what we talked about all summer, right? Which is to say, nothing at all. At least this means something. At least it's real." Janice considers this quietly, thinking that it is, perhaps, the wisest thing Margaret has said in weeks. Everything is in the open, all her ugliness out for display and discussion, and even though it *is* ghastly, leaving Janice feeling raw and naked, somehow it isn't as painful as she'd imagined it would be. She smiles wanly at her daughter.

They lapse into silence. The news ticker on CNN informs them that back-to-school sales start this weekend. That New York City has broken heat records. That a cyclone in Texas uprooted six houses and left fifty-two homeless. Janice closes her eyes, and when she opens them again she asks Margaret, "You and Bart broke up, didn't you?"

Margaret stares at the TV screen, and for a moment Janice thinks that Margaret hasn't heard her. Then she swings her gaze to Janice. "Yes," she says. "In the spring. He left me. He's dating a movie star now."

"And . . . *Snatch*?"

"Over and done."

"Why didn't you tell me?"

Margaret looks down at her hands. "Because telling you would have made it real. And I didn't know what would be worse—your disappointment in me, or my disappointment in myself. Plus, you hated the magazine."

"I didn't hate it," Janice says. She pauses. "Mostly, I just found it frightening."

Margaret looks at her queerly. "I'm not sure what you mean by that."

Janice tries to come up with an explanation, but she can't figure out how to start. Instead, she stands and goes over to Margaret and sits down next to her in the orange bucket seat. She takes Margaret's hand from her lap and squeezes it in her own. Margaret leans her head on Janice's shoulder and sighs. The sound makes the hair on Janice's arms stand on end; she closes her eyes and feels the weight of Margaret in her bones.

"I don't think you're a disappointment," Janice says. "I admire your ambition. And you're only twenty-eight. You can still do anything you want."

Margaret's chest rises and falls heavily with her breath. After a minute, Janice hears her voice, muffled. "Are you lonely without Dad?" asks Margaret.

"Yes," says Janice, realizing, though she hadn't considered it before, that this is true. The thought of fall's impending arrival, with Lizzie starting school and Margaret's inevitable departure, frightens her. "But I don't miss him," she adds.

"We're going to lose in court next week, aren't we?" Margaret asks, her head still resting on Janice.

Janice smiles wanly. "Most likely," she says. "Your father has very expensive lawyers."

"I can't believe he could love you so little," says Margaret.

This stings. "It's more complicated than that," she says. "Your father is a selfish man, but he loved me in his own way. It's just, I think he realized far too late that he didn't want what he'd thought he'd wanted from me. Maybe I can't blame him for that. Or maybe I can, I don't know. It was my decision, too."

"You didn't ever think that marrying him was a mistake?"

Janice pauses, then admits the truth. "No, I knew it might have been," she says, thinking back to college, to pills wrapped in foil, to Paul's resigned knee sinking into the soil. "I knew it before I even married him. I just chose to ignore it because I wanted something else—I thought I wanted stability, security— more. It's what I thought I needed. And there was you." She looks down at Margaret, twenty-eight and single and in a financial mess but totally unencumbered, and admits to herself (even if she will never say it out loud) that what she has long felt in her daughter's presence is envy.

Margaret squeezes Janice's hand, once, and sits up. The ghostly impression of her head remains behind on Janice's shoulder, where the skin tingles. "We can't let him win," she says.

"It doesn't matter that much anymore," says Janice. "I'll have enough to live on. It will just take some adjusting to."

"It's the principle of the thing," argues Margaret. She rolls the *Sunset* magazine into a tight cylinder and raps it against her thigh. "And I hate to see him . . . diminishing you like that. Especially in public."

"Well, it's not *that* public," says Janice. "No one needs to know. It's not like we're having a press conference. It's not like our friends and neighbors will be visiting us at divorce court."

Margaret turns to her mother and stares at her. She appears to be thinking very hard, and Janice wonders what on earth she said that is so difficult to comprehend. As she watches, Margaret uncoils before her, pushes herself to the edge of her seat, slaps at the chair one last time with the rolled-up magazine, and then drops it to the floor so that she can rummage in her shoulder bag. "What?" Janice asks. "What?"

Margaret has her hands buried deep in her purse. The bag, a battered brown leather thing that looks as if it lost all of its shape back in 1972, smells moldy even from where Janice sits. Margaret extricates a used Kleenex, an empty tequila bottle—Janice clucks in protest—some illegible receipts and a mesh coin purse filled with pennies, and drops them in her lap. Finally, she unpeels a small rectangle of paper, stained by dark liquid, and flourishes it triumphantly. "Can I borrow your cell phone?" she asks.

"Who are you calling?"

"I'll tell you later," says Margaret.

Janice hands Margaret her phone and watches Margaret slip through the automatic doors of the waiting room and into the parking lot. Through the glass, Janice sees Margaret talking, the cell phone pressed to one ear, her thumb plugged into the other to block out the noise of an incoming ambulance.

Watching her, Janice envisions an alternate universe—still a viable universe—in which Margaret is a crisp and efficient businesswoman, making deals on her cell phone as she jets from city to city. She can be anything she wants to be.

As Janice observes Margaret through the doors, Lizzie appears in the waiting room, wearing a paper bathrobe and holding a fistful of forms. Around her wrist, a blue plastic band; her feet are still bare. She looks anemic, her tan drained away with the blood in the pool. Her first few steps into the room are unfocused and slow, and she weaves a bit as if she might collapse right there on the dirty linoleum. But then Lizzie sees her mother and her face lifts into an expression of such guileless relief that tears come to Janice's eyes. She rises from her chair just in time to catch her daughter as Lizzie tips forward, letting the weight of her body fall against her mother and come to a rest. They stand there, pressed together, breathing in time. Somewhere behind her, Janice hears the ambulance paramedics shouting commands to each other as they burst through the automatic sliding doors and into the waiting room with a man on a gurney, a chaotic tangle of dripping IVs and plastic tubes and bloody limbs. Janice barely notices.

For the first time in longer than she can recall, she feels happy.

fourteen

they catch her in the driveway, when she
goes out to pick up the morning paper. "Margaret Miller?"
she hears and she turns, surprised. For a hallucinatory
minute, she thinks that the man striding up the drive might be
an admirer—a fan of *Snatch,* perhaps, coming to pay his re-
spects—and she instinctively smiles, despite the fact that he is
not at all her readership's demographic: male, for one, but
also middle-aged and wearing cowboy boots and a baseball
cap. But perhaps he's a journalist? Could they have arrived already? She stands there, blinking in the yellow dawn, still half
asleep. He walks toward her and says her name again, his voice
raspy and demanding. "Margaret Miller?"

Margaret nods before she can think better of it, and he
steps in, so close that she can smell the peanuts on his breath
and see the graying stubble on his chin. "You've been served,"
he barks, and his hand jerks forward until the document he
holds is just a millimeter away from her chest, quivering with

proximity. Shocked, she looks down at the smudged envelope—her name unmistakably typed on the front—and takes it from his hand. The man wheels around and walks back down the driveway, his boots crunching through the gravel.

She reads the summons in the kitchen as she drinks a cup of coffee. Visa is suing her for the $32,448.23 balance on her card. This is just the first of a series of summons coming her way in the upcoming weeks, she realizes. She imagines them, tripping over one another in the race to her door, hordes of process servers leapfrogging up the driveway. Looking at the September court date written there on the document, she discovers that it is a relief to know that the end is finally here. She is tired of waiting.

The kitchen is quiet. It is early, and her mother is still sleeping upstairs, compensating for a summer of insomnia. Pushing the court order aside, Margaret opens the *New York Times* and turns to the business section. There, on page C4, she finds the story she's looking for. "Applied Pharm CEO in Divorce Suit," the headline reads, and seeing those words gives Margaret a little jolt. Despite the fact that she knew the article was going to run, it still surprises her to see it in print, so concrete, so *final*. And so fast. It's an impressive tribute to Kelly Maxfield's talents, if leaking gossip can be rightfully considered a skill.

Kelly had been at a Mommy and Me music class when Margaret reached her on the phone the day of Lizzie's miscarriage. In the background, Margaret could hear a hollow clanging and lightbulb-shattering wails and screeches. She had to yell her name into the receiver twice before Kelly—saying, "Who? I can't hear you! Who?"—registered who it was on the line. As she stood in the parking lot of the hospital, Margaret worried that the publicist had remembered her drunken rant at the movie theater and was pretending not to recognize her name. But finally Margaret's voice broke through the din of crying toddlers. "Margaret! Hi! I didn't think you'd take me up on my invitation!" Kelly screamed back, and Margaret could hear genuine pleasure in her voice. Even when Margaret confessed that this was not, in fact, a social call, Kelly didn't seem fazed. "Of course!" she said, as if Margaret's request for help screwing her own father was the most natural thing in the world.

When Margaret told Janice her idea of going to the press with their case, Janice went pale. "It's vulgar to be so public with your personal matters," she said. "Nice people don't." It wasn't until Margaret mentioned Kelly Maxfield's name that Janice relented. Still, it took the better part of a morning for Kelly and Margaret to convince Janice that she wouldn't have to talk to anyone personally or reveal anything other than the legal details of the situation, that she would, if anything, emerge blameless and righteous and deserving of justice. Still, her mother would have nothing to do with the planning, as if ignoring it meant it wasn't happening at all.

So Kelly and Margaret met without her. On Friday, they devised their strategy in Kelly's home office, a sunny room strewn with baby toys and piles of press kits for companies like HyperGiz and InnoModo. The baby itself—a fat little ball of flesh named Audrey—slept in a Bugaboo stroller that Kelly pushed back and forth with her foot while she rapped out e-mails on her BlackBerry.

Kelly called their PR campaign a "public shaming" and noted that this tactic had worked very effectively for Jack Welch's wife when she'd revealed the astonishing details of his GE perks. "She walked away with half of his net worth, which was a flipping fortune," Kelly said as she pulled newspaper clippings out of a file cabinet. "Your mom—poor woman, I just feel so *bad* for her—is going to get tons of sympathy. God, I can only imagine. Anyway, we'll start by getting a story Monday in the *New York Times,* for legitimacy. What the *Times* will write won't be as *colorful,* but we can leave that to the also-rans that will pick up the story Tuesday." The stroller zipped back and forth, the baby's head wobbling sleepily from side to side.

Margaret, lulled into a hypnotic state by the movement, nodded. "How much will this cost?" she asked.

Kelly hesitated. "Usually I charge two hundred dollars an hour," she said. "Three hundred for corporate. But I'll do this for you pro bono, as an old friend. At least for the first twenty hours. Sound good?"

"That's great," said Margaret. "Better than great."

"We'll need a statement from your mother."

Margaret pulled a folded paper from her purse. "I have one. I wrote it for her."

Kelly released the stroller and read it. "This is *perfect,* Margaret!" she said. "'Pained beyond words.' Like something from a movie! God, I hate writing statements, it's always such a *minefield.* Maybe you should consider a career in PR—you're a natural!" She dipped into a bowl of jelly beans on her desk, picked through them, and proffered a few pupalike remainders. "Do you like the banana ones?"

Margaret found herself admiring Kelly's focused efficiency, as Kelly commandeered the legal documents the newspapers would require, briskly composed a half dozen e-mails, and set two assistants in her central office to the task of collecting relevant press clippings. If she had hired Kelly as her CFO perhaps *Snatch* wouldn't have been such a financial disaster, she found herself thinking, and she warmed to this woman, despite the fact that Kelly, complacently suburban and content to live in the shadows of other people's renown, was the antithesis of everything Margaret had ever wanted to be.

"Thanks," she said, recalling how dismissive she'd been of Kelly at the movie theater. "You didn't need to be so nice to me."

Kelly fluttered a hand, as if shooing away a fly. "I always

looked up to you in high school," she said. "I can't say it's not an ego boost to be needed."

The baby woke up and began to cry. Kelly swept her up with one hand, calmly unbuttoned her ruffled blouse, and clamped the baby to her nipple. The baby suckled greedily, as Margaret averted her eyes. "I should change her and get started on calls," Kelly said.

Margaret rose quickly and moved toward the door. Kelly followed, propping the front door open with a hip, and as Margaret squeezed by she gripped her elbow with her free hand. "You know, I always run into these creeps who dump their wives for trophy girlfriends after they make it big," she said, looking down at her blissed-out baby. "They're crawling all over the tech conferences with skinny pretty little assistants who follow them around carrying their briefcases, fetching their coffee, acting like they're gods. And they treat us—their publicists—like maids whose only purpose is to cover for their mistakes." She paused and looked up at Margaret. "I know I shouldn't say this, because he's still your father, but I always thought your dad was an egotistical opportunist. I admire your balls." And she swept Margaret through the door.

For a while, Kelly's words kept Margaret floating on a cloud of vindication—she was doing the right thing—until yesterday morning, when she woke up in a panic thinking she had made a terrible mistake. How could she betray her father so completely? If he was dismissive of her before, she could only imagine how he would feel about her after this. *You don't care,* she told herself, but twenty-eight years of habit informed her otherwise. Now, as she looks at her words in the *New York Times,* she knows that it doesn't matter either way because it's too late to stop this train.

The story is six short paragraphs on the bottom corner of the page—barely an article at all—across from the Nasdaq listings, where APPI appears at 134½ a share. She had hoped for a front-page exposé or, at the least, a photograph. It is deflating to see that what felt to her like an epic—a six-hour opera of Sturm und Drang—did not merit even a cover blurb.

Paul Miller, CEO of Applied Pharmaceuticals, is due in court this Friday for the first hearing in a divorce suit against his estranged wife, Janice Miller. According to court documents, Mr. Miller is seeking to prevent his wife of 29 years from splitting his stock grant from Applied Pharmaceuticals, valued, at today's share price, at $376.6 million.

Central to the suit is an unusual "postnuptial" document—signed by Mrs. Miller at the time of Mr. Miller's assumption of the CEO position—that cedes any rights to Applied Pharmaceutical—related assets, including stock and stock options. Mrs. Miller asserts that she was unaware of the contentious one-paragraph clause, inserted into a 411-page document otherwise intended to address the logistics of Miller's compensation package from Applied Pharmaceuticals. She is countersuing for half of all joint assets, citing California divorce law.

"My client was coerced into signing documents that were presented to her as standard Applied Pharmaceutical documentation and, trusting her husband, she failed to employ counsel that might have noted this disadvantageous wording," said Mrs. Miller's attorney, Lewis Grosser. "What person in the world would have signed away that much money had she not been deceived? More importantly, what kind of husband would do such a thing to his wife?"

Janice Miller offered a written statement, via her attorney. "I am pained beyond words by the dissolution of my family and am optimistic that the California legal system will be fair and just."

Margaret reads that line again, now hating the florid flourish of "pained beyond words"—she would never have let that
cliché into the pages of *Snatch,* so why did she think it was appropriate for the *Times*? It doesn't sound like something her
mother would say, even if Janice had signed off on it. She
reads on:

> According to divorce filings, which the *New York Times* has
> obtained, Mr. Miller plans to offer $72,000 a year in
> alimony to his wife, plus $4,000 a month in child support.
> The Millers have two daughters, Margaret, 28, and
> Elizabeth, 14. Mr. Miller's current compensation is listed
> in S-1 filings as $489,000 a year, with an additional
> 2.8 million shares of Applied Pharmaceutical stock.
> Coifex, Applied Pharmaceutical's much-anticipated hair-
> regeneration drug, is due to arrive on pharmacy shelves this
> fall, after clinical trials showed an unprecedented 96 percent
> success rate. Due to delays, Applied Pharmaceutical (APPI)
> shares have dropped from a height of 148.75 a share in the
> weeks after Applied Pharmaceutical's IPO on June 28 to a
> current share price of 134½.
>
> Mr. Miller declined to comment. Applied Pharmaceu-
> ticals spokeswoman Linda Lockly said, "We don't discuss the
> personal matters of our staff."

And it ends there, abruptly. It seems so inconsequential—
just words on paper, disposable pages that will be lining bird-
cages and starting barbecues before the end of the day.
Probably nothing is going to come of it all. And yet, looking
at this tiny little blip of a story, she remembers the glow of accomplishment she used to get when a new issue of *Snatch* came
back from the printer's and she held the pages for the first
time, lifted the bales of magazines off the delivery pallet and
lined them up in towers on the living room floor. There they

were, her words, manifested as a physical *thing*, ready to go out and make an impact on the world. She should pop open a bottle of champagne, she thinks bizarrely, and wishes someone—her mother, Lizzie, James, anyone—was there to celebrate with her. But Lizzie is upstairs in bed, and James is long gone to Mexico, and Margaret suspects that Janice will not be eager to raise a toast to the airing of the family's dirty laundry in public.

Margaret refolds the paper and leaves it lying on the kitchen counter as she takes a tray holding a bowl of cereal and a glass of orange juice up to Lizzie's bedroom. Lizzie is propped up on a mound of pillows, watching soap operas. Five days after her miscarriage she is no longer confined to bed rest, but she has been wallowing in the role of invalid anyway, and no one is stopping her. When Margaret walks into the room, she emits a tiny moan.

"Uhhhhhhhhh. My stomach is *killing* me." She eyes the breakfast tray. "Is there any bacon?"

"Mom isn't up yet," says Margaret, as she fits the tray over Lizzie's legs. "And I don't fry."

Lizzie lifts a spoonful of soggy cereal to her mouth and slurps it down. "So," she says. "Did they print it?"

"The story?" Margaret says. "Yes."

"Was it good?"

"I'm not sure 'good' is really the right word to use. But I think so. I'm not sure."

"Is Dad going to, like, freak out?"

"Maybe," says Margaret. "Don't answer the phone. Can I get you anything else?"

"Something to read, maybe?"

"Sure," says Margaret. "What about something by Joan Didion? Have you read her yet?"

Lizzie hesitates. "I was thinking more like . . . the new *Us Weekly*?"

Margaret considers the libraries of fine literature that Lizzie is never going to read, the great philosophers Lizzie will never ponder, all the feminist thinkers whose names Lizzie will never remember. She thinks of her sister's brain cells, winking out one by one, like insects drifting into a bug zapper, as Lizzie wastes the rest of her life worrying about movie stars' love lives and pondering the secrets of Hollywood personal trainers. "Anything you want, kiddo."

Lizzie beams, and Margaret swims for a moment in her sister's guileless pleasure. "Thanks," Lizzie says. "I promise I'll read a book next."

Downstairs, Margaret finds her mother in the kitchen, dressed and drinking a cup of coffee. She is still pale and thin in her jogging suit, but the hollows under her eyes are starting to vanish and she looks sturdy again, like a sailor rediscovering his sea legs. She stands over the kitchen counter, skimming the front page of the newspaper and blowing on her steaming cup of coffee. The business section sits next to her, still folded. Margaret pours herself a cup of coffee and sits down beside her at the counter. She picks up the entertainment section and flips through it, past a full-page advertisement for *Thruster* ("Pumping, thrusting summer fun!"—*Sioux City Journal*; "Johnson is a real man's man!"—KKBX, Fargo), a story about reality television stars who launch their own clothing lines, and a profile of a twelve-year-old boy whose novel has just made the best-seller list. A concrete-mixing truck growls by out front, en route to a construction site down the road.

"Aren't you going to say something about the article?" Margaret finally asks.

Janice looks down at the business section at her elbow, as if noticing it for the first time. "I'd rather not read it," she says. "I only want to know when it's over."

The phone starts to ring, and Margaret lunges for the receiver, realizing as she does that this is probably the first time in months she has been eager to find out who might be on the other end of the line. "Hello?" Her eyes meet Janice's across the kitchen island. Janice peers at her over the top of her mug, where it has frozen just below her nose. Tiny tremors vibrate across the surface of the coffee.

"Hi there, I'm calling from CNBC?" says a woman's voice. "I'm trying to get in touch with Janice Miller?"

by midmorning it is clear that the story has
had more impact than five inches of type might have implied. The *San Francisco Chronicle* calls, and so does the *Wall Street Journal.* CNET. CNN. Janice will not answer the phone, so Margaret does it for her, referring each call to Kelly Maxfield, saying nothing except "no comment" (an infuriating phrase, because of course she has comments, lots of them, and it is physically painful to hold them back). Through the kitchen window she can see Janice sitting in the garden, her ramrod back the only sign that her mother is listening, intently, to every word Margaret speaks into the receiver.

At the close of the stock market, when Margaret checks on-line, shares of Applied Pharmaceuticals have dropped from $134\frac{1}{2}$ a share to 128. She considers this—normal market fluctuation? or a sign of her father's impending doom?—before clicking away to Google. There she types in the phrase "credit card debt," then chooses the button "I'm feeling lucky." The summons lies on the desk beside her, still creased from her pocket.

She ends up at a Web site called Debt-B-Gone.com. Here Margaret can order a series of tapes for $99.99 that will teach her how to consolidate her credit card debt and outmaneuver her creditors. For $799.99, she can meet on the phone with a special counselor who will help her come up with a "lifetime affluence plan." "Face your debt demons one step at a time," the Web site offers, and Margaret thinks that modern life is just an endless series of traps, each one lying just beyond the last. There is no safe, direct path anymore, no bread-crumb trail to follow. Existence has become an evasive maneuver.

In the hallway she hears her mother's footsteps, and then Janice appears in the door of the study with a plate of sliced fruit. "Summer peaches," she says, looking down at the fruit. "It's almost the end of the season, so you should enjoy them while you can." She comes over to where Margaret sits at the desk and then stops, her eyes drawn to the document near her daughter's hand. Margaret watches as her mother scans the summons upside down, not even bothering to be discreet about her curiosity, while the plate in her hand makes a steep trajectory toward the desk.

Clunk. The plate takes a hard landing, the peach slices rocking back and forth on the white china as they sweat sugar syrup. "I want to give you the money," Janice says, and the words erupt from her with a vehemence that surprises Margaret. "Even if I don't win the lawsuit. I'll liquidate some assets."

Margaret looks down at the summons and then up at the granite expression on her mother's face. She can see now that saying yes to her mother would be, in fact, a kind of gift—not for her, but for Janice. Yet she still can't do it. "No," she says. *Don't say it,* her mind tells her, too late. She forges ahead nonetheless. "No. I don't want you to do that."

"It'll be a loan, Margaret. You'll pay me back."

"Thanks, Mom," she says, feeling her tentative conviction gathering force, the hazy decision that's been germinating in the back of her mind hatching itself as fully formed words for the first time. "But I've decided that I'm going to declare bankruptcy. It's the cleanest way." Her mother's eyebrows spring toward the ceiling, and Margaret hurries to explain herself. "It's not going to hurt that much, really. I don't really have anything for them to take, except maybe my car, and somehow I doubt they'll want that."

Janice purses her lips, and Margaret can tell this was the wrong thing to say. "You'd rather declare bankruptcy than let your mother—let *me*—help you? Is that what this is about?"

"This is *not* about you. I just . . . I just want to feel like I'm starting fresh, not beholden to anyone, not riding on anyone else's coattails. Does that make sense? If I take your money I'll feel even smaller than I already do, and I don't need that pressure. Honestly, Mom, you handed me my life on a silver platter and I really appreciate it, but you don't have to give me this, too. It's my fault, not yours."

Janice touches the summons with a thumb, rotating it so that she can read it more easily. "I understand that, Margaret, I do. But I'm your *mother.* I wish you'd reconsider. It will destroy your credit rating—it will be on your *permanent record.* I don't know how you'll ever buy a house!"

Margaret laughs, a sharp, bitter bark. "Somehow I really don't think that's my biggest problem right now."

"You'll need a lawyer."

"I know."

Janice sighs and shakes her head. "Sometimes I just don't understand you," she says. "Really, I don't."

by the time margaret wakes up the following morning, the story has made the local newspapers. On the cover of the business section of the *San Jose Mercury News* is a photograph of Paul—from the day Applied Pharmaceuticals went public—and a far more satisfying inch-high cover line: "NASDAQ DARLING IN DIVORCE SCANDAL." The *San Francisco Chronicle* skips the picture but adds a graph depicting the declining value of Applied Pharmaceuticals stock, a jagged

line that finishes in an arrow that points ominously downward.

By ten A.M., the stock is at 119.

The online and television news journals chime in as the
day passes, and Margaret is surprised to discover that her father's life is, in fact, a story of national interest. MSNBC
quotes an "unnamed member of the board of directors of Applied Pharmaceuticals who has registered his disappointment
that the personal life of the CEO is 'tarnishing the good name
of Coifex.' " CNN mentions "concerns from Applied Pharmaceuticals investors that the details of executive compensation and company finances will be dragged through the press."
Only Fox News has aligned itself firmly with Paul Miller's side
of the case: A pundit describes Janice Miller as "a greedy Silicon Valley housewife who hasn't earned a buck in her life and
expects everything given to her gratis." There is much con-
jecture about Coifex's delayed arrival on store shelves: Is
the FDA withdrawing approval? Are side effects being suppressed? Margaret wonders if this speculation is somehow
Kelly's doing.

That afternoon, there's a defensive press release from Applied Pharmaceuticals itself: "Coifex is on track to arrive in
pharmacies this fall. Any delays are strictly procedural." Media gossip Web sites publish the news that Paul Miller has hired
bulldog New York publicist David Farikow, a specialist in PR
disasters. From Paul himself, however, there are no statements, no denials; there is no public blustering whatsoever.
Her father does not call. The stock dips further: 112, and then
110, before the market closes.

The trial date looms just three days away: ten A.M. on Friday. The answering machine fills with messages from re-
porters, lawyers, neighbors, talent wranglers for network news
shows, even a few strangers (women, always) calling to "offer
support." Janice considers accepting an interview with Larry

King, but Kelly advises against it. "I have a feeler out to Oprah," she says. "Let's wait for her. It's a better match."

"Oprah?" Janice says. "Oh! I love Oprah." And Margaret notices a hard new gleam in her mother's eye—tempered with a twitch of shame, still, but steely with vengeance and self-righteousness. Against her will, she realizes, her mother is capable of enjoying this.

Margaret herself makes only one call, to Los Angeles. Josephine answers her cell phone with a wheezy "Hello?" She pants into the receiver, taking great winded gulps of air, as if she's running. Margaret can hear dogs barking in the background, the faint plaintive wail of a fire engine.

"What are you doing?" Margaret asks.

"Hiking in Runyon Canyon. Where are you? Where have you been? It's like you vanished off the face of the earth."

"At my parents' house," Margaret says. "You hike with your cell phone now?"

"I *know,* it's awful, but I'm expecting a phone call from my agent." Josephine gasps for breath. "Okay, I'm stopping. I just read the news this morning about what's going on with your family. Oh my God. Are you okay? No wonder you took off."

"Well, that wasn't the only reason. *Snatch* went under—Stuart Gelkind didn't buy it after all."

There's a hesitation on the other end. "Yeah, I kind of figured that out. There was a big feature about him in the *L.A. Times* last week and *Snatch* wasn't even mentioned, and everyone put two and two together."

"Oh," says Margaret, feeling queasy. "The jerk put me into bankruptcy."

"I am *so sorry,* Margaret," Josephine says. "*Snatch* was great, and he was stupid if he didn't see that."

Margaret indulges in a moment of self-pity. She swallows. "It's been a pretty lousy summer, Josie," she says.

"Oh! Honey!" Josephine's voice grows throaty with emotion. "Well, maybe this will make you feel a *little* better: Ysabelle van Lumis dumped Bart. Apparently she was cheating on him with Bobby Masterston the whole time."

"Oh," Margaret says, surprised. She sends out feelers along her body—to the tips of her toes, the back of her neck, the thumping muscle in her chest—trying to sense some residual anger, some pain, some hope. Something. But there's nothing, just a pinch—but only a pinch—of sadness. Perhaps a smidgen of schadenfreude. Did she ever love him in the first place? she wonders. Or was she just seduced by an aura of ambition? It doesn't really matter now. "I still owe him twelve thousand dollars," she tells Josephine. "Did I ever mention that? Another thing I need to sort out."

"He doesn't need it," sniffs Josephine. "You're coming back soon, right? I know *Snatch* is done, but you could take a screenwriting class or something—I bet you'd be great at it. You shouldn't just stop writing; that would be such a waste. And you're totally welcome to live in my guesthouse. I insist. It would be so much fun to have you around."

"Thanks, but I think I'm going to stay here for a while, until I figure out what I want to do next. It's a marginally less poisonous environment, you know?"

"You think we're poisonous?"

"That's not really what I meant. But do you really want me lurking around your house, all sour with envy? Besides, I can't even afford to come back right now."

"Well, if you need quick money I could hire you to help me with some things. I really need an assistant. I got a pilot and I'm totally overwhelmed."

Margaret laughs, despite herself. "Josephine, you're really missing the point."

Josephine sighs. "I just miss you, you know?"

"I miss you too," Margaret says. She looks out into the manicured garden, thinking of the hard bright light of Los

Angeles, of the wild Santa Ana winds making the palm trees bend over in obeisance, of the nighttime helicopters hovering with their spotlights trained down on the wide boulevards below. For a moment, she thinks she should go back now, as soon as possible, before she loses her momentum entirely. And then she pours herself a glass of lemonade and goes upstairs to watch a DVD with Lizzie.

things take a turn for the worse on wednesday, when Applied Pharmaceuticals announces that it has a release date for Coifex. The drug is being rushed to market and will be available within two weeks. Oprah declines the interview with Janice, and the commentators, distracted by a new product announcement by Apple, start to abandon the story. What press coverage remains is tainted by backlash. "The media furor over Paul Miller is pointless," says one middle-aged (and balding, Margaret notes) pundit on *Hannity & Colmes,* his livery mouth snapping at a sour young blonde who has been weakly defending Janice with an arsenal of feminist tropes. "The personal lives of executives have no bearing on their ability to run a company. If anything, Paul Miller's financial ruthlessness proves that he has the makings of a great CEO."

By the end of the day, Coifex stock has risen again, all the way to 125, and Janice stalks through the house with her mouth pressed into a grim horizontal line. The feeling of defeat in the air is palpable, thick like pea soup. The phone has stopped ringing, and even when Lizzie and Margaret and Janice are all in the same room together they are mostly silent. Around dusk, the Groupers walk slowly by, taking an evening constitutional with their dog. Margaret watches them through the kitchen window as they stare blatantly at the house. The Bellstroms follow them a few minutes later, and yet no one comes up the drive to ring the bell and offer words of support. Margaret wonders if they are afraid that failure is contagious; she senses the neighborhood shrinking back, in fear of an infection. She can see that she has, unintentionally, raised the stakes: If they don't win this lawsuit, the fallout for her mother will be hideous, and not just financially. She imagines Janice in the supermarket, people whispering behind her back even as they smile to her face, offering sympathy and yet secretly wondering whether Janice somehow deserved what she got. She'll be ostracized, inevitably, and it will be Margaret's fault.

The unexpected coup de grâce comes on Thursday, the day before the trial begins, when an anonymous e-mail ping-pongs around the Internet, linking to a Web site that purports to have "Paul Miller's Secret Sex Tapes." Kelly is one of the first to see it, and she calls early in the morning to warn them.

"It's about to get ugly," she tells Margaret. "I'm looking into it. In the meantime, don't answer your phone. They're sharks, and they've smelled blood. Journalists live for these moments."

Margaret hangs up and looks over at Janice, who's been standing at the kitchen island with a magazine in her hand, pretending not to listen. She feels as if she's just been asked to hit her mother with a baseball bat. "Mom," she says slowly. "There's a sex tape."

"What?" Janice blinks rapidly.

"A sex tape, Mom. Of Dad. And Beverly."

"Oh God." Janice presses her hands into the granite countertop, shoulders locked tight. "This is more than I signed up for," she says. She picks at an invisible spot of food with her fingernail.

"I'll watch the video and tell you anything you need to know," Margaret says, knowing that this unpleasant task is small penance for the humiliation she has unwittingly brought down upon her mother.

"Do you think it's too early for a drink?" Janice asks. She

lowers herself into a kitchen chair and sits there, staring un-
enthusiastically at the cover of *Bon Appétit*.

margaret pours herself some scotch from her
father's neglected wet bar (ten A.M. is not too early for a drink
at all, she decides) and draws the blinds in the study. The
computer whines to life, the dust on the screen sizzling as
the monitor warms up. She pauses before hitting "Play" on
the video file, remembering something that happened when
she was in grammar school. She woke up in the middle of the
night thirsty for a glass of water and, passing by the partly open
door of the master bedroom, glimpsed her mother and father
mid-coitus. She watched in silence for a minute, frozen in
terror by what looked to her like a violent wrestling match taking place on the bed, and then, even as it dawned on her what
was going on, she was struck by a curiosity about which of her
parents would win. She couldn't decide who she wanted to
lose. The fear of getting caught eventually compelled her to
move away from the door and go back to bed, where she stayed
awake all night, replaying the scene in her mind with growing
horror.

She will need a hot bath when she is done with this, she
thinks, her hand hovering reluctantly over the mouse.

The grainy video is the size of a thumbprint and just as in-
criminating. A blurry white blob bobs up and down and then
comes into focus. It is a naked rear end, bouncing in and out
of frame. There is another smear of movement as the camera
is shifted. The new angle is strange, and for a few seconds
Margaret can't quite identify the body part she's looking at,
until she realizes that Paul has picked up the camera and is now
pointing it straight down his torso in order to capture, for
posterity, his erection.

Margaret looks away, nauseated, and when she looks back

the camera has been deposited on what must be a bedside table. Now the two bodies are clear, their heads visible: Paul and Beverly on a well-appointed king-sized bed, their naked lengths stretching away behind them. Margaret can practically count the hairs on her father's head. It is not an attractive view.

Their sex is strictly missionary-style—nothing kinky, nothing weird, Paul on top, Beverly below. Their bodies, squashed flat by gravity, have the middle-aged consistency of old custard. Beverly appears to have breast implants; they are the only part of her body that doesn't droop. For a while, Margaret thinks the video has no sound, and then she hears their quiet breathing and realizes that they are just having unexciting sex. The only audible noise comes toward the end—after a brief, and rather dull, four minutes—when Beverly squeaks a few times. Paul wheezes out a word that sounds like "Urg!" before he collapses. And that's it.

She watches the video clinically, trying to think of the figure on-screen not as her father but as an anthropological subject to be analyzed, only it's not that easy. She is repulsed but, even more, ineffably sad. She had made the assumption that Paul had left her mother for something more exciting, something wild and abandoned—a lure she could understand. The truth, it seems, is more mundane, and therefore less comprehensible. He threw us away for *that*?

And yet, at the same time, she feels an unexpected sympathy for her father with his dreary little sex tape. If it wasn't excitement that drew him away, what was it? Maybe it was love, and for that, she could possibly, someday, forgive him.

As Margaret sits there, sipping at her scotch in the glow from the computer screen, Lizzie wanders into the study, wearing sweats. She sits in the club chair gingerly, as if she's settling down on a very delicate egg. Margaret switches the computer off, but Lizzie already has a strange look on her face.

"Is it the video?" she asks.

"What video?"

Lizzie rolls her eyes. "Puhleeze. I'm not dumb, Margaret."

"Seriously," says Margaret. "How did you know about it? Did Mom tell you?"

And only now, observing the expression on Lizzie's face, does Margaret stop to wonder where the video has come from. The corners of Lizzie's lips vibrate slightly, and her eyes bulge as if from some hidden pressure. It dawns on Margaret that her sister knows something that Margaret does not. "Did you have something to do with this?" Margaret asks.

"No!" says Lizzie, drawing her legs up below her. "Not really. *I* didn't do it."

"What does *that* mean?" asks Margaret.

"Mark found the tape in a shoe box in his mom's closet," Lizzie says. Margaret is taken aback, envisioning Mark trying on his mother's shoes and lingerie, an aspiring drag queen in the first throes of self-discovery. And then she realizes what he was more likely to have been doing: sniffing his mother's shoes to catch the familiar earthy aroma, a lonely kid in an abandoned closet. It is too depressing to dwell upon.

"And he told you about it?"

"He showed it to me."

"Wow, Lizzie, that's really twisted." She recalls, now, the two kids in the family room, their guilty shrieks. "Is that what you were watching last week? The day that . . . ?" She can't quite finish the sentence: *you caught me having sex with James.*

Lizzie picks at a scab on her toe and nods. "And then Mark sent it to a lady from some Web site who called their house looking for his mom." She pauses as the scab flakes off to examine the bead of blood that wells up in its place. "Pretty dumb, but I think he has, you know, abandonment issues? I told him that it wasn't going to make anything better and it certainly wasn't gonna make his mom change her mind, but he said that wasn't the point. I guess he has to work his anger out. His mom doesn't live at home anymore, and he's pretty pissed off. You know."

"Oh," says Margaret, somewhat floored by this speech.

"I think she lives with Dad now, at the hotel," Lizzie continues. The sisters are silent for a minute, mulling this over. "I went with Mark to the post office. I thought maybe I'd talk him out of it, but honestly? I didn't try that hard. I guess I must have abandonment issues, too. Do you think Dad will find out, Margaret? You're not going to tell Mom, are you?"

"Don't worry," she says, thinking that despite the damp ink on the treaty between her and her mother, there are still certain things Janice just doesn't need to know. Then again, maybe Janice would have the number of a good psychiatrist. She imagines the two kids tipping a brown paper package into the post office mail bin and is reminded of those stories about children who, brainwashed by anti-drug advertising campaigns, turn their parents in to the police for growing a pot plant in the basement and end up in foster homes while their parents rot in jail. Someday when they are slouching toward middle age, Margaret thinks, Mark and Lizzie will spend a fortune on therapy trying to process what they did. The sooner Lizzie starts working through her baggage, the better.

"Are you okay about all this?" Margaret asks. "What with all the stories in the paper, all the attention to Mom and Dad."

Lizzie lifts her hand in front of her face and examines the chipped pink nail polish on her thumb. "I dunno. It's weird. I guess I've had a lot of other things to worry about, too," she says. She slumps down in her chair until she's nearly horizontal. "Do you think the newspapers will write about what happened last week? I mean, the . . . thing . . . in the hospital?"

Margaret shakes her head. "They couldn't know."

Lizzie picks a flake of nail polish from her pinkie finger

and lets it drop on the floor. "I'm going to get Mom to transfer me to St. Gertrude's for my sophomore year," she says. "She said I could, if I really wanted to."

"The Catholic school? With the nuns? And catechism classes?"

"They have a really good swim team," says Lizzie. She sits up again. "Do you think they care if you're not really Catholic? I mean, you only have to believe in God to get in, right? Do you think *God* cares?"

"You're weird," says Margaret.

"Maybe I'll get Mark to transfer, too," Lizzie says. "He *hates* Fillmore High."

"Is he your boyfriend now?"

Lizzie shrugs, but pulls the edge of her sweatshirt up over her mouth to conceal a smirk. There is something incestuous about that coupling, Margaret thinks. But seeing Lizzie's smile, she says nothing.

Lizzie lets the sweatshirt drop. "Anyway, I'm never going to be able to go back to Fillmore again," she says. "I'll be, like, a total outcast. I already am."

Margaret pushes the scotch aside. "This is going to be of no consolation whatsoever, I know, but just so you're aware, a lot of the popular kids in your class are actually peaking right now. In ten years you'll go to your reunion and they'll have three snot-nosed kids apiece and live in trailer parks. And when you get to college you'll find out that geeks and weirdos are the ones who end up really running the world."

"Is that what happened to you?" asks Lizzie. She hoists a skeptical eyebrow, plucked within an inch of its life. "Are you running the world?"

"Not exactly," Margaret says, wishing now that she had said nothing at all. "But I'm an exception to the rule."

Lizzie snorts, rolls her eyes, and leaves. Margaret watches

her thump out of the room and thinks that when her sister is just a little bit older, she is going to be a force to contend with. Maybe she already is.

despite kelly's warnings, no one calls immedi-
ately, and Thursday morning passes at a glacial pace. The sex tape isn't mentioned in the day's papers, and the only story about Paul at all is a small squib on the back page of the *New York Times* business section about the upcoming ad campaign for Coifex, a story that only briefly mentions the trial. Margaret watches the morning news but has to turn to CNBC before she finds anyone talking about Coifex, and then it's only to relay the fact that Applied Pharmaceuticals stock has stabilized back at 134.

It's impossible to concentrate on anything. With each minute that ticks by, it seems more likely that the gamble isn't going to pay off. The media has lost interest in the lawsuit, no one is going to pay attention to the sex tape, and her father won't budge from his position. They will go to court tomorrow, and her mother will lose. Margaret walks out to the pool to stare at her reflection. The water is still—no one has gone near the pool since Lizzie had her miscarriage there—and a thin layer of brown sediment has settled on the bottom of the deep end. Margaret thinks of James, somewhere on the beach in Mexico, and wishes that she'd thought to get a joint from him before he left.

She flops down on the lawn and stares blankly up at the blue sky, where the last wisps of the overcast morning are being burned off by the heat of the midday sun. Her back itches from the freshly mowed grass, and she thinks she can feel the faint curvature of the earth beneath her spine. A plane flies by, and she watches the ghostly vapor trail it leaves until it has vanished completely and the sky is once again empty and clear. Inside the house, the phone rings for the first time that day, like an alarm bell shattering the silence. The answering machine clicks on, but the message is too muffled for Margaret to hear it from out here. A few minutes later, it rings again. Margaret remains motionless, as if sudden movement might break a spell. Eventually she falls asleep.

In the early afternoon, Janice comes out and stands above her, blocking out the sun. "Your sister and I are going to play a board game," she says. "Would you like to join us?"

"Sure," says Margaret, and stands up. The backs of her legs are imprinted with blades of grass.

"Your father's charming video is all over the news," Janice adds. She rubs an eye with the palm of one hand and closes her eyes against the sun. "The telephone has been ringing off the hook. Everyone wants to know how I feel. How do they think I feel?"

"I'm sorry, Mom," says Margaret. She reaches out and impulsively rubs her mother's shoulder through the thin fabric of her poplin shirt. Janice's muscles are tight and knotted. "Really."

Janice shakes her head. "It's not your fault. I'll make us some iced tea. Want to pick out a game? We were thinking Monopoly."

Margaret can't remember exactly where the games are kept—when was the last time she played a board game with her family? It must have been years. In the family room she opens one cupboard, then another, each exposed shelf a little window into her mother's world. Cupboards of family albums, going back all the way to the discolored Instamatics of Janice's youth. Hardback best-sellers with the corners folded over as placeholders. Home videos labeled in Magic Marker: MARGARET RIDING 1ST BIKE and PAUL TEACHES LIZZIE TO SWIM and HAWAII 2003. An entire history in these cabinets, and as she runs her hands over the dusty tops of the videotapes she feels the loss of those memories acutely. Janice will never be able to look at these again without the specter of the future darkening them. None of them will. She wonders when her mother will start purging the house of Paul's belongings.

She opens a fifth cupboard and stops. There, lined up in a neat row, are twenty-three issues of *Snatch:* every one she ever published, in chronological order, their spines slightly creased. She stands there, looking at them, and has to suppress the urge to cry. Her mother had saved them, after all; perhaps had even read them. She plucks out an issue—"The Celebrity Issue," from two years ago—and opens it to a random page but finds that she can't read the words. Was it ever any good? She doesn't want to know, right now. Perhaps with time she'll have enough distance to judge.

Lizzie comes up behind her and looks at the magazine in her hand, then up at the array on the shelf. "Oh," she says. "I was wondering where they'd gone."

Margaret puts an arm around her sister and kisses her, impulsively, on the apple of her plump cheek. "Can you tell me where we keep the games now?" she asks.

they gather around the card table in the fam-
ily room, each gravitating to their usual pieces. Lizzie: Scottie dog; Margaret: boot; Janice: thimble. The seat to Margaret's left gapes emptily, where Paul (top hat) normally sat. Paul would be winning this game, if he were here. He usually did, peremptorily and without the gleeful gloating other family members displayed when, by luck, they managed to wrest the board away from him. He took his winnings as a matter of fact, tucking the stacks of wrinkled paper money under his edge of the board with a smile. "Them's the breaks," Margaret remembers him saying once as he bankrupted her with a hotel blockade.

They roll the dice and move their tokens around the board, but it is hard to concentrate with the phone ringing constantly. "I should take it off the hook," Janice says once, but she doesn't, and so they listen with half an ear as a fact-checker from the *New York Post* leaves a message and Matt Drudge calls for a comment and a talk-show booker suggests that Janice come on the show to "work things out" with Paul and Beverly on the air.

Lizzie lands in jail three rolls in a row, as her cash dwindles away. "This game sucks," she says. "Why can't we play Uno? I'm good at that game."

"We're getting used to the feeling of losing money," says Janice, squinting down at the sheaf of bills in her hand.

Margaret stares at her mother, trying to decide whether she means this as a joke or whether she's just offered a glimpse of how bitter she really is. Janice looks up to see her watching and smiles tightly. "Just some levity, Margaret. I'm trying. I'm really trying."

"This is serious," Lizzie says. "It's not funny, Mom." But it's not clear to Margaret what her sister is referring to. Lizzie rolls the dice again and is marching her pewter dog toward Park Place, where Janice has built a barricade of little green houses, as the phone rings yet again. Margaret is only half-listening to the machine when she realizes that the voice echoing through the speaker belongs to Lewis Grosser.

"Janice, give me a ring on my cell as soon as you can," he begins. *Hssst!* Static crackles across his voice as his words cut in and out. "I've heard from Paul's lawyers and they *hssst!* to postpone the hearing tomorrow morning and talk settlement. I think he might be. . . . *Goddammit, use your turn signal!* Sorry, I was saying, the media *could* finally be working to our advantage. Too much scrutiny *hssssssssst!* the company bottom line and all that. We have a good. . . . *Dammit . . .*" His last word echoes over a soundless void for a moment, and then the answering machine clunks to a stop and clicks off.

Margaret watches her mother, who is staring at the machine as if Paul himself might be about to jump out of the phone. Pink blotches bloom on her neck.

"Was that something good?" Lizzie asks.

Margaret looks at her mother. "It could be. Mom? Aren't you . . . ?"

"Lizzie, you owe me thirteen hundred dollars," Janice says, and holds her hand out for the last few bills in her daughter's bank account. She picks up the dice and skitters them across the board. Three and four. *Tap tap tap* she moves the thimble across Free Parking and Chance to land on B&O Railroad. "I think I own that."

"Go ahead and call the lawyer back," Margaret says gently. "We can finish the game another time."

Janice looks at the neat stacks of miniature money she's just tucked under the edge of the board. "No," she says. "Let's finish our game first. It's your turn."

Margaret wants to scream at her mother: *Call him! Finish this! Don't take any more chances! They will screw you if they can!* She frowns at Janice across the table, but something about the look on her mother's face stops her. The late afternoon light refracted through the window catches in an iridescent line of moisture that rims her mother's lash line, and Margaret is terrified that if she says one word more this speck will gather itself into a tear and then her mother will be crying and crying and crying, for things that Margaret won't ever really understand.

Instead, Margaret rolls the dice and lands next to Lizzie on Park Place. "Crap," she says. "You cleaned me out too."

"Did I just win?" Janice asks, looking down at her properties.

"I hate this game," says Lizzie.

"Ice cream," Janice says. She stands up. "I think we should have ice-cream sundaes."

She disappears into the kitchen while Margaret and Lizzie

clean up, stacking the money into piles and rubber-banding the properties together and plinking the plastic hotels back into their bags. In a minute, Margaret can hear the refrigerator door opening, an appliance whirring. She puts the lid back on the Monopoly box and stares down at its faded cover for a minute, trying to manage her impatience.

"What's going on?" Lizzie whispers. "Mom is acting weird."

"I think Dad might be giving her more money," Margaret whispers back.

"Oh!" Lizzie brightens. "Well, maybe she will take you shopping if she wins. You need a new dress. You need a haircut, too."

Margaret flicks her sister in the leg. "Very funny," she says. "This coming from a girl who wears purple glitter eyeshadow without irony." But she looks down at the nap of the terry-cloth dress, worn almost smooth from constant wear and safety-pinned together, and for the first time in many weeks feels compelled to put on fresh clothes. To take a shower and apply makeup and ready herself for the assault of the outside world. Fall is arriving, and in the fading light of summer she can feel the brisk undercurrent of coming change.

"I'm going to go give Mom a hand," she says.

In the kitchen, their mother is loading three bowls of mint chip with fudge sauce and whipped cream onto a tray. Each bowl is garnished with a tiny sprig of fresh mint. Margaret stands next to her and watches.

"Can I help?"

"There's nothing left to do," Janice says. "But thanks for asking."

"Why haven't you called Grosser back yet?"

Janice pauses and looks at Margaret, her eyes hard. "Let Paul wait and wonder," she spits. "Let him learn what that feels like."

Margaret examines the perfect round scoops of ice cream, ice crystals glittering as they begin to liquefy in the heat. "What are you going to do if he gives you the stock after all?"

"I'm going to sell my shares before the stock drops," Janice replies, and lifts the tray up. "No pill is *that* magical. I just don't believe it. Let's go eat this before it melts."

they sit on the big couch in the family room,

facing the French doors that look out at the garden. Lizzie turns the television on but leaves it muted, and in the slanting light from the low sun they can see their shapes reflected back in the screen, but no one gets up to pull the curtains closed. Janice sits between Margaret and Lizzie, and digs in to her ice cream with a determined expression on her face.

"Delicious," she says.

As they eat in complicit silence, they watch muted advertisements for Cadillac, for Visa, for Oil of Olay anti-aging cream, for low-interest mortgages. Janice rests a hand on Margaret's thigh and looks at her intently. "You know, you'd be very good at PR if you ever wanted to try it. I bet Kelly would give you a job."

Margaret imagines herself in an Ann Taylor suit, trotting around booming conference centers with an armful of press releases and a plastic smile and shudders. "I can think of nothing I would enjoy less."

"I thought," Janice begins. Her hand bounces on Margaret's leg. "I thought that maybe you'd want to meet a career counselor."

"Mom, don't. Please."

"She should go to a psychic," Lizzie says. She curls her legs up underneath her, exposing her dirty toes. "Becky went once and they told her she was going to be a famous doctor when she grew up. And marry a guy with brown hair."

"Both of you, just stop it. I don't need a career counselor or a psychic," Margaret says. "No input from anyone, please."

Janice turns back to the TV. "I just want you to be happy," she says quietly. "I think you could do so many things."

Margaret is tempted to feel sorry for herself, for the fact that she'll be twenty-nine in just five weeks and then, then, it will be just a short march to thirty, and she'll still be alone and a nobody and starting a career again at zero—less than zero, even, because she'll still have to crawl out of bankruptcy before she can start to build anything again. Is it too late for her? Is she standing on the shoreline watching the boat sail away with all of her successful peers aboard? Maybe. But right now—at least for this minute—as she sits in this buttressed den with her sister and mother, cosseted by their illogical faith, there isn't enough space for fear. She'll come up with something, surely. She has to.

They demolish their desserts in silence. Evening is falling outside, the shadows creeping across the lawn, the light in the family room waning, as Janice, Lizzie, and Margaret sit watching but not watching the mute television. Lizzie leverages a spoonful of melting ice cream to her mouth, and a drop plops onto the couch. Janice reaches over and wipes the ice cream up with the hem of her sleeve.

"Mom, what's the stock worth anyway?" Lizzie asks, smearing whipped cream off her chin with the back of a sticky hand.

Janice pauses. "More than I'd ever be able to spend," she says at last.

In the garden, the oak trees rattle as the evening breeze stirs their limbs. They release a dusting of dead leaves into the pool below. Margaret watches through the window as the leaves dance on the surface of the water and then are drawn, slowly, toward the drain. She closes her eyes and lets the sweet, warm chocolate sauce dissolve over her tongue, and listens to the orchestra of lawn mowers in the distance.

ACKNOWLEDGMENTS

If it weren't for the weekly ministrations of Darcy Cosper, Benjamin Hewitt, Carina Chocano, and Colette Sandstedt— along with my frequently saintly husband, Greg Harrison—this book would still be a folder on my laptop. There's no way to adequately express my gratitude. For their support, judicious feedback, and occasional free housing, I am also indebted to Heather Collins and Tim Kaeding, Leslie Schwartz, Alexandra Grant, Bruce Falck, Guin Doner, both Laura Millers, Dawn MacKeen, and Elisha Cooper; not to mention my parents and sister, Pam and Dick Brown and Jodi Carter, for encouraging this madness for three decades. Finally, a thousand thanks go to my editor, Julie Grau, for her creative vision and infectious enthusiasm; and to Susan Golomb, truly the agent of my dreams.

all

we ever wanted

was

everything

JANELLE BROWN

A READER'S GUIDE

Random House Reader's Circle has acquired a transcript of a group therapy session, recently conducted between Janelle Brown, author of *All We Ever Wanted Was Everything,* and Janice, Margaret, and Lizzie Miller.

THERAPIST
Everyone comfortable?

JANICE
I could use a glass of wine.

THERAPIST
I'm sorry, I discourage drinking during therapy sessions.

MARGARET
Mom, isn't it better that you maybe lay off the intoxicants for a while? Considering—

JANICE
Considering what? I told you, I'm fine now. Anyway, I blame *her* for all that . . .

Janice, Lizzie, and Margaret swivel their heads to stare at Janelle, who shrinks farther back into her seat.

THERAPIST
Well, this is as good a place as any to start. The reason we're here today, Janelle, is that your characters would like to address some of their concerns about the book you wrote about them. They feel that you were, perhaps, not very *sensitive* to their feelings . . .

JANICE
We were all perfectly happy until she started tinkering with our lives for the sake of her "novel"!

THERAPIST
Were you perfectly happy, though?

Margaret snorts. Janice examines her manicure; Lizzie flips through an US Weekly *on the coffee table.*

THERAPIST
As I suspected. Janelle, why don't you start? It does seem like you threw these women into an awful lot of turmoil. Why don't you explain what your intentions were.

JANELLE
Really, I didn't set out to be a masochist. I just wanted to explore the ugly underbelly of the boom years in America's affluent suburbs: the dysfunctional relationships, the skewed priorities, the underlying emptiness of a life defined by money and the pursuit of success. And the drugs, sex, religion, and infidelity all struck me as interesting and comic ways to unveil that. So maybe I put you all through the ringer—but it all turned out okay in the end, didn't it? Sort of?

She smiles, but is met by stony silence from her characters.

JANELLE
Anyway, I've always loved narrative-driven novels—books like *The Corrections*, or *White Teeth*, or *Little Children*, which not only have colorful characters and rich themes but also boast twisty, turny plots that keep you up reading until the wee hours of the morning. Books that you can't put down, but that make you think while you're turning the pages. That's what I was hoping to do with *All We Ever Wanted Was Everything*.

MARGARET
Which reminds me. Would you please explain why you co-opted the title of my high school valedictorian speech as the name of your novel? Isn't that plagiarism? Or at least wildly unoriginal.

JANELLE
Well, you could say we both plagiarized the title of a song by Bauhaus, a goth band that was very popular with the teen alterna-crowd in the eighties and early nineties. I always loved the wistfulness of the title, which suggests a chronic dissatisfaction—because who ever gets *everything* they want?—but also the pathos of hope and longing. It seemed to sum up the mentality of the last decade, when Americans believed that everything was within our reach, and yet it never really was as close as it seemed.

LIZZIE
All *I* really want is, you know, for people to like me. And maybe to lose ten pounds and have a boyfriend.

JANICE
Hmmph. I blame your father for somehow teaching you that sex equals love. God knows that's what that *thing* with Beverly was probably all about. . . .

THERAPIST
Janice, you seem to still have a lot of anger towards Paul—

JANICE
And you wouldn't? He not only dumped me for my best friend, but he tried to cheat me out of half of the money he made from Applied Pharmaceuticals! It was mortifying.

MARGARET
Honestly, Janelle—why did my father have to be such a jerk? Do you have a thing against men or something? Not that I would blame you if you did, but . . .

JANELLE
Actually, I saw Paul as an archetype—a symbol of the endgame of self-entitlement. There's this kind of Ayn Randian libertarian mentality that you see among captains of industry: success is the ultimate endgame, and who cares who you step on along the way? I like to imagine Paul as a kind of cross between Bernie Madoff and Dick Cheney. That said, what he did to Janice was incredibly coldhearted, and I do feel a little bad about that—

JANICE
As you should!

JANELLE
—but I certainly don't have a thing against men. In fact, some of my favorite characters in the book—like James, the morally ambivalent, drug-dealing, Zen-spouting poolboy—are male. When it came to the men in the book, though, I was mostly interested in how the Miller women look to men for their validation. Even Margaret, the ardent feminist, drops everything to follow a man to Los Angeles. I think that's more common

than women would like to admit—even in this post—"grrl power" era, when feminism has permeated so *many* aspects of our lives, men still often wield a level of emotional control over women's sense of self-worth and identity. And certainly the boom years were driven by male-dominated industries: banking, entrepreneurialism, and technology.

THERAPIST
Interesting. So you self-identify as a feminist?

JANELLE
Of course. In fact, I cofounded a feminist women's Web magazine, back in the 1990s, which could probably be described as a less strident version of Margaret's magazine, *Snatch*.

MARGARET
So, wait, you're saying that I'm based on . . . you?

JANELLE
Not at all. The book is entirely fictional. Although there are definitely some points where my own biography hews closely to Margaret's—I, too, was once a struggling twenty-something feminist editor—and I also grew up in suburban Silicon Valley. In fact, that's what inspired me to write this book. I lived and worked in the area as a technology journalist during the dot-com boom, writing for publications like *Wired* and *Salon*. I was both fascinated and appalled by the influx of this ludicrous wealth and how it was changing the nature of communities and families, and their definitions of ambition and success. Silicon Valley became the American Dream on steroids, distorted beyond recognition into something vaguely monstrous.

MARGARET
Amen, sister.

JANELLE

Yes. I wanted to explore how people cope when they realize that they can't live up to that inflated idea of success, or the expectations and achievements of their peers and families. In Margaret's case, she decides to outwardly reject financial success (even as she secretly longs for it). That's her way of coping emotionally with her own failures: to repudiate the world her parents live in completely.

In Janice's case, she obsesses over the outward appearance of things in order to suppress the dark feelings of failure entirely. She can cook a stunning six-course meal, plant a gorgeous garden, be the quintessential wife and hostess; but those routines merely mask her fear that she married the wrong man in the first place. I felt readers would be able identify with a woman who spends her time perfecting surfaces in order to conceal what she doesn't want to see underneath. God knows we all do that sometimes.

THERAPIST

Ah, yes. And it would seem rather evident that Janice's use of crystal meth was another form of emotional sublimation.

JANELLE

That's why I chose crystal meth as Janice's drug of choice. The appeal of crystal meth to Janice is that it makes her feel even more like herself: more capable, more in control, more productive. It makes her the uber-housewife. Of course, it also gets her terribly addicted and increasingly out of touch with reality—

JANICE

Excuse me? I'm sitting right here. You don't need to talk about me as if I don't exist.

JANELLE
My apologies.

LIZZIE
What about me?

THERAPIST
What about you?

Lizzie throws down her magazine.

LIZZIE
Aren't we going to talk about me too? For once?

JANELLE
Sure. In a way, I think you're the simplest character in the book, and the one that I think everyone can relate to the most. How many of us *didn't* feel unloved or friendless as a teenager? In Lizzie's case, she *is* neglected, because her family is too involved in their own little dramas to realize how lost she is. Which is why she turns to sex first, and then religion, in order to fill that hole.

In fact, Lizzie was the easiest character for me to write, perhaps because she was the one I could identify with the most. Her pain was so clear to me, and I've always loved the wry humor that can be wrung from teenage melodrama.

THERAPIST
If Lizzie was the easiest, why didn't you write the book entirely from Lizzie's point of view?

JANELLE
I really wanted to explore the novel's themes from the POV of three different generations: Janice's generation is still rooted in more traditional American ideals, the notion that a woman's

primary place is in the home. And then there's Margaret, who was raised in the postfeminist era, where female equality and male hegemony were taught in every liberal university. And then there's Lizzie, from the age of media oversaturation, who is simply perplexed by all the conflicting things she hears.

THERAPIST
Let's discuss the recession. Obviously, times have changed quite a bit since the novel was written.

JANICE
Well, yes, we are having to tighten our belts a little bit. But one thing I know from growing up the way I did is how to make a dollar stretch. It might even be good for us. For example—Margaret's trying to convince me to swap out the Porsche for a Prius when the lease is up. Anyway, as long as we can hang on to the house, that's what's most important.

THERAPIST
Janelle, how do you feel about this book, knowing what you do know about the economic crash that was to come?

JANELLE
In a lot of ways, I see the experiences of the Millers as a harbinger of what was to come in late 2008. Their lifestyle and expectations are a microcosm of our greater society's priorities over the last decade. And just as the bubble eventually pops for them, it's since popped for the rest of America. So I kind of think of *All We Ever Wanted Was Everything* as a depiction of the mentality that led us to where we are today.

JANICE
And yet you wrote this "novel" before there were any signs of the crash?

JANELLE
Yes, but—at least to me—the crash felt inevitable. I started working on the book in 2003, and finished it in 2007, when things were already starting to feel unsustainable—the Dow was boggling high, the price of real estate was through the roof, and handbags cost $2,000. I think of the book as a time capsule of those years.

The therapist checks her watch and clears her throat.

THERAPIST
Our time is up, unfortunately. Perhaps what we can take away from this session is that Janelle put an incredible amount of work into this novel, and hopes that you—the Miller women—can accept her good intentions?

The three Miller women grumble, and then nod.

MARGARET
It *was* a pretty entertaining read.

JANICE
I have to admit, I was rather pleased that Paul at least got his comeuppance in the end. Even if it had to come at my expense.

THERAPIST
So, are we all feeling okay now?

The women nod, smiling.

LIZZIE
Is this when we do the group hug?

1. Discuss the epigraph by J. M. Barrie and its meaning in the novel. How are the notions of failure, success, and personal fulfillment examined in the book and are they complicated by the expectations of family, culture, and society?

2. This novel is centered on three very different women. Explore the concepts of femininity and feminism in the novel and the ways in which Janice, Margaret, and Lizzie reinforce and challenge those models.

3. Location plays an important part in the novel, magnifying and thwarting characters' aspirations. Examine the setting in this novel. What do Santa Rita, Los Angeles, Silicon Valley, and California itself symbolize? Could this story take place anywhere else?

4. In the first chapter, Janice dreams of buying a piece of art with her new fortune: "She covets a Van Gogh, one like those

she saw a few years back. The violence of the paint applied in furious layers so thick that she could see the impressions of the artist's fingers, clawing at the canvas—she felt like she'd been slapped. The color! As vivid as a hallucination." Is this object of desire an obvious one for Janice? What can we glean about Janice from her choice of a Van Gogh, in particular?

5. After he requests a divorce, Paul tells Janice, "You don't need me. You've never needed anyone in your life." Do you find truth in Paul's statement? Does Janice come across as completely self-reliant or hopelessly dependent? Or is Paul projecting his own feelings onto her, trying to justify leaving the marriage?

6. At the beginning of the novel, Janice and Margaret seem to be antagonists. Does this remain the case throughout the story? By the end of the novel, do Janice and Margaret merely understand each other, or have they grown more alike?

7. At first glance, Bart seems like an odd choice for Margaret's affection. Why does she fall for him and how does she reconcile her love with her neofeminist principles?

8. The Miller women cope with their predicaments through various means—the accumulation of material objects, money, drugs, religion, ambition, and sex. How effective are these ultimately and what do they have in common?

9. After an unsuccessful and desperate attempt to score *It*, Janice races to the hospital to meet Margaret and Lizzie, who has just been released from the emergency room. The text reads, "For the first time in longer than she can recall, [Janice] feels happy." In many ways, this is such a low moment; explain what the author means.

10. *All We Ever Wanted Was Everything* is a satire. What or who is the object of the author's critique? Some early readers likened the novel to the film *American Beauty*. Do you see a similarity between the two works? What is Janelle Brown's message to her readers?

ABOUT THE AUTHOR

Janelle Brown is the author of the novel *All We Ever Wanted Was Everything*, published in May 2008 by Spiegel & Grau, as well as in a dozen other countries across the world. An essayist and journalist, her writing appears regularly in *Vogue*, *The New York Times*, *Elle*, *Wired*, *Self*, the *Los Angeles Times*, and numerous other publications. Previously, she spent five years as a senior writer at *Salon*, covering a diverse range of subjects—from Internet culture to the war on drugs, pop culture to style, public policy issues and the digital music movement—and began her career as a staff writer at *Wired*, working on seminal Web sites like HotWired and Wired News during the heyday of the dot-com boom. In the 1990s, she was also the editor and cofounder of *Maxi*, an irreverent (and now, long-gone) women's pop culture magazine. She lives in Los Angeles with her husband, filmmaker Greg Harrison.